CHOICES AND CHANCES: A CADE TAYLOR NOVEL

MICHAEL HEARNS

BEATI BELLICOSI

BEATI BELLICOSI PUBLISHING A DIVISION OF BEATI BELLICOSI MEDIA

ISBN: 979-8-9897279-0-2 Paperback
ISBN: 979-8-9897279-1-9 Electronic Book Text
ISBN: 978-1-7344075-9-4 Hardback

Library of Congress Cataloging-in-Publication Data
Name: Hearns, Michael, author
Title: Choices and Chances: A Cade Taylor Novel/Michael Hearns
Description: First edition. Miami: Beati Bellicosi (2024)
Identifiers: LCCN ISBN

First Edition: February 2024

Editor: Julie Hutchings
Cover Design by Dillon Hearns
Author Photo by Ricki Witt Braswell

For additional information and speaking engagements visit Michael Hearns on the worldwide web: http://www.MichaelHearns.com

Beati Bellicosi Publishing a division of Beati Bellicosi multimedia.
Copyright 2024 by Beati Bellicosi
Printed in the U.S.A

Also by author Michael Hearns:

"Trust No One"
2020 Beati Bellicosi

"Grasping Smoke: A Cade Taylor Novel"
2021 Beati Bellicosi

"One More Move: A Cade Taylor Novel"
2022 Beati Bellicosi

Acknowledgments

I would like to thank the legion of Cade Taylor fans who have made the writing process and the storytelling experience so rewarding not only for me, but for all the readers. The growing enthusiasm for the Cade Taylor book series has been nothing short of a wondrous amazing journey for me.

I must give an abundant thank you to my editor Julie Hutchings. She has been refining and coaxing the bends and twists of the Cade Taylor novels like an accomplished maestro in front of a preschool holiday pageant, a wizened sea captain in a hurricane gale, and a graceful bullfighter during a stampede. She has managed and handled everything I have thrown at her. Her abilities and experience outpace anyone else in the editing field.

I would like to thank my son Dillon Hearns for everything he is and for everything he is to me. The legacy of our lives transcends the material and superficialities of life. The heart swelling love and proud feelings I have for him are indescribable.

Most importantly I want to thank my wife Ricki Witt Braswell. She is my muse, and my everlasting love. We should all be so lucky to have a person of her caliber in our lives. I am fortunate, blessed, and eternally grateful for the love and support she has brought to my life. If I had known I was going to spend the rest of my life with her I would have started living the rest of my life sooner.

I am honored and humbled that you have selected me to be your chosen author. I thank you the reader for providing that privilege to me. I hope you are settled in and comfortable as you prepare to read this novel. Check your seatbelt.

To Ricki and Dillon. I love you both.

Chapter One

"**Y**OU GOT A cigarette?"

"I don't smoke." I said.

"You should start," he said, looking past me at the idling Miami Dade Crime Scene van. The green, white, and gold paint glinted in the early morning South Florida sun.

"Should I take credit for your slightly extended life span?" I asked him.

"You? Cade? *You*?" he said, casting me a look reeking of demeaning disbelief.

The nicotine-deprived fellow was Homicide Detective Lloyd Trentlocke from the Miami Dade Police Department. Fifteen years earlier he and I had attended the police academy together.

"If you think you can beat back two ex-wives and a kid who barely knows me then yeah, maybe you can qualify as some sort of life extender. Short of that, unlike all of you conforming believers waiting for some great divine to decide your fate, I'm choosing my exit at $5.25 a pack. Taxable!" he said with the confidence of one who repeats the flawed lethal logic to themselves, even if it is encased in woefulness.

The life of a homicide detective can be incredibly difficult. You investigate and chronicle the dead, all the while fully knowing the stress, emotional carnage, and the inordinately long, difficult hours of the task will shorten your very own life. Compound the grind of the job with doing it in Miami Dade County exacerbates, accelerates, and instigates the inevitable career burn-out and its companion, the inglorious premature aging of your mind, body, and soul. Mix that with a smattering of PTSD that haggles nightly with the gruesome sights and sounds that only you can see and hear as they carom through your head at 4am, and you have a great formula for an early death, either by the hand of God or by a gun in your own hand.

Up until ten months ago, I hadn't seen Trentlocke since our police academy graduation. At our last encounter, I noticed his forehead had furrowed noticeably and the gray in his hair was spreading rapidly across his temples. He now stood in front of me again. It seemed as if he was aging even more quickly, and not in a good way. When I last cast eyes on him he was with two other Miami Dade homicide detectives. Inwardly to myself I had nicknamed the two detectives "Pudgy" and "Dumpy." It was in the middle of a balmy February night, and Trentlocke requested that I show up on his homicide scene. He was investigating the murder of one of my drug informants. The nocturnal investigation of the death of my informant couldn't have come at a worse time for me personally. I was in the throes of a divorce that seared into me like a burning spear. Compounding my stress was the fact he and his Miami Dade Homicide compadres were all eyeing me as a suspect in the informant's murder. It was a very rough week for me, dealing with Llyod and his supervisor, Captain Teofilo Zambrano.

"I'll take you into the scene. Give the uniform officer your business card," Trentlocke said to me.

"I don't have business cards. Remember?" I said back to him.

He rubbed his chin ruefully. He looked down at the ground and transitioned his hand from rubbing his chin to rubbing the back of his neck. He looked up at me, remembering the calamity that I and business cards had caused him ten months earlier. He motioned to a uniformed Miami Dade police officer standing just outside the yellow crime scene tape. The sagging tape wavered in the early morning breeze.

"Yes, sir?" the officer said to Detective Trentlocke.

Trentlocke squinted at the officer's name tag. "Officer Montalván, this is Detective Cade Taylor from the Coral Gables Police Department."

The young officer looked at me questioningly but kept listening to Trentlocke intently.

"I know. I know. He doesn't look like a cop but believe me he is a cop. He's S.I.S with the Gables."

"It's V.I.N in the Gables," I interjected accentuating the letters between the periods mocking Trentlocke's tone.

Trentlocke stopped his introduction and shot me a "does it really matter" look.

"I'm Cade Taylor, with the VIN unit at Coral Gables. VIN's an acronym for Vice, Intelligence, and Narcotics. I'm undercover and I'd like to keep it that way. If you know what I mean," I said to officer Montalván.

I could see the young officer processing my appearance as I stood in front of him. My blue jeans and a threadbare subdued Reyn Spooner print shirt did not in any manner say, "I am a police officer." Not here. Not anywhere. My shoulder-length hair was pushed back under my black Hartford Whalers hat, and with my full goatee and earrings I didn't look like any cop Officer Montalván had probably seen in his young career.

"So…keeping that in mind officer, please note him as on the scene here and allow him access as long as we're here," said Trentlocke.

Officer Montalván nodded affirmatively and wrote the briefest of notations in his notebook. Both Trentlocke and I crossed under the crime scene tape, taking a few steps into the very large crime scene. We stood on a patchy swale adjacent to Old Cutler Road on Conde Avenue in Coral Gables. The traffic on Old Cutler Road was minimal. It was promising to be a sunny December day in South Florida and although early in the morning, the sun was increasingly scaling over the largest palm trees east of where we were standing. The Saturday morning was greeting us both with streaking rays of sunshine rising further east and cresting over the rooflines of the houses closest to Biscayne Bay on Conde Avenue.

"This is your city," he said.

"This is your county," I replied.

"So, does Conde Avenue go all the way to the bay?" Trentlocke asked me.

"No, it dead ends with a small section of Nogales Street," I said, pondering once again why I'd been summoned to a Miami Dade homicide scene.

Especially another one being conducted by Llyod Trentlocke.

"You have streets that go north and south? In the county streets go east and west," he said to me.

"Like you said, it's my city." I was wondering what all of this was leading up to. "We're Coral Gables. You can't park a pickup truck in your driveway overnight. We zealously code-enforce the residents into resigned compliance. Yes we have streets, circles, courts, boulevards, drives, parks, places, and avenues that go in nearly every direction counter to the county's numbering system. Hell, we even have an Alhambra Place, Alhambra Plaza, Alhambra Circle, Alhambra Court, and a street called South Alhambra that's miles away from all the other Alhambras," I said.

"Cade, it was a simple question. I don't need the Rand McNally map of your overly manicured Godforsaken city. Just answer the question."

"Remind me to give you a map." I looked past him at all the assembled personnel and vehicles.

Because once again Trentlocke was investigating a homicide in Coral Gables, the powers that be at the Coral Gables Police Department summoned me to the scene. Truthfully there really were no powers that be. There was only one power that be, and he be my immediate supervisor and the current acting Chief of Police of the Coral Gables Police Department: Major Theodore "Ted" Brunson.

Major Brunson was the longest tenured employee in our department. The few times he ever used the police radio, the dispatchers that answered him often sounded confused. His radio number was predicated on his city employee number which was very low compared to the rest of the police department. He was a very rigid police officer who may not have seen everything, but I could guarantee he'd seen more than most of the department in his career. Our police chief, Robert McIntyre, was practically ambulatory and trying to recover from a near-fatal stroke he'd suffered just over a year before. The city's maniacal, fiscally conservative city manager prolonged the appointment of a replacement for Chief McIntyre to save himself from paying another police executive salary. He kept Major Brunson in the acting chief position and if he was allowed to do so, the city manager would keep him there indefinitely.

Brunson was far from warm and fuzzy. He was acidic, caustic, nearly devoid of proper manners, and he used profanity so frequently that to the uninitiated it seemed that all he ever did is swear, and then swear some more. Prone to vent his anger on inanimate objects, he often kicked waste baskets, slammed doors, and threw wads of paper in disgust. The coursing animosity in his veins might actually have been the propulsion his blood needed to circulate. He collected and sampled hot sauces from all over the world and sampled every one of them regardless of the Scoville heat level. I learned a few months ago not to underestimate his ability to harness and decipher information. He often pointed out to the department's non-believers that he sat in the biggest office in the building for a reason—that reason being that he had a finger on the pulse of the department, its employees, and anything to do with the agency. He could use that very same finger and shut off any sustaining artery of the agency that he wanted to. His phone call to me earlier in the morning was brusque and short.

"The fucking county's in the south end. Go find them and either help them out or kick them out. Either way, get there and see what the fuck the clowns in the brown gowns are doing making a mess of my morning. Keep me appraised."

The brown gowns was a direct remark about the medium

mocha-colored brown uniform the Miami Dade County Police wore in direct opposition to the State of Florida. Every other county sheriff in Florida was mandated to wear dark green, white, or gray. Although they referred to themselves as a police agency they were in fact the sheriffs' department of Miami Dade County. In 1957 the county politicians, fed up with their inability to influence an elected sheriff, shifted the agency from the "County Sheriff's Department" to the more palatable "Public Safety Department." It had been a tug of war of discord with Miami Dade County and the state government in Tallahassee ever since. That wasn't my concern or my problem. I was trying to determine if what I was doing now on this warm Saturday morning should have me concerned, and more importantly would it be my problem.

"You were wearing a Hartford Whalers hat the last time I saw you, too. They're not even an NHL team anymore. Is this some sort of thing with you?"

"A guy can hope, can't he? The way I see it, they haven't lost a game this year," I said.

"But they aren't a team anymore," he said with a perplexed tone.

"Unlike all of you conforming believers waiting for the league to decide your fan base, I'm choosing my team. Faithfully!"

"Cade, ten months ago you pushed my patience and fraternal benevolence to the point of exhaustion. I woke up today exhausted. I don't have it in me to try and make sense of your loyalty to a defunct hockey team."

"Yeah, well Lloyd, my long lost academy classmate, if you think standing here on a Saturday morning with you is more preferable to me than settling into my couch to watch the University of Miami Hurricanes play football against UCLA on TV, you are sorely mistaken. I got sent out here by someone not in your department, not in your county, but from *my* city. You see those street-marking white headstones with the black ink on the street corners? You're in Coral Gables now, buddy."

As Llyod stepped a little closer to me his cigarette tainted breath preceded him.

"Coral Gables is in my county."

"The back of my identification card says State of Florida. So fuck you," I said.

"You're still disenchanted over last February. Cade, follow the bouncing ball here. Recommended things needed to be done that required us to get the requisite results we wanted," he said.

"Disenchanted? Disenchanted is when you find out the prom queen stuffs her bra. You, and your loser Captain Zambrano made my life a complete hell. You put me smack in the middle of your murder investigation; an investigation, need I remind you, that had a bullseye right on my chest. Was that a requisite requirement?"

"Cade, I'm just a cog in the wheel. You need to get on the inside of the wheel like the rest of us. Spinning on the outside is how you get run over by the wheel."

"No thanks. I'll take my chances out here with the unwashed masses while you adjust the thermostat of your life and stay safe with your pocket protectors and Styrofoam cups of coffee."

"People gotta die, Cade. It's simple. With the dead, I don't have to deal with their voices, their explanations, their excuses, or their bullshit. I don't have to look for cases like you. The phone rings and I leave my comfortable desk. Sometimes I wait a bit for traffic to ease up. It's not like they won't be dead when I get there. You, on the other hand, are living on doper time. Three in the morning is just as important as three in the afternoon. You have no control over your day. Your life spins like a wayward Soviet satellite with flawed hardware. You're always trying so hard to find your orbit."

My orbit? If there was such a thing. The life of a VIN detective is consistently inconsistent. I'd been an undercover detective in the Coral Gables Police Department's Vice Intelligence and Narcotics Unit for nearly nine consecutive years. Nine years of intersecting and often colliding with people in the ever-changing sphere of societal ills. In the last year specifically, there'd been one short marriage and one even shorter divorce, which produced one lingering gargantuan heartache.

Nine years.

In Miami.

Undercover.

I'd been working large-scale cocaine deals and high-volume money laundering cases the entire time. Nine years felt like nine lifetimes crammed into each and every one of those long years. A lot had happened in that time. After nine years you'd think that I'd have a stronger handle on the nuances of the job. Some sort of control. A better grasp of the knot on the bucking bronc of my life. Not so. The dynamics of money and cocaine are without instructions, spiral-bound manuals, or any sort of collegiate tutorial. You learn as you go. Those who don't learn the lessons quick enough, simply go. Either to jail or to a burial plot. I'd been detached from the police department to the Drug Enforcement Agency (DEA) for the past seven years. I was rarely even in my own police station. There were Coral Gables police officers who'd been working a heck of lot longer than Officer Montalván who had never seen me before. To many of them I was just a name on a piece of paper.

If that.

My trips into the VIN office were predicated on necessity or being summoned. I'd been engaged in so many big cocaine and mountainous money laundering cases that with each one it felt like the outcomes, and the players all changed. It was a never ending array of faces, names, locations, circumstances, and cases. There isn't anything simple about the drug world. Unlike Llyod Trentlocke, nothing was simple about my job. The VIN environment was not for the faint of heart. There were no laws of nature in narcotic work. You can't have principled laws in a lawless environment. The drug world was fueled by greed, profit, supply, and demand. There was no allegiance or loyalty. International borders were a mere obstacle, or at best a dotted line on a map. Cocaine infiltrated the Florida coastline like a surging, unending white tide. Cocaine works off of a three to one principle: one kilogram of cocaine generates three kilograms of cash. That is the law. As surely as the moon will come out tonight and the sun will rise tomorrow. The velocity of money is unimaginable to the uninitiated. Currency becomes a fast-growing byproduct of the cocaine trade that compounds and exponentially grows so fast that the storage of cash became a bigger dilemma than the actual accruing of money. I've seen jacuzzi bathtubs brimming over with cash, money stacked on pallets, and hefty bags stuffed with one and five dollar bills because the money was too cumbersome to count. The temptation of the narco dollar taints multiple levels of society especially at the judicial level. Judges are bribed, juries are bought, law enforcement is highly susceptible to ineptitude, corruption, and complicity. Trust and loyalty are just vapid concepts.

Trentlocke was right. Homicide had a scientific component to it. Death has principled laws. Once the body has died, rigor mortis, decomposition, and body decay follow a predictable progression. Not so in the drug world. There were no predictable elements of time and circumstance. There also are no alarm clocks, t- ball sponsorships, or assigned parking spaces. The drug world is a different dimension of life, an altered lifestyle. It is surreal, sexy, and sublime. It is also dangerous, detrimental, and deadly.

Police work is rudimentarily regimented in replication, and redundancy. There are documents to sign repeatedly, and procedures to follow constantly. Repetition is a mainstay in police work. The drug world is unregimented. Living, and for the better part, thriving, in the drug world while meeting the standards of police work is a precarious balancing act. As an undercover detective I am expected to meet the standard archaic demands of the police agency, all the while living my days and nights without the merest resemblance of any discernable rules to follow.

I turned my attention back to Trentlocke.

"So what do you have here?"

"You mean what do *we* have here," he said.

"There are too many *we*'s in this *you*. You're homicide. I'm narcotics. Remember? So what do *you* have here?" I asked him again.

He squinted in the rising sunlight, looking at the bustling crime scene in front of us.

"I'm not exactly sure myself, and I'm not so sure you aren't included," he said.

My stomach immediately knotted. This was not going to be a "kick them out" morning for me after all. There was a mixture of resources within the outer crime scene tape. A Coral Gables fire truck was one of the largest pieces of equipment. The truck was parked alongside the north fence line leading into Conde Avenue from Old Cutler Road. I could smell the faint whiff of smoke and wondered if we were investigating a fire or arson. Two Miami Dade Police cars and a Coral Gables police car were parked off to the side in the driveway of 680 Conde Avenue. The uniformed officers from both jurisdictions chatted amongst themselves in a close cluster outside their cars. Across the street by a tall stand of bamboo were three Miami Dade Crime Scene technicians having a somber discussion with the lone Coral Gables crime scene investigator. The height of the bamboo and its proximity to the road provided them shade from the rapidly rising sun. Further east there were a few people, including gray-jumpsuit-clad Coral Gables firefighters walking in a tight row, looking down at the ground. A tight grid search was underway. The firemen weren't here for a fire and I would venture to guess they had been called out because of their large number of on-duty personnel. Trentlocke called out to them as we walked past.

"Anything turn up yet?"

A firefighter on the end of the line closest to us looked up briefly. All he said was "Nope."

Trentlocke and I continued walking slowly east into the curve of the road. As we came around the bend, I could see more investigators milling about. We were still half the length of a football field from where most of the activity was. We walked in silence down the tree-shaded street. As we neared the intersection of Conde Avenue and Nogales Street, more and more of the local residents were milling about on their front lawns and porches watching the activity east of us. They were in various stages of dress from athletic wear to bathrobes and house slippers. Whatever had brought me out here on this early Saturday morning had obviously brought them out of their comfortable homes as well.

I saw three thin yellow tarps on the ground. Two of them were on Conde Avenue and the other one was on Nogales Street, right where the roads converged. The tarps were concealing the carnage from prying eyes. But even with the tarps, there was enough blood to warrant "carnage" as an accurate description. Splotches of blood stained the tarps. Blood splayed across parked cars and the trunks of palm trees. Blood was seeping out from under the tarps.

"Three?" I said to Trentlocke. "You didn't tell me there were three victims," I said, my eyes widening in disbelief.

We entered the inner perimeter of the crime scene.

"There aren't three victims. There's only one," he said.

"He's in three pieces."

Chapter Two

"**P**IECES? YOU MEAN like, hacked up?"

"No. It's more like, as in, splattered into pieces," he said with a dour demeanor.

"Splattered? How does that happen?" I said scanning the treetops around us.

"He was discovered by a resident at 6:54 this morning. Our victim has injuries indicative of a fall from an elevated position," Trentlocke said matter-of-factly.

"An elevated position? What are you talking about?" I asked with an incredulous lilt in my voice. "This ain't some New York City sidewalk, Llyod. How does a guy *fall from an elevated position* with enough force to *separate* his body when there is no elevated position to fall from?"

"My guess is a from an airplane," he said.

I was paralyzed, looking at the three tarps. I began to see them with an entirely different perspective. Oozing rivulets of blood were visible leaching into the ground in different directions. There were droplets on mailboxes, streaks of blood across the pavement, and viscous pools of blood seeping from underneath the tarps. The first tarp concealed a leg and an arm. Judging by the bulges under the tarps, I deduced that the second tarp concealed the victim's torso, a leg, and his head. A leg with a dusty boot stuck out of that blood smeared tarp. The third tarp had a smaller lump under it. It must have been the other arm.

Trentlocke squatted by the first tarp. I kneeled and leaned forward, resting my hands on my knees, looking down. He lifted the tarp. Initial responding police units had placed the separated arm and leg underneath this tarp.

"They didn't have enough tarps. They marked where the arm was found with that yellow cone over there." said Trentlocke as he motioned with his head towards a yellow cone about fifteen feet away.

When the tarp was pulled back, revealing the lone leg, shorn from the hip, I could see the pants were torn from his body when the leg was ripped away. The man's foot was still encased in tight lace-up boot. The toe of the boot and laces had a fine white, coarse dust on them, as did the bottom of the boot. The same dust was on the cold gnarled hand. The hand was grotesquely bent in an odd position. It looked like it had been broken at the wrist. Wordlessly, Trentlocke softly draped the tarp back over the leg and arm. We moved on to the next tarp.

This tarp concealed a larger mass of the victim. The torso appeared to be at least skeletally intact—although in seconds I could see that was not accurate. The first look was very deceiving as entrails and the digestive tract were burst through the skin. They laid partially under the shirt, the rest smeared on the asphalt. The ribs were broken like tinder sticks. The chest was completely caved in, rendering the body cavity flat and compacted. The head and face were nearly unrecognizable as human. Brain matter was compacted into the skull and embedded in the ground like a splattered, dropped melon. The left eye had popped out of its socket. The leg was bent under the body with the femur jutting through the ripped pant leg. His other boot was partially on the foot. It too was caked in the white dust we saw on the other leg.

"You okay?" Trentlocke asked me.

I just nodded.

"The third tarp is the other arm."

"Does it have a watch on it?" I asked.

He looked at me and immediately realized what I was alluding too. We went to the third tarp, and he pulled back enough of it to reveal the dusty hand. The arm did indeed have a watch on it. The watch was shattered, but it clearly showed the stopped time as 5:22.

"I think we can clearly assume time of death as 5:22 this morning." he said.

He covered the tarp and stood upright.

"You got anything?" he asked me.

"If at first you don't succeed, skydiving is not for you," I muttered to myself.

Trentlocke looked at me, rubbing the back of his neck as if by doing so he could liberate thoughts.

"Cade, there ain't no parachute."

"No parachute?"

"Well, let me rephrase that. As of yet we have not found a parachute in the tree lines or anywhere else. The body also doesn't seem like it had been wearing one from what we know so far."

"So what does that mean?" I asked him.

"It means we have a long morning in front of us. If our John Doe here did in fact come back to earth in a manner different than when he left, then we have one of three scenarios. The first scenario is that if he jumped out of a moving airplane without a parachute, we could have a suicide on our hands. If he was trying to fix something through an open door on the airplane, he may have slipped; then we have an accidental death. That's highly unlikely. The third scenario is he was pushed or thrown from the airplane. Then we have a murder."

Thinking about what Trentlocke said, I found myself looking up at the sky, shielding my eyes from the bright rising sun. I kept looking up to the sky then back down at the tarps. It was a reflexive act. As if I could figure out how this person landed here and how he got so viciously dismembered. It made no difference how much

I contemplated or tried to mathematically calculate height and distance, none of this was making any sense to me. The neighbors who lived on the quiet street were amassing in clumps, congregating in front of their houses, barely mindful of the yellow crime scene tape to the point they were often leaning over or against the fluttering nylon barrier.

"We need to separate these lookie-loos before they start telling each other the same rumors and stories. Cade, I'll give you first choice. You want to interview the woman in the Bed Bath and Beyond housecoat, or do you want the guy in the denim jacket?"

Standing outside of the crime scene tape was a woman in a garish paisley-patterned cotton robe talking to a man wearing a denim jacket and dark blue floral board shorts.

"I'll take a chance on the guy in the Canadian tuxedo," I said.

Trentlocke wasted no time hurrying towards the woman. He called out to her and quickly walked her away from the man in the denim jacket as I went to him.

"Sir, I'm Detective Cade Taylor of the Coral Gables Police Department. I was hoping you'd talk with me about what you may have heard or seen." I said.

"You're a cop?" he said, looking me up and down.

"Yes. I am a cop and yes, I am a detective." I tried to disguise the exasperation in my voice. I rarely ever told people who I was, and yet here I was in the bright morning light, feeling that I was telling everyone who I was from Miami Dade Officer Montalván to this bewildered resident with a phenomenal cowlick-infused bed head.

"Sir, can I get your name please?"

"My name?"

"Yes, your name," I said once again masking my exasperation.

"Jason."

"Jason?"

"Jason Cordicio."

"This is your house here, Mr. Cordicio?"

"Yes. 601 Conde Avenue."

"How long have you lived here?"

"This house?" he said, glancing back towards at the yellow stucco and glass residence.

"Yes, this house. How long have you lived here, Mr. Cordicio?"

"Since February of '93. We got it for a steal after Hurricane Andrew. The previous owners were freaked from the hurricane. They wanted to sell quickly."

"How are you doing with what occurred here this morning?" I asked him.

"This whole thing has been a complete shock. I woke up hearing Tessie screaming wondering what the heck was going on. I gotta tell ya, it scared the crap out of me. My wife said I needed to go check. I must admit I wasn't so sure if that was a good idea, but I did it anyway. The sun wasn't up yet. I couldn't tell exactly what was going on, but Tessie was here practically in our driveway screaming."

"Tessie?" I asked him.

"My neighbor. She's talking to the other cop you walked up with," he said, tilting his head towards the woman in the housecoat with Trentlocke.

"Was she saying anything about what she may have seen, or just screaming?"

"She was screaming like a banshee. I mean, this blood-curdling shrieking! There. Right there. She was standing right there near my mailbox. She has a pet iguana. I thought it might have been something to do with her iguana. The freaking thing is getting to be as big as a Komodo dragon. It's got claws like a bear. I swear. She's always picking hibiscus flowers off of our bush to feed the thing, does it in the early morning when its dark. She thinks we don't know she does it, but we do. Besides, we don't care. I just can't figure why she would want one of those things for a pet when we have so many running around here wild. They eat them in Trinidad. Did you know that? They barbecue them. They call them chicken of the trees."

There was a man in pieces fifty feet away and yet Mr. Cordicio had focused on the inanest thing. Fear and shock will do that to a person.

"Mr. Cordicio let's get back to what brought you out of your house. Aside from your neighbor Tessie screaming, did you hear anything or see anything before that?"

"No. I didn't hear anything. I was sound asleep."

"How about your wife, do you think she heard anything?" I asked him.

"I have a deviated septum. I snore a lot. My wife oftentimes moves to the spare bedroom in the middle of the night. I don't know if she heard anything or if it was Tessie who woke her up."

"Is it just the two of you in the house? Is anyone living here besides you and your wife?" I asked.

"We're partial empty nesters. Our youngest son is a sophomore at Temple University. He's in finals now, he'll be home for Christmas break next week."

"He's your youngest? What is his name?"

"Lucas."

"Lucas Cordicio," I affirmed.

"Yes. Lucas. The oldest is our daughter Lanie. She's in healthcare, but she doesn't live here. She lives out of state in Haddonfield, New Jersey."

"Mr. Cordicio, what is your wife's name?"

"Lucille Amanda, but we call her Lucy."

"May I ask what occupation you are in, sir?"

"Finance and Mergers. I help Venture Capitalists identify suitable acquisitions."

"Does your wife work?"

"No. Now what does this have to do with the fact there are body parts in my street?" he said with rising anger in his voice.

"Mr. Cordicio these are just routine questions I'm asking on a morning that is anything but routine for both you and I."

I turned to look back towards Trentlocke. He appeared to be getting an animated version of events from the woman identified as Tessie.

"Excuse me for a minute, Mr. Cordicio," I said as I started to amble over towards Trentlocke.

Tessie was still excitedly talking to him, clutching the top of her bathrobe to her chin to keep it from opening. In mid-sentence she stopped talking to Trentlocke and looked straight at me as I entered their conversation space.

"Who are you?" she asked me tersely.

"I'm Detective Cade Taylor with the Coral Gables Police Department."

"No you're not. You're not a cop," she said with a dismissive wave of her hand.

"Actually, I am. I'm here with Detective Trentlocke."

"I don't believe you," she huffed.

"Ma'am, a man fell from the sky this morning. There are cops and firemen here. What makes you think I'm not who I say I am? Do you think I just wandered under the yellow tape to stand next to a detective and play pretend here? What do you want to see? A badge? A donut? What would convince you?" I said the frustration in my voice rising in clear relation to the absurdity my morning had taken on.

Trentlocke pivoted away from the woman and leaned close to me.

"Cade, give her a moment, she was the one who actually discovered our victim first," Trentlocke softly said to me.

I reached for the chain around my neck and pulled my badge up from under my shirt. She stepped closer and looked at it intently.

"Nice. White gold with Yellow gold. Looks good. I used to work in jewelry at the Seybold Building before my husband passed away," she said with a much calmer voice.

"Cade, this is Teresita Esteban DeHoya. She lives at 600 Conde, right across from the man you were speaking with," said Trentlocke.

"Yes. Jason and Lucy live across the street from me. I was here first," she clarified with emphasis.

"I'm sure Detective Trentlocke asked you if you heard or saw anything prior to your unfortunate discovery this morning," I said to her.

"No. Nothing. But when I came out this morning to get the newspaper I saw these piles in the road. I thought at first the newspaper guy dropped his papers by accident. I mean it was dark and all so I really couldn't make out what they were, then I got closer. I thought it was a pile of clothes or rags. You know? Your mind will try and answer questions it doesn't understand. Then…" Her eyes welled up with tears and she fanned them with her hand. She struggled to regain her composure. "I saw a leg with a foot inside a boot. I got really freaked, I thought it might be a crocodile or something that did it. You know they're all over here. That's why I don't go in the water behind my house."

I tried to change the direction of the conversation briefly to give her some time to collect her emotions.

"You have water behind your house?" I asked.

"Barely, but yes. It's more like a brackish tiny narrow canal. A mosquito no- tell motel my husband used to say. There are frogs and turtles there too. The crocodiles like the bay. They'd probably like to come in this close, but the mangroves are too thick for most of them. Once past the mangroves and the rock pit it is open ocean behind us. They say that when Coral Gables developed this area of the city they mined the limestone and coral from the rock pit and used it as a buffer to keep the salt water from intruding into the underground aquifer."

Trentlocke saw an opportunity to understand where best to search for the parachute.

"Ms. Esteban-DeHoya, we'll be looking for a parachute from our victim, so what exactly is behind your house?" he asked her.

"Like I said, really thick mangroves. At least forty acres of mangroves. Then the bay. You have to go in from Campana Street so you can hook around the mangroves. You got to know your way around or you'll get lost. Off of Marin Street there's a footpath to the rock pit. The rock pit is about six acres wide and ten acres long. It's a big rectangle. My husband and I used to walk around it in the evenings and catch the sunset. East of the rock pit there are more mangroves and then Biscayne Bay."

"So even though it's still Coral Gables, it's pretty wild between your house and the bay..." Trentlocke said, smirking at me.

"It's pretty wild all the way past Chapman Field."

"Chapman Field is about three miles south...in the county juris-diction," I said with a sly smile to Trentlocke.

"Don't you live down there somewhere?" he asked me.

"I'm in the Royal Harbour Yacht Club, you know Paradise Point," I said.

"Excuse me, Detective, is there anything you need from me? I'd like to check in on my wife." said Jason Cordicio who unbeknownst to me had walked up behind us.

"No, Mr. Cordicio. We will let you know if we need any further questions answered. Please convey our sentiments to your wife. Thank you," I said.

"Do you have a business card, Detective?" Cordicio asked me.

Trentlocke chuckled, knowing full well I didn't have any business cards. He pulled one of his Miami Dade cards and gave it to me with a pen. I wrote the Coral Gables Police Department's main number on the back of Trentlocke's card. I handed the card to Jason Cordicio. He turned to leave and then gave Tessie a sympathetic soft pat on her back before walking pensively back to his house. Once again Trentlocke rubbed his chin ruefully. He looked down at the ground and transitioned his hand from rubbing his chin to rubbing the back of his neck. He did this a lot, some sort of nervous tic when he was thinking. He looked up at me for a moment.

"I think I'll have to call Aviation on this one. We might need to get up in the helicopter and see what we can find."

"Lloyd, I told you earlier there are too many *we's* in this *you*. I don't need to be in any helicopters this morning. This wasn't in the brochure."

The argument about whose city and whose county started again, while Tessie watched us bicker with rapt attention. In short order, Trentlocke put an end to the bickering.

"Listen Cade, it's simple. I need another spotter beside myself and right now you're it. So clam up. I'll see if they can meet us in the parking lot on the point in Matheson Hammock Park. Its big enough there, they can set the chopper down there easily. When the helicopter gets here, get in, buckle up, keep your eyes open, and your mouth shut."

Tessie shifted on her feet and moved closer to Trentlocke, subconsciously viewing him as the victor in our conversation. Llyod turned his attention to Tessie.

"Ms. Esteban-DeHoya, is there someone who can spend some time with you? Would you like me to have one of our victim social advocates come talk with you?"

"My daughter lives in Cutler Ridge, she's on her way up here. This has all been so bizarre and scary at the same time. I'll be okay. I just don't expect these type of things in Coral Gables."

"It's still Miami," I said.

"It is Miami, right? Things happen," she said, wistfully looking down at her hands.

"*Oye Mamma!*" a young woman in a flowered print dress called out to Tessie from the other side of the crime scene tape.

"That's my daughter. Veronica," said Tessie with a teary-eyed smile.

Trentlocke called out to Officer Montalván and told him to allow

Veronica into the crime scene. Mother and daughter embraced and then…then Tessie really started crying. I quietly suggested to Trentlocke to call social services for a counselor to come to Tessie's house and maybe the Cordicio residence as well. He agreed, making a note for himself in his small binder.

"Cade, this is a terrible scene to wake up to but there's probably a logical explanation. If we get eyes in the sky we might find a parachute or ultralight aircraft in those mangroves."

We both started walking back towards Old Cutler Road. The firefighters were no longer in a grid search. They were standing clustered around their fire truck. Jokingly, I said to one of the firefighters, "How'd you find your way here? I'm surprised you guys even know where this street is."

"We get called here all the time. That woman you were talking to always complains about her neighbor burning logs in a backyard firepit," said the firefighter.

With a shake of my head and a shrug of my shoulders, I fell in line walking with Trentlocke. As we neared the outer yellow crime scene tape a dark sedan pulled up, braking hard inches from the outside of the taut yellow tape, kicking up a cloud of dust. The male driver and his female passenger stepped out of the car. The driver, a fair-skinned man in a blue polo, flung the door closed, clearly agitated.

"Which one of you is Lock Trench?" he bellowed simultaneously to everyone and no one on the inside of the tape.

"I'm Miami Dade Homicide Detective Llyod Trentlocke, and I'm in charge. How can I help you?" Llyod asked the man.

The man pulled off his aviator sunglasses and hastily tucked them into the breast pocket on his polo shirt.

"Not anymore. You're not in charge. I am!" he exclaimed.

Chapter Three

"**B**UDDY, I DON'T know who you are, but until I find out who you are don't even think about crossing under this crime scene tape," Trentlocke said.

The man was just under six feet tall. He was wearing desert sand-colored 5.11 tactical rip-stop BDU pants. His dark blue polo shirt was tucked neatly into his trousers. He had a military style haircut although based on his manners, I ventured to presume he was not and never had been in the military. His lack of civility betrayed a college education and quick ascent into a government job. In yellow scripted lettering across the left breast of his shirt was the name "Dreyer." He trained a steady gaze on Trentlocke, and I could tell he was mulling over in his head whether or not to test the seasoned Miami Dade Homicide Detective. Before he could say anything, his female partner who was clad in the same attire, rounded the front of the car.

"Detective, I am Addison Hope, and this is my colleague Lawson Dreyer. We're with the National Transportation Safety Board. You know? The NTSB."

This seemed to embolden Dreyer.

"Detective, let me remind you…better yet, *inform* you that the NTSB is an independent federal agency charged by Congress with investigating every civil aviation accident in the United States and its territories. We are the premier investigative agency for significant events in other modes of transportation too. All types! We supersede all investigative entities. Our domain includes railroad, transit, highway, marine, pipeline, commercial space... If it flies, floats, or flings we oversee it," he pompously bellowed.

"My father always said if it flies, floats or fucks, you should rent it. Come to think of it he was kind of like you guys in some ways." I said.

"Who exactly are you?" Dreyer said leveling his eyes at me.

People asking me who I am had become the morning theme, and quite frankly one I was getting tired of answering. There was too much hostility for this hour. Unfortunately, I was a decent contributor to that animosity with my contentious attitude toward Trentlocke. I was still angry about the events nearly a year ago when we last saw each other. That was most apparent to both him and I, but here with some blue shirt butt boy demanding to take over the investigation, I was siding with Trentlocke. It was Trentlocke who stepped over Dreyer's question and with as much diplomacy as he could muster, he addressed Addison Hope.

"Ms. Hope, thank you for clarifying who you are and who you're with. Do either of you have credentials with you? If so, would you be so kind as to present them so I can address you both properly."

Trentlocke was smooth as a river stone. The years of conducting interviews and dealing with grieving survivors of homicide incidents had fostered a professional polish to his mannerisms. Something I obviously lacked. Dreyer was committed to maintaining his arrogant position. He turned his body to show Trentlocke the bold letters "NTSB" written in yellow across the back of his polo shirt. The lettering was so large I seriously thought that even Stevie Wonder could see them.

"Right there. See it? NTSB!" said Dreyer.

"I see man in a polo shirt who's much more agitated than his partner," Trentlocke coolly replied.

It was Addison Hope who once again proffered a calm détente as she presented her credentials to Trentlocke. She held open her wallet that held a photo identification card and an NTSB badge. Trentlocke and I could clearly see it.

"Detective, we are aviation and accident investigators for the NTSB. We are part of a 'go team' stationed at our national headquarters in Ashburn, Virginia. Our teams operate out of Ashburn, but Lawson and I are TDY'ed here in Miami for South Florida and Puerto Rico deployment. I recognize you're Homicide, but if this death occurred due to an aircraft, then we do relegate your investigation behind our own. May we now enter *our* crime scene?" she said.

Trentlocke appreciated her comments, but he was a wizened veteran.

"Investigator Hope. I see exactly what you mean. As of now we have a body on the ground behind us. Granted, the body is in pieces, but we haven't determined if it came from an aircraft or fell from a construction crane. So as you can see, even under the barest OSHA standards we cannot release the scene to you or any other investigative agency until our preliminary investigation determines what exactly occurred to cause the termination of our victim's life."

Like I said, he was smooth as a river stone. Using the Occupational Health and Safety Administration (OSHA) as an ally would buy Trentlocke time. The NTSB did not want to battle with OSHA, an agency that competes for the same congressional funding sources. Aside from jurisdictional comeuppance, I was perplexed why Trentlocke wouldn't be agreeable to the NTSB taking the investigation over. It would free up both of our mornings and alleviate a plethora of potential future headaches. I could see Lawson Dreyer was not the type to stand down. Even if it was in his best interest.

"Bullshit. There is no construction crane and there never was one!" he said.

"Says you. As of right now I can't rule out any possibility," Trentlocke said, stonewalling both NTSB investigators. "This scene contains a body. No wreckage, no sign of any mechanical apparatus.

Detective Taylor here and I will be doing an aerial canvass of the area within the hour—"

Dreyer cut him off mid-explanation.

"Just how do you plan to do that?"

Trentlocke was briefly taken aback by the strong line of questioning, but he maintained his calm demeanor.

"Miami Dade Aviation is enroute from our Intercoastal station near Aventura. Our helicopter should be here in twenty minutes or less. We'll be meeting them just north of here at Matheson Hammock."

"No you're not. I have put a hold on airspace for every aircraft within three miles of here. I might have a dangerous windshear in the lower atmosphere," Dreyer said smugly.

Trentlocke lost it.

He quickly slipped under the yellow crime scene tape and grabbed Dreyer by the collar of his smooth polo shirt. Lifting Dreyer onto his toes, Trentlocke walked him briskly backward to the NTSB car. He bent Dreyer back over the hood of the car. Dreyer wasn't expecting the swift action and change in temperament that overcame Trentlocke. Dreyer's eyes were wide with fear. He fumbled awkwardly with his arms as if some magical handrail could keep him from being bent back over the car.

"I'm going to airspace a wind shear right through your throat," Trentlocke hissed at Dreyer. "Don't you ever come out on my scene and tell me what you can do and what I can't do. Because I will *can do* you right through the front grille of this car. You hear me?"

Dreyer was so scared, his mouth just opened and closed instead of answering. The firefighters looked between Trentlocke and me, expecting me to do something.

"Hey Dreyer, I hope you bought some actual hope with you besides Addison Hope, because I'm serious as a heart attack he will kick your ass if you don't answer him," I said to Dreyer.

From his contorted spinal twist across the car's hood, Dreyer blurted, "Okay! Okay. I hear you; I hear you."

Trentlocke released his grip on Dreyer and the ruffled NTSB investigator righted himself and smoothed his wrinkled shirt. "I can have you arrested for assaulting a federal officer! I have plenty of witnesses."

With that declaration, the assembled firefighters and other support personnel slowly turned away and walked further into the crime scene, away from the fray. Dreyer could see that his veiled threat was not going to be implemented and that maybe…just maybe he had driven up to the wrong police investigator on the wrong morning.

"You locals are all the same. Thick as fleas on a mangy dog. You'd never make it in the federal system, I can tell you that."

"What you can tell us is that you're going to lift the airspace ban so we can do our job. That's what you're going to do," I said.

"Oh now you want to jump in on this too!" he barked at me.

"Listen, buddy this ain't about you and the Feds and you're microphones and podiums at every airplane crash. We're not having a stellar morning here, so dial it down a notch. Since the dead guy and his parts, which are on the ground by the way, constitute this as Miami Dade's homicide until they release it to the NTSB, you aren't taking over anything. Now we ordered a helicopter to pick us up. You can ride along or stay here pouting, but one of you in the matching Garanimals outfits better open the airspace before we penetrate it and proverbially kick you in the nuts again," I said.

I looked at Addison Hope and offered a half sincere comment. "No offense."

"We still don't know who you are," she said eyeing me with slight perplexity.

"I'm Cade Taylor. I'm a detective with the Coral Gables Police Department."

"A detective? What kind of detective are you?" she inquired.

"I'm Vice Intelligence Narcotics. I'm a VIN detective."

She persisted further "Just why are you here?"

All morning I'd been asking that same question myself. Major Brunson summoned me out here and it had been a cavalcade of exasperation and bewilderment from the moment I arrived. I found myself dealing with a former police academy classmate I didn't really like, and now defending him against an arrogant NTSB investigator I liked even less.

"We're in Coral Gables, and Coral Gables is in Miami Dade County, so that is how both me and the 'Miami Mauler' here, are on scene," I said with a slight dig towards Trentlocke's quick penchant for aggressiveness.

"May I propose a compromise?" suggested Hope.

All three of us testosterone-charged agitated males stopped and looked towards her.

"Detective Trentlocke, I can attest as surely as I'm standing here that at some point, and most likely very soon, we at the NTSB will take over this investigation. This I know to be true. Posturing and pontificating by you and Lawson won't get us anywhere. Your command staff will mandate that you not only supply us with whatever resources we ask of the Miami Dade Police Department but also of yourself. Although Lawson didn't mention it, I *am* his supervisor. You could have deduced that since I wasn't driving, but your powers of observation are not to be brought into question—at least not yet. I'll lift the air restrictions. I have no issue going up in the helicopter, but Lawson tends to get a little blue around the gills when flying."

Lawson Dreyer became sheepish. He looked away for a moment in shame.

"So my compromise is I take Chad here with me…"

"Cade. It's Cade. Cade Taylor."

"Whatever. I take Cade with me, and we'll get an aerial perspective. You and Lawson learn to play nice and come up with some answers while we're gone, try to get an idea on how this death occurred."

Trentlocke and Dreyer looked at each other. With barely

contained reluctance, Trentlocke lifted the crime scene tape and Dreyer stepped under and into the crime scene.

"Officer Montalván, will you please log in our newest addition to the investigation?" said Trentlocke over his shoulder to the waiting officer. With the two of them moving on into the crime scene it left myself and Investigator Hope standing outside the tape.

"Since it is your city, and you know your way around, how about you drive?" she said.

Internally I was cursing Major Brunson, Llyod Trentlocke, Tessie, Jason Cordicio, the dead guy, and anything and anyone else I could blame for interrupting my Saturday morning. I gave her request a brief thought and then gave in to the obvious logical conclusion. I simply nodded my head in the direction of my car. She retrieved binoculars and a notepad form the NTSB car and quickly caught up to me.

"I see that chivalry isn't dead," she grumbled, slowing down beside me.

"You really can't have it both ways, lady. You show up with that blowhard cartoon in matching Goodyear tire store outfits and you expect some sort of preferential treatment. Did you even think to ask if I *wanted* to go up in the helicopter?"

"The last time Lawson flew with me he puked in my binocular case. Do you need a barf bag too?" she teased.

"No. What I need is to quit answering my phone on Saturday mornings and getting dragged all over God's green earth and his big blue sky because some knucklehead trying to be Icarus found a way to confuse us all by falling out of the air."

We were now standing at the rear of my mint green 1999 Toyota Land Cruiser. All of our undercover cars were supplied to us from three small independent Miami rental agencies. Ramon, the manager from the agency, had secured the Land Cruiser for me a few days ago. Months ago he said a midnight blue IROC Z-28 was good for my image. I figured image went out the window when I traded in the Z-28 for this Land Cruiser that he had pushed on me. "All the dopers in Miami have one!" he said. I never gave my image much thought but the years of being undercover imparted the necessity of perception, reality, and how perception becomes reality. Fitting in with Miami's drug underworld is essential to being a successful undercover VIN detective. Yet every time I thought I had it all figured out, I once again found myself stumbling and tumbling into another only-in-South Florida type of convoluted dangerous mystery. I opened the driver's door and unlocked her door with the automatic button. She opened the door, stepped into the Toyota, and slammed it behind her. With us both seated I turned on the ignition.

"Did you have a mother?" she asked me.

I was taken aback by her question.

"Yes. Of course I had a mother."

"Well, she must not have been from the south or she would've taught you to open a car door for a lady," she said with a tinge of admonishment.

I turned the car off.

"My mother was from Old Orchard Beach, Maine. She met my father here. So no, my mother is not from the south. She never said anything about opening doors for ladies. She did teach me to walk though. I'm sure your mother taught you to walk. You should get out and walk back and get the car keys from Motion Sickness Boy or start walking to the point at Matheson Hammock Park. Its only about two and a half miles from here. Make sure you have bug spray."

"You're serious?" she asked incredulously. Before I could reply she answered for me. "I know. Serious as a heart attack." She unbuckled her seat belt and reached for the door handle when I interrupted her.

"Just stay. Besides, I don't think the pilot wants to wait for you to find your way there any more than I do."

I once again started the car.

I eased the car from the shoulder of Old Cutler Road and started north towards the Matheson Hammock Park entrance. To try and break the tension that had crept into the car with us, I started talking.

"Are you from the South?"

"Yes," was her terse answer.

The razor-sharp tension barely lifted. I figured I better try a little harder. We already had one unfortunate guy fall from the sky; I didn't need to go up in a helicopter with an angry NTSB investigator and end up being the second.

"So, where in the south?"

"Prosperity, South Carolina."

"Prosperity? Your name is Hope and you come from a town named Prosperity?"

"Yes."

"I never heard of it. Where in South Carolina is it?"

"Believe it or not it's in Prosperity, South Carolina. Now if you're asking me what it's near, it's about forty miles north of Columbia, the state capital."

"Yeah, that's what I meant. What is it near. That's what I meant to say."

"Words are important, Cade," she said again with another tinge of admonishment.

"Is it a big place?"

"When has prosperity ever been big enough for anyone? Actually, it's pretty small. It was originally called Frog Level because of its low lying flood areas. There were a bunch of ponds and mudholes, so they called it Frog Level. Then the town burned down like a hundred years ago, so for good luck they renamed the town Prosperity."

"You're serious?" I asked her.

"Like a heart attack."

"So where was college? I mean, to be with the NTSB you need to have a degree, right?"

"Coastal Carolina University. Before you ask, it's about fifteen miles from Myrtle Beach."

I nodded in acknowledgement. Normal conversation usually

flows with the other party asking you about yourself. She neither cared to ask or simply didn't care at all. That was fine with me. I like it that way. There is something safe and clean in the silence. No complications and misconstrued comments. I thought of an expression I once heard an attorney say after a lengthy courtroom deposition.

"Silence is golden. Duct tape is silver."

As we turned into the entrance of Matheson Hammock Park, I was actually happy with the silence. It gave me some time to ponder just how our victim came to be splayed and split all across the pavement. I also didn't feel the need to explain the history and vastness of the 630 acre park, beach, and marina. It was Hope who broke the silence.

"Old Orchard Beach, Maine. Where is that?" she asked me.

"Believe it or not it's in Old Orchard Beach, Maine. Now if you're asking me what it's near, it's about twelve miles southeast of Portland." Before she could say anything I finished with, "Words are important, Addison."

She quickly understood the tone of the conversation and asked me as we were pulling up towards the idling helicopter. "Are *you* from Maine?"

"No, I'm from Miami," was all I said as I eased the Land Cruiser to a stop away from the rotor wash of the helicopter.

The helicopter was set down and awaiting us in the enormous empty parking lot near the Red Fish Grill restaurant. The Miami Dade Police helicopter is a Eurocopter AS350 Ecureuil. Nicknamed "The Squirrel" it can hold between four to six passengers. Addison opened the car door and started walking towards the idling whirly bird. The helmeted and mirror-visored pilot could see her NTSB shirt clearly. He nodded as she walked, bent forward to avoid the rotating blades of the chopper. She opened the door to the number two seat and climbed aboard the noisy aircraft. I could see her shaking hands with the pilot as I approached the helicopter. The pilot motioned with his thumb to take the seat behind him, and I too bent at the waist and crouched towards the noisy flying machine. I thought to myself, *Is this really necessary?* I saw lots of people do it in movies and on TV but was it truthfully necessary to lower your height profile by fourteen inches to avoid accidental decapitation? The answer was visibly obvious as I could see the slower rotating blades droop, but still I felt I looked like some sunbaked tourist searching for shells on a beach as I scampered across the asphalt looking at my shoes. I clambered into the helicopter through the open side door and pulled the heavy square door shut behind me.

The pilot looked back into the cabin interior using his large rectangular mirror. Even with his visor obscuring his eyes, I could see he was staring at me. I pulled my badge from under my shirt and held up the thin chain around my neck long enough for him to know I was a cop. He might not know who I was or maybe even from what agency, but he knew I was a cop. He motioned for me to put on an olive green headset hanging on a hook near my seat. Addison already donned her headset. It seemed to cover her entire head. She reminded me of the infamous picture of Massachusetts senator and presidential candidate Michael Dukakis wearing an oversized tank helmet for a photo opp. Either that or the Great Gazoo from The Flintstones.

Once I had my own headset adjusted I could hear the pilot talking with Addison. He looked again in the mirror and saw that I was buckled in, my headset was on.

"Hey long hair, you got a name?" I heard in the headset.

"Cade. Cade Taylor. I'm with the Gables?" I spoke into the attached small microphone.

"Gables? Where's Trentlocke? I thought he was going up."

It was Addison who answered.

"Detective Trentlocke is staying on the ground with the rest of the NTSB team."

Team? I don't really constitute two people as being a team. Not even beach volleyball or doubles tennis. I'd think of them as more of a partnership than a team.

I needed to keep my focus on the task at hand. I was allowing the trivialities of the morning get in the way of my thinking. Even though I was getting more disheartened by the minute about how this morning was turning out, I needed to shut out all the little agitations that were nibbling at me inside.

"I want to have a clear understanding of what we're doing. Before we lift off, how about a refresher?" asked the pilot.

Addison said, "We need to get a better perspective of the scene from an airborne position. We think there may be a parachute or personal ultralight aircraft down in the mangroves east of our scene or maybe even in Biscayne Bay."

"How did our victim die?" asked the pilot as he threw switches and fastidiously checked dials.

"The mechanism of death we believe to be an unplanned terminal event initiated by an unintentional height influenced rapid acceleration causing *exitus momentatus* by abrupt impact with terra firma," she said.

He looked at me in the mirror hoping for a simplified explanation.

"Basically the cause of death was Florida," I said with a shrug.

Chapter Four

BEFORE A HELICOPTER lifts off from the safety of the ground there's a brief waver that to the uninitiated passengers makes them wonder, *Is this thing really going to fly?*

I saw the Land Cruiser become smaller as we ascended up and above the parking lot. The pilot smoothly turned the helicopter towards the Arvida Channel in the Coral Gables waterway and then banked the surprisingly quiet craft northeast out towards downtown Miami. As we headed northeast he quickly had us soaring high above Biscayne Bay.

I heard him say through my headset, "Winds and currents are running northeast towards the ocean. I suggest we start out by Stiltsville and work our way in. There could be something bobbing out there."

Addison was chattering in the headset about how much meteorology plays in these type of searches. I didn't feel like talking and would have loved to mute her. I just gave him a thumbs up from the back. I then started scanning out the wide window watching the blue-green water of Biscayne Bay. Within two minutes we were circling over Stiltsville. In the 1930s a number of small shanty-type structures were built in the area on stilts over the water. The shanties were high and dry, elevated above the aquamarine bay. The only way to access the recreational dwellings was by boat. At one time there were nearly thirty of the homes in Stiltsville. Due to the unrelenting pounding from decades of hurricanes, rampant vandalism, and simple owner neglect there were now only a few houses in Stiltsville. In 1985 this portion of Biscayne Bay on down to the Monroe County line became Biscayne National Park. Repairs and new builds became prohibited. The National Parks system in true slow as molasses form, is hoping for time, and the elements to eventually erode the remaining structures. Then they would be no more. The ones still standing had wraparound decks and were painted in fading hues of baby blue, pink, and seafoam green. Pelicans and Anhingas shared the rooflines of the few remaining houses. They appeared to be drying their wings in the morning sun. We circled the houses and shallow shoals around Stiltsville looking for any sign of a parachute, ultralight aircraft, or God forbid, another victim. Addison and I kept our eyes trained on the smooth water and neither of us were seeing anything. Feeling that he had seen all he could, the pilot started to fly due west towards the shoreline. Once we were over the shoreline he would turn the helicopter east and travel a mile offshore, then back west again. He repeated this pattern, doing a grid search of Biscayne Bay. After multiple passes and seeing nothing of consequence, the pilot started doing concentric circles over the crime scene. Addison and I kept our eyes trained on the mangroves and small cut-out channels east of the crime scene.

Tessie was absolutely spot-on with her description of the area. Indeed, there was a vast tract of mangroves that extended from behind her house and with increasing thickness on out to Biscayne Bay. The gnarly rooted trees provided an immense ecosystem for wildlife. In the distance looking south I could see that the mangroves created a jagged shoreline-influenced buffer along the coastline south, past Deering Bay. The mangroves jutted in and out right to where I was currently living at Paradise Point. The pilot kept the helicopter in a steady tight circle. Still, below us there was no sign of any parachute or any type of an ultralight that could have dropped, pushed, shoved, shaken, or even stirred our victim out of it. The large rectangular rock pit that Tessie mentioned was very prominent from our elevated position. Over the crime scene, I could see through breaks in the tree line: the Coral Gables fire truck, people milling about, and because of the large NTSB on his back, an occasional glimpse of Lawson Dreyer. Steadily circling the area, the pilot was very patient, silently waiting for Addison to say we'd seen enough from our whirring perch in the sky. Her silence was either a testament to her dogged determination or cringing ignorance to the obvious. Eventually it wasn't the pilot or her that made that decision. The decision was made for us by a low fuel light on the cockpit console.

"Okay campers, we're going to have to make a run to Tamiami for fuel," I heard the pilot say in my headset.

"Can you drop us off first?" I asked knowing a run out west to the Kendall Tamiami Executive Airport would easily add another hour to my already interrupted Saturday.

"No can do. County policy. When the light comes on, we go for fuel," was the reply from the pilot.

Tamiami airport was nearly a straight line west from where we were. It had once been on the western fringe of the populace of Miami Dade County but with the county's unplanned development, hurried growth, and rapid expansion it was now surrounded by houses, townhomes, businesses, and warehouses. There was a long-established little pub called Keg South just across from the airport fence line. A cold beer and some Buffalo wings would be ideal, but I didn't think the pilot nor Ms. NTSB would appreciate me turning this impromptu airborne assignment into an impromptu Cade Taylor wing and beer run. Within ten minutes we were over the airfield at the busy municipal airport. The Miami Dade Aviation hangars are near the southeast section of the airport. The helicopter skids gently touched down on the helipad. I could hear the rotating blades slowing to a stop. With the engine turned off and the noise drastically reduced, the pilot took off his helmet. He put on some mirrored sunglasses, which quite frankly didn't change his incognito appearance very much.

"You both might want to stretch your legs; besides it can get hot in here. It should only take about twenty minutes for us to get some Go Juice," he said as he stepped out of the helicopter.

Go Juice.

I was trusting my safe return to Matheson Hammock to a man who refers to aviation fuel as "go juice."

The day had started with such promise. A balmy December morning, two good football teams on TV, and then once the phone rang from Major Brunson the fuckening started. Once the crap started with Trentlocke I knew the fuckening was coming. Although even with my sharply honed sardonic mentality I could not have imagined this morning of body parts, a crying house-coat clad woman, haughty NTSB investigators, and a pilot who called me "long hair."

I climbed out of the helicopter. The pilot was already gone and out of sight. There was a support team that didn't seem to be in any hurry to fuel the aircraft. Addison and I ambled into the hangar and used the bathrooms inside. When I came out she was nowhere to be seen so I went outside and decided to look around at all the machinery and spare parts stored on pallets. Addison Hope walked out and joined me as I stood in the now mid-morning sun. There was a picnic table under the shade of some small bottle brush trees near the hangar's parking lot.

"Want to sit down?" she said as she walked past me towards the picnic table.

"I thought the whole idea was to stretch our legs." I said to her as she passed by.

"He didn't say we had to do it here, standing so close to the helipad."

I fell in behind her and we sat on opposite sides of the picnic table facing each other. I wanted to rest my elbows on the splintered tabletop, but the crackling paint and weather-worn wood made that a less than savory option. Sitting straight up would eventually create an aching back. I leaned back with my arms folded against my chest.

"Defensive?" she asked, nodding at my posture.

"No, I'm just resting my back," I replied.

"You look defensive."

I tried to contain my sigh of exasperation.

"What's on your mind, Investigator?" I asked.

"We have some time here, and I just thought we could talk. I'm intrigued. How long have you been with the Gables?

I saw no sensible reason that a question about my time with the Coral Gables Police Department had anything to do with body parts, but I tried to not be rude.

"About eleven years."

"Did you ever consider going federal?"

"I've been detached to the DEA the past nine years so I'm kind of doing the same work. What about you? What made you decide the NTSB was for you?"

"I don't know. Aviation and aviation investigations were the furthest from my mind when I was in college. I met my first husband my senior year. He was applying everywhere in the federal system. I don't think he really cared who would hire him, it was like a 'more is better' approach. I was helping him with his applications, and he was printing multiples at the library. You know, in case he made a mistake or something. If you think these agencies don't talk to each other you're in for a rude awakening. They compare applications and resumes. The first discrepancy and one of them will rat you out to the other. Then after that agency drops you the one that ratted you out will job offer you. Our little kitchen table had all these printed blank applications, so I sent a few in myself and I was selected by the NTSB."

"Anybody else job offer you?" I asked her.

"Two other offers. One was the Federal Communications Commission, and the other was the Federal Accountability Office. I mean, serious dullsville. So I went with the NTSB."

"You chose mass casualty plane crashes over dullsville?"

"Yeah, I know it's not something you really consider until you find yourself on a hillside somewhere, pulling bloody metal shards out of the bottom of your boots. I once had a woman's finger wedged in the thread of my boots. That was a serious rethink-the-whole-career moment." Her eyes were unfocused, staring past me.

In the silence, she continued looking past me. She delicately tucked a wisp of her brown hair behind her ear. Her mind was somewhere else reflecting on something that very few can imagine.

"You said your first husband. Have you been married more than once?"

She snapped back from her reverie.

"No, just once. It was a very short marriage. More like an extended prom date actually. I lost track of him years ago and I'm sure he's lost track of me too. How about you? Is there a Mrs. Taylor home darning your socks and keeping the home fires burning?"

"No there is not a Mrs. Taylor," I scoffed. "There was once, but she decided that a life with me was not something she wanted to do until death do her part. So she did her own part of leaving and that was that. The home fires burning has a whole different meaning to me. My marriage and subsequent divorce was more like a fire sale. I just didn't get the sales notice, burn permit, or the flame retardant suit. It was very quick and easy. At least, for her it was."

"Where there any signs at all? I mean you saw the red flags at some point, right?"

"I thought it was a carnival," I said with a lift of my eyebrows.

"Funny. How long has it been?"

"About a year."

"What was her name?"

I briefly mulled over if it was pertinent and necessary to say her name. Hers had become a name I focused on not saying.

"Gina. Her name is Gina. What was your husband's name?"

"Dan."

There was an awkward silence. I felt like the conversation had quickly turned to two people comparing hidden scars under our clothing. She broke the discomfort by transitioning the conversation back to work.

"What do you think happened to our victim today? I mean, we know he fell from either an airplane or helicopter. But what do you think happened?"

I was thankful for the redirection.

"Have you ever seen a case like this before?" I asked her.

"Without a parachute? No. Detective, do you know about pressure?"

"Pressure? Like pressure to pay bills, pressure in my job, pressure that comes from living in Miami. What kind of pressure?"

"No, I know those are real pressures. I'm talking about atmospheric pressure."

"I lived through Hurricane Andrew, and I saw a lot of structural things related to the pressure of the hurricane."

"No, no, no, I'm talking about every day, in the air, normal atmospheric pressure."

I uncrossed my arms and leaned forward with my palms resting on top of my thighs. I looked at her, indicating she should continue talking. She started talking animatedly with her hands like a middle schooler standing in front of her classmates giving a speech on meteorology.

"Atmospheric pressure is directly affected and approximated by equally strong hydrostatic pressure. It's caused by the weight of air above a defined object. In most cases, that's the air pressing down on the fuselage of an aircraft. As an airplane increases its elevation, there is less layering of atmospheric mass, so it's an inverse reaction of atmospheric pressure decreasing with increasing elevation."

I silently tried to understand what she was saying.

"So what you're saying is that at slower speeds and lower altitudes, there's more pressure on an airplane than one that's higher and traveling faster?" I proffered.

"Exactly," she said with a smile, pointing at me. "Nearly every airplane disaster occurs at landing or take-off because there are so many variable factors occurring at one time. The airplane is ascending or descending, there are flight adjustments by the flight crew, but the never-changing constant is that the atmosphere is thin. I mean, thin in relation to the Earth's total radius. The density of the atmospheric pressure at low altitude in conjunction with the Earth's gravitational acceleration is relatively constant."

"That's why NASA rockets need all that propulsion to get the actual space capsule high and above in the sky," I said.

"Exactly!"

She liked to use that word a lot.

"So what are you getting at, Professor Addison?"

"What I'm getting at is that our falling Wallenda here did not fall from a tightrope or a circus ladder. He also didn't open an aircraft door at a low altitude and jump out. You ever see those sky diving airplanes? They all land and take off with the door open or even totally removed. Our victim, I suspect, was either pushed or fell accidentally out of an open door of a low-flying aircraft."

"Low-flying aircraft. Aren't there rules about altitude and residential areas?"

"Yes, unless you're on approach to an airport," she said making an obvious overt gesture of looking around.

"You think he fell from an airplane destined for this airport?" I asked her.

"You saw for yourself. It's nearly a straight line from where he landed to where we are."

"Wouldn't there be a record of all landings and take-offs?"

"Yes. I think we should start with the landside ops office here and see who came in early this morning. How about I give you a proposition? I'll use my NTSB authority and go see what I can find. I'll call Lawson and have him pick me up. You can fly back with the pilot, and I'll let you know what I find out."

Desirous to pick up my Saturday where it had been so rudely

interrupted I put it back on Miami Dade Homicide. "Actually…this is still under the purveyance of Miami Dade Homicide. You'd be better off just letting Llyod Trentlocke know what you discover. I'm sure he and Lawson Dreyer have created a cozy bond by now."

"Yeah, like us," she said facetiously.

As a matter of professional courtesy, she and I exchanged telephone numbers. I entered hers into my contacts on my cell phone.

I caught a glimpse of the pilot now walking from the hangar. He was carrying a white paper bag in his hand. My initial thoughts about the expediency of the support crew fueling the aircraft were proven wrong. The pilot saw us and called out as he was walking.

"You folks ready to go?"

Addison shouted back, "I'm going to stay but Cade will be going back. He needs to get his car."

"Let's go, Cade. Let me show you again the fine art of the depart."

I got up from the picnic table.

"It was nice meeting you. Good luck with your investigation."

"I'll let you know."

"Don't. This isn't my case, and it isn't my department. Trentlocke. Remember? Trentlocke."

I made sure to approach the aircraft from the nose and not walk behind the helicopter where the tail rotor was already spinning. I climbed in next to the pilot and immediately could smell Buffalo chicken wings. I closed the door, buckled myself into the seat and put on the headset.

"I stopped over at Keg South and got some wings for my lunch later," said the pilot.

The fuckening continues.

Chapter Five

ON THE WAY back to my car I thought about what Addison had said—that the airport was nearly a direct line from the crime scene. I noticed the route was almost razor straight. As we neared the parking lot at Matheson Hammock Park the pilot became concerned for two reasons: There were more cars in the parking lot and the winds had changed.

"Look at the kite surfers," he said, pointing to the sky. "The winds have picked up and are switching back and forth," I heard him say through the headset.

Multicolored windsurfer sails and fast moving kite surfers were vying for the dashing winds just offshore. The fluttering nylon sails were a pageantry of swirling rainbow hues. Unfortunately for me their cars, large trailers, pickup trucks, and vans were haphazardly parked in the parking lot making a parking lot landing for us impossible. The erratic parking was for the ease of offloading their gear. I'm sure none of them expected a helicopter to need a landing zone when they showed up to chase the soft winter breezes of Biscayne Bay.

"You ever do a flying fish drop into the water before?" he asked me.

"A what?" was my astonished reply.

"I'm just messing with you, but I am going to have to let you down at the furthest east parking lot closest to the bay on the southside of the marina. You'll have to walk over the bridge to get to your car. If you cut across the marina parking lot it will save you a few minutes."

The fuckening continued.

He set the helicopter down at the furthest parking lot, a rarely used square of sun-bleached asphalt. I stepped out of the chicken wing-smelling cockpit. With a wave of his hand he said goodbye. He lifted off.

It was a much longer walk back to my car then the pilot said it would be. *Much* longer. I was drenched in sweat. I'd neglected to bring my cellphone with me. I didn't think I would have a use for it up in the helicopter. I couldn't have foreseen that we'd be going out to the Tamiami Airport. When I got into my car there were two messages on my phone. The first was from Trentlocke telling me they had broken down the crime scene. Lawson had told him Addison had authorized the removal of the body and the clearing of the scene. He let it be known in no uncertain terms that he would have rather talked to me but obviously I couldn't "bother to pick up my phone."

The second message was from Major Brunson. He too, was angry at me for not notifying him of the situation. He ranted about why he had to hear about the situation from a patrol sergeant and not from me. I put the phone down. The coolness of the air conditioner in the car was helping me to settle into the driver's seat and contemplate how the day started. I reasoned I had no control over how it started. That was past history. I did have control over how it would end. I could still catch the University of Miami and UCLA football game on TV. The Miami Hurricanes were annihilated by Syracuse last week and UCLA was 10-0. The oddsmakers had the Bruins crushing the 7-3 Hurricanes soundly.

The other pastime I could indulge in was having a few cold beers in the community swimming pool at my development. With the sweat still trickling down my back, the swimming pool was currently ahead of the football game in the Cade Taylor Potential Things to Do Today calendar. The aroma of chicken wings still tickled my nose. My hunger was getting the better of me. I briefly wavered between beer and football and seized upon what I thought was a brilliant idea. I didn't have to drive back out to Tamiami Airport to get wings. There was a Keg South near where I lived, just a short drive from where I currently was. It was very confusing to me, having two restaurants with the same name. I always phoned in takeout orders into the wrong establishment. Today that wasn't my concern. I knew where I was going and that was all that mattered to me.

The restaurant was at the intersection of Killian Drive and US-1. You could look at it ten times and not see it. It was a small, wood-framed and cinderblock house with a dull blue paint exterior. The house had been converted in 1968 into the pub. Nestled covertly from the road behind large dense hedges and a wooden fence, it was as though the proprietors couldn't care less if you showed up or not. Parking was tight in the rear alley, with limited spaces. There were more signs warning patrons of cars being towed than there were actual parking spaces.

I was able to get one of the highly prized spaces.

It may have been the alleviation of the fuckening. The parking space was a prize, but the parking lot itself was so oddly shaped and small that my saying it was a prize was at best, a consolation prize. Many a patron has pulled in straight and then hours later backed out crooked, mostly due to their intoxicated state. Walking in, I sidestepped the Harley Davidsons crowding the door. It was a twisty, turning shimmy for me. I even sucked in my abdomen to get past a pair of turned handlebars that jutted into the entryway. A guy with a faded American flag baseball hat sat outside on a bench smoking a cigarette, a half-drank Pabst Blue Ribbon bottle propped against the leg of the bench. The uneven asphalt of the parking lot put the bottle in a precarious balancing position. He wore a sleeveless t-shirt and poorly cut-off jean shorts. He nodded at me as though we knew each other.

We didn't.

Daytime drinkers seem to forge immediate bonds with those they perceive as other daytime drinkers. Often by the time night falls the same bonded drinkers become adversaries due to their shared inebriation. Differences in politics, sports, or even stupid subjective opinions could be a drunkard's flashpoint. Something as stupid as who was hotter, Ginger or MaryAnne, led to drunken stumbling fisticuffs. Day drinking would take you into the twilight of the day and unfortunately to the twilight of your mind. I just nodded my head back at the daytime drinking bench dweller. I didn't consider myself a daytime drinker. I was actually more of an anytime drinker which once the ambiguity of day and night was factored in. That probably made me worse than a day drinker.

I stepped inside, into near darkness. The rectangular, backlit stained glass sign behind the bar helped my eyes adjust. It wasn't artful but it did say all you needed to know. Written on the sign was "The Keg South Bar & Grill est. 1968" sloppily wrapped around an oozing keg of beer and a beer mug overflowing with more beer. There were scatterings of patrons at some of the hard bench booths. Two young men were preoccupied playing a game of pool on the place's only pool table.

Inside the pub, the whooshing sound of cars driving on US-1 still seeped through. The pub's decade-old walls were the only barrier as the cars zoomed just feet from the nonchalant patrons. I figured that a seat at the bar was a better place to be than one of the booths near the wall. The thinking was inherently flawed but the idea of a patron with chicken wing grease on his fingers getting pulverized by a careening car crashing into me made it seem like a safer place. The bartender looked like a young kid, barely over twenty-one. More than likely he snuck in here months ago with a fake I.D. and now that he was of legal age he was working here. He wore a black Keg South T-shirt and had a white bar towel slung over his left shoulder. He sauntered over to me.

"What can I get ya?"

I looked past him at the beer tap selection. They were mostly mass-produced national brands like Budweiser and Miller. I did see the familiar Heineken tap and opted for the only import in the bunch.

"I'll have a Heineken, a dozen medium wings, and some fries. Please."

"Wings come in ten, twenty, thirty and fifty."

"Make it ten."

He wrote the order down and placed it in the cook's window. Thankfully he briskly returned with a very cold mug of Heineken beer. As I savored the beer I marveled above me at the lacquered British Union Jack-painted electric guitar posted above the bar. I was on my second Heineken when the scrumptious wings were placed in front of me. The wings and the fries were delicious, and the football game would be starting soon. Two young men were standing by the pool table. One was casually tossing a football up in the air with his right hand and catching it repeatedly. It was only a few inches. They weren't really bothering anyone, but the bartender made a point to tell them to be careful with the ball.

My cellphone was lying on the bar, and it began to ring.

It was Major Brunson.

I picked it up on the second ring.

"Cade!"

"Yes, Major?"

"Be in the office at ten tomorrow morning. The county called. They got an I.D. on our victim."

"Tomorrow is Sunday," I said with a hint of protest.

"Cade, for some damn reason do you think I don't have a clear understanding that tomorrow is fucking Sunday? I mean, I'm sure there *is* fucking on Sunday but for you and me and everyone else who will be there it is just fucking Sunday…"

"Major, is there some sort of urgency…"

"Goddamn it, Cade. Bees don't spend their day explaining to houseflies that honey tastes better than shit. I don't need to explain to you that you need to have your ass there tomorrow. Be there!" he snapped as he hung up.

We would all like to be friends with our boss. At the very least you can hope your boss is friendly. That is not how it was with Major Brunson. He was neither a friend nor friendly. He said, "our victim." The urgency of being in on a Sunday and using the term "our victim" told me that this was not going to be a pass-it-on-to-the-county situation. Miami Dade was not going to release this case and the NTSB would also vie for it. Whoever took the lead on the case was immaterial to me. I was mandated to be there so I'd just have to fall in line with whatever the meeting tomorrow dictated.

I set the phone back on the bar and just looked at it for a beat. A beat to be sure he wasn't calling back. After seeing a guy's internal organs that morning and the imagery of his popped-out eye, I figured some more numbing agents would be nice. A third Heineken would not be out of order. It came just as frosty cold as the previous two. I hated going into harried, rushed meetings not knowing anything. Certainly Trentlocke would be at the meeting and maybe he could give me a heads up of what to expect.

I called Trentlocke. There was no answer. The need to know what had unfolded in this case was thumping in my mind. I didn't want to appear needy or weak and call him again. I *had* added Addison Hope's number just a few hours earlier. *I could call her, see what she found out at the airport, see if it goes anywhere from there.* Against my better judgment I dialed her number. She picked up on the third ring.

"Hello."

"Addison, this is Cade Taylor. I was wondering what you found out from the landside ops at the airport."

"I thought this wasn't your case, or your department, and I should be in touch with Trentlocke, not you."

She had me on that one. I needed to reverse my approach.

"It isn't my case or my department, but I still have to file an incident report because of the city resources that were called in."

"Uh huh," was her *I'm not buying it* response.

Then she continued.

"It doesn't matter because for some reason which I cannot

understand I've been pulled from this case. They're keeping Lawson and bringing in another investigator down from Ashburn tonight. I was told to be at our Miami office at 9:30 tomorrow. Obviously you or Trentlocke threw me under the bus."

I didn't take kindly to being accused of having her bumped from the investigation.

"I didn't throw you under the bus and I don't think Trentlocke did either. Besides, if you *were* thrown under the bus, isn't that something you would be investigating anyway?"

My comment was answered with a *click* as she hung up on me.

The bartender was doing double duty as restaurant manager and bartender off to my left. On the bar he had twenty to thirty open saltshakers on a cafeteria-type tray. He was delicately holding a very full plastic pitcher filled with table salt, carefully pouring it into the shakers.

"Some people put grains of rice in the shakers to keep the salt from binding up in humidity," I said to him.

Without taking his eyes off of his task he explained that there weren't any menu items that had rice in them. It was at that moment that the football the young men had been lightly tossing came whizzing past me and hit the pitcher of salt in the bartender's hand. The pitcher took on a life of its own as it fell from his hand and bounced twice on the bar, knocking over the saltshakers and spewing salt all over the bar and bartender. The bartender was immediately red-hot incensed. Before he could even get around the bar one kid retrieved the football, and the two young men ran out of the pub. It was more than likely an honest accident but it didn't stop the bartender from letting out a litany of vile cursing. He took a moment to collect himself. The pitcher nearly empty of its contents laid on its side on the bar. The bartender took the pitcher, held it to the surface level of the bar, and began using his hand to scoop the spilled salt back into it. Crystalline salt was all over his body and arms and hands. The bartender's hands and arms had the same powdery-looking residue as was on the victim's boots and hands.

It looked like white, coarse dust.

Chapter Six

I LEFT CASH ON the bar to pay my tab. The bartender was literally too salty and infuriated to even care. I stepped out into the parking lot where the same sleeveless, day-drinking smoker was on the bench. At this point the only difference between us was that I had sleeves and I wasn't smoking.

"You leaving, buddy? How about a dollar for watching the car for you?" he called out to me.

I pressed a five dollar bill into his hand.

"Thanks buddy! For that I'll even help you back out."

He stood up and with a wobbly walk stepped into the alley with his arm outstretched in front of him as if he was stopping a herd of wild bison charging at him. His theatrical actions were a bit over the top and truthfully unnecessary, but everyone needs to have a purpose even if it's just the feeling of having a purpose. I could see him giving me a thumbs up in my rearview mirror as I drove away.

I picked up my cellphone and called the police station.

"Coral Gables Police and Fire, Operator J.R. Richards, how can I direct your call?"

"Jeanie Rae, this is Cade Taylor."

"Cade? Calling on a Saturday? Please tell me you aren't going to load my day with tons of things. Did you know the Hurricane game is staring in a few minutes?"

"Yes and no."

"Yes and no what?" she asked with trepidation in her voice.

"Yes I know the Hurricane game is staring in a few minutes and no, I'm not going to load your day with tons of things."

"Good," she said, breathing out a sigh of relief.

"Who's the desk sergeant today?" I asked her.

"Scott Rainer. Do you want him?"

"Yes. Please."

I heard the phone being placed down. I could barely discern her asking for Sergeant Don Rainer and also telling someone else… *Thank God. Every time he calls it's a fiasco and giving a damn doesn't go with my outfit today.* Upon hearing that I reflexively looked in the rearview mirror and got a glimpse of myself, like by looking at myself I could discern if I was an actual fiasco or if she was exaggerating. To my core, I silently thought she might be right. The past year had been one heck of year. The agency had to contend with some tension and anxiety concerning some of my cases. I heard her pick up the phone.

"Just a minute, Cade."

I mustered a quick, but polite thank you as I stored her recent comment in the back of my mind.

Shortly, a male voice said, "Sergeant Rainer."

"Scott, I thought you were working midnights?"

"Filling in for Blanchard. He's got tickets for the game today."

"I thought you'd want to go to the game."

"Me? Why would I do that? They've got a TV here and they pay me overtime to sit in front of it—unless I get called away to take a phone call or something. Know what I mean, Cade?"

"Understood. Do we have marine patrol on duty today?" I asked him.

"Of course we have marine patrol today. It's the weekend. How else will the waterside residents know we have a Marine Patrol if we don't parade them up and down the waterway when the residents are home?"

"They're dive certified, right?"

"Cade, why are you asking these dumb questions, minutes away from me, sitting in the communications section in front of the TV with a Dr. Pepper and a sad bag of Cheetos?"

I needed to stop with the ambiguity and just declaratively say what I needed.

"Have them meet me in ninety minutes at the rear of the last house on Marin Street. Waterside. They need dive gear and at least one long weapon. Expect them to be out of service the rest of the afternoon."

"Wait. What? Cade, we don't need this today we got plans…"

"I have plans, too. Ninety minutes. Thank you. By the way tell Jeanie Rae the fiasco continues. Bye."

I said ninety minutes to give me a chance to metabolize the three Heinekens. I also wanted to save the marine patrol from embarrassment if their dive gear wasn't on the boat. The time would give them a chance to get their supplies. It may be Biscayne Bay, but our marine patrol treated the open water as if it were the high seas. Anything could happen.

I headed back towards the crime scene from this morning. I had a hunch that the day, and possibly the night, were going to be long ones. I tried to call Trentlocke one more time. Still no answer.

Just north of where the crime scene had been I turned into the gated community of Hammock Oaks. The uniformed guard waved as I went through the paper tiger security on Campana Avenue. I drove past the manicured stately homes and turned right on Marin Street. I followed the short street to its most southern end to the turning circle. Directly adjacent to the turning circle was a house with a for sale sign on the lawn. There was a stack of U-Haul boxes in the trash pile in front. I took a chance the house might be empty.

I parked in the driveway, keeping my car inconspicuous from

prying eyes, and got out. I walked around the circle a few times looking for signs of tire tracks, or where grass may have been flattened by heavy objects. I wasn't able to determine there were any. Through the unkept mid-shoulder high Podocarpus bushes, I saw a small opening. Once clear of the bushes there were lots of pine needles on the ground but none of them appeared to be disturbed or flattened. The tall Australian pines towered over me. The sea breeze lightly blew through them, making an orchestra wind and sway that most don't ever hear. South Florida locals could often tell the changes coming in the weather by the slight variation in pitch of that sound. Today was a calm day. Under the fallen pine needles, there were loose rocks of limestone and a smattering of small coral pieces.

The trail was just as Tessie had described.

The rock pit was a serene, dark, brackish rectangle of water. A decently discernable trail was on the west side, under the Australian pines.

The first thing I wanted to do was see how the rock pit was being filled with water. Along the sharp, jagged coral rock ledges of the bank was a thin green algae line—a clear indicator that water in the rock pit rose and dropped with local tides. To my left, a small channel of bluish green water cut through the mangroves and led out to Biscayne Bay. Waterside residents had docks built behind their homes to tether their boats. Between the rock pit and the bay channel was a thin land bridge comprised of hard-packed limestone, coral, and sediment. I walked along the land bridge scanning the channel for any small signs of a flow of water. I also looked for tarpon or mullet gathering near the flow to catch a sea morsel as it was carried by the undercurrent. Midway down the land bridge I saw the small bubbles and lack of underwater fauna near a submerged intake pipe. I laid down and peered over the side of the bridge to see a very rusty grate welded into the submerged pipe. The water from the bay was flowing directly underneath me and into the Coca-Cola-colored water. The grate told me that there shouldn't be any saltwater crocodiles in the rock pit.

Unless they crossed over the land bridge or mangroves.

Small fish and turtles could pass through the large openings in the grate, but if they grew inside the rock pit, they probably couldn't get out. The rock pit was probably a backwater fisherman's dream. Stocked and replenished by nature and plentiful, anglers would enjoy plying it for good times and fishing adventures. I was glad to see the grate, but it only told me half of the story. If there was an abundant food supply in the large rock pit, then there could conceivably be a very large crocodile in there.

Drawing my handgun and carrying it at my side, I walked back to the northwest corner of the rock pit, staying vigilant for rattlesnakes, water moccasins, and yes, the potential encounter with a crocodile. I snapped my head up, watching the hanging tree branches for the large spiders and webs that were surely there. Still, the ground did not appear to be disturbed and there were no signs of footprints, wheelbarrow tire treads or anything else denoting people had been on the trail recently. The walk along the trail afforded a view of the water in between the gnarly Australian pine tree trunks. Midway down the trail was a large gap between the trees. The bank of the rock pit was lower and the drop into the water was not as steep as other places along the path.

There were five large ceramic floor tiles next to each other on the bank near the water's edge. *Floor tiles? Why?* Due to the occasional king tide that raised water levels higher than normal, there was dusty green residue where the tiles had been in the water and then dried in the hot sun. Algae probably formed and then died off a few times each year.

Squatting near the tiles, I looked at each one carefully. There wasn't anything odd about the tiles except for where they were. The location was perfect for slipping into the water and actually, the tiles were ideal to place SCUBA tanks upon. You could sit on the bank of the rock pit with your legs in the water and don and remove the tanks from your back with ease. I looked for anything else that would support my hypothesis. No cigarette butts, soda cans, candy bar wrappers, or anything else. I was just starting to doubt myself when amongst a pile of pine straw I saw a used, sun-faded chem light. My heart immediately raced.

Chem light.

Children call them glow sticks. Some people know them as light sticks. Rave party attendees call them rave sticks. Military and first responders call them chem lights. A chem light is a self-contained, short-term light source. It's a translucent plastic tube that houses isolated chemical substances. When the pliable stick is bent, emitting a crisp *snap*, the isolated chemicals comingle and create light through chemiluminescence. The light cannot be turned off and the stick is useful for only one time. It will provide light for a couple of hours in or out of the water.

I left the chem stick where I found it and continued along the path until I got to the southernmost corner. Here, the trail was not as easily passable as the west side. Traversable enough, but I'd seen what I need to see. I backtracked to the bridge and waited for the marine patrol. Thankfully, the mosquitos were dormant this time of year, as were the no-see-um bugs. They were called no-see-ums because they're so small you can't see them, but they sure can bite. Twenty minutes went past before I could hear the slow-moving sound of the two 200hp Mercury outboard engines on our marine patrol boat, a 1998 Boston Whaler 23 Outrage. One of the marine patrol officers saw me. He put the boat's bumpers over the bow and portside of the vessel so as not to scratch or damage the boat. He threw the bow line to me and I tied the boat to a sea grape tree branch hanging over the water.

The marine patrol officer was Charlie Tresserman. Charlie had been with the department fifteen years and been on the boat for the past ten. The other officer was a young woman I hadn't seen before. She piloted the boat with ease and had it safely right against the rocky ledges of the land bridge, then she cut the engine. It was silent and once again I could hear the wind blowing through the pines.

"Cade, I ain't gonna lie. This better be good because today is *not* a day I feel like doing a whole lot."

"Charlie, what day do you ever feel like doing a whole lot?" I asked him.

He laughed and straddled the side of the boat. I noticed he was wearing neoprene water shoes as he stepped onto the rocky land bridge. The female marine officer also disembarked from the boat and stepped up next to Charlie. She also had water shoes on that zipped up to her ankles and they both had on dark blue short wetsuits with medium blue Coral Gables Marine Patrol long sleeve T-shirts over them.

"Cade, you met Shea before?" he asked me.

"No. I'm Cade Taylor. I'm in VIN," I said, extending my hand to her. Shaking my hand, she said, "I'm Shea Pope. I'd heard of you, but I've never seen you."

"Most people have heard of Cade and not all good, right buddy?" Charlie said with a big guffaw and an even bigger pat on my back.

Shea just looked at me and then glanced around the area, taking in the lay of the land. Her frosted blonde hair was pulled back in a ponytail—necessary, given the speed of the boat and the winds on the bay.

"Hey, were you out there this morning? It was right near here. Right? I heard it was a gruesome mess," said Charlie.

"Yeah, it was pretty bad," I said.

"Is that why we're here?"

"I think so," I said.

"You *think* so? What do we got here, Cade? We ain't looking for any body parts are we?" he said, astonishment making his voice rise higher and higher.

"No. I'm pretty certain they recovered all of those."

"Good, *that's* a relief. I don't need some guy's jawbone getting tangled in my buoyancy compensator. Then what *do* you have us looking for? A submerged shopping cart? You lost a priceless necklace, and you want us diving for it?"

I said, "I think we have the Real McCoy here."

Chapter Seven

"CADE, *WHAT ARE* you talking about? What's the Real McCoy?" he asked me.

"The Real McCoy means authenticity. Like the real deal, right? When something is true, you know? "

"You mean legitimate," said Shea.

"Legitimate. That's a good word. We say it all the time, but many don't know what it means."

"Cade, she just said it. It means legitimate."

"No, no I get that, but it actually has an origin. The Real McCoy was actually derived from William 'Bill' McCoy. He was a prolific booze smuggler during Prohibition times. This guy was the king of bootleggers. He was real crafty. He'd load up liquor from Nassau and stay in international waters. He'd let the rum runners in speed boats come out to him and load up. He never took the chance of being caught. But he was known for one other thing. He made a choice that he wouldn't water down the alcohol. He didn't mix it with any impurities. When you bought and smuggled hooch from Bill McCoy you were getting the real thing. The *Real McCoy* they called it."

"Cade, I'm not sure how this necessitates you taking both of us out of service to go bottle hunting for you," said Charlie.

"McCoy was not only smuggling liquor, but he was really inventive and very good at concealing his product. Keep in mind, this was a waterborne operation. There were logistics and due to the volatility of the ocean, transportation was tricky. Back then they had run-of-the-mill, conventional, sometimes rickety wooden crates that they stacked the bottles of alcohol in. Because of sea swells and waves they were losing product when the bottles broke against each other. It wasn't very efficient, especially when transferring from one ship to another ship. So, McCoy got inventive. He developed something called the smugglers' "ham." In the ham, he'd stack bottles, tightly wrapped in cut-up old sails, burlap, anything to hold it together. It reduced the weight. The "hams" would be stuffed with salt as well, which in the case of being caught by the Coast Guard, allowed smugglers to throw the contraband overboard without getting caught. The weight of the salt would cause the ham to sink, destroying any trace they were in the smuggling business. This was only temporary though, as the salt would eventually dissolve, allowing the ham to rise back to the surface. The smugglers would then come back and reclaim their illegal goods later."

They both looked at me with blank stares.

"I haven't seen the autopsy report but our victim this morning had all of this white dust on his boots and hands. I think it was salt."

"You think it was salt. You ever think he might have been a crop duster and it was fertilizer? Don't you think you should have these facts before calling us out here?" said Charlie with angry skepticism.

"No, it was more crystalline than fertilizer. NTSB talked about atmospheric pressure. Our guy fell out of a low-flying slow moving plane. I think he was a kicker."

"What's a kicker?" asked Shea.

"A kicker is the guy who when the airplane is over a drop zone, pushes or kicks the load out of the airplane. In this case I think our victim today was a kicker who kicked some product into *this* rock pit."

"Why this rock pit and not offshore?" asked Shea.

"Because this is contained. It's easier to retrieve. Less chance of it floating away or another boater finding it. It's also in a direct line with Tamiami airport. Let me show you something, where I think the retrievers are putting on their gear and slipping into the rock pit. It's right down this trail here," I said, motioning with my arm.

Charlie looked at me and then at Shea. She also looked at him for some sort of verbal cue.

"I'm going to grab the tanks. You wanted a long weapon—I've got a Ruger Mini 14. Shea, let's get back on the boat. You grab your dive bag and go with Cade. Cade, take my bag and the Ruger. I'll be right behind you."

"Charlie we might need some rope that you don't care about getting wet," I said.

He nodded and they both went back onto the boat. While Charlie collected the SCUBA tanks and respirators, Shea handed me Charlie's dive bag and the Ruger. She stepped off of the boat carrying her own dive bag and we started walking towards the spot where the tiles were placed on the bank of the rock pit.

"So how long have you been with us?" I asked her.

"I started about six years ago. I did a year of uniform patrol in the north end of the city. When they had an opening for marine patrol I put in and got it. I think my Spanish language helped. Charlie can barely speak Spanish."

"Are you Hispanic?" I asked her as we both ducked under a low-hanging tree branch.

"Hardly. I came out of high school kind of wondering what I was going to do. I ended up being accepted to a small college in Mount Vernon, Iowa. Cornell College. Ever hear of it?"

"I've heard of Cornell University in New York but not Cornell College in Iowa."

"Yeah, no one has ever heard of it. I played on the soccer team. After graduation, one of my teammates suggested being a teacher in Costa Rica. That sounded pretty cool, so I did that for five years. That's where I perfected my Spanish. I did a little work for Habitat for Humanity down there, too. I got the nonprofit bug from that experience and bounced between upstate New York and Georgia working for nonprofits. I then realized that I really wanted to be a cop. I applied and Coral Gables accepted me. So here I am."

"Quite a background. Do you like being on the boat?"

"I love the boat. Charlie can be a little cranky sometimes. He says I'm never on time. I don't think he knows there's *actual* time and Charlie time. Two different things. At the end of our shift I park his crankiness and go home and spend time with my dog, let the trials and tribulations of the day slip away. It's not easy being on a twenty-five foot boat everyday with the same person. It's like being intermittently shipwrecked every day."

I laughed. "Yeah, Charlie can be a little sea salty," I said after ensuring I was out of Charlie's ear shot.

"What's your dog's name?"

"Jones. Away from work we're inseparable."

"That's nice. That's good."

She listened to my theory and then inspected the tiles. On one tile she detected a dinner plate size ring impression in the dirt and algae residue. Charlie walked up with the tanks and the rope. She put one of the tanks over the ring and it was very close match. I repeated my theory to Charlie. He had more doubt than Shea but when he saw the chem light he reluctantly agreed to go into the rock pit with her to see if they could locate anything.

"I'm thinking there'll be a load with a tethered rope or nylon line with a bunch of these sticks already snapped. If the load is packed in salt, there should be some rising from the bottom as the salt dissolves. The loads may not be on the bottom but somewhere slowly floating to the surface. I'll keep an eye on you both with the Ruger just in case we have a crocodile in here."

Shea's eyes widened. "Aren't they a protected species?" she asked.

"Not if they get close to us, they ain't. Cade, we got the wetsuits on remember that. Anything else that moves in the water you shoot that sucker," he said as he helped Shea don her tank, weight belt, and respirator.

Once she was outfitted she helped him with his gear. I stayed on the rock pit bank with the rope near my feet. I kept the Ruger in the ready position and scanned the surface of the rock pit for any signs of a swimming croc while they slipped into the rock pit. Within seconds they were completely submerged. I saw them briefly in the murky water and then was only able to track them through their air bubbles. They were underwater for about ten minutes when Shea surfaced first. She spit the respirator from her mouth.

"I think we got something!" she shouted to me.

Charlie surfaced thirty seconds later, unable to spit out his respirator fast enough in his excitement.

"Cade! Cade we got a few of them. I'll swim over to you, throw me the rope!"

"A few what?" I shouted back.

"Hams. Real McCoys. There's a *ton* of packed salt in them. I used my knife on the first one to loosen the salt and they started rising. It was just like you said! They're suspended about three feet from the bottom. You could tell they'd been resting on the bottom because the silt is disturbed. They're rising. They look like kilos packed in Styrofoam."

In Miami, kilos means only one thing. Kilos means cocaine.

He swam closer and I threw him the rope, holding one end of the line. He swam further out with the other end in his hand. He dove down again. I felt a big tug on the rope. I started pulling. It was *heavy*. I alternated between pulling and walking backward holding the line and soon I saw a large object break the surface. A large red plastic covered mass with Styrofoam haphazardly wrapped around it. I could see the large swatch cut out of the red plastic where Charlie had released salt from the orb. I thought I was doing a good job pulling the kilograms of cocaine up from the deep; unbeknownst to me Shea was swimming on the other side of the tethered package, pushing it. I was thankful for her help. Chem sticks jutted randomly out of the Styrofoam. A strip of linen was attached like a tail to the odd-shaped red creature from the deep. The strip was most likely from a torn bed sheet. About seven chem sticks were tied into the ripped linen.

Shea was excited as she got to the bank of the rock pit. With her pushing from the water and my pulling from land we were able to get the encased plastic sheet bundle up on the trail. It looked like a World War II nautical mine with its round shape and squares inside of it pushing against the taunt plastic covering. I looked closely at it, searching for any telltale markings. The plastic had some fine print labeling written in Spanish. I untied the rope from the clump of kilos.

Shea stayed in the water. I gave her the end of the rope and she dived deeper down, out of my sight. After about seven minutes I felt another hard tug on the rope. Both Shea and I repeated the same process bringing up the second load and eventually the third and final load. All three were packaged the same way. The slits that Charlie had made in the plastic sheeting provided me an opportunity to see how the cocaine was packed. It looked as though thirty to forty kilograms were stacked in the sheeting in a ring. Copious amounts of salt and broken slats of Styrofoam were packed tightly into the void. Layers of the red plastic sheeting were wrapped around the kilograms. It was similar to saran wrap but stronger, with a red tint. Layered over itself made it appear to be a darker red than it actually was, like blood. The chem sticks were activated. I clasped my hands over them and in the darkness of my cupped hands I could see they were still emitting light.

After we had gotten the third parcel on the canal bank, Charlie swam over and hoisted himself up onto the tiles.

"That's it. The chem sticks made it easy to find them. What do you think, Cade? Maybe 100 kilos here?"

I silently studied the three sopping misshapen loads. I needed to formulate a plan before darkness fell upon us.

"Charlie, I'm going to need you to help me here. I need two people to stay with the kilos at all times. Can you take the gear and air tanks back to the boat? Once you get that stuff secured, raise dispatch. Have a unit and a certified drug K-9 dog and the handler waiting for you and Shea at the marina in forty minutes. Get the stuff put away *before* you call dispatch. We need to have this timed right. Don't let them send you just a K-9 car, we need two cars. Then come back here with a property receipt and a Polaroid, bring as much film as you have."

I expected a little bit of a pushback from him, but to my surprise he agreed readily. He was an iron man. With a dive tank on his back, another dive bag slung over his shoulder, carrying the other bag, and a tank in his hands, he walked back towards the boat.

Shea was looking at the cocaine, wide-eyed.

"Is this the most cocaine you've ever seized?" I asked her.

"I've actually never seen cocaine before," she said.

All three of the parcels had deep slits in their sides where Charlie expelled the salt from them. The large slashes definitely helped the kilos to rise to the surface. I reached through the jagged rip into the sludgy salty interior and pulled out a kilo. It was wrapped in a muslin-type thin cloth that had been taped over repeatedly. The outer wrapping and tape probably added half a pound to the cocaine brick. I handed it to her. There was a distinct look of awe in her eyes as she looked at it.

"How does it feel? Does it feel about three pounds?"

"Yes," she said, still looking at it.

"The kilo is about 2.2 pounds but with all the soaked wrapping it's probably about three pounds. These would have needed to dry in the sun or under a heat lamp for a few hours."

She turned the kilo over, and on the underside was a clear marking. Someone had drawn on the kilogram. A large rectangle resting on a small circle under one corner and another small circle under the opposite corner. The number 215 was in the center of the rectangle.

"What is this marking. Is it the true weight?" she asked.

"They know the weight. Anyone tries to sell something under-weight they won't be in the business long—or alive for very long.

That marking is probably who the kilo is designated for. It tells the off loaders who to give the kilos to. As we get into these loads the marking will either stay the same, meaning it's one intentional load… or if there are other, different markings then we have a combined customer load and they shipped the kilos all together. Once Charlie gets back here we'll have a better idea. Right now I don't want to mess with them too much."

Fifteen minutes later, Charlie came walking back with a Polaroid camera, extra film, and a property receipt.

"Dispatch is sending a road unit and K-9 handler, Mark Streit and his dog, Newton. Their ETA is about thirty minutes."

Charlie took a series of pictures of the three red-wrapped loads. He and Shea then used their knives to open the slits they had cut even deeper. We took a parcel each. We pulled out the kilograms. We laid the kilograms on the ground. They looked like oblique pale paving stones. Each one of the kilos had the same rectangle over two small circles marking with 215 in the center of the rectangle. Each red-wrapped shipment had held thirty kilos, ninety total. The Polaroid camera whizzed with a mechanical whine as picture after picture slid out of its housing. We took a lot of pictures. Shea and Charlie asked me to take pictures of them with the kilos laid out in front of them. Glory shots are not uncommon. For someone like Shea who was just starting her career this was a big moment. I snapped a trophy picture of her holding a kilo and handed her the picture. I snapped a picture of a singular kilo on the ground. I kept that one. I had Shea and Charlie each sign the back of a picture of the loads and the ninety kilograms. I put the picture of the singular kilo, and the picture of the ninety kilos in my pocket.

I filled out the triplicate-form property receipt and listed the items as three red plastic wraps and ninety "suspected kilograms of cocaine." Many a case has been lost in court because property seized, or arrests made, were based on what authorities thought was contraband prior to having it officially tested in a laboratory. Having officer Streit and his dog Newton alerted to the cocaine in the marina would be an additional step in the investigation. Both

Shea and Charlie initialed the property receipt. I kept my copy and they kept theirs.

We then herded the kilograms back into the red wrapping. We each took one of the odd-shaped bundles and tried to walk to the boat. Charlie and I bunched up the top of ours. We tried carrying it like a suitcase. I switched hands after a while, but managed to carry my bundle to the boat. Shea tried to carry hers like a grocery bag against her chest, but she didn't get very far. Charlie and Shea exerted a lot of energy but managed to quick walk their parcels to the boat. When we got to the boat Shea properly secured the dive gear.

"You two head to the marina. Officer Streit and his dog Newsome—"

"Newton," corrected Shea.

I gave very explicit instructions, down to the letter.

"Right, Have Streit run Newton all over these loads. Make sure he files his own K-9 report. Then put the cocaine in the trunk of the other marked unit. Have Streit lead you back to the station. Put him in the lead car. The cocaine in the marked unit will be the second car. Shea, you bring up the rear in the marine patrol SUV. Treat it like a dignitary escort. When you get to the station, get the kilos and all the wrapping into the evidence property room. Remember, this has about a two million dollar street value. Lots of people have died in Miami for a hell of a lot less. Keep your escort tight and be on your toes. No stops for anything. From here you go straight to the marina. Keep it all on the down low until I get a chance to talk with Major Brunson and see how he wants to play this. I'm heading to the station. I'll meet you there. If I get there first, I will get things ready for your arrival. Got it?"

"Got it, Cade," said Charlie.

Shea took a sharp breath, and I think she started getting a sense that there was way more to these types of cases than she'd at first perceived.

I helped them cast off the bow line. Shea motored the boat east through the channel while Charlie sat on the stern taking off his aqua socks and drying himself with a yellow towel. I watched them until they cleared the first curve in the channel and were out of my sight. I reached for my cellphone to call Major Brunson. It was then that I remembered we had left the Ruger behind. My first inclination was to call Charlie back to me but that was in direct opposition to the very explicit instructions I just gave them.

I cursed Charlie but then quickly recognized that I had asked for a long weapon. They supplied it to me. This stupid act of forgetfulness was solely on me. The sun would be setting behind the western tree line in about twenty minutes. It might not be a complete South Florida sunset but from where I was, the tall Australian pines would make it seem as though the sun had dipped in the western sky for the night. I walked with a purpose to retrieve the Ruger. Halfway on my way to the weapon was when I heard the distinct sound of dirt bikes coming my way.

Chapter Eight

I STARTED RUNNING TO get to the Ruger. Low-hanging branches brushed against me, slapping me in the face and chest. Running in the near darkness of the trail was treacherous. The growl of the dirt bikes was getting louder, definitely riding on the ragged trail right behind me.

They were closing in on me quickly.

I had the station on speed dial, number five. I needed some help, and I needed it now. On the run I put the phone to my ear. I never stopped running. The bikes were so close I was concerned that the station wouldn't be able to hear me unless I shouted, revealing myself to my pursuers.

I needed someone to pick up the ringing phone at the station immediately.

I kept running and weaving, evading tree stumps, downed saplings, and bushes in my way. Finally the phone was answered.

"Coral Gables Police, Sergeant Rainer."

"Scott! Its Cade Taylor!" I huffed into the phone.

"Cade, hold on, Miami's about to score," he said, followed by the *clunk* of the phone being placed down on a hard surface.

"No, wait!"

He was gone.

I was so far down in the south end of the city, and had already taken two units out of service to meet Shea and Charlie at the marina. There was no cavalry coming for me. At least not in time to be of any help. When seconds count, cops are minutes away.

I finally reached the spot where the tiles were. On the run, I scooped up the Ruger by the barrel and kept running with it. I dove behind a massive tree as the motorcycles rolled up. The tree's thick trunk was gnarled and bent; its roots embedded into the edge line of the rock pit. I tried to muffle my heavy breathing. The cellphone had been my lifeline. Now it was a useless appendage to carry. I was worried that Scott might call me back, the ring announcing my hiding spot. Moving quietly behind the tree, I put the Ruger between my knees and switched the phone to silent. Fearing any unnecessary movement might reveal me, I pushed it down the neckline of my shirt and let it rest against my stomach.

The engines turned off. It sounded like there were three of them.

They were only about twenty feet from me. I could hear the thud of their boots hitting the ground as they dismounted from their motorcycles. They were talking amongst themselves. Two of them definitely had Hispanic accents and the other one was distinctly Anglo. They stopped at the tiled spot—so they were the retrievers of the cocaine. I wasn't sure where they were in the food chain. They could be the owners of the cocaine. They could be the distributers of the cocaine. Or they could be low-level mopes tasked with retrieving the cocaine. Either way they weren't recreational motorcycle riders. After Charlie and I spent so much time struggling to carry the kilos these guys knew to bring dirt bikes. They more than likely had trailered the bikes. They'd done this before.

I silently adjusted my position and peered around the tree trunk where a thick undergrowth of kudzu vines and wild bramble were growing. Twilight was nearly upon us, and I could barely see them. I leaned back further behind the safety of the tree.

Your mind will rationalize and also fool you in precarious

situations. I needed to get my breathing in order and assess my advantages. I needed to minimize any noise I made. I assumed that the three of them were armed. I had no idea what type of weaponry they might have but since they came in on motocross-type bikes, necessitating both hands on the handlebars, they probably didn't have a long weapon with them. It was of little comfort.

Guns kill.

Any gun can kill. I might have superior firepower with the Ruger but there were three of them and only one of me. I was disadvantaged with my back to them. I needed to face my potential adversaries. I slowly and with as little noise as possible moved into a position where the tree gave me concealment and cover, but simultaneously allowed me to face in the direction of the three men. There was comfort in having my body against the tree. Tactically, it wasn't best for me to stay in the comfort spot, so I eased myself as low to the ground as I could to minimize my profile and my size. There *was* a possibility these three riders were just recreational motocross enthusiasts. As of that immediate moment they hadn't committed any crime. Rising up, identifying myself in the developing darkness of the night would be pointless. If they were in the drug trade, which I believed them to be, killing me in this remote spot would not phase them in the least. It might actually be a pleasure for them. I decided to stay covert and listen.

Retreat was not an option.

Charging at them was also not an option.

I was where I was. I was prepared to fight and engage them, but it wasn't a prudent move at that time. I hoped to gain some intel by listening.

"Yo, *Dedos!* Line them bikes up in a row. I don't want no problems trying to get outta here and be all tangled up with youse," said the Anglo.

Dedos? Dedos in Spanish means fingers. One of the Latin guys must have been nicknamed "Fingers." Listening as intently as possible, I heard a kickstand being pushed up and then the motorcycle wheels slowly rolling over twigs and pine needles. The kickstand was harshly lowered again. Whoever Dedos was, he moved one of the bikes.

When a person is trying to intently hear something they often close their eyes. I couldn't close my eyes. I was fearful one of them would come upon me and ambush me. I kept my eyes open and furtively continued scanning around me. I heard the third voice tell the Anglo that the tiles were soaking wet.

"Whatta ya mean they's wet?"

"Wet. They are wet. Everywhere. Not from rain or anything. I think someone has been here."

It sounded like the Anglo had walked over and was inspecting the tiles.

"They's wet alright. Sonsabitches. Youse guys get the tanks on and get in the *wooder*. See if we's got a problem here."

No one spoke, and I could hear the clanking and clicking of tanks being put on the backs of two of the divers. I assumed it was Dedos and the other Hispanic guy going in because as they geared up I heard the first voice say, "This ain't good, this ain't good. Hurry up get that jawn on."

This solidified my assumption they were here to retrieve the ninety kilograms of cocaine. I heard a loud splash, then a second loud splash. The two divers who entered the rock pit were nowhere near as careful about entering the water as Charlie and Shea were. I wasn't relaxed at all. Even though there was only one person on shore, and it reduced my odds, it still was a precarious situation to be in.

I gave myself over to the reality that I was in a seriously bad place.

The two divers could surface anywhere, including right where I was laying prone along the shoreline with this tree as my biggest protector. I clenched the Ruger even closer to my chest, my finger wrapped inside the trigger guard. Sweat trickled down my temple.

One of the divers broke the surface of the water and my stomach dropped.

"*No esta, no esta, no luce no esta!*"

"What? What's you say?" came the voice just a few yards from me.

"Nothing. *Nunca.* We swam the whole drop zone. No lights. No nothing."

"Ah Jesus this is ain't no fucking good. It ain't good for me and it ain't good for youse two. This ain't good at all, Mackarryo. We gonna get hosed on this! Youse know that, right? Holy mutha of shit. We's fucked! You knows that right, Mackarryo? You two sea monkeys gets youse selves outta there. We gotta think this out."

Mackarryo? He must mean Macario. A fairly common Colombian male name. Three guys. One named Dedos, one named Macario and the leader of them who sounded like he was standing in the line at Geno's waiting to order a hoagie. I could hear the divers swimming closer to shore. They might discover me first, but they weren't my current biggest threat. The guy on shore with the heavy Philadelphia accent was my greatest threat. If either of the divers saw me, it was Rocky Balboa I would take out first. I kept my ears perked but my eyes on the water. I could tell by the ripples in the "wooder" that they were exiting the rock pit at the tile spot. I kept the Ruger close and ready to extend it and fire. I could hear the tanks being plopped onto the tiles.

"Put all that jawn aways and let's get our story right."

The three loads we seized were heavy. They must have had small mini SCUBA tanks, carried in on small backpacks. I'm sure they'd intended to make two quick runs back to their truck with gear and the kilos. Tonight it would be an empty run carrying something even heavier than the ninety kilograms of cocaine.

Fear.

In the drug business excuses and explanations are not tolerated. It didn't matter that they were trumped by me and the marine patrol. When the owner of the two million dollars of cocaine found out the load was lost, any comment about being stuck at a red light or stopping off to get Gatorade before making the jaunt out there would definitely lead to Ben Franklin and the Colombian aquanauts being murdered. These guys were in the hotpot, and I directly put them there. The two Latin divers were quiet. It just sounded like gear being put away.

"Dedos. Dedos!"

"*Si, Jefe* ."

"You and Mackarryo ain't holding out on me, are youse?"

"*No. No, Jefe.*"

"If youse two think that I'm some sort of gringo you can fuck over I'm gonna put a bullet right in youse both. *Right* in youse both."

Then Dedos was pleading for him to put the gun down.

I was stuck. I couldn't let him kill the Colombian diver. If I stumbled or misfired it would take minimal effort to have the very same gun trained on me. I didn't know exactly where they were. It was too dark to guess. If I sprang from my position they might all three start shooting in my direction. Any one of those rounds could kill me. Hope is not a strategy, but it was all I had at the moment. Dedos was nearly crying, begging the Anglo to put the gun down.

It was then that I heard Macario exclaim, "Look!"

That was it. I was sure they had seen me.

I braced myself for the rounds to come into the bramble. I prayed the tree was large enough to stop the first rounds and give me an opportunity to rise up and at least fire back. I didn't want to die without even getting a shot off. I rose up on my elbows. I needed to keep my backside down to avoid quite literally having my ass shot off. It was at that moment I heard Macario again.

"*Mira, mira agui rojo. Rojo.*" [Look. Look here, red. Red.]

I wasn't sure, but it sounded like the gun was being pushed into a waistband or a holster. So it had been taken off of Dedos.

"Gimme that," said the Anglo.

I deduced that Macario had found a swatch of the red wrapping on the ground where we'd cut open the plastic to count the kilograms.

"You're one lucky bou, Dedos. Mackarryo here thinks enough of ya to think about your life," he said to Dedos.

"Mackarryo, when youse was in the islands what did you use to wrap it all up in?" he asked the concerned smuggler.

"Red wraps. Plastic sheets that were red. We used that and the Styrofoam just like we always do," he answered with a shaky voice.

"Don't ja be lying to me, Mackarryo. Last times it was blue. Remember? Maybe I's should put my gun to your head instead."

"It was only blue because that custom inspector held us up on the red sheeting. We had to use blue on the last one. We always use red because of the white stones," Macario replied his voice a little higher pitched than before.

"Red like this?" he said.

"That's it. *Exactemante!*" said Macario.

"*Mas, mas, mas,*" said Dedos.

In the darkness, he had discovered more pieces of the red wrapping. The three men studied the tattered pieces of the red plastic.

"Look at the writing!" said Macario.

"You know I don't read no Spanish. What abouts it?"

I recalled what I had seen when we pulled the three parcels ashore.

"*The plastic had some fine print labeling written in Spanish.*"

"It's the plastic we used to wrap the *yayo*. I got it from my uncle's shop. You can see the manufacturer here in the writing. This is from the load. Someone was definitely here before us and ripped it off. They got the cocaine! You saw it with your own eyes! The tiles were wet, and now there's our wrapping in pieces. Someone stole the load."

The Anglo wasn't completely satisfied.

"How'd they knows it was here? Huh? It ain't like we's in the middle of Veteran's Stadium and the Phillies is playing. How'd they know? I swear to everything that's fucking holy I'm gonna kill whoever took our coke. They're dead! They's so dead they will have to bury them twice."

It briefly got quiet. I assumed they were thinking of their next move.

"What will you tell Emmanuel Servais?"

I made a mental note to remember that the three of them answer to someone named Emmanuel Servais.

"I don't know, Mackarryo. Right now the way I see it youse bous didn't deliver. We always got along with youse guys but this ain't a me problem. This a youse two problem. When youse bring it up from the wooder it comes on me and my bous. That didn't happen. Youse two will need to deal with Emmanuel Servais. I can tell ya this, we ain't paying for a loss like this, and the next load in we's gonna want a discount because ya just left us and our customers in Montco and Delco in the wind. Luckys for youse it ain't summa cause those bous down the shore would go ape shit without theys favorite nose candy. It's getting darker than the Hershey factory here. Let's get us outta here. Get them bikes loaded. We don't need whoever found the cocaine calling the cops and dealing with thems showing up. Youse both bring them red strips with ya. Emmanuel Servais is gonna need some convincing."

For the next three minutes they hurriedly got their gear together and then mounted the motocross dirt bikes The engines turned on with an ear-splitting grumble. I could hear them filing out down the trail. I waited until the sound was in the distance before I rose from my hiding spot. I wanted to catch up with them, get a look at them or the truck waiting for them on Marin Street. Running in the dark with the Ruger in front of me in case I needed to quickly use it was hazardous. I nearly tripped twice on raised tree roots and small rock boulders.

I could no longer hear the motocross bikes. I didn't think I was going to able to catch them.

Nightfall had come upon me. I walked cautiously down the trail worried about falling, snakes, scorpions, and any other crazy thing that invaded my mind. I used my cellphone to illuminate my path and saw there were no missed calls. Scott Rainer didn't even try to call me back.

I got to my car and put the Ruger across the passenger seat. I stopped at the guard house on Campana Drive on the way out of the neighborhood Noticing the glass doors on both sides of the guard house, I threw a towel over the Ruger to keep it from the guard's prying eyes. The same hand-waving guard I saw on the way in opened the door. I was debating whether to identify myself or try and keep my intentions from the guard. I'd heard the Anglo mention they'd been in here picking up loads of cocaine before.

"Don't ja be lying to me Mackarryo. Last times it was blue. Remember?"

Two-million dollar loads of cocaine can buy a lot of loyalty from hourly wage security guards. I decided to try and learn what I could from the guard without identifying myself as a cop.

"Evening," said the guard.

"Evening," I replied.

"How can I help you?"

I took a chance that the house on the end of Marin Street that I'd parked at had sold and the new owners weren't moved in.

"I just moved into the house at the end of Marin Street by the circle. Did you see a truck towing some motocross bikes come in?"

"They did. They come in from time to time."

"Yeah, well they parked in our driveway and my wife is pretty particular about things. It seems they dumped oil on our new pavers. Do you know who they are?"

"No sir. I don't know them. I've just seen them once or twice."

"Does your gate have cameras?"

"Not yet. The HOA is getting ready to accept bids to have them installed," he said.

"Did you write down their license tag?"

"Sir, HOA rules state I can only provide that information to—"

I cut him off.

"—to the HOA and its board. Do you know who your newly elected HOA president is?" I bluffed him.

"No sir. I don't."

Remembering the Anglo and his thick Philadelphia accent and the reference he made to the Phillies baseball team playing in Veteran's Stadium, I took a swing at a Woody Harrelson barbecue pitch.

High and outside.

I invoked the Phillies baseball gods and used the name of retired Baseball Hall of Fame Philadelphia Phillies pitcher Steve Carlton.

"Let me introduce myself. I'm Steve Carlton, the new HOA president. Nice to meet you," I said with a big smile as I extended my hand out the car window for a handshake.

The guard shook my hand. He slightly bowed his head. He was conciliatory.

"Can you tell me their license tag number? I'd rather handle this nicely. Keep my wife, the HOA, and especially the company you work for out of it. You know how HOA boards can get if they think we let *just* anyone in here. Next thing you know they want new guards, or heaven forbid, even new guard companies. Everybody wants to rule the world."

He understood my implication. Without hesitation he reached back inside the guard house and retrieved his clipboard.

"CP9-70Z."

"Is that the truck or the trailer?"

"That's the truck. The trailer is "JJM-05H"

"Thank you. I'll be back in a few minutes. I need to make a run to an ATM," I lied as I drove away.

I so desperately wanted to head south and go home. Instead, I turned north onto Old Cutler Road and drove to the police station. The four-story police and fire station was on Salzedo Street, sandwiched between Sevilla and Palermo Avenues. The Coral Gables

Police station had a lovely address on Salzedo Street. A beautiful Mercedes dealership diagonally across from the front door. The Guatemalan Consulate with its landscaped rooftop deck was directly across the street. The building that ran north of the police station on Sevilla Avenue was the international headquarters for Del Monte. It was a nice commerce "neighborhood." So long as you overlooked the dilapidated and crumbling eyesore of a building that was the police station.

The building was a short, four story-concrete and brick monstrosity that had all the aesthetics of a long-neglected, poorly constructed commercial office space. Over the years it had been retrofitted by numerous low-bidding contractors, each one putting their own layer of shoddy workmanship on the unattractive edifice. Each time I saw the police building, I was struck by the sheer lunacy and inept architectural design of it. The building was designed sometime in the early seventies. The most notable feature was a glass atrium on the west side. The windows were poorly UV-rated panes of glass that seem to accentuate the scorching sunlight. Even when the windows were finally provided with a level of tinted material, the workmanship was poorly applied. Within months the tinted film baked, bubbled, and curled in the broiling sun. The windows permitted ultraviolet rays to pour in. You could get a sunburn just standing in the lobby for an hour. The building steamed and hell-fired all its inhabitants in the unrelenting South Florida afternoon sun. The brilliant construction minds put their heads together and came up with a remedy. The remedy was to become incredibly environmentally unfriendly and crank the air conditioning system to such a blizzardly frigid temperature that was icy cold. Each and every morning as people walked into the building, the opening and closing of doors fluctuated the building's temperature. Condensation on the windows streams down the walls and puddled on the floor. Eventually entire walls need to be replaced, over and over again due to the spreading mold. Every civilian employee wears a borrowed winter jacket from a road patrol officer, or they wear their own choice of sweater or jacket making the corps of employees look like a gaggle of kindergartners on picture day. I would venture to say the strongest part of the building was the bright blue ribbon they cut during the opening day ceremony.

Politicians wore hardhats at the groundbreaking ceremonies where they use tin and aluminum shovels to flip over a spade of dirt from an already unearthed pile of soil. The ridiculousness doesn't stop there. Hard hats aren't needed to turn over a few inches of dirt, they weren't needed months earlier when those same politicians sat in dark tufted leather booths at a downtown steak house and accepted envelopes stuffed with cash as bribes to get those very same construction projects approved.

Now decades later, walking into the Coral Gables Police Station, I would be comfortable wearing a hard hat especially with the brick façade on the southside of the building randomly dropping bricks onto the sidewalk below. I parked on Sevilla Avenue, and I walked into the building. It was bad enough I had to be in the building, but I could spare my car the indignity of parking in the crumbling parking garage. I took the elevator outside the back entrance door. It took me up to the third floor parking lot. I exited the elevator and went in through the third floor parking garage door. Coming in this way afforded me the quickest route to the VIN office and to the evidence room where Charlie and Shea stood at the open door. The three red bundles were stacked and ready to go inside the secure evidence room. They saw me and they broke into huge smiles. I silently handed Shea the Ruger. Just inside the evidence room door, who'd opened it for the officers, was Scott Rainer. Everyone was in a celebratory mood. With a smile I walked up to Charlie and Shea. I silently motioned to them to step back. Their mood was giddy. Silently they moved away from the open doorway to let me through to where Scott Rainer stood.

"Hey Cade," he said with a big grin on his face.

That's when I hauled back and slugged him right in the center of his forehead.

Chapter Nine

I DIDN'T HIT HIM hard enough to break the skin of his forehead or to hurt my hand. He was emotionally stunned. He was also highly surprised. Rotund and in an ill-fitting uniform, he looked comical staggering back from the blow. He stumbled back into an old fingerprinting table that was being stored in the evidence room.

"Cade, what's your fucking problem?" he yelled at me.

Charlie and Shea quickly filled the open doorframe. Their confused faces told me they may have heard an altercation, but they didn't see one. I glared at Scott. He was red in the face. He was angry. He was embarrassed. He also wasn't going to defend himself. Forging a career hiding behind a desk from the rigors of police work will do that to your fighting spirit.

"I'm writing you up! You just crossed one line you can't come back from," he threatened me.

I picked up a pen from the top of the unused fingerprint table and threw it at him.

"Use this one. I'm sure there's still enough ink in it to write me up, and add the part about how watching TV on duty is in direct violation of the desk position SOP. The phone lines are recorded Scott." I reminded him of his own words. "What was it you said?

That they're paying you overtime to watch TV, right? Unless you get 'called away to take a phone call,'"

I remembered his exact words.

"Me? Why would I do that? They've got a TV here and they pay me overtime to sit in front of it—unless I get called away to take a phone call or something. Know what I mean Cade?"

He looked at me, mulling his options.

"I made that phone call. I made that call, Scott! The one that should have pulled you away, as three drug runners descended upon me, but you put me on hold because according to you '*Miami's about to score.*' So you go ahead and write me up. I can tell you it will not end for you nearly as luckily as it did for me."

"Are you saying after we left some guys showed up?" asked Charlie.

I turned to face Charlie leaving my animosity with Scott.

"Three of them. Two Latin, one Anglo. They never saw me. I hid behind a tree while two of them went in the water looking for the cocaine. They obviously came up empty-handed, and they were pissed. Charlie, don't put me on any of this paperwork. Make this a marine patrol seizure. Marine patrol only. You and Shea take the stat and the glory. I think I'm going to need to have some distance on this. I haven't even talked to Major Brunson yet."

"You can bet your bottom dollar I'll be talking to him," said Scott, still visibly angry.

I whipped around at him. I actually considered punching him again. It was Shea who broke the stare down.

"How do you want us to write the report?"

"Start the report narrative with '*based on a law enforcement source...*' Don't get too specific. Just write that an unnamed law enforcement source directed you to investigate the waterway for submerged or partially submerged kilos of coke. It will only come up in discovery if someone comes forward and tries to claim ownership of the cocaine. We all know that won't happen. We just don't know how many eyes in the judicial system will see this report so keep me one hundred percent out of it."

"I'm still going to talk to Major Brunson," interjected the increasingly whiny Scott.

"Scott. Look at me. Seriously, look at me. Do you think I give a shit if you call Brunson?"

I started to leave the evidence room but stopped and pulled a handful of the red plastic off of one of the packages. I stuck the swatch into my front pocket.

"That's evidence, mister. You can't take that. I'll be sure to tell that to Major Brunson too," Said Scott.

"Officer Shea Post, have you written your report yet and transferred the evidence from your case completely into the evidence room?" I asked Shea.

"Um…no… I mean at least not yet."

I looked back at Scott Rainer.

"It's not impounded yet, not officially evidence, it's still being investigated by the officers who discovered it. Besides I'm taking this to the Miami Dade Crime Lab to be analyzed."

"That's my job!" Scott shrieked.

"Your job is to oversee the desk. Not watch TV, especially when a fellow officer in dire need calls and you're too busy watching football to properly handle it."

Shea stayed in the evidence room. Charlie followed me as I walked out.

"Cade, I get it. You're okay in my book. Thanks for not handing us up for forgetting the Ruger."

"Everything happens for a reason. The Ruger was my best chance out there. I was glad to have it. Charlie, I need you to do me a favor."

"Yeah of course. What is it?"

"I'm being called in here tomorrow by Major Brunson for some meeting about our free-falling dead guy. You and I know the cocaine is related. This will probably light up like a house of straw. I think

Scott and the dispatch crew aren't fully engaged with what's going on. Too many TVs, manicures, magazines, and a 'someone get the phone I'm busy' mentality up there. I need some distance from all of this, at least for now. I'm asking you to run two tags for me and get as much information as you can. Push dispatch to look for Scoff violations, outstanding tickets, all that kind of stuff. Can you do that for me please?"

"Absolutely."

"Thank you. The first tag is CP9-70Z, it should come back to a truck. The second should be on a trailer. JJM-05H. Can you put it in co-mail and have the information dropped into my mailbox tonight?"

"Absolutely," he replied again.

"Oh, one other thing: throw one of the Polaroid pictures of Shea holding a kilogram into the envelope please."

I shook his hand, and I left the building. I was tired. I was hungry. I just wanted to go home.

The past six months home for me had been 6211 Paradise Point in the Royal Harbour Yacht Club. A very desirable address in South Florida, the entire complex is an opulent waterside utopia nestled amongst beautiful trees and tropical foliage. It's a straight east drive on Coral Reef Drive to the bay. The land is a peninsula that juts into Biscayne Bay. The complex is a tranquil oasis tucked away from the high energy of South Florida. Living there, I feel fortunate. Unfortunately, that's as far as my feeling of being fortunate goes. It's owned by a doctor who was a friend of a friend. He'd purchased the unit for his mother. Prior to her moving in she broke her hip in the Dominican Republic and suffered a series of medical setbacks afterwards. She stayed in the Dominican Republic being attended to by private nurses and caregivers. The doctor, knowing of my bombastic divorce, offered it to me as a temporary place to stay until his mother recovered. Her slow recovery has enabled me to stay longer than both the doctor and I expected. So far it hasn't been an issue. He is happy to have someone he can trust watching over the place. The condominium is appointed with expensive furniture and artwork for his mother, and furnished with an interior designer's obvious influences. There are plush large, comfortable couches and burnished wood built-in shelves that are polished to a high sheen. Pre-Colombian art pieces decorate the common living areas. There are two imitation Luis Botero pieces. The Botero sculptures dance for your eye's attention with paintings from Sebastian Spreng, Alberto Pancorbo, and Connie Lloveras hanging on the walls of the hallways and living room. There is even an imitation lithograph of Wifredo Lam's 1944 painting *Les Fiancés* in the den. I only knew these artists and what the pieces are because the doctor left a binder describing the artwork and the artists.

Anyone who actually knows of this bayside haven simply just call it Paradise Point. With the exception of the beautiful, scripted sign attached to the coral rock entrance by the guard house entrance, no one ever calls the tight row of townhomes Royal Harbour Yacht Club. The spelling of Harbor with the addition of the Bahamian and British addition of a "u" lends an air of exclusivity. The entire enclave was high end, highbrow row house condominiums, each adjacent to the next one by a shared external wall. Each residence had surprising depth, and each unit was, at minimum, two stories high. Most, including my unit, had a third level used as an outdoor deck. From the outdoor decks of these houses manatees and dolphins could be often seen swimming in the narrow channel that leads directly out to Biscayne Bay. My unit was on the southside of the tree-canopied lane. The view from my unit was an unobstructed spectacular vista of trees, mangroves, and Biscayne Bay looking south towards Boca Chita Key, Elliott Key, Chicken Key, and the rest of Biscayne National Park.

I was anxious to get home. I was also starving. Traffic moving south on Lejeune Road was easy and quick. When I arrived at Cartagena Circle where Lejeune Road, Sunset Drive, and Old Cutler Road converge, I picked up my phone and dialed my favorite Italian restaurant. I was motoring out of the circle south on Old Cutler Road when someone at the restaurant answered.

"Papa Ricco's."

"Hey there, I'd like to order a large pizza."

"Pick up or delivery?"

"Pick up."

"Okay what do you want on it?"

"Sausage, mushrooms, and green peppers."

"What's the name?"

"Cade."

"Okay. Twenty minutes," he said as he hung up.

One of the staples of life in South Florida is that no matter what restaurant you order from, it is always "twenty minutes." Not fifteen. Not thirty.

Twenty.

I placed the phone on the passenger seat, and I tried to refocus myself. On my way to get the pizza I was going to literally drive by all the places that unfurled my day into absolute chaos. I was trying to get my mind into a proper place. Psychologists call it compartmentalizing. The definition of compartmentalization is:

"*Compartmentalization is a human defense mechanism in which people mentally separate conflicting thoughts, emotions, or experiences to avoid the discomfort of contradiction.*"

Contradiction?

There isn't much contradiction in body parts ripped away from a human being, or hearing a gun being put to someone's head. With the life I was leading, I might need to rent storage space for all the compartments I should be using. It was a matter of personal sanity, career longevity, and keeping the memories and experiences in check somehow. That was when my phone rang. It was Major Brunson.

"Hello."

"Cade, goddamn it! I don't think I know anyone whose balls I'd rather fucking smash in a mailbox right now more than yours!"

Compartmentalization just got put into a tiny, sealed envelope and thrown out my car window.

"Yes, Major."

"Did you really punch Scott Rainer?"

"Yes, Major."

"Cade, have you ever looked at someone and knew the wheel was turning, but the hamster was dead? That's fucking you. What the fuck is going on in that loopy brain of yours?"

"I can explain—" I protested.

"I don't want your explanation. I don't want a damn thing from you. Actually, let me correct that. I do want something from you. I want one of those old fashioned candy necklaces but instead of candy I want you to string it with Tums and Ibuprofen for all the fucking aggravation you give me."

"I can explain," I proffered again.

"Did you not hear what I just said? I don't want your fucking explanation! I swear to everything that pretends to be sacred I can't believe you're the sperm that won. Listen, my source of unrelenting constant and ongoing fucking aggravation, Rainer says you punched him without any provocation. You just walked up to him like some sort of lunatic and punched him. Hey dumbass, you know that's considered battery on a law enforcement officer?"

"Yes, sir."

"Did you have your fucking gun on you when you punched him?

"Yes, sir."

"*Wonderfuckinful.* Now it's *aggravated* battery on a law enforcement officer. Everybody has the right to do stupid things, but you are really abusing that privilege. Luckily for you, he called me instead of someone below me."

"How's that?"

"Because I'm the fucking acting Chief! That also makes me an at-will employee unbound by any of the constraints of the FOP or any other police unions. This won't come across my fucking desk because it came across my fucking phone. There is no fucking paperwork."

"What are you saying?" I inquired.

"I'm saying that for all the fuckery that goes on I still run a pretty tight shipwreck. He told me. I listened. I then reminded him of all the stupid shit he has done that he thinks no one knows about. Yeah, sorry to break it to you. You're not my only fucking problem child. That's why I sit in the biggest office in this *shitastrophy* we call a police department. I have a solid memory and drop my cards only when needed. I just dropped a low card to save your scrawny ass. Granted it wasn't like it was an ace or anything. I still hold those cards. Nonetheless, he said if you're okay, he's okay. So you two imbeciles find a way to play nice on my playground or as God is my reluctant witness, I will have you both walking Miracle Mile looking for pedicured dogs shitting on our lovely fucking pink sidewalks. You understand?"

"Understood."

"Now, I hear that Charlie Tresserman and Shea Post discovered ninety kilograms of cocaine somewhere off of Marin Street."

"Yes."

"We still have a ten in the morning tee time with a bunch of people I'd rather not see on a Sunday. Including you. Be in my office at nine-thirty so we can discuss. I don't need the full fucking details right now. I'm trying to enjoy what every TV talk show host calls domestic bliss. The reality is they can all bliss my ass on that one."

With that declaration the phone went dead as he hung up on me.

Whatever mountain top of composure I was trying to reach I just lost my sherpa, provisions, and safety line with that phone call. There was just no reasonable dialogue to be had with raging animosity.

There was also no reasonable excuse for me punching Scott Rainer.

It initially felt good. In the back of my mind I knew that since he'd been a desk sergeant for so long, he hadn't seen the streets for so long, he probably didn't even know we had a street called Marin.

I could not have adequately explained my predicament or position to him in time to keep "Philadelphia Freedom," Dedos, and Macario from descending upon me. Even if I could, there was nobody within four miles of where I was. Two police units meeting the marine patrol at the marina more than likely depleted the south end of the city of adequate police coverage. I was on my own with or without Scott Rainer doing his job properly. Desperation and the relief that comes from its alleviation sets up a great psychological Serta-perfect sleeper for anger, resentment, and revenge to softly land, only to spring up as a verbal or in my case, a physical reaction.

I was wrong. It wasn't the first time, nor would it be the last time if my track record continued on its familiar trajectory. My day started with Major Brunson calling me with a profanity laced phone call. It looked as though it would end that way too. In between the profane calls I found ways to anger a long tenured Miami Dade homicide detective, antagonize a woman who woke up to a dismembered body in her street, irritate an NTSB investigator, watch two million dollars' worth of cocaine plop to the surface of a dark water rock pit, nearly piss my pants from fear as I hid from three drug runners, pass myself off as an HOA president by invoking the name of a Major League Baseball CY Young winning pitcher, and then punched a fellow long-time police officer.

Yeah, it had been a banner day for me.

There was no one to blame but myself for all the "Cadetastrophes" I'd brought upon myself. The upheaval and calamities of my life could be attributed to the living breathing byproduct of being a VIN detective in Miami. Introspectively, I had to ask myself how much of this was the VIN lifestyle and how much of it was my own functionality in it all. Major Brunson told me, "you're not my only fucking problem child." How many of his problem children were living like I was? How many were divorced and adrift in a world of distrust and deception? How many of them stared into the dark death funnel and kicked life pebbles down into the endless hole? The dissolution of my marriage to Gina, the failed post-divorce relationships that were never given the proper igniter to properly flourish, the disappointments, disillusionments, and dysfunction of the VIN lifestyle were easy to point that solo finger at, but in the end I had to acknowledge there are four more fingers pointing at me. It would be easy to say, "just learn from your missteps, mistakes, misadventures and move on." What happens when the manifestation of those missteps, mistakes and misadventures morph and come back around in many forms?

Looking at cars traveling in the opposite direction on the road, I wondered how many of them have had the kind of Saturday I have had? *Is this normal?* Was their day a trip to Home Depot to get batteries for the garage remote control and no other errands or responsibilities? Would they even be able to fathom what my day had been like? Would they even believe that there were ninety kilograms of cocaine seized that I believed was related to a stranger who fell from a moving airplane? Was that something they could even conceivably comprehend? The absurdity of my life was probably the only constant in my life.

As I neared the Kings Bay Shopping Center I could see the Saturday dinner crowd had filled many of the available parking places. A little-known maneuver I'd learned years before was to cut south down the delivery alley behind the McDonald's that anchored the plaza. Papa Ricco's was in a covered alcove in the "L" corner of the shopping center. I parked in the rear alley by a large electrical meter room. It was a quick step out of the car through the open breezeway and I was at the front door of Papa Ricco's. The small bistro was packed with happy clientele all enjoying their meals. The interior décor was an eclectic mix of photos, memorabilia, and posters of sports and entertainment legends. I walked up to the small counter. There was a young woman behind the register. I told her I was picking up a large pizza for Cade.

"Pick up for Cade!" she yelled to the chefs behind her.

"Up top," was the quick response.

She retrieved the white pizza box from the top of the oven and within minutes the car was filled with the aroma of the expertly crafted pizza as I drove away. My hunger was getting the better of me. Rather than going home, I drove west through the alleyway and turned onto US-1. The Toyota was a bit wide on the U-turn I made. I went to the Coral Reef Drive traffic light and turned into the 7-11 on the corner. Within minutes I had a chilled six pack of Amstel Light in my hand. Immediately adjacent to the parking lot was the ramp to the rooftop parking lot belonging to the corporate building next door. Since it was Saturday night, the lot was empty of cars. I backed the Land Cruiser into one of the west parking spaces. I opened the rear hatch and sat on the bumper area under the raised rear door. The surprisingly light traffic sounds on US-1 rose up from below. In the near distance I could see Deering Hospital. Across from the hospital was the Palmetto Golf Course. The lights from the driving range lit the western sky. I couldn't fully see the children playing roller hockey on the public outdoor rink near the busway, but I could definitely hear their excitement and voices. It was an odd dichotomy. The pleasures of golf and suburban life were an easy nine iron shot from a hospital where I'm sure some people were having the worst day of their life. I also reckoned that there were some people in the hospital having the best day of their life too. The swirl of life doesn't provide designed favoritism or intentional anguish. It carries on and carries us with it. We like to think we have control over our lives but at any given moment you could be in a helicopter craving chicken wings or falling from an airplane wishing you had wings.

The sounds of the children playing roller hockey brought a measure of peace to me as I ate the pizza. I swigged down the first bottle of beer. The pizza was delicious, and I devoured it entirely. I opened a second bottle of beer, and it went down as smooth as the first one. I sat on the back of the Toyota amongst the soiled napkins and empty pizza box from my *al fresco* dining experience. I slipped my thumb into the neck of one of the empty bottles. My forefinger went into the second empty bottle and I clinked them together in a rhythmic beat. At least it sounded rhythmic to me. The clinking and clanking of the bottles filled the air with a lilting beat that reminded me of the Bahamian junkanoo bands at the annual Goombay Festival in Coconut Grove. My mind went back to the memories of the beautiful, scantily clad, long-legged dancers who turned Grand Avenue's center median into a sizzling outdoor asphalt dance hall. The gyrating men in wildly colorful painted masks moving to the calypso beat as they set the tone with rake and scrape music added to my remembrances. The night air would fill with whistles blowing and cowbells clanging. It was always such a fun weekend of pageantry, music, and local food. The food was incredible. Conch fritters, pigeon rice, crayfish chunks, and johnny cakes. The carefree atmosphere brought on by one too many Goombay Smash drinks was a time of my life that seemed so far away from where I was now.

Now I was spending my weekend with body parts and drug runners.

Was this the way I envisioned it when I was elected into the VIN unit? That's the process. You make your intention known that you want to do the work, and then through a series of interviews and a career review you can be tapped for the position. You *choose* to be chosen. Could I have foreseen the toll it would rain down on me? The implosion of my marriage? The optics don't stretch that far in a young man's eyes. Horizons are to be pursued, another one after the previous one. It's when we're older that the horizons come at us with increasing frequency. I felt my life transitioning from a young man to a premature older man. Time is a cruel mistress. It taunts and deludes you into thinking you have an abundance of it. As a VIN detective I waded into the murky pond of life that most sensible people step around. It wears on a person. It wore on me.

I wasn't too far from home. Another beer for the ride wouldn't be out of order. Sensibility briefly took hold. I bundled up the pizza box and napkins and dumped them into a nearby trash bin, then closed the liftgate to the Land Cruiser, securing the four unopened beers in the cargo area away from my reach. I drove down the parking ramp and turned east onto Coral Reef Drive. It was figuratively, and literally a straight drive to Paradise Point. As I passed the front entrance to Westminster High School I started thinking about the four beers I could hear rocking together in the cargo area. I pressed the remote control affixed to my passenger visor and entered the community through the resident gate, giving the guard a customary wave.

My headlights illuminated the dense fig vine that framed the darkly painted green wooden garage door of my unit. The previous owner had trained the vine to grow thick and full across the entire upper external staircase and around the garage opening. Whoever the doctor hired to maintain the property had continued the beautiful topiary. I never parked in the garage and always chose to park in the herringbone brick driveway. I retrieved the still-cold beers from the cargo area of the Land Cruiser and went up the outside flight of stairs into the condo. I put my keys, wallet, badge, and gun on a long white credenza in a cobalt hand-blown glass bowl that I'd deemed my drop spot. The bowl was probably more valuable than all the things I put in it. I was grateful to have the opportunity to live in the condominium, but I knew it wouldn't last forever. I was going to have to find my own place soon. I'd lived in the deep southern part of the county for quite some time, and it was where I felt most comfortable. Eventually the doctor would want to move his mother to the United States. This condo may have been suitable before she broke her hip but I questioned if the multiple layers and three stories of stairs would be a good for her now. That wouldn't bode well for me as the doctor would probably sell the condominium that had been my home for the past eight months. Decisions were going to need to be made by me. That was in the long term. In the short term I needed to decide if I was having another beer or not. I decided to pass on another beer.

I'd have two.

I went up to the master bedroom with an opened Amstel in each hand. I went into the lavishly marbled tiled shower and turned on the water, placed an Amstel on the shower bench and took the other to the terrace outside the master bedroom. I looked out at the darkened sea and sky, trying to see Chicken Key and Elliott Key. The moonless night provided zero ambient light to see any of the spoiler islands. I drank the beer quickly, stripped and entered the shower. I sat on the bench and drank the beer in the shower with the warm water raining down upon me. I started to think about all that happened that day. Then I began to shake.

Uncontrollably.

Chapter Ten

TRAFFIC ON A Sunday morning can be startlingly light. The biggest obstacle on a Sunday morning was the road clotting with identically dressed recreational cyclists who thought the flat smooth paved roads of South Florida were their own *Tour de France*. Many of these same self-inflated riders would have a coronary event if they ever had to ride the elevations of North Carolina or Colorado. After passing the denizens of sweaty lycra-clad enthusiastic but delusional cyclists, the drive into the police department was uneventful. I arrived at 9:15am. I parked in the shaded paved alleyway between the police department and the multi-story Regions Bank building. I had no idea how long I would be there. If it was for an unforeseeable and more than likely inordinate amount of time, I wanted to keep my car in the shade as long as I could. Parking in the deteriorating building's basement parking garage would ensure shade. I just abhorred the idea of my car down there with the leaky pipes, puddled water, and greasy surfaces of the basement garage. I opted for the Miami natural shade of large concrete buildings built on the foundation of forged building permits, bribed inspectors, and encroaching lot lines.

I walked into Major Brunson's office at 9:25. I was early enough to not be late, but close enough to be in his office at 9:30 so I could be here to as he said discuss. The early arrival I hoped made me appear to not be anxious.

Major Brunson's office was actually two offices. The smaller inner office was cojoined by a door to the larger office where Major Brunson's desk was. Mondays through Fridays his secretary, Charlene Muscanera, sat at a desk in the inner office. She acted as Brunson's gatekeeper. She was also the one who could gauge his explosive temper sooner than anyone else in the police department. She long ago developed a knack for knowing when his temper was escalating or if whatever brought you to his office would be the topic to set him into a profanity-laced tirade. A tirade which usually culminated in him kicking a garbage can or anything readily near his swinging leg. Without her there to forewarn me, I was potentially walking into a powder keg of a situation. I stopped in the open doorway, looking at Charlene's empty desk, taking in the peacefulness. Although technically not in the office, I don't think I'd ever felt such calmness in the office. The door between the two offices was open. My reverie was soon disrupted when Major Brunson called out:.

"You think I can't hear you breathing out there like some thirteen-year-old kid at his first school dance? Get your ass in here. What the fuck are you doing?"

Instinctively I looked to the ceiling as if some sort of absolution would fall down upon me. I passed Charlene's desk and stepped into his office. Major Brunson was behind his desk, a stack of papers before him. There was a bottle of hot sauce on the corner of his desk: "Voodoo Prince Death Mamba."

He wore a long sleeve white shirt and a navy necktie. Suit and tie on a Sunday. Whatever I was here to discuss, I sensed was far and away beyond whatever I thought today was going to be. He nodded at an empty chair across from his desk. I'd been summoned enough times to his office to know the look to the chair was a direct way of telling me to sit down. I sat down.

"My wife has told me I'm going to hell for constantly overusing the word 'fuck.' I've rented a bus if any of you fuckers needs a ride," he said to me by way of greeting.

"I've always heard that every man paves his own way to hell," I said.

"Yeah? Well I've got a fucking steamroller for that theory, too. Charlene here yet?" he asked me. Charlene on a Sunday? If she was called in for this then whatever this was, it wouldn't be a normal Sunday for any of us. I'd never heard of her, or any civilian being called in on a Sunday unless it was a hurricane. The weather was clear, and we were now one month past the end of hurricane season. Before I could answer, he answered his own question.

"Of course she isn't here yet. I told her 9:45. She wouldn't come in a minute sooner than necessary due to my sunny disposition. Actually, I'm more like a goddamn scorching solar flare, but you get the fucking idea, Cade."

I just sat there, trying to make sense of what was potentially unfolding.

"Cade, as you know we have a meeting set for ten this morning. I asked you to come in earlier because I wanted to hear from you about yesterday."

"Yesterday? A lot happened yesterday," I responded.

"No shit, Sherlock. Let me help you along here. How did you know there were ninety kilograms of cocaine in the rock pit off of Marin Street?"

I thought it was prudent to start from the beginning.

"You called me yesterday and told me to find out what Miami Dade County had going on in the south end of the city. When I got there they were investigating a found body. It was actually a body dismembered in the intersection of Conde Avenue and Nogales Street—"

"I do believe I told you to call me back once you found out why they were there," he said, interrupting me.

"I saw our fire truck, firefighters, crime scene unit, and patrol units on the scene when I arrived so I assumed—"

"Cade, when you assume you make an ass out of 'u and me'. Next time I say call me and keep me apprised you better fucking believe I mean call me and keep me apprised," he interrupted me again.

I stopped and looked at him knowing full well there really had been no need for me to call him. He was definitely kept apprised of the situation. The circular conversation was tiresome so early in the morning, but I had to have faith there was a reason for it.

"Cade, have you ever thought to consider that the conversation between you and me wasn't about you conveying information to me, but me conveying information to you?"

There it was. Faith restored.

"Understood," I said.

"You say that often, Cade. You *imply* you understand but you don't put yourself in the answer. You don't say 'I understand.' You say 'understood' and there's an implication you're on the same fucking page as everyone else, but I have seen you fucking go off script so many times that I'm not sure if you fucking *understand* what it is I'm even telling you now."

He stopped talking and stared at me.

"I understand," I said.

"Today is going to be full speed. There will be a lot of moving parts. Since I'm the lead mechanic, I need to know all the parts. Now I'm going to circle back. Without all the *I was standing here, and he was standing over fucking there* just tell me how you knew there were kilograms of cocaine in the rock pit?"

"It was calculated chance. The victim from yesterday morning had white crystalline dust on his hands and all across his shoes. I didn't know what it was. When I got in the helicopter with Miami Dade Aviation I saw that the rock pit was a direct line to Tamiami airport. There's a smuggling technique called a 'Real McCoy.' Contraband is packed with salt and airdropped or thrown overboard a ship into water. When the salt dissolves the contraband floats to the surface. At that time of morning a low flying airplane on its way to Tamiami, well, it doesn't deviate from its flight path. The rock pit, although fed from the bay, ensures nothing will drift out with tides. It's a good kick spot. Open the airplane door and just kick the load into the water. We had marine patrol working in the afternoon. I had a choice to make and I took a chance."

"You took a chance?"

"Yes, sir."

"Well, I'll give you high credit for your instincts and being correct."

It was at that moment that Major Brunson saw Charlene enter the inner office through the open doorway. "Charlene. We have people coming. I thought you'd be here sooner."

"Yes, I know. They're already here, I was meeting them and getting them seated. They're waiting on you in the basement meeting room," she said.

He looked at me and with an animated facial motion and his eyes said that both he and I better get going. He hastily jumped up from his seat. He retrieved his suit jacket hanging on the back of his chair and very quickly put it on as he walked out of the office.

"Cade and I are on our way down now. Stay by your phone," he said as he passed Charlene's desk.

We were moving with a sense of urgency, and I had no idea why. He was out the door and walking briskly towards the elevators. I looked back at Charlene for some sort of indication of what I was getting into but she just waved her hand at me in a dismissive manner as if to say *get going and take him with you*.

We stepped into the elevator. He pressed the button with the "B" on it.

Government builders.

Even the elevator buttons need to be simplified for the wandering morons that can't understand that "P" stands for parking and "B" is for basement. When they put an "M" button for mezzanine it caused all kinds of havoc. We rode the elevator to the basement in silence.

Human nature can be weird sometimes. He'd just been asking me to explain how the ninety kilograms of cocaine were recovered and now some sort of societal protocol necessitated an odd no talking stance as we traveled to the basement.

The elevator doors opened. The public information office was in the basement. The small area outside of the elevator had tables along the walls, covered in boxes overstuffed with pamphlets and brochures. Before we exited the elevator Brunson turned to me.

"Don't say a word. Don't say a fucking word unless I ask you myself. You got it?"

"Understood."

He gave me a hard glare.

"I mean I understand," I said.

We stepped off of the elevator. We took only a few steps and turned into the basement meeting room. The room had rows of long tables and accompanying chairs. It was a multi-use room for police instruction, police award ceremonies, employee baby showers, employee birthday parties, soon-to-be-former employees retirement parties, and for the assembly of alpha bravo platoons of officers during a hurricane. This time it was a quiet room with a small smattering of people inside waiting for Major Brunson. I was Kato to his Green Hornet. Nobody was waiting on me.

Major Brunson went to the podium at the center of the room. Llyod Trentlocke stood off to the side of the podium. Lawson Dreyer in his ever-present bold-lettered NTSB shirt was seated in the front row of seats with another NTSB fellow. Addison Hope was not in attendance. There was one other man in a suit sitting in the front row. There was one open seat in the front row. It would be in bad taste to sit in the back of the room where I actually wanted to be, so I sat in the open seat next to Lawson Dreyer. We said very quiet hellos to each other. Major Brunson started the meeting.

"Gentlemen, we're here with regard to the incident that occurred yesterday. In that incident a male was found deceased in Coral Gables at the intersection of Nogales Street and Conde Avenue. The deceased was discovered by a local resident. An area canvas was conducted with no witnesses or additional evidence. The body was…well, why don't I have Homicide Detective Trentlocke from the Miami Dade Police Department take it from here. Detective?"

Llyod Trentlocke stepped up to the podium.

"Thank you, Major. The deceased was discovered in the early morning hours yesterday. His injuries were indicative of a fall from a high elevated position. It is theorized he fell from an airplane. The body was severed upon impact with land and was discovered in three distinctive parts. Internal temperature of the body did not find any trace of oxygen deprivation or frost accumulation—"

"What does that tell us?" asked Brunson.

Before Llyod could answer, Lawson Dreyer sitting next to me did.

"It means he wasn't in the wheel well of a commercial airliner and fell thousands of feet. He wasn't frozen, and he wasn't oxygen deprived due to high altitudes."

"As Investigator Dreyer has clearly stated, our victim was not frozen, nor did he suffer from a lack of oxygen. His death was caused by impact with the ground. The deceased was wearing size eleven shoes. They were American made, Herman Survivors men's Boulder waterproof six inch steel toe work boots. They can be purchased in nearly every sporting goods store or major retail outlet like K-Mart, Sears, Walmart, and the like. The shoes had a considerable amount of pre-calcified non-iodized salt across and on the bottom of the shoes. The same pre-calcified non-iodized salt residue was on the victim's hands—"

"What does that mean?" asked Dreyer.

Major Brunson looked at me. I understood his look. I kept my mouth shut.

"Right now our crime lab and the medical examiner's office are doing further testing. The deceased is a white male. He was six feet one inch tall, and he weighed 188 pounds. In his pocket was a single one hundred gulden bill, or using the proper pronunciation a *hunderd gulden* bill. There was a single *vittig gulden* which is the equivalent of a fifty gulden bill, and seventy-five cents in Netherland coins. All the currency in his pockets is from the Netherlands. He was wearing thin dark pants comprised of a cotton and polyester blend and a thin cotton button down shirt. Toxicology is not fully complete but as of now we have not discovered any alcohol or drugs in his system. We are still actively trying to understand the events that led up to his death."

"Led up to his death?" Dreyer guffawed. "I saw this once in the Mojave Desert. It's a thrill seekers death. They like to throw the parachute out of the airplane then jump out after it. They put the parachute on as they descend. Only in this case, I don't think our victim was able to catch up to the only lifesaving thing he threw out and quite simply, he died. The parachute, still compact and tightly packed, probably sunk in the bay somewhere. I've seen it more times than I want to recall. All this newfangled get-on-TV stuff is making these daredevils put their lives in the hands of fate, and everyone thinks they're so cool. Idiots if you ask me."

"Actually, I didn't ask you," said Trentlocke from the podium.

I could see that the seated unidentified man in the suit was looking down at his shoes portraying an act of nonchalance, except the vein in his temple was pulsing. He was opening and closing his fist which he tried to conceal by holding his hand down by his side.

Lawson Dreyer said, "It doesn't matter. We at the NTSB oversee this investigation. We're certain that's what happened. It's Sunday, I don't think me or my colleague need to be here any further. Detective Trentlocke, can you forward all of your investigative reports to my office? I would like to put a bow on this and close our investigation. Thank you all for your time and efforts from both me and the NTSB. Sincerely. Thank you."

Dreyer and the other NTSB investigator stood up. He patted me on the back as he squeezed past me on his way out. Major Brunson rose up from his chair and picked up the telephone mounted on the wall. He pushed a few numbers. "Call me when they've left the building," was all he said, then he sat back down. Trentlocke stayed positioned behind the podium. No one spoke. It was eerie. Four grown men sitting in silence. A few minutes passed, then the phone on the wall rang. Major Brunson picked it up.

"Yes Charlene? Uh huh. Okay. Thank you."

He hung up the telephone and turned to the rest of us.

"They're gone. Let's start the real meeting."

Chapter Eleven

THE REAL MEETING?

Whatever was about to happen would do so without the NTSB. Just before leaving the room Lawson Dreyer said, "We at the NTSB oversee this investigation."

Something was certainly amiss.

Major Brunson motioned for me to join Trentlocke at the podium. I got up from my seat and stood at the front of the room. Major Brunson took a seat next to the man in the suit.

"Cade, sitting next to me is Special Agent Phil Zammit. Agent Zammit is with the Drug Enforcement Agency, and he's the head of OPBAT. Agent Zammit, maybe you'd like to tell us a little about OPBAT so we can follow the bouncing ball of this meeting," said Brunson.

Agent Zammit stood up, unbuttoning his jacket and meeting each of our eyes.

"First of all, thank you all for being here today. I'm Phil Zammit. I'm a special agent with the DEA. I currently serve as the regional supervisor for OPBAT. OPBAT is a combined DEA, U.S. Coast Guard, U.S. Customs and Border Protection and Government of Bahamas partnership to combat drug smuggling to and from the Bahamas. OPBAT is an acronym for our joint task force *Operation*

Bahamas, Turks. Our operations center is in Nassau. We're responsible for initiating and prosecuting law enforcement cases in the Bahamas and Caribbean. The Bahamian area is our primary AOR."

"AOR?" asked Trentlocke.

"Area of Responsibility. We have a robust ongoing cooperative effort with the governments of the Commonwealth of the Bahamas, the Turks and Caicos Islands, as well as the U.S. Coast Guard, U.S. Customs and Border Protection. The joint task force is enacted to deny drug traffickers the ability to operate effectively in the Bahamas. Our efforts so far have dented and dismantled many smuggling operations who want to use the nearly 700 islands of the Bahamas as a staging area for transshipment of drugs, mainly cocaine into the United States. I happened to be stateside when the information came to us that the Coral Gables Marine Patrol Unit seized ninety kilograms of cocaine last night. Major Brunson and I have been in close contact since last night. Per our discussions and after hearing the rest of the news we decided to call this meeting and strategize a plan."

I squirmed a little further knowing that whatever Zammit and Brunson had schemed was going to involve me at some point. Major Brunson spoke next.

"Phil, with us is Cade Taylor."

Major Brunson asked me to recant the events of the day before. I briefed Agent Zammit about my being on the scene and then leaving with NTSB investigator Addison Hope. I talked about flying in the helicopter with her and how we made an unanticipated stop at Tamiami airport. I spoke about the straight line of flying from the rock pit to the airport. I verified that I too had seen the white dusting on the deceased's shoes. I explained the smuggling method of making hams in a Real McCoy. It was a stretchable leap that our deceased person was what we call a "kicker" in the drug trade, and that he may have been pushing or kicking the kilograms of cocaine out of an open airplane door when he met his demise. I informed them about notifying the Coral Gables Police Marine Patrol and how with a few dives in the rock pit they were able to find the cocaine.

I described the markings on the kilograms, and I noticed Zammit perk up. I gave a detailed dissertation about the three individuals who came to retrieve the cocaine, and I mentioned that I'd asked Officer Charlie Tresserman to run the truck and trailer license tags through the NCIC and FCIC system and to put a copy of the findings in my mailbox. Major Brunson got up and picked up the wall phone again.

"Charlene, go to Cade Taylor's box and bring us down whatever envelopes are in there."

As soon as he hung up the telephone a man in a dark well tailored suit entered the room. He looked frazzled and a little stressed. Major Brunson looked at him as he came in.

"Agent Mitchell?" he asked the stranger.

"Yes. Yes. Good morning. I'm Brad Mitchell. I'm so sorry for being late, I just flew in from Key West and there was a delay leaving. The agency and I are incredibly distressed over this whole situation. I met our jet at Naval Air Station Key West. My driver got a little lost in Coral Gables. He got us here as soon as he could."

Trentlocke gave me a knowing look concerning the geography of Coral Gables.

Brad Mitchell sat down in the nearest open chair. He seemed a bit flummoxed and confused. His tousled hair conflicted with his crisp starched shirt and gleaming Cole Hahn shoes. We all looked at him and then we turned our eyes to Major Brunson who introduced us all to Agent Mitchell. With a noticeable jolt Brad Mitchell realized the social faux pas and stood up nearly as quickly as he sat down.

"Once again, I'm Brad Mitchell from the U.S. Department of State, I'm the Regional Director of the Diplomatic Security Service Special Agent Division. Many walks of life, even in law enforcement aren't familiar with who we are and what we do, so let me explain. We refer to ourselves as the DSS SAs. The DSS SA office is tasked with securing embassies and consulates. We do dignitary protection for diplomats, conduct investigations, and take on all foreign threats to the sovereignty of our nation. We also investigate international criminal networks that work in and outside of our borders. We're in 275 cities in 135 countries. Our network is beyond vast."

He sat down nearly as quickly as he stood up.

"You're a black passport," Trentlocke said to Mitchell.

Mitchell nodded affirmatively. A black U.S. passport is a diplomatic passport, the rarest passports issued by the United States. To have one, you must be an employee of the U.S. Department of State either as a diplomat, an ambassador, or an embassy staff member. Major Brunson asked that I stay at the podium with Trentlocke, but I was finished talking. I saw no need to keep standing there so I left the podium and sat down in the front row of seats. I turned my attention to Trentlocke. He bit his lip and then he was lost in thought for a moment as if he was trying to gauge his comments. Trentlocke then started talking.

"So what we have here is a deceased individual who, through fingerprints and dental record identification, we have identified as a DSS special agent."

When he said that the entire room became quiet. For me this whole situation had just taken a wide turn on a narrow curve. My thoughts immediately went from was the DSS special agent corrupt or was he working undercover, and was he pushed out of the airplane? The realization of the loss Brad Mitchell must be feeling wafted over all of us.

"I think I speak for everyone here in the room when I offer my condolences to Brad Mitchell for the loss of one of his agents. Upon finding out he was a DSS special agent I went the extra mile to try and process the crime scene. NTSB investigator Lawson Dreyer was more of a hinderance than help on the scene. Agent Mitchell, Investigator Dreyer was here earlier, you just missed him. Dreyer is holding onto a theory that I, as a homicide detective, find to be without merit. Dreyer's rigid conviction that it was a thrill seeker who dived out of an airplane to try and retrieve a parachute in the dark and attempted to put the parachute on as he fell to earth does *not* pass the smell test. First, it was dark when the event occurred. Secondly, no parachute was ever found, and third it would have been too dark to film the stunt. It wouldn't be the first time an almighty authority with a penchant for coiffed hair, teeth veneers, and standing behind a bank of microphones was wrong. I think we can all remember two years ago when the FBI totally botched the Centennial Olympic Park bombing in Atlanta during the Summer Olympics. They fingered that poor security guard Richard Jewell as the bomber and nearly ruined that young man's life. Even when other agencies demonstrated to the FBI they were incorrect," said Trentlocke.

Charlene walked into the room and quietly handed Major Brunson the envelopes that were in my mailbox. She just as quickly left the room. Trentlocke continued talking.

"As I just said, I went the extra mile to try and process the crime scene. The boots were inspected inside and outside. The manufacturers of his clothing were researched. Nothing about his clothing stood out. Except we may have gotten lucky. I mean we may have gotten *very* lucky. He was wearing a Fossil black leather belt with rectangular silver medallions. We used the best crime scene technician we have to print all of the silver medallions and the buckle. We did get plenty of the deceased's prints; But we also got a partial right index finger on the right side rear medallion, and a left thumb print on the left rear medallion. They were sent to the automatic fingerprinting identification system or what we call 'AFIS' for comparison. I'm happy to say we have a match. The prints came back to a known cocaine trafficker. A Colombian national named Macario Santos Higuera."

When I heard him say Macario I knew deep in my heart the very same Macario from the rock pit had to be the one to leave the prints on the DSS special agent's belt. He didn't fall from an airplane—he was pushed. That explained why Major Brunson and the others were content with letting the NTSB bull their way with their assertions. This wasn't an accident. It was murder, and the NTSB has no say in the investigation, regardless of what they said or thought. I still didn't understand why Addison Hope was pulled from the case and was summoned to her office at 9:30 that morning.

Trentlocke went on: "It seems Higuera was arrested in 1993 by the DEA on a freighter off of Andros Island in the Bahamas. He was the only Colombian national on the ship. The rest of the crew was Cuban. He claimed he'd been on a motorboat that stalled in the ocean and he abandoned it. The freighter picked him up. He claimed he wasn't part of the Cuban crew. A judge in Nassau believed him and let him walk."

"The judge believed him or the judge was bribed?" asked Agent Zammit.

"Your guess is as good as mine. He did spend some time in Fox Hill Prison in Nassau until he was released," said Trentlocke.

Zammit grimaced. "Fox Hill? Fox Hill is without a doubt one of the most deplorable prisons I have ever seen. The place is infested with rats, maggots, and disease. The conditions are beyond horrible. There could be as many as six prisoners housed in a cell meant for one or at the very most, two. You can forget about sanitary facilities and clean running water. The place is literally hell on earth."

There was a brief respite of silence. It was Zammit who spoke again.

"It's just the five of us here. Let's stop this stand-up-and-give-your-book-report shit. Let's all sit at the same table and lay it out there. We have a DSS special agent we suspect of being murdered. Major Brunson, let's bring the envelopes and our collected hypotheses together and just hash it out."

We all gathered around one of the tables. It was the first time I got a good close up look at Brad Mitchell. He seemed very pensive and solemn. Major Brunson put the envelopes on the table. I found some paper and pens in the PIO office and dispersed them to everyone.

"My house. I'll start the quorum here," said Brunson.

"What do we know so far? We have a DSS special agent who was kicking kilos into an enclosed rock pit adjacent to channels in Biscayne Bay. Cade deduced the rock pit was a direct flight line to Tamiami airport. Any air traffic controllers from Miami International

Airport or even Tamiami Airport would discern no disruption in altitude, air speed, or direction."

I was actually impressed that he said the entire statement without cursing.

"So this fucking dirtbag asshole Macario we think was on the airplane…" he continued.

Being impressed is overrated, I thought to myself.

"Cade saw the salt residue on the agent's shoes and hands and took what he called a 'calculated chance' and deployed our marine patrol to dive the rock pit, where they discovered kilograms of cocaine packed tightly with salt. He also was present when the dope runners came to retrieve the coke and came up empty. There were three of them. An American with a Philadelphia accent, one called Macario, and one called Toes."

"Fingers. It's not Toes. It's Fingers. In Spanish he's called *Dedos*," I interjected.

"Can you identify these three men?" Mitchell asked me.

"No. They came in on dirt bikes and the trail is narrow. I needed to get some concealment and I hid behind a tree. I just heard them."

"You hid?" he said, arching his eyebrow.

"There were three of them and until they actually stopped and tried to get the coke I couldn't make a stand against recreational motocross riders. It was when they tried to get the coke that I knew what they were there for. By then I had no back up available, and it was low-light circumstances."

Brunson stepped in: "I would have done the same fucking thing. Three against one in the fading light with cocaine missing. Fuck yeah, I'd a done the same thing. Cade was able to get the license tag from the truck and trailer they used to haul in the motorbikes."

He unsealed the envelope that Officer Tresserman had put in my mailbox and briefly looked over the paperwork.

"Florida license tag CP9-70Z, the one on the truck, is not on file. No record of it in the Florida system," said Brunson.

"Nothing in the system? I'll try and see if our state department channels can find anything. This is our biggest priority," said Mitchell as he wrote down the license plate number. The intensity of Mitchell's urgency was palpable. *He's a loyal guy*, I thought.

"License tag JJM-05H, also a Florida tag, comes back to a 1998 Trail Lite seven-by-fourteen aluminum trailer. Registered owner is Macario Santos Higuera…"

The room erupted with a collective shout of "Yes!" from myself, Trentlocke, Zammit, and Mitchell. Brunson continued reading.

"Registered address is 514 West Flagler Street, Miami, Florida."

Trentlocke wrote the address down and asked Major Brunson if the phone on the wall could make outside calls.

"Dial zero first, wait for a dial tone, then call."

Trentlocke rose up from his seat and made a call while Major Brunson and Zammit exchanged knowing looks. Brunson showed Mitchell the photograph of Marine Patrol Officer Shea Pope holding the singular kilogram of cocaine. Mitchell inquired how far the West Flagler address was from where we were. Trentlocke returned in about three minutes.

"I'm assembling a team to check out that address. My lieutenant says he can have people in place by one this afternoon, and a warrant signed by two. I know it's Miami police jurisdiction, but Miami sits in my county. So we're doing this without Miami."

Phil Zammit said, "I recognize the marking on that kilo. We had an informant in Great Inagua. The proximity to Cuba and the narrowness of that strait makes it an easy entry point for cocaine into the Bahamas and eventually into the U.S. Matthew Town is the center of commerce on the island. Going as far back as 1600 the island is best known for producing something. Can you guess what?"

"What?" asked Brunson.

"Salt. Just like the non-iodized salt that Detective Taylor spoke about. Our informant was born and raised in Matthew Town. It's also where we found him dead eight months ago. He was shot sixteen times and left in a corroded barrel behind a poultry processing plant.

He provided some drawings of these same markings to us. He'd seen them. He'd seen other shipments of kilos with these markings. I remember the briefings when he drew them for us. We still haven't figured the moniker on the kilograms, but it doesn't matter because we know where the kilos are going and whose organization it is. Our Philadelphia field office has seized a few of the kilos in South Philly. These kilos you seized yesterday belong to the Caruso crime family in Philadelphia, headed by Ray Caruso. I don't have much to say about Ray Caruso. I wish I did. I mean the guy is like a phantom. No one, not us, not the Pennsylvania State Police, not the Philadelphia Police Department, not the local smaller agencies, nobody has any pictures of him. No driver's license, no credit cards—at least any that come back to him—nothing. He doesn't attend funerals, weddings, christenings, I mean nothing. This guy is feared by the entire organization. Every mobster we've ever pinched refuses to even acknowledge he exists. Wiretaps and UCs that have been able to get inside the organization all confirm his existence, but we have zero intel on Ray Caruso other than the stories of his quick brutal lethality. He's harder on his own crew than on his enemies. We think he's responsible in the past decade for nearly every mobster killed in Philadelphia and New Jersey. He's gone against one of organized crime's biggest tenets of omerta. He has no issue running a drug operation. Trenton mobsters defer to him over the crime families in New York. I mean, he has *major* juice! Word on the street is that even the Gambino and Lucchese family won't stop for *gasoline* in Philadelphia. The city of brotherly love is locked down tight by Ray Caruso and no one, I mean no one, wants to go against him."

"If he has Philly guys doing his bidding they'd stick out like a sore thumb in the Bahamas," said Trentlocke.

"If his pasty white boys, or as they say in Philadelphia 'bous,' even stepped off a trawler, catamaran, yacht, or a jet ski in the Bahamas, we'd know. They're using intermediaries to move the coke through the Bahamas."

Zammit's explanation of the pronunciation of "bous" clarified what I'd heard the Philadelphia thug calling Dedos and Macario Santos Higuera.

It was Brad Mitchell who put the cherry on top.

"Phil, Major Brunson, detectives Taylor and Trentlocke I cannot express fully how thankful I am to all of you for your solid, incredibly fast, and thorough investigative work. Detective Trentlocke, you especially went into hyper speed when you found out the victim you were investigating was one of our own. You helped to arrange all of us here today and in accordance with the cooperation of Major Brunson and the Coral Gables Police Department I just feel overwhelmed with gratitude for everyone in this room. In the sense of fair play and to bring justice for my fallen comrade I feel it necessary to put my cards on the table and help you all to help us."

We waited as he searched for the right thing to say.

"Let me start by saying our operative originally started with us, assigned to our Atlanta field office. In our profession you could find yourself living abroad for nearly fifty percent of your career with us. He had assignments in Helsinki, Istanbul, and his most recent assignment was in Saint Eustatius. Until I was promoted, I myself was assigned practically everywhere. If it has a ski mountain, a desert, or is surrounded by water I've done embassy time there. You get the idea. Saint Eustatius is in the Netherlands Antilles. The Dutch pronunciation is *Sint Eustatius*. There are only about 4000 permanent residents on the island. Our agent felt that he could do more from Saint Eustatius than he could from the ABC islands. The cruise ships and tourists were actually a headache for Colombian smugglers because of all the comings and goings they brought to the islands. Those are the southern quadrant of the Netherlands Antilles. The northern quadrant is three islands. Those islands are Saint Eustatius, Saint Martin, and Saba."

The mention of Saba reminded me of someone I once knew who was now living in Toronto. I had a brief fond remembrance of her but snapped back to the task at hand.

"Our operative infiltrated a mid-level group tasked with collection and redistribution of cocaine in the islands. According to the intelligence reports the cocaine was being brought in from Colombia, primarily coming in from Cartagena. It was being airdropped in a remote area of Sant Eustatius called 'The Quill.' It's a poorly patrolled national park that covers most of the southern part of the island. Our operative was trusted by the intake smuggling team. He'd ride with the smugglers either by boat or airplane to Great Inagua where the intake team would pass the cocaine off to the redistribution team—one member of this redistribution team was known to our operative as 'Macario.' In Great Inagua they'd encase the cocaine in dense packed salt, then they moved it to the U.S. doing air drops from deep in southern Miami Dade all the way up to the Lake Worth inlet. Our operative was being paid for the intake and the redistribution. He was the human funnel it was all going through. His reports told us the cocaine profits were being gathered by a northeast crime family who had designs on the 2000 presidential election. A candidate who can win early primaries with a fat budget powered by cocaine money could upend the probability of a non-compromised candidate getting into the White House. It's all about who gets out in front first. No one looks too deep at the political contributions of a candidate until they're becoming the party's nominee. This northeast crime group isn't planning to fund the entire campaign. They want to just inject enough money to make a front runner. A compromised U.S. President can wield a lot of power with getting casinos built in states like Pennsylvania. The group's plan is to take the risk now, pump and dump the cocaine money to get their guy into office, and then use the future cocaine sales to fund a big fat juicy casino in some farm town in Bucks County. Within five years you're out of the drug business and in the casino business. Think about it. Who wants to go to seedy Atlantic City when you can have the green hills of Pennsylvania?"

"Let me get this straight. The Ray Caruso organized crime family of Philadelphia wants to tilt the presidential election of 2000 with narcodollars so that Ray Caruso can put more narcodollars into casino licenses in Pennsylvania, eventually making even more money than cocaine sales on the blue hairs they bring in on buses to gamble? Is that what you are saying?" asked Zammit.

"Pretty much. The product that was seized yesterday will hit them, but it won't cripple them. Macario more than likely pushed our operative out of the airplane not knowing who he was, hoping to become the intake and redistribution connection so he could fatten his own bottom line. Unfortunately for them they've just kicked a hornets' nest that will rain the wrath of the DSS on Ray Caruso's criminal empire. This is war to us, and we're going after them."

"This doesn't sit well with me or the DEA that you knew this and kept the DEA out of it," said Zammit.

"Phil, with all due respect, the State Department doesn't check with any arm of the Justice Department. National security supersedes. The big issue is how do we bring down the Ray Caruso crime family and avenge Dan."

"Dan?" I asked.

"The DSS special agent. Dan Stallings. You met his ex-wife yesterday," said Trentlocke.

I looked at Trentlocke quizzically.

"Addison? Addison Hope from NTSB? Dan Stallings was her ex-husband."

Chapter Twelve

I SLUMPED BACK IN my chair. It was as though the wind had been taken out of my lungs with a strong gut punch. I recalled what Addison Hope told me at Tamiami Airport about her ex-husband. That he was applying everywhere in the federal system, and he didn't care who hired him. She was helping him with his applications, printing multiples at the library. I was thinking of how she was summoned to her NTSB field office probably to be told her former husband was dead. Eventually that information would filter to Lawson Dreyer. He more than likely would want to amend his daredevil theory and inject himself back in the investigation. It would be up to Major Brunson and Llyod Trentlocke if they'd allow him back in. I didn't foresee that happening. This was now looking very much like a drug-related homicide. A homicide of a federal agent. Even though Addison said she'd lost track of her ex-husband years ago, surely the news of his death would be a shock to her, especially since she was on the crime scene yesterday. She hadn't crossed under the yellow cordoned-off area, but I was sure she saw the tarps covering the body parts from the helicopter.

Zammit went on: "I think our best approach is to go with what we know. We know they're feeling the loss of the kilograms. We have an address. Let's start there. I'll redirect our enforcement stronger in Great Inagua, and I'll be in contact with my Dutch counterparts to start amping up enforcement in the Netherlands Antilles. If what you're saying is accurate we have a very dangerous snake in our Caribbean back yard whose bite could reach as far as Washington. We need to kill this snake before that happens." Zammit finished with a hardened jaw and a stiff upper lip, ready to go.

"Let's see if we can find Macario Santos Higuera. I have a TNT team being activated. The Tactical Narcotics Team is the best of the best for these types of things. I'll be coordinating the advance on the address at 514 West Flagler. I'll be on scene, and I expect Cade to be there as well," Trentlocke said, slyly including me in his plan.

"I'd like to get some of my people on that as well. This is a federal agent we suspect was pushed from an airplane," said Mitchell. "In the meantime, our office is going to send a delegation to the NTSB to talk with Dan Stallings' ex-wife. She needs to know the entire State Department and myself are supporting her and we'll bring Dan's killer—or killers, for that matter—to justice. Detective Trentlocke, I'll call you when I get people placed with your group," he said as he handed his business card to Trentlocke, then cards to the rest of us. With a solemn goodbye he left the four of us in the room. Major Brunson sat in his chair wringing his hands. He didn't look very happy.

"I don't like the way this is going. If we get this Macario fellow today that only solves one part of the problem. We still got the Ray Caruso mob out here in South Florida and the Bahamas bringing cocaine into the U.S. This doesn't solve anything for me and Phil," said Brunson.

"We need to draw them out," Zammit said.

"We don't even know who these guys are. We heard what Phil said. Ray Caruso is a vapor. He's a myth. He doesn't leave a trace anywhere. I say we go with what we got and see if it leads us to Ray Caruso," Trentlocke said.

"I'll call our Miami field office and try to get some DEA support there as well," said Zammit. "While you and your teams are at the

Flagler Street address, me and Major Brunson will devise a plan that will get the attention of the Ray Caruso crime family."

Trentlocke left Phil Zammit a business card. "When you get your agents assembled have one of them call me. This will be somewhat done on the fly, but it's more of a knock and announce. If we get any pushback on our consent search we will have a warrant within the hour. As soon as Cade and I get out there we'll set up a place to stage and decide on the team set up for entry to the house." Then to me, "Whose car are we taking?"

"Yours. We're nearly halfway there now," I replied.

Once at Trentlocke's car, he asked me, "Did you hear that?"

"Hear what?"

"Your Major Brunson and Phil Zammit. Did you hear what they were saying? I think they have a bigger plan in mind, and it might just include you. I could be wrong, but my inner voice says they want to go for the whole enchilada on this. Me? I'm Homicide. I get the guy who killed Agent Stallings and I'm out. You narcotic guys…you got a lot of ground to still cover. I'm going to suggest we keep you out of this as much as we can. Keep you in a support of the support position. In the rear with the gear, let TNT and DEA do all the work. I'm thinking of keeping the DSS guy on the outside, too. We don't need any vigilantism or overkill. Cade, I mean literally over-kill on this. These guys you encountered yesterday are just retrievers. Macario Santos Higuera could have sold Dan Stallings the belt, or who knows what or how his prints are on the belt. We need to play this by the book. Right down the line."

"So you want me to sit in a car blocks away, while you guys do all the glory work?" I said.

"Exactly."

"Fine with me. I get paid whether I sit or sweat."

We got in his car and he had us gunning down the parking ramps in no time. Once we were streetside I knew I had made a tremendous error in judgment. His car was a rolling black lung. The actual ashtray was overflowing with cigarette butts, and gray pungent ash. I wanted to wretch from the noxious smell of stale tobacco. Looking around, ash was everywhere. Even the headliner of the car looked like it had a slight burnish amber color to it.

"I thought they stopped making cars with ash trays?"

"They did. This is one of the last ones. The motor pool wants me to change this car out for a newer one, but I need an ashtray."

"Do you really need an ashtray? I mean, can't you just put your cigarettes in a coffee can or something?" I asked him.

"Cade, you have no clear understanding of an addicted mind. If the auto industry, one of the biggest industries in the world, can provide me a place for my crushed and used cigarettes than smoking must be acceptable, you know? The reasoning of the mind. It may be illogical to you but it works for me. Look at this car, it even comes with a lighter," he said as he actually lit a cigarette with the car's push-in lighter.

"The surgeon general has a disclaimer on cigarette packs that tells you of the health risks associated with smoking," I said.

"Ah, just get the packs that don't apply. Like the warnings for pregnant women, I try to get those."

Trentlocke was like a one-man band. The drive to 514 West Flagler Street was short but along the way he made and received at least eight cellphone calls. He hung up his last call and turned to me.

"There's a church on the corner of Northwest 7th and Flagler Street. The address is 670 Flagler Street. Church services are done for the day. My guys say the parking lot can accommodate all of us. The church is called 'The Soldiers of the Cross Church.' A few of my people are there now. They say I can't miss it, big Spanish tile-roofed A-frame with a full wall of stained glass. My guys also say there's a big forty-five inch TV mounted outside the church's front door with a full color LED message board."

"Nothing says 'I am the light of the world. Whoever follows me will not walk in darkness, but will have the light of life.' like the illumination from a big screen TV," I said.

"You know your Bible pretty well, Cade."

"As a kid I was an altar boy. All the serving of mass I did, I don't think I need to go to church for about nine to ten years. They owe me time. As my life progressed I do believe I've gone from an altar boy to an altered boy."

Trentlocke gave me a sideways glance and a chuckle. I opened the window to let in some fresh air. He, in turn, intentionally opened his window causing a small vortex in the car which lifted a lot of the cigarette ash and blew it across both of us and the interior of the car. He thought that was hilarious and had a really big laugh.

"There you go buddy, just like our police academy days. Remember? Basic Law Enforcement Class 117. BLE 117. Remember our class motto? *BLE 117 first and ready on the scene!*"

"For you it should be BLE 117 first in line at the cigarette machine!" I said trying to wipe the ash off my shirt.

We pulled into the church parking lot. There were officers from both the DEA and from the Miami Dade TNT team. There wasn't an agent from DSS. I perceived that as a win for Llyod as it was one less person he'd have to integrate into the team. On such short notice there may not have been time for Brad Mitchell to get one agent, let alone a team of agents together.

We all exited our cars and joined the others in a loose huddle in the center of the parking lot. Introductions and pleasantries were exchanged. It was a mixed bunch of people. The agents and detectives were men and women all of different ethnicities, but all here for the same purpose. Trentlocke thanked them all for being here especially on a Sunday, making a point of saying that three times. The operational plan they created consisted of a mixture of DEA and TNT. One group of agents and detectives would cover the rear of the address. They'd be clearly designated by their tactical vests with adorned Velcro strips emblazoned with "Police" and "Policia" attached to the front and rear. Similarly dressed detectives and agents would accompany Trentlocke and two plain clothes TNT detectives. They'd approach the front of the building. The front door team would hold back a few paces and allow the plain clothes detectives and Trentlocke to try contacting whoever might be inside. Trentlocke was a proponent of trying to enter the address with pleasant conversation instead of tactical force. If they didn't make any contact, then with the warrant in hand, they'd institute a forced entry.

He made a point to stress that although DSS Special Agent Stallings had died, it was not fully known if it was a homicide. If Macario was inside the building he didn't want to overplay his hand.

The decision was made to send the rear team ahead by five minutes so they could get in position. I'd seen more thorough operational plans but given the short notice and the pedestrian aspect of knocking on a door as opposed to busting it down, the plan was simple in its design.

I would be staying back in the parking lot. Fine with me. The expression "out of sight and out of mind" is one that I'd learned to embrace, especially when working with an acerbic police major like Brunson.

The teams were quickly mustering up. Since they were called in for this, they were anxious to get the task done so they could get on with their Sunday. Many of the rear coverage members piled into two SUVs, leaving the other cars in the parking lot. I was tasked with watching over the cars. Trentlocke and the two other plain clothes detectives would walk the short distance to the front of the building while a three-person team in tactical vests quietly walked a few yards behind them. Road traffic was light, and the walk was short. Trentlocke left me his car keys so I could sit in the cool comfort of the car's air conditioning. They all walked away and around the corner out of my sight.

The cool comfort of his car.

The car smelled like a bouget of charcoal briquets. Just sitting on the seat caused a plume of smoke to puff up. I tried. I tried to stay in the car, but it was unpalatable. Driving over with him I had no control of the arid choking smoky smell, but sitting in the car now made me feel like I was sitting on a bale of cured Virginia tobacco. I decided to take my chances with the sun's ultraviolet rays and sat outside on the trunk. It was very quiet. The clouds passed slowly overhead, and the afternoon felt just the way the Young Rascals sang."

"Just groovin' on a Sunday afternoon."

I listened to the murmured sounds of the street and nearby downtown Miami. The palm trees above rustled. I thought of how my career would have been different had I been a cop in Pittsburgh, Boston, or some other freezing-in-December-city. I was here in the warm sunshine on a quiet day just feeling the vibe of the tropical day. The Dolphins were playing the Raiders in Oakland. The game started in an hour. It might be nice to watch the game on TV, maybe catch it at an outside waterside bar. Maybe Mike's Venetia, or Tugboat Annie's.

"Just groovin' on a Sunday afternoon
Really, couldn't get away too soon.
We'll keep on spendin' sunny days this way.
We're gonna talk and laugh our time away."

It was pointless to have me out here today. The assembled cars in the parking lot really didn't need my watchful eye. My cellphone rang. It was Trentlocke.

"Cade?"

"Yeah."

"Good news and bad news. The good news is the trailer is here. License plate JJM-05H, just like you said. I'm looking at it right now, it's parked at an odd angle. It has the three motocross bikes on it. We need to get the warrant so we can tow the trailer out and fingerprint the bikes. The bad news is there's no one here and we can't tow the bikes without that warrant. I'm sending the rear team home. No use in me screwing everybody's Sunday here."

"Including mine?"

"Stop whining. I'm here, so you're here. You should have driven your own car."

"You're telling me!" I said.

"Speaking of which, I could use a smoke. I left my cigarettes in the car. Drive up here so I can get my cigarettes."

"Are you asking me or telling me?" I asked him.

"I'm asking you but if I go another ten minutes without a cigarette I'll be telling you. Did you know that in the 1920s this place was a funeral home? Can you imagine how many people have died here?"

"I'm sure they didn't die there; they were dead when they got there. Words are important," I corrected him.

"You get my point. This place has seen a lot of death. Crazy, right? Okay, enough yakking. Cigarettes. We're in the back."

"Meet me out front," I said as I hung up.

I walked back to his car and with wincing reluctance I opened the door. I slid behind the wheel of the nicotine mobile. I actually thought about holding my breath while I drove, but I was not now nor ever going to be a world underwater swimming champion. I gritted my teeth, put the key in the ignition and drove around to the front of the church. Traffic was light. I stopped at the red light at Northwest 6th Street and cursed the red light the whole time as I could feel the tobacco odor permeating my clothes. I caught a glance at a black Chevrolet Silverado 4x4 extended cab pickup truck turning from 6th Street onto West Flagler Street. It stayed to the right and avoided the Flagler drawbridge. I looked at the license tag on the bumper.

"CP9-70Z."

The same Florida license plate the security guard had provided to me last night.

I gunned Trentlocke's car through the red light, causing a faded blue Chrysler Lebaron entering the intersection to lock up its wheels. The driver laid hard on his horn as he struggled to avoid hitting me. Smoke and loud obscenities quickly followed. I could see Trentlocke walking from the rear of the business and approaching the front sidewalk. He was with one of the DEA agents. The pickup truck looked as though it was slowing to turn into the business. The noise from the Chrysler laying on his horn caused Trentlocke and the DEA agent to look towards me.

The driver of the pickup slammed on the brakes as well and the truck heaved and lurched to an abrupt stop. All of these vehicle noises distracted the DEA agent and Trentlocke as the truck's driver opened his door and sprung out, brandishing a dark handgun. He was very fast as he spun towards the driver's side bed of the pickup truck. He fired four gunshots at Trentlocke and the DEA agent over the truck bed.

The DEA agent fell back.

At that close range it would be highly implausible that one of the four shots wouldn't hit. Trentlocke turned his torso quickly, trying to avoid the hail of bullets and still draw his weapon but the DEA agent fell back hard into Trentlocke, knocking them both to the ground. The truck driver hurriedly jumped back into the truck. The transmission made a grinding noise as he hastily shifted into drive. Rather than stay on the side access road to West Flagler he cut the wheel hard to the left, driving over the curb, truck bouncing, until it landed heavily on the grassy swale. The tires fought to gain traction on the uphill grade of the median. Once his front tires gripped onto the sidewalk on the other side of the grass, he was bounding east onto the West Flagler Street drawbridge that spans the Miami River. He gunned the truck hard, leaving tire tracks across the low elevated swale of the Flagler Street Bridge.

I'd been eastbound on the West Flagler storefront side road heading to Trentlocke. I made a split-second decision to push the pedal down as hard as I could. I veered left to go after the shooter in the pickup truck.

I was closing in on him fast. Had his wheels not gripped into the grassy uprising so quickly, I could have rammed him. I gritted my teeth and cursed letting him slip away from us as the truck sped eastbound on the bridge.

As I passed the building, other detectives were running out to attend to Trentlocke and the DEA agent. He was now ahead of me and cresting to the top of the bridge high above the Miami River. As he crested the drawbridge he briefly went out of my sight.

An ear-splintering crash shuddered the ground ahead of me. White smoke rose up on the horizon. I crested the bridge. I saw that the pickup truck had rear-ended a Ryder rental truck. The front of the pickup truck was mashed and crumpled under the bumper of the Ryder truck. Hot green radiator fluid was spilling all along the underside of the truck. The radiator was releasing hot steamy white smoke from its compacted coils. The impact lifted the Ryder truck's back end, with the pickup wedging even further underneath it. The shooter tried to put the truck into reverse. The backup lights glowed and the tires spun but the pickup truck was firmly lodged under the Ryder. Both trucks, conjoined by their twisted, damaged parts, had come to a rest at the top of the bridge facing northeast. The Ryder truck had been pushed across the center double yellow line and was blocking the westbound lanes of traffic.

I slammed on the brakes of Trentlocke's car, hard. The brakes made an ungodly sound and white smoke from my own rear brakes quickly blew across the front of the car. When the front wheels of Trentlocke's car contacted the steel grating at the top of the drawbridge, the brakes worked even harder to grip. A loud bang reverberated through the car from somewhere underneath it and the car lurch violently to the left. I surmised something on the front axle must have snapped off.

The car stuttered, hopping and sliding hard into the back of the pickup truck. The impact was forceful enough to make the passenger airbag deploy. For some uncanny reason the driver's side airbag did not deploy. I braced my arms against the steering wheel. There was a millisecond where I remembered that was not the best way to absorb an accident, but my muscles reacted in defiance. Fortunately, the right side of Trentlocke's car took the majority of the crash. The rear bumper separated from the pickup truck and crashed onto Trentlocke's hood. My own radiator and engine block sustained serious damage as they shifted back towards the passenger compartment, causing them to rise and further bend the hood of Trentlocke's car like a boy scout's pup tent. My seatbelt kept me in the seat, but it also locked against my torso, knocking the wind out of me. The shooter in the pickup truck wearily pushed the creaky, crumbled driver's door open.

He was wobbly on his feet as he got out of the truck. He leaned inside and rummaged around the floorboard, looking for something. He emerged from the truck now holding the same handgun.

My seatbelt may have saved my life but now it was locking me in where he could shoot me and end my life. I struggled to get the seatbelt out of its rigid latch, wiggling and sucking in my abdomen before getting enough tension released to finally get it unhooked. The passenger airbag had deflated but the passenger door was crushed inward from the front. I could immediately see that I wouldn't be able to get out of the car by crawling across the seat to the passenger door.

My only way out was through the driver's side door which would put me directly in his line of fire.

The shooter was still partially dazed but like a prizefighter who takes a big hit to the jaw and stays on his feet, he seemed to be getting his legs under him. I tried to open the door, but it was wedged closed. I threw my left shoulder into it. I banged against it with my body in three quick successive, painful hits until it creaked open partially. Leaning to my right, I started kicking the driver's door with both legs. Each kick opened the door more and more. I briefly looked up through the cracked windshield and dented hood.

My actions had drawn the attention of the still dazed gunman.

I nearly had the door open enough for me to slip through. One more big push and the door squealed open.

That's when I was surprised by Trentlocke's dashboard emergency blue light on the floorboard, apparently stashed up against the driver's seat. The police blue light and its coiled cigarette lighter plug tumbled out and rolled across the grating of the draw bridge. The driver's eyes flickered right to the blue light rolling across the bridge, and must have immediately realized I was a cop. He leveled the gun at me as I laid across the mangled compartment of Trentlocke's car.

Chapter Thirteen

I SQUIRMED FRANTICALLY. I spun my body, keeping myself low on the car seats, trying to use the wrecked front of Trentlocke's car as a shield from the armed driver. I'd try to crawl, or at the very least dive out of the car rather than be encased in this Detroit auto assembly line-created tomb. Then came the screeching of brakes. When I thought it couldn't get any worse, I sensed another car careening into me. I just held onto the seat. I huddled under the steering wheel, waiting to be turned into a human accordion with the rear of the car crushing me into the already-wrecked front end of the car. I closed my eyes as I anticipated the collision.

Later, I surmised the driver of a red Mazda Miata had been rocketing up the bridge when he got scared out of his mind by the wreckage before him. He tried, as I did, to avoid colliding with the cars in the accident and skidded to the left—narrowly missing me in Trentlocke's car. I say narrowly because he was mere inches away when the *whoosh*ing screech slid past my side of the car, shearing the crumpled driver's door completely off. I opened my eyes just as the door was ripped away, violent and fast. I was frozen as Trentlocke's car was now filled with bright daylight. As I laid across the seat I looked up and saw blue sky. A red flat metal surface was just outside the door.

The deafening gunfire immediately followed. One bullet tore

through the already shattered windshield. The second bullet also went through the windshield, causing a sizeable junk of glass to break away and fall on my leg. The rest of the windshield fell inwards and hung over me, held together only by the rimmed rubber gasket that framed it.

I pushed with my legs on the seat and scrambled out of the open doorframe onto the red flat metal surface. It was the trunk of the Miata. Slithering low across the rear of the Miata, I landed hard onto bridge's metal grating, searing hot from baking in the bright sunshine. I rolled across it onto the concrete abutment. The concrete was only slightly cooler. I wavered, as I tried to get to my feet. It was almost surreal.

The entire sequence of crashes and gunfire had happened so fast. The Miata driver was curled under his own dashboard. I suspect he was trying to avoid the bullets. The Ryder truck driver had also heard the gunfire and was now running back towards Trentlocke and The DEA team at the bottom of the bridge's rise. I finally got a better glimpse of the shooter: dark hair, dark slacks, light purple polo shirt. He surprised me when he ducked down low and then scampered deftly under the Ryder truck. I lost sight of him as I started running towards the Ryder truck. He'd climbed into the truck's passenger side and was attempting to start it. The truck had been pushed too far across the double yellow line. He wouldn't be able to back up because of the pickup truck still wedged under the backend. There wasn't enough turning radius for him to turn on the bridge. He quickly abandoned that idea escape plan.

The bridgetender's station was on the northside of the bridge a mere fifteen yards from where all of this was happening. He bailed out of the Ryder's passenger side and took off running, heading right for the bridgetender's station. He hesitated as he appeared to be weighing whether going into the station or down the station's emergency stairs. He opted for the latter. Keeping a watchful eye on him, I threw myself up against the front of the Ryder truck. I knew he'd seen the blue light, and I most definitely knew he tried to shoot me twice. He knew I was a cop, but I needed to give this chaotic mess every opportunity to end as peacefully as I could. He still had the gun in one hand as he grasped the blue railing of the staircase with the other hand.

"Stop. Police!" I yelled.

His whipped around, hastily firing two more rounds at me. Both rounds struck the Ryder—one hit the front hood I was using as cover. The bullet penetrated the thin metal of the hood but found an inertia-killing resting spot somewhere in the engine block. I poked my head up just in time to see him galloping down the bridgetender's station's steel external staircase. The frightened face of the bridgetender watched me through one of the grimy, smeared, street-side windows. Behind me the sounds of sirens resonated off of the deep dark waters of the Miami River.

I bolted towards the bridgetender's station thinking there might be a straight ladder down to the bottom. There wasn't one. The staircase the shooter was on was the only way down.

The stairs were nearly vertical with five landings to break up the treacherous descent. I held back at the start of the stairs, quickly peeking my head over the rail to see where he was. He was already two levels down and moving rapidly.

I started bounding downwards after him, my Glock already drawn when I was on the bridge. Holding the rail, I hopped down three to four stairs at a time trying to catch up to him but I was falling behind. At every landing I was more exposed than on the actual stairs, forcing me to slow down on each landing.

He reached the bottom. The staircase ended, facing Northwest North River Drive. Behind the stairs along the seawall of the Miami River was a large wooden fence. He only had one direction to go— out to the street.

I landed hard on the last series of stairs and could feel the jolt in my knees. He had turned and was running in a straight line down the broad sidewalk. He approached the intersection of Northwest First street, but he continued running on the sidewalk, with me following, feeling the effects of the car crash and jumping down the stairs. I was about thirty yards from the staircase when I took a tactical position at the side of a large two story fish market.

"Right there! Stop right fucking there!" I yelled at him.

He responded by turning to his right and ducking behind a palm tree in the narrow, weed-choked, barren patch of grass that paralleled the sidewalk. He fired a quick two rounds at me. I kept myself as protected as I could, utilizing the building as cover. His rounds traveled somewhere past me down the sidewalk. I returned fire, three rounds. One hit the palm tree he was standing behind near head height. Small particles and chunks of the tree blew out in all directions, spraying him. Some of the dusty stringy particles got in his eyes and he stumbled out from behind the tree onto the sidewalk, gun still in his hand.

He leveled the weapon in my direction.

From the safety of the building and at about twenty-five yards, I hit him twice in the chest. He spun completely around and collapsed. First on one knee, then down on both knees before falling over flat on his face against the side of the same building that I was using as cover.

I stood there for a moment. I kept my gun trained on him. I was catching my breath, making sure he wasn't playing possum. *I told him three times to drop his gun. He never responded.* I speedily side-stepped into the street and approached him from the intersection of Northwest First Street. If he was going to shoot at me he'd need to turn his entire body towards me.

I was determined that if he even twitched, I would shoot him again. No questions asked.

The sirens up above on the bridge were getting louder. I heard more from ground level somewhere on Northwest North River Drive.

From the intersection of the two streets I approached him slowly. I maintained a step and drag approach to him. Stepping forward with my left foot and then dragging my right kept my gun steadily leveled on the shooter. I got within a foot of him. I was now standing over him pointing my gun down directly at his head. His gun was still in his hand. I stepped on his hand locking it and his gun under my foot. Leaning down, I placed the barrel of my gun against his head and with my left hand felt for a pulse in his carotid artery. There was none.

He was dead.

I straightened up and looked around me. There wasn't anyone on the street. The sirens were getting closer but I didn't think they were coming for me. They were City of Miami Police patrol units looking for a way onto the bridge above me.

Directly across from me, chipped into the wall in a decorative font was a quote, framed in a perfectly chiseled two-inch-wide rectangle.

CAPT. TOM SAYS:-
THIS MARKET WAS BUILT
FOR THE BENEFIT OF THE GENERAL PUBLIC
SO THEY MAY BUY FISH AT REASONABLE PRICES.

I didn't know who the dead shooter was. I didn't know if he shot Trentlocke. I didn't know if he killed some innocent people with his reckless driving. I *did* know he shot at me.

Six times.

What I did know was he died face-down splayed against a 1930's era fish market.

I lifted my shirt and tucked my gun into my holster. I stared at him, wondering if whatever possessed him to shoot at a clearly identified DEA agent was worth his life. He might have killed the DEA agent or Trentlocke. The thought that one of my police academy classmates might be dead brought tears to my eyes. No matter what our post-graduation experiences were, we still had a shared history.

This quiet Sunday had burst into absolute bedlam.

A Miami police car was tearing ass over wheels, swangin' and bangin' down Northwest North River Drive, approaching with lights and siren spinning and shrieking the whole way. I thought about stepping into the road and flagging the patrol car down, but the Miami officer was driving so fast he might just accidentally hit me and put the proverbial thin blue line right through me. I pulled my badge out from under my shirt and held it aloft in my hand as I put one foot in the street. I kept one foot in the gravel-speckled swale in case I needed to jump back.

The patrol car appeared to be gaining speed rather than slowing down. I waved my arms wildly to get the driver's attention.

As the police car neared me I could see it was a female officer driving the car. She had a more important place to be. Little did she know that where she was heading was personified in me as I frantically waved at her. She drew abreast of me, and it was only then I think she saw the badge in my hand. She slowed considerably as she passed me before pulling a wide U-turn under the bridge. She drove back towards me. When she got within twenty yards of me she jumped the curb, nearly hitting the old, shuttered fish market. She turned her wheel to the left and used the car and the exterior wall of the market to shield her as best as she could, then popped out of the car. Through the compact opening of her car door against the fish market wall she drew her duty-issued Glock. She pointed it directly at me.

"Let me see your hands!" she commanded of me.

My hands were still up in the air from trying to catch her attention.

"How do you not see my hands? I'm Coral Gables—"

"Don't you move a muscle!" she shouted at me.

"Hey! I'm Detective Cade Taylor from the Gables. Put your gun down!" I screamed back at her.

"How do I know that? Where's your I.D.? You're just someone with a badge."

"Couldn't I say that about you?" I countered.

"Don't be an asshole. You see this uniform. You see this car. You know who the hell I am. How do I know you didn't just take that badge from the detective?"

"Hey Speed Racer, I'm the guy who flagged *you* down. Remember? You wouldn't have even seen me if I didn't step out to get your attention with my badge," I said exasperation dripping from my voice.

"If you're a cop then you know code. What's a forty-five?" she asked.

"A forty-five? A *forty-five*? It's a deceased person. This right here is a forty-five," I said pointing at the dead shooter. "He's fucking dead!"

Another Miami police car pulled in behind her and a mustachioed burly officer stepped out. Seeing her back-up arrive, she holstered her weapon and quick-walked around the back of her car and approached me.

"Keep your hands up. What did you say your name was? Tate Caylor?"

"Cade Taylor. I'm Cade Taylor from Coral Gables. The people up on the bridge can verify me."

She spoke into her lapel microphone. She told the dispatcher she was at 28 Northwest North River Drive, mentioning me by name. She said there was a *forty-five* on the ground.

"Where's your weapon?" she asked me.

"In my holster under my shirt."

"Give it to me," she said.

"No."

"What do you mean *no*?" she said, putting her hand on her holstered Glock.

"I mean no. I just killed this guy. You want your fingerprints on my gun?"

"Put it on the deck."

"No."

"No? I said put it on the deck!" the ire in her voice rising.

"Yeah, no," I said dismissively.

She contemplated what to say or do next. She obviously wasn't used to having her authority challenged. We were in a Miami version of a Mexican standoff.

"Listen, you also understand that if I did that, I'd be putting a major piece of evidence from this investigation carelessly on the ground. In minutes, dozens of people dressed just like you will be here taping this whole area off. I'm *not* leaving my gun inside a crime scene especially since the shooting team will want it. You already have a backup here. I can still hear the sirens. Why don't you just tell your dispatcher to slow down the units before one of them gets in an accident because *you* neglected to say the situation was in hand?" I said calmly to her.

With her eyes still locked on me she used her left hand to pull her lapel mic closer to her mouth.

"Unit 244, slow down the other units," she said as she stepped a little closer to me.

I could see the name tape on her dark Miami uniform. "A. Baker. What does the A stand for?"

"Antonia."

"Well, as you know, I'm Cade. I'm going to lower my hands now, okay?" I said as I slowly did so.

She nodded. I just wanted to keep her from ramping up again. I kept talking to her, trying to keep her from getting excited. More Miami police cars were arriving, the officers getting out of their cars, seeing the *"forty-five"* and not wanting to venture closer. They stayed on the fringe ringing the two of us. None of them wanted to be dragged into being part of a possible four-to-five hour investigation so close to quitting time for the day.

"You told me to put my gun on the deck. You obviously have either worked in corrections or the military," I said.

"I did two years at MDC corrections," she said.

"Very noble. How long have you been with Miami?"

"Three years. So what happened here?" she asked.

"You ever been in a shooting before?" I asked her.

"No."

"Well, if you had then you'd know that anything I say is considered evidentiary. So all I can say is I am law enforcement, and *he* is not. I'm alive and he is dead."

"That's it? I'll need more to write my report."

I had turned my back to the street to look at the dead shooter.

"You won't be writing this one," I said softly.

Chapter Fourteen

S TREAMS OF LAW enforcement officers from different agencies rolled into the area. The crime scene boundary was designated by yellow crime scene tape. Outside of the yellow the hordes of on-scene police personnel moved with the unison of a pile of ants moving a dead bug.

Lots of walking, cellphone talking, pointing, and congregating.

Some were from the DEA, but most of the officers and detectives were from the Miami P.D. and the Miami Dade County P.D. The entire area was closed off. Traffic was being rerouted away from Northwest North River Drive. Everything inside the yellow taped area was considered part of the crime scene including officer Antonia Baker's car and Officer Antonia Baker herself. It was getting hot out and she was noticeably perspiring.

I was sequestered outside the restricted area, sitting in the passenger side of a cozy air-conditioned Miami Dade patrol car. A uniformed Miami Dade Police Lieutenant was standing outside the car keeping everyone away from me, and invariably keeping me away from everyone. I sat there wondering whether Trentlocke or the DEA agent or both were dead or alive. It was weighing heavy on my mind. I kept replaying in my head all the events that led up to the pickup truck pulling up and the driver shooting at them. I ran through all the ways it might have gone differently. *What could I have done differently?* I kept asking myself.

The lieutenant outside my car door had a cellphone clipped to his belt. Being a lieutenant, he didn't carry the requisite gear many road officers carried. He had room on his belt for the cellphone and judging by his ample weight and girth I wouldn't be surprised if there wasn't a place on his belt for a spork. His cellphone rang and he answered it. He looked at me. He motioned for me to lower the passenger window. I did so and he handed me the cellphone. I took the phone from him and raised the window for privacy and to keep the car comfortably cool.

"Hello?"

"You crazy lunatic you wrecked my fucking car!" shouted Trentlocke into the phone.

I was so relieved to hear his voice, it was an emotional moment that I fought to suppress deep down in my soul so it wouldn't be detectable.

"I'll buy you another rolling ashtray," I said in my best deadpan voice.

"I don't want another one. They're going to give me some fancy deluxe thing with no lighter. I'll be buying Bic lighters the rest of my fucking career."

"I'll get you one of those stainless Zippos so you can deflect bullets," I said.

"I don't need one of those, I'm better at dodging bullets. The DEA agent caught one in his vest, though. Knocked him right over. I mean, like *hard*. He fell right into me. I thought he was dead. The vest stopped the bullet. Advice to the wise—don't buy cheap bullets. He has a hematoma the size of a frisbee. They took him to Jackson Memorial; he'll be discharged and home probably before we get to leave here."

"So who's working this?" I asked him.

"Me. But not me," he said.

"What does that mean?"

"It means I drew this play up in the sand so I have to stay and quarterback it. Seeing as now I'm a victim of an attempted murder on a law enforcement officer I can't investigate your scene, my scene, or the scene on the bridge. So when these three scenes are finished being investigated I'll have them rolled into our original case. In the meantime, you know the drill. Say very little and when asked, say even less."

"Gotcha."

"We got the trailer and motorcycles loaded and we're heading back to our crime lab to print them. Our crime scene guys always start with the gas cap. Everyone leaves prints on the gas cap. They'll process the rest of the motorcycles for comparisons. You know how bikers straddle their bikes with their hand on the side of the gas tank and sway the bike to feel how much gas is in there? Perfect palm prints each and every time. I got two of our accident reconstruction members and one of our ballistic people coming out of Station Five to handle the shooting on the bridge. There'll be two more from homicide coming from headquarters your way to process your scene down there. They're good guys. Let them do their thing but don't get lulled into the whole brotherhood thing. Don't get in their way, and be nicer to them than you are to me," he said.

"I am nice to you."

"No you're not. I asked for cigarettes and you wrecked my car. I'm stuck here in front of this old mortuary now turned greasy garage. No one here smokes except for one of our female officers and I'm bumming Virginia Slims from her. Virginia fucking Slims. That is what my life has come to." he said as he hung up.

I lowered the window and thanked the Lieutenant and handed him back the cellphone. I stayed seated in the cruiser as the events played out in front of me. Watching through the windshield it was in many ways like watching a TV show unfold. As time went on the scene filled with more and more individuals. They even brought out refreshments for the personnel working on the scene. The lieutenant had gotten tired of standing outside and he was now off to the side talking with other cops and drinking a Diet Coke. I immediately recognized Lieutenant Charlie Maddalone from the Coral Gables Police Department. He was wearing an aqua and orange trucker's hat with the Miami Dolphins logo on it along with a polo shirt and blue jeans. The shooting must have pulled him from his own TV. I stepped out of the car to help him find me sooner. I thought I'd be doing him a favor by letting him conduct his business quickly.

"Over here. Over here," I said waving at him.

He walked briskly towards me, carrying an aluminum Haliburton case that glinted in the afternoon sun.

"Taylor. Taylor! How many times do we have go through this with you? Have you ever gone through an entire year, no strike that, have you ever gone through an entire ninety days without killing someone?"

Whenever a member of our police department has a firearm discharge—or in my case, a discharge that results in a fatality—Lieutenant Maddalone is tasked with going to the scene and taking possession of the firearm that was used in the shooting. The gun would either be brought back to the police station for testing to see if it was a malfunction, or in a situation like this it would be handed over to the Miami Dade Police Department's homicide unit for processing. He was also mandated to provide the involved officer with a replacement weapon.

I wasn't feeling charitable with my words and wanted to keep the talking to a minimum, and his inevitable lecture to even less words. I unholstered my weapon and put the Glock down on the hood of the patrol car. He in turn, put the case on the hood next to my gun. He unlatched the small case. Inside the charcoal foam rubber inserts was a loaded forty caliber Glock. He handed me the replacement gun and donning latex gloves, he then put my recently fired Glock in the case. He had me initial and sign a transfer weapon form.

"I should have these forms preprinted with your name," he said gruffly.

"Did I pull you away from the game?" I said, purposely ignoring his dig at me.

"You know full well you did. It doesn't matter what you pull me away from. You just *do*. You pull me away all the time. I swear on my wife's grave you bring me more misery than anyone else in the department."

"I thought your wife was alive."

"She is. But if I'm lying just to keep my word, I'll kill her. You, Cade, are a menace. A state of Florida-licensed law enforcement officer menace."

He looked around at the gathering clusters of investigators, technicians, and officers.

"We will talk in our own city on a day this week when Dan Marino's not shredding the Oakland Raiders. This is not my circus. These are not my monkeys, but I certainly recognize plenty of the clowns here. Now if you'll excuse me, I have done what I was sent here to do. I plan to get out of here as soon as I can. You sir, are on your own," he said as he brusquely slammed shut the case and walked off towards the Miami Dade Police Department's mobile forensic RV.

Sweat beaded on the back of my neck. I retreated to the coolness of the Lieutenant's parked police car. The engine was still running with the A/C on. I was content to sit inside. I vowed not to get out again for anybody. I sat with my arms folded thinking about what Lieutenant Maddalone had said about me being a menace. It's easy to judge when you've never had to make the kind of decisions I had to make that day.

An imposing detective from the Miami Dade Police Department had arrived on the scene. The other investigators and officers seemed to give him wide berth as he walked amongst them. He stopped to talk with a huddle of detectives and crime scene investigators. Someone must have said something because he looked in my direction. He locked eyes on me and the patrol car from thirty yards away. He started walking towards me, never taking his eyes off mine, his huge stance getting bigger and taller as he came closer. He was older than me and the gray in his short, cropped hair was overtaking the dark black it must have been at one time. He walked in front of the car, opened the driver's side door and sat in the driver's seat causing the car to rock under his weight. He slid the seat as far back as it could, then tilted the seat back even further so his large frame could fit with marginal comfort. It was odd to see so many adjustments being made to the seat especially since the car was assigned to the heavyset lieutenant. Closing the car door, he brashly heaved his clipboard up on to the dashboard. His entire body was enormous. The clipboard was dwarfed by his hands.

"I think if I had to drive one of these every day, I'd stick a cocktail fork right through my ear," he said by way of saying hello. "I'm Richard Borkowski. I got twenty-one years on and have spent the last twelve in Homicide. Nice to meet you. Okay, tell me what happened."

He was physically intimidating and his voice was deep, it seemed to fill the entire car with its resonance. His abrupt and quick introduction had surely psychologically disarmed many people he'd interviewed before.

"I'm Cade Taylor. I got twelve years on and have spent the last nine in Vice Intelligence and Narcotics. Nice to meet you. Okay, tell me my rights."

I don't think he was accustomed to not getting his way. He was very familiar with using his monstrous presence to bull his way through his interviews, and more than likely his job as a whole. He went to an alternate plan: stare at me and make me feel uncomfortable. I noticed his eyes were slightly crossed.

"You know, Florida State Statue 112.532. I like the part under subsection one about legal counsel being present," I said.

"Let me back this up a little," he said. "We have eyewitnesses on the bridge. Namely, the bridgetender who says you clearly stated you were law enforcement. He said you asked the deceased to stop running, all the witnesses saw the blue light from the Miami Dade car. They knew you were a cop. I can make a safe assumption our deceased individual knew it too. The drivers of the Mazda Miata and the Ryder rental truck were in fear for their lives as the deceased discharged his gun four times, twice I might add, directly at you after you had identified yourself verbally as law enforcement. Our investigation on site here where the shooter met his demise has retrieved one round we believe from your weapon lodged in a palm tree. The deceased appears to have died as a result of being shot twice in the upper body, once again, we suspect by you. I see this as a good shoot," he said.

"There should be two rounds further west on the avenue. I fired five times. Two missed, one hit the palm tree, and the last two went into the deceased. Also note those rounds were fired *after* he'd fired twice at me. So there should be two rounds from his weapon further east on the avenue."

He reached up and grabbed his clipboard. The pen looked like a mascara brush in his large hand. As he made notations on his clipboard, I heard the back door of the patrol car open. A young woman with long dark wavy hair quickly sat behind Detective Borkowski.

"Damn Richard, you got this seat so far pushed back I can't even fit back here. How am I supposed to be watching him if I have to sit behind him? This won't help us with the good cop/bad cop routine."

Borkowski looked in the rearview mirror at the scrunched woman in the backseat.

"Detective Taylor, this is bad cop homicide detective, MEC the Navy Wreck," he said, once again by way of an odd introduction.

"Don't listen to him, he's nearly senile. You can barely see where the Lilliputians had him tied down."

"Very funny," said Borkowski.

I looked over my left shoulder as she squirmed to slide across the seat and sit behind me. I caught a glimpse of a black ink tattoo of a seashell on her left wrist. I deduced she was a lover of the ocean. She more than likely had other tattoos elsewhere on her body.

"MEC the Navy Wreck?" I asked her with legitimate curiosity.

"MEC. Those are my initials. Meaghan Elizabeth Clifford. Before

I was a cop I served in the Navy. Mr. Big Laughs here likes to tell everyone I'm 'MEC the Navy Wreck.'"

Borkowski interrupted her. "Meaghy's been in Homicide now five years. She's on our team and she is truthfully a big asset to the unit. She's sitting in as we talk about what happened today. Meaghy, what's your I.D. number again?"

"82595."

Borkowski scribbled some more into his clipboard. I assumed he was adding Clifford and her I.D. number onto some of the many notes and forms that are used in a large-scale investigation.

"So you were in the Navy?" I asked her.

"Yeah I was a corpsman for a few years. I thought medicine was my future, but back home nearly every medical position was looking for a nurse practicioner. I didn't want to go through more school. My last assignment was at the Navy Operational Support Center in Miami. Actually, it's really Hialeah. That fact alone you think would have sent me screaming back home to South Deerfield, Massachusetts, but no not me! Not super smart me! I decided to forgo seven more months of government-sponsored medical training and opted for four months of the Miami Dade Police Department's police academy. A few quick tours in uniform in Liberty City and Hialeah Miami Lakes, then I got promoted into Homicide just so I could meet fine gentlemen like yourself and work with debonair gentlemen like Richard here. So because I passed on the Navy, Richard here, calls me 'MEC the Navy Wreck,'" she said with a sarcastic smile.

I never asked for the amount of detail she gave but people always seemed to tell me way more information that I wanted. I must have had that kind of face.

Borkowski pulled out a palm-sized recorder. In his large hand it barely met the description of "palm sized." He pressed the record button and spoke into the recorder's built-in microphone.

"I am Detective Richard Borkowski of the Miami Dade Homicide unit, with me is Detective Meaghan Clifford of the Miami Dade Homicide unit. We're joined by Detective Cade Taylor from the Vice Intelligence and Narcotics unit of the Coral Gables Police Department. It is Sunday December 6th, 1998, at 4:47pm. We are currently at a homicide scene located at 28 Northwest North River Drive in the City of Miami. Detective Taylor was involved in a law enforcement firearm discharge. It is believed the discharge from Detective Taylor's city-issued weapon resulted in the demise of a lone white male. Detective Taylor, will you state your name for the record?"

He turned the recorder towards me. I lowered my head and spoke clearly into the recorder.

"Cade Taylor. C-A-D-E T-A-Y-L-O-R."

"Detective Taylor, in your own words please elaborate on what occurred here today."

"In my own words? Okay. What occurred here today was I reminded Detective Borkowski of Florida State Statue 112.532 which is also known as the Police Officer's Bill of Rights. Detective Borkowski has opted to ignore the parameters of the state statute, so I am saying *sayonara*." I opened the car door, leaving the portable recorder and the two detectives behind.

Detective Clifford was first out of the car. Her lithe body was to her advantage as Borkowski was still struggling to extract his large frame from the car.

"Detective Taylor! You take another step and as an ordained bad ass *sinister* from the church of hard living, by the power vested in me I will pronounce you so *very* fucked!" she yelled at me.

I turned back to face her.

"Listen Ensign Meaghy, I'm not sure how your life on the high seas was, but there ain't no brig here. Both you and Gorilla Morilla over there are going about this all wrong. I don't have to sit and talk to any of you without legal counsel. I don't have to sit in a car because somehow you think it replicates a designated office. I also have the right to see all statements from witnesses before talking with you. The way I see it, you and the Hulk there have weeks ahead of you canvassing and interviewing everyone within eyesight of the bridge, this street, and the building back there on Flagler Street where the DEA agent was shot. All before you can even start talking to me. This isn't my first kite that got stuck on a powerline, you know."

She studied me for a few seconds.

"After all these years, you know the law," she said.

"After all these years, I think the law knows me."

Chapter Fifteen

THE MEDICAL EXAMINER had removed the body. The crime scene was being disassembled. There was a three-person team looking for the two rounds I fired that missed the shooter. Another squad was looking for the rounds he fired at me. Antonia Baker and all of the City of Miami police officers and resources were gone. Borkowski made a huge production of stomping around and referring to me as "that Coral Gables asshole" to anyone who would entertain his opinion of me. Clifford went about her business but did give me a knowing smile. She knew I was correct. Her and Borkowski would have an opportunity to interview "that Coral Gables asshole" sometime in the next two weeks. My bigger concern was getting back to the Gables police station to get my car. The Miami Dade lieutenant whose car I'd been holed up in drove me back to the police station. I thanked him and took the elevator to get my car.

I'd kept my cellphone shut off to keep Miami Dade Homicide from saying an attorney or someone else was meddling in their investigation. When I turned it on I saw that I had two missed calls from Major Brunson. It was better to face the winds of profanity now than later. I called him back.

"Cade? You okay?"

"Yeah. It's been a wild twenty-four hours or so but I'm okay."

"You sure? You want me to call Reverend Messon for you? I can see if he'll spend some time with you?"

Bob "I Just Bless 'Em" Messon.

Reverend Messon was from the Saint George Antiochian Orthodox Cathedral, which was about a seventy-five step walk from the police department. Being the police chaplain, he'd actually been provided a uniform and full access to the police department. He was a very good man. No doubt. But the way I was currently feeling, unless the good reverend came with a government warning on the label, a fragrant cork, or a bottle opener he wasn't what I was seeking.

"It's getting late and I'm sure he is full up on his duties seeing as it's Sunday. I can talk another time with him if I need to. I'm just going to get comfortable and pull the plug on today," I said.

"Cade, I reviewed the preliminary reports of what happened today. This will wash over very quickly. I can't believe this shitiot had the balls to shoot at a clearly identified DEA agent. Last I heard, the DEA agent was discharged from the hospital and is home eating linguine and clam sauce. Lieutenant Maddalone said you were very composed and not at all rattled. Then again, as he reminded me for ten long fucking minutes, you have been in this position before. He likes to point out that you've put him in this position too. Listen, we got this thing locked down. It's a good shoot. We got an I.D. on the one you put down today. It was Macario Santos Higuera. Same guy from the rock pit and the one that Trentlocke said had done time in Fox Hill Prison in Nassau. The math is simple here. Good guys one, bad guys none. In the meantime, stay out of the damn office at least for tomorrow. Agent Zammit and I are putting together something we think will flush out these Philly mobsters and the Colombians working with them. We'll need you to get onboard for the ride. Rest up!" he said as he hung up.

Get onboard for the ride.

He said it as if I had the chance to have a choice in the matter. I didn't. That was one thing I'd learned in the past few years of my career. Being a VIN detective, I had the choice to take chances and the chance to make choices. Today the shooter had a choice. His chance was to shoot at Trentlocke, the DEA and me. My choice was to chase him. I made the right choice. He took the wrong chance. It had become the yin and yang of my VIN existence. It's either choices or chances. Leveraging experience and resources to have the best outcome that you think will be in your favor.

Today it worked in my favor. There would be time to reflect on it all later. Before reflection set in, I wanted to pack it away for now. Pack it deep down.

I'd turned the Land Cruiser west, away from the police station. I was looking for dark, and alone. The alone part I would have to work on. The dark part I might be able to find. I kept driving west across Lejeune Road. The sun was nearly set. Through the tree canopy I could see the iconic tower of the Biltmore Hotel in the distance, lit against the darkening sky. Turning north, I continued across Coral Way. My journey took me to South Greenway Drive. I ventured only two blocks west to the intersection of Red Road and South Greenway Drive, putting me directly in front of Duffy's Tavern, its mortared red brick exterior and big green awning beckoning to me. Many a drinker who has patronized Duffy's and inadvertently parked in front of a neighboring business has come out of the well-known Irish bar and grill to find their car towed. The towing of cars near bars seemed to be a Miami thing; or maybe it was just the bars I frequented. Experienced drinkers knew to park on South Greenway Drive and cross the double yellow line into the beckoning green neon lights of the bar.

I parked on South Greenway Drive.

Duffy's is a gastro drinking Miami institution. It has been in business since 1955. By Miami standards that's ancient. The United States Marines named it a "TUN Tavern" for their military members. It made no difference to me. The beer was always cold, and the Duffy death dogs were a true hot dog lover's treat. It had a fully stocked bar. I crossed over the double yellow line leaving the city for the county as I did so. I briefly wondered how many suspected drunk drivers had been asked to walk heel to toe on this very line. Many a midnight police officer investigating a suspected drunk driver would refer to it as "line dancing." That term was surely vastly different than what went on in Honky Tonks on the westside of Nashville every Saturday night. Voices and music boomed and droned inside. Some of the diehard Miami Dolphin fans were still in the bar. It wasn't much of a football game; Miami beat Oakland 27-17. I opened the door and had only taken one step into the bar when my cellphone rang. I stepped back outside to look at my phone and decide if I wanted to answer it or not.

Addison Hope.

This was not going to be an easy phone call to take. I looked at my phone as it rang, debating whether to answer it or not. I let the betterment of valor get in my way and on the fourth ring I answered it. The green neon lights of Duffy's bathed me in a surreal glow.

"Hello."

"Cade, it's Addison Hope. Is this a bad time?"

"I should be asking you the same thing," I said.

"You heard?"

"Yeah, I heard. I'm sorry for your loss."

"Dan was a special man at a special time in my life. Our marriage was short but he was once still my husband…once. Our lives changed and my life changed. He went on to be special elsewhere in the world. I'll always love him."

There was brief awkward pause on the phone. I wasn't sure what I should say.

"Addison, what can I do for you?"

"The NTSB pulled me when they found out it was Dan."

"Addison this isn't an NTSB investigation," I said.

"I'm haunted. I mean, full-on wracked with guilt that I was just yards away from him as he lay under those tarps and I didn't know it was him."

I looked to the sky past the bar's green neon bulbs, searching for the right words to come to me. I decided to give a carefully thought-out brief version.

"We determined that although an airplane was involved, it's a murder investigation. We got a lead on some guys who may be connected. Forensics is trying to determine identities. One of them we identified as a known cocaine trafficker. He shot at Detective Trentlocke and a DEA agent this afternoon. He's dead now..."

"Cade. Cade, listen to me. I want—no, I *need* to get in on this."

"Addison, this really isn't my investigation," I partially fibbed to her.

I had no idea what 'get onboard for the ride' meant, but as far as I was concerned Trentlocke said it was his investigation. He drew the play in the sand and he was going to stay on and quarterback it. My involvement, as I had hoped since yesterday morning, would be minimal at best. At least that's what I told myself. Deep in my core I could see that wasn't going to happen. Still, it seemed like Trentlocke, Major Brunson, and Agent Zammit were quite happy to watch the NTSB walk out the door. They even called it the "real meeting" when the NTSB left.

"They're gone. Let's start the real meeting."

They would be as agitated as an ant pile that got peed on if I brought Addison Hope in on the investigation. They'd say all of the correct things.

"She has no jurisdiction."

"She's too close to the source."

"It might compromise the integrity of the case with her personal connection."

I genuinely felt bad for her. I empathized with her feelings for wanting to find the killers of her former husband. I was not immune to what she was feeling—it just wasn't my party. I couldn't invite someone to a party I wasn't hosting. The question of her coming into the investigation lingered on the line.

"Cade, I'm a source of information. I can cut through the

government channels and red tape. I can do things. Cade, I can *do* things. Don't shut me out," she pleaded.

I briefly closed my eyes. I opened them again. Red Road was quiet. There were no cars on the road, drunk or sober. I looked at the Land Cruiser parked across the street. Against better judgment I heard myself say into the phone, "Where are you?"

"Home. I live in the Roads section?"

"You're in the Roads?" I asked her.

"Yes. Twentieth and Second Avenue in the Roads. It's a house owned by a one of our execs from Reston, Virginia. Are you nearby?"

The Roads was known for its older homes, long-tenured private schools, and its tree-covered streets. The Roads was very close to Downtown Miami and the bustling commercial area of Brickell Avenue. She wasn't too far away and with traffic reduced on a Sunday evening it would be a short drive to Duffy's. She repeated herself on the telephone.

"Are you nearby?"

"No. I live way down south," I said.

"Are you home?"

"No, I'm not home."

"Where are you?"

"I'm kind of near the Gables," I said as I once again looked across the street at my car parked in Coral Gables.

"That's kind of near. It's just up Coral Way…"

"Actually, Addison I'm on the west side of the Gables."

"Well, if you'd just tell me where you are maybe I could come by and try and tell you why it's so important that you let me in on the case."

More silence.

"Please, Cade. Don't make a fine southern woman beg."

"I'm at Duffy's on Red Road," I said as I hung up the phone.

It almost didn't sound like my voice. I don't know why I told her where I was. I turned the phone off. I didn't need to give her directions. I reasoned if she got lost on the way then maybe it should stay that way.

A missed opportunity.

A lost chance.

A wise choice.

That's what I told myself. It might have been the recent events of the past days, it might have been fatigue, it might have been hunger, it might have been sympathy, it might have been empathy, or it might have been my own shadows of loneliness...For whatever reason I told her where I was.

I went back inside the bar. There were a few dirty tables, mostly with great views of the large TV's. Crumbled paper napkins and baskets of half eaten burgers and wings foretold that big groups of Miami Dolphin fans must have been at the tables. A young waitress in dark long pants and a green Duffy's polo shirt was cleaning the table. I caught a glimpse of the back of her polo shirt.

Duffy's Tavern: Where the elite meet to eat.

License plates were penny-nailed frame to frame, encasing the entire bar in a mostly-Florida homage to the DMV. The walls of the tavern were equally filled with numerous sports pictures and beer advertisements. There were very few spots not clustered with pictures, signage, and color. Just inside the front door was a framed picture of Ted Hendricks of the Oakland Raiders closing in on Miami Dolphin quarterback Don Strock. The Hall of Fame linebacker was inches away from crashing into Strock. The picture was taken easily a decade earlier. With a brief whiff of nostalgia I recalled that I was at that home game in the Orange Bowl. The play was in the west end zone of the stadium. Strock was able to release the ball but "Terrible Ted" knocked him fifteen feet back into the field goal netting behind the end zone. It took Strock a good minute to extract himself from the netting.

There was a section of the bar where the stools were open. I sat down in the middle, trying to assure myself of no distractions unless of course Addison Hope should arrive. The bartender was a young man in his mid-twenties.

"Ya here for the special?" he asked as he put a coaster down in front of me.

"What's the special?"

"If you buy twenty-five wings you get a free domestic pitcher. Only on Sundays."

I mulled over the prospect of wings two days in a row. I had actually thought that a Duffy's Death Dog would be my choice for dinner. From the kitchen the wings sure did smell good.

"I'll have the special. The wings grilled. Can you make them half buffalo the other half barbecue?"

"Absolutely, and the beer?"

I looked over at a table of three college-age young men and the nearly empty beer pitcher on their table.

"Whatever they're drinking, just give them the pitcher. I'll have a Jameson, neat please."

The bartender gave me a knowing smile. He put a beveled shot glass in front of me and did a healthy pour of the Jameson with a flourish before bringing a pitcher of beer to the young men. Smiles and hoots of appreciation ensued, to which I acknowledged with a toast before I powered the Jameson down like some sort of desperado in a 1970's western. The sound of the empty glass hitting the wooden bar attracted the attention of the bartender who walked to me holding the Jameson bottle. With a combination look of gratitude, acceptance, and desire I gestured to fill my glass again. He did so, this time leaving the bottle behind the bar closer to where I was sitting to shorten any future trips of accommodation he might need to make on my behalf. He may have been young but he was experienced.

This hit of Jameson I chose to drink a little slower. The first shot was meant to keep the demons from the day held back. The yearn for the burn of the Irish whiskey was intended to scorch any eruptions of thought or reflection. This next pour settled in front of me to hopefully help keep the hardier of the demons locked down. I looked back over my shoulder at the young men enjoying their free pitcher of beer. To them a free pitcher of a beer from a stranger at the bar was like mana from heaven. I wondered if they knew the benefactor of their sudsy lager had killed a man earlier in the day. I wondered if they knew that the hand that motioned to the bartender to bring the pitcher of beer had actually held a smoking gun just hours earlier.

I envied their concern.

Free beer!

I envied their lack of concern.

Free beer!

I thought about how carefree my life was over a decade earlier when I saw Miami Dolphin Quarterback Don Strock get thrown into the netting and be a proverbial fish out of water. The innocence of that time and of my life was gone. Long gone. Pack up the moving truck and drive away gone. The excitement over free beer was gone. The carefree feelings of not discerning consequence of action was gone. My life was no longer an open road of endless possibilities. I now recognized why there's a painted double yellow line in the road. I knew what happened when you cross the line at the wrong time.

Boundaries in life, and boundaries in my own life were rigidly defined, deciphered, and deduced. I comprehended the limitations and frailties of myself and others. I knew weakness and I knew strength. I had also come to know the strength in weakness and weakness that comes with strength. The possibilities of life and death were all too clear to me now. Graphically clear. The difference between choices and chances was without a doubt understood now.

I sipped on the Jameson as I waited for the wings to come out from the kitchen. My fingers slowly caressed the glass as I stared into the amber colored whiskey like some sort of catatonic soothsayer searching for an answer for a perplexing life quandary. The conversations of the day played over and over again in my head. I jostled the glass ever so slightly causing minute ripples in the alcohol as I self-mesmerized myself into a blank mind. I tried to squash the thoughts of seeing a DEA agent being shot, my belief that Trentlocke had been shot, and ultimately, me using my own gun to remove a soul from this earth.

"Good guys one, bad guys none."

That's what Major Brunson had said. The cavalier mention of it all was no different than a scorekeeper at a bowling alley counting spares and strikes. Pins up and pins down. Hold your hand over a puny hot air blower as you wait for your gaudy painted ball to roll up from the bowels of the ally, and then go do it again. Nothing matters. Just the jotting of numbers and hash marks on a score sheet matters. Keeping score.

If only it was that simple. People aren't tally marks on a score sheet. Unlike bowling pins, people bleed. They moan, they flail about, they scream, they shudder, they shake, they go supine and then they go silent.

Forever.

I felt the enormity of my day welling up again. Like an overflowing bathtub I sensed the level rising up inside of me. As I said to Major Brunson on the phone, I needed to get comfortable and pull the plug on today. I needed to pull the plug on the rising tide of emotions. I downed the remainder of my shot and motioned to the bartender for a third shot. I could see his look morphing slowly from one of contented personal affability to concerned professional accountability. He dutifully poured me a third shot of Jameson as he reminded me that the wings would be out "any minute now." It was a subtle reminder that food might be more in order for me than Dublin, Ireland's biggest export. His apprehension was palpable but nothing buys complicity quicker than comradery and currency. I looked back over at my shoulder as the young men had nearly emptied the free pitcher of beer and asked the bartender to send them another pitcher on my tab. The bartender was agreeable to my proposition, and the young men were agreeable to my generosity.

Comradery and currency.

My third shot of Jameson arrived with the mouthwatering chicken wings. I ate the wings in relative silence, only speaking to ask the bartender for more napkins. I think he was pleased to see me eating the wings while leaving the Jameson untouched. He could think what he wanted, but I knew the current situation wouldn't last. Soon the wings would be gone and so would the Jameson as well.

I voraciously tore through the majority of wings and left five of them uneaten. I asked for a small to go box for the remaining wings. The bartender packaged up the wings. He cleared the remnants and bones away. He even wiped down the bar in front of me. I appreciated that. I like drinking in a clean space. I can drink in filthy places, dingy bars, and creepy dives but I like a clean surface in front of me. The young men behind me were now full of beer and were a little loud, but it was okay. Their laughing and chattering gave the bar an ambience I found pleasant. Satiated by the wings, I raised the third shot to my lips. Then I heard Addison Hope's voice near my ear.

"You smell like booze and bad choices. Come sit by me."

Chapter Sixteen

I TURNED IN THE direction of Addison Hope's voice but she was already walking towards an open table away from the beer drinking fellows. I glanced back at the bar to see the bartender looking at me with a *well, look what we have here* smile. I think he assumed Addison was my wife and I might be in some sort of domestic trouble for pounding Irish whiskey on a Sunday night when I should be home watching *60 minutes* on CBS. With wholly unnecessary bravado and a *take that* attitude I threw my head back and gulped down the Jameson.

Motioning to the table Addison had chosen, I said cheekily to the bartender, "Could you bring me another one to the table and whatever my parole officer over there wants as well?"

I left the box of wings on the bar when I slid off the bar stool and went to her table. One of the beer-swigging young men jumped up from his seat to high five me. Addison took notice of the fraternal drinking action. I sat down across from her.

"Do you know those guys?" she asked.

"No."

"Why is he high fiving you?"

"Because I bought them beer," I said.

"You bought beer for them? They aren't middle school kids

standing in front of a liquor store looking for some cheap ripple. Do you always buy strangers alcohol?"

"It's a bonding moment," I said.

"What? Drinking in an Irish bar with license plates as wall art? This is how you bond?" she said glancing around.

"No, actually I create my best bonding moments with people my own age who, like me, are also walking around parking lots trying to remember where they parked their car," I said.

It was at that moment that the bartender placed the fourth shot of Jameson in front of me.

"What will the lady be having?" he asked Addison, addressing her directly but in the third person.

"I'll have an Old Fashioned with Maker's Mark please," she replied.

When he was out of earshot I reminded her that although I didn't consider her a complete stranger I would be buying *her* drinks too, and if she wanted to, she could high five me as well.

"I appreciate all of that but I don't need a Cooter Brown to buy me drinks. I can pay for my own drinks."

"What does a Cooter Brown mean?" I asked her.

"It means half in the bag, hammered, sloshed, a drunk," she said.

"I'm not drunk. I'm just whiskey enhanced. As for buying your own drinks, I'm sure you can," I said as I got up with my drink in my hand.

"Where are you going?" she asked.

"You're a big girl. You're big enough to pay for your drinks and you're big enough to sit by yourself."

I made my way back to the bar and pulled out the same high back bar stool I'd been sitting in previously. The bartender was putting the finishing touches on Addison's drink.

"Trouble with the misses?" he nearly whispered as he applied an orange peel garnish to her drink. Before I could even answer he said very quickly, "Incoming."

The stool next to me was being pulled back. Out of the corner of my eye I saw Addison climbing onto it. The bartender put the drink in front of her before she was fully in the stool.

"You know what, Cade Taylor? You sure have a highfalutin' opinion of yourself."

"What does that mean?" I asked her.

"It means you think the sun rises just to hear you crow. Like it's all about you. Like you're some sort of catch—"

"Actually, I'm more of a catch and release," I said, cutting her off.

She took a sip of her Old Fashioned while I stared into my shot of Jameson. There was a pause in conversation that was tinged with regret and unspoken apologies.

"Maybe you aren't fully aware that I was informed today that my ex-husband was murdered," she said with a waver in her voice.

"Maybe *you* aren't fully aware that I was the man today who killed your ex-husband's murderer," I said, still staring at the Jameson.

She emitted a gasp. She stared at the bar for a few beats then took a huge swallow of her drink.

"What? How? You didn't say on the phone you killed Dan's murderer," she said as she grasped my forearm.

"I said that we got a lead on some guys who may be connected, and one of the guys shot at Detective Trentlocke and a DEA agent this afternoon. I told you he was dead. I just didn't say I was the one who killed him."

"I don't mean to throw a hissy fit but don't you think that part is relevant to telling the story?" she asked me.

"I didn't want you coming all the way out here because of concern. You actually shouldn't be here with me now. Having you near this investigation can only be an ignition point for trouble."

"What's that supposed to mean? Concern or no concern, I'm the one who practically pleaded with you to tell me where you were. Need I remind you I'm a federal investigator who has access to sources?"

"You were also directly involved with the biggest aspect of this case. Not just *involved*...you were *married*. It can get, how do you say in the south...*mighty sticky* for everyone? There's case integrity to be maintained, and other investigators who are part of this now. The man I killed today tried to kill Trentlocke and a DEA agent. Counting your ex-husband, the guy on a cold slab downtown in the morgue with my bullets still in him, didn't have a lot of high regard for authority or law enforcement," I said.

"Let's roll back the hounds here. Just how was it that you and whomever determined the man you killed actually killed Dan?"

"Your former husband was wearing a Fossil brand belt with silver medallions interspersed along its length. Dan's fingerprints were on it but so were the fingerprints of a known Colombian drug trafficker. They weren't everywhere, but they were on the belt tabs aligned with the hips. We think he pushed Dan out of the airplane. I'm sorry."

Tears welled up in her eyes. She downed the entire contents of her drink and then held the glass aloft for the bartender to see. I really wanted to drink my Jameson but I showed restraint, at least temporarily.

"How did you find this known drug trafficker?"

I decided to hold back on telling her about the rock pit and the license plates. I opted to say that information was provided from a law enforcement source. Although I was the source. She didn't need to know that. Such a broad blanket comment I hoped would deter her from probing. She looked at me for a long moment.

"So can you tell me at least how it all came to be today?"

"It was really out of the blue. Trentlocke and the DEA were checking an address in Miami that they thought might be connected to the suspect. I was blocks away. Trentlocke asked me to meet them at the address, and a pickup truck pulled up in front of the address alongside them. The guy jumped out, started shooting at Trentlocke and the DEA, then he got back in the truck and started driving away. I chased after him. He hit a Ryder truck on a bridge. He shot at me. He actually shot at me a lot. I returned fire and he died."

She stared at me intently. Now it seemed she was searching for the words to say something. After a long pause she spoke.

"I'm sorry you had to go through this—but I'm not sorry that heap of manure is dead. I'm heartsick over Dan's passing. Just heartsick. He was lying under a tarp yards away from me and I had no idea. This guilt and regret will stay with me my entire life." Tears rolled down her cheeks.

The bartender set the drink in front of her and shot me a disdainful look, thinking I was the reason she was crying. It was a few minutes until she had a handle on her emotions. Her tears were authentic. I felt like my heart was submerged in sludge. I was sorrowful for the ordeal she was struggling with. I stayed quiet, giving her a moment to collect herself. I took a sip of the Jameson and my body eased up again. She needed a few minutes to pull herself together. I waited until she seemed to be composed.

"Heap of manure?" I said to her with a chuckle.

She dabbed her eyes with a cocktail napkin and gave me a slight smile.

"You know nothing about southern culture or politeness. We southern women have a vengeful fury in our DNA and the only way y'all stay safe in this world is because of our own self-moderation. A good southern woman can be your worst nightmare if lightning strikes her shoe buckle or she gets a bee in her bonnet."

"Addison, if I may, sometimes you say things that I think would be coming out of Minnie Pearl's mouth in the Grand Ole Opry."

"What do you know about Minnie Pearl? You ever see her off stage?" she asked me.

"No."

"Well, I have. Believe me you, a Medicaid card and a mini skirt should not be on the same woman."

"You're really all about being from the south, aren't you? Will you ever be able to shake that off?"

"Cade, were you hit with a branch from the stupid tree or did you get whacked by the whole damn forest? How exactly am I supposed to, as you say, *shake off* my entire upbringing? You ever hear of a chart-topping multi-Grammy winning band called *Alabama*? Well, like they say: 'southern born, and southern bred.' That's me, sugar!"

"So you are all biscuits, sweet tea, magnolias, and pee-can pie?" I said.

"Pee-can? Did you say pee-can? It's pe-*cahn*. Pecan pie. A pecan is a nut from a tree. A *peecan* is something you take with you on a long car drive."

"Words are important, Addison. Words are important."

"That goes for you as well. Cade, like I've been telling you, I can find things many can't. The DEA is good, but not everyone is in the drug trade. The FBI is good, but not everyone is in the crime world. People travel. They use passports. They buy travel tickets with credit cards. The NTSB has back door portals you might not be aware of. Bring me in, Cade. Who was the man you killed today?" she said.

I gave it a passing thought and relented.

"Macario Santos Higuera. The DEA arrested him in 1993. He was on a freighter with some kilograms of cocaine off of Andros Island. That's all I know. I don't know his date of birth or anything else."

She took a pen out of her bag and wrote down his name. I noticed she underlined Andros. She put her pen and paper away. There was a large, laminated menu off to the side. The bartender noticed her looking at it.

"Folks, kitchen's gonna close in fifteen minutes. It's getting slow and they're sending the cook home early."

"Thank you, I just need a moment to look over the menu," she said.

"There are some wings in the box."

I slid the box to her.

"Are they any good?" she asked me.

"Would I offer them to you if they weren't?" I replied.

She graciously accepted the wings. She arched her eyebrows after her first bite into the succulent chicken wing. She was very pleased with the combination of Buffalo style and sweet barbecue sauce coating on the remaining wings. The sweet savory sauces were on her fingers and she actually stuck her thumb in her mouth to extract the tasty sauce.

"Licking fingers? Is that a southern thing too?" I said, being sarcastic.

"Oh honey you have no idea how good barbecued things will make a good southern woman do bad things," she said. "Since you told me about the man who killed Dan, I will tell you this. Does this name ring a bell—" but the bartender interrupted her.

"I was just in the back. The cook has his car keys on the counter. If you want something you need to order quickly."

"Um. Okay, I'll have the hickory barbecue burger with cheddar and fries. Can you please see if the cook can use the same barbecue sauce on the burger he did on these wings?" she asked the bartender.

"You were going to tell me a name?" I said to her.

The bartender was temporarily held in place as I held up my finger. I wanted to order something but didn't want Addison to lose her train of thought.

"Emmanuel Servais," she said.

My pulse quickened. I remembered the name from the rock pit. I sat fully back in my barstool and immediately recalled what I'd said to myself.

The three of them answer to someone named Emmanuel Servais.

The bartender looked at me with urgent expectancy.

"I'll have the Death Dog."

Chapter Seventeen

"So what do you know about Emmanuel Servais?" I asked her.

"I really don't know anything," she said.

"Addison don't play coy with me. Now's not the time. If you know something you need to tell me everything!"

"I was married to Dan. We went different ways. The divorce was handled by a law firm in Conway, South Carolina. There was nothing to contest—I wanted to move on and so did he. We married very young. I reasoned it just wasn't the right time for the right people. I lost track of him, I'm sure he lost track of me too or he wouldn't have sent the card to my parent's house."

"Card? What card?"

"Two weeks ago. My parents got a Christmas card addressed to me at their house in Prosperity, South Carolina. It was from Dan. My parents put it in an envelope and forwarded it to me here in Miami."

"How do you know the name Emmanuel Servais?" I asked her.

"You go first," she said.

"Addison, you're practicing bitchcraft with me. I'm not playing a game of *you spin I spin* to see who goes first. You want in on this investigation, then you need to get it out now."

She half looked towards the kitchen hoping the food would come out as a distraction. When it wasn't she seemed to resign herself to playing her biggest card and hoping I'd still keep her in the card game.

"Dan wrote in the card he was sorry for the way our marriage ended. He was *sorry*. He took all the blame himself for the failure of our marriage. He and I both know that's not true but he was falling on his sword. He didn't say anything really telling about his life or job, just that he was working at the federal level. That's what he said, 'the federal level.' He said nothing about what agency or where. I don't think he even knew I was with the NTSB. He said he was into something really big. He said it was 'Watergate big.' He said if anything ever happened to him to tell the authorities he was chasing a criminal named Emmanuel Servais. If anything ever happened to him the authorities need to find this guy, Emmanuel Servais. That's it," she said, once again dabbing the tears from her eyes with a paper napkin.

I listened to her intently. I repeated her words in my head as she spoke so that nothing would be lost in translation. It became my turn to tell her how I'd come to know the name Emmanuel Servais. I let my next sip of the Jameson sit against my lips just before I drank it.

"The same law enforcement source heard three people talking about a lost cocaine shipment. One of the three people was Macario Santos Higuera. They were all fearful of angering someone named Emmanuel Servais. I mean, like *really* scared of this guy, Servais. Next thing we know Macario Santos Higuera rolls up and starts shooting at cops."

The three young men who had been drinking beer on my dime had departed twenty minutes earlier. The bartender came out of the kitchen with her hickory burger and my Death Dog. We were the only two patrons in the bar. The bartender wanted to close our tab out and against her protestations, I paid the bill. Looking out the bar windows the street outside was nearly devoid of any traffic. The meal had helped tamper down the alcohol buzz I had been looking to create. I held the door for her as we stepped outside.

"You're learning," she said as she stepped out into the night.

The next thing she said was less than congenial.

"You have got to be fucking kidding me?" she shrieked.

Off to the left, in front of an adjacent business was her car. It was parked almost equally between the No Parking tow service signs. Her government-issued Dodge Intrepid had a big yellow metal boot attached to the front driver's side tire. The tow company must have been too busy to tow her car and booted it for immobility.

"Why I declare! I didn't know a good southern woman cursed?" I teasingly said.

"Cram it, Taylor. There's a lot about *good* and *southern* that you'll never know."

She pulled out her cellphone and dialed the tow company's phone number that was on the sign. I walked across Red Road and opened the rear of the Land Cruiser. I retrieved the heavy, curved single bar tire iron from the back and returned to her car. She appeared to be on hold with the tow company. I tried to pry the heavily locked metal boot off of her tire.

"Don't! You're going to damage the rim," she said just before talking with the tow company.

She pleaded her case for getting the boot removed. There was a back-and-forth exchange where she even threatened to have her own tow company come out and tow the car, negating the profit for the company who booted her car, in addition to having them lose their attached metal boot. A compromise seemed to be reached. She finished her conversation with "It better be off by the morning or I'm going to have the state attorney review every one of your commercial contracts and if there's just *one* that isn't up to date, I'll have your license pulled," she said as he hung up.

"What's up?" I said.

"What's up? What's *up* is that the tow company is really short staffed. The tow driver decided to boot my car rather than tow it. He *meant* to come back but now he's out near Southwest 120 and Kendall on a bad accident. He won't be back this way for hours. But for my *inconvenience* they'll remove the boot sometime between now and morning. No charge. She thinks I'm a push-over. They don't care about inconveniencing me, they're in the inconvenience *business*! I'll need to call a cab."

"I can take you home," I said as I dropped the tire iron and fumbled for my car keys in my pocket.

"Me? In a car with *you*? Are you out of your feeble snockered mind? How many Jamesons have you had?"

"More than you," was my glib answer.

"I wasn't *drinking* Jamesons! Besides you shouldn't be driving anyway!" she yelled.

I bent over to pick up the tire iron and it felt like the earth was moving up to meet me. That's when I toppled onto the asphalt. Addison helped me up from my low altitude face plant. I wasn't hurt but I was plenty embarrassed.

"Which is closer, your place or the Roads?" she asked me.

"My place."

"Give me your keys. I'm driving. I don't want to hear *any* back talk," she said.

This whole "anger a southern woman, make a southern woman happy" thing was an exercise that I clearly wasn't good at. I sheepishly handed her my keys.

She opened the Land Cruiser with the remote and settled in behind the steering wheel. I got in on the passenger side. She made it very apparent with a huff that the opening of doors was gender-specific in the south.

"I'm *so* angry. The tow truck dispatcher couldn't care less…at first. I set her straight. I need to remind myself it isn't her fault she wasn't raised right," Addison said as she started the engine.

"Go south, right at the light then turn south on 67th until the road ends at Coral Reef Drive, then turn left. S'where I live," I said, feeling myself become less articulate with every word.

She started driving to Paradise Point in the Royal Harbour Yacht Club. I was still holding the tire iron between my legs.

"Unless you got ideas of making some sort of a horror movie, how about you put that hard thing between your legs in the backseat, and yes, I am talking about the tire iron," she said.

I laid the curved single tire iron across the backseat.

"So why we are both here in this quiet car, can you fathom any idea who Dan was talking about when he said he was close to a 'Watergate big' case?" she asked me.

"Addison, you aren't part of this investigation. I mean I'm onboard to help you with…and I'll be delicate by saying *your insightful queries* but there are things I just don't know and other things I need to be careful discussing," I said, putting the words together carefully.

"Why?"

"Let's take it back a little. Do you know who Dan was working for?" I asked her.

"I told you already. All he wrote was that he was working at the federal level."

"Well, he most certainly was at the federal level. He was a black passport," I said.

"State Department?" she said raising her eyebrow.

"He was Diplomatic Security Services of the State Department. A DSS Special Agent. We were told he started his career in their Atlanta field office."

"Dan had wanderlust in his soul. If he was state department DSS there's no way he stayed in Atlanta," she said.

"His most recent assignment was in Saint Eustatius in the Netherland Antilles." Every one of those many s-words was slurred.

How much should I say to her? She may have had federal security clearances but she was still an ex-wife, and possibly the last person that DSS Special Agent Dan Stallings communicated with outside of his agency before he died.

"Cade, not now. Don't hold back. Not now. I need to know," she pleaded with subtle southern dignity.

"It was relayed to us that Dan was working on an investigation dealing with a large cocaine importation group. He was undercover. We think he was a kicker—"

"What's a kicker?" she asked as she drove south on 67ᵗʰ Avenue.

"A kicker's the person who, when the airplane filled with cocaine flies over a drop site, actually pushes or kicks it out of the open airplane door. We think working in his undercover capacity he was kicking cocaine out of a low-flying plane off Biscayne Bay. We think the man I…killed today, Macario Santos Higuera pushed Dan out of the airplane door."

"Why? Why would he push Dan?" she said with misty eyes, clutching the steering wheel.

"Dan had infiltrated the organization to such a level that he was handling the initial cocaine entry into Saint Eustatius from Colombia. He was also overseeing the redistribution of the cocaine on the air drops. We think Santos Higuera wanted to be the top dog and thought that by killing Dan he could rise up in the organization," I explained.

"How is this a "Watergate big' case? I understand everything you're saying—even when you slur your words—but *how*? How is this Watergate big?"

"We think the cocaine is being sold to a big crime family in Philadelphia. The crime family is using the profits to prop up a presidential contender for the 2000 election. Primaries are still almost a year away but this family is building a war chest to finance a candidate through the early primaries. To make the candidate a front runner they can control when he wins the presidential election. I think Dan knew this. And the guy who stands to gain from it all is Emmanuel Servais."

"Up until now everything you've been saying 'we believe' and 'we think.' Now you're saying *I* think," she was quick to point out.

"The crime family is run by a mobster named Ray Caruso. He's reputed to be ruthless. Every wise guy who ever gets popped and every FBI agent and law enforcement agent they've tried to get inside the Caruso crime family says Ray Caruso is a guy who rules with an iron fist. He's merciless. He's also a phantom. I mean, like *no one* can describe him. No one ever *sees* him. They all just feel his wrath. Not just the Philadelphia mobsters but the Gambino, Lucchese, Colombo, Bonanno, Genovese... Every crime family, every part of organized crime lay off any claim to Philadelphia. He's put the fear of God in all of them. If the Caruso criminals can get their guy in the Oval Office than I think whoever this Emmanuel Servais is, well... he's going to benefit greatly from it too."

She gave some thought to what I told her. The landscape outside the car window was now palm trees and mango trees shadowed by the moon in the sky.

"Was there a post stamp on the envelope?" I asked her.

"Yes. It was postmarked in the Bahamas. I remember the stamp. It was very formal. It was a commemorative Bahamas Independence stamp. It had beautiful Bahamian flag colors and a black and white portrait of the guy who wrote their national anthem."

"Did you happen to notice the island it was postmarked from?"

"No. Sorry."

"Is there anything else about the card you might have neglected to tell me?"

She bristled a little but shook it off. "Just what I told you. I can get it tomorrow and show you. It's at my place in the Roads. There...was an odd phrase that he wrote at the end of the card."

"What was that?"

"He wrote 'I soon reach.'"

I soon reach. I was mulling over whether I should explain that phrase to her when she beat me to the punch and asked me. In for a penny, in for a dollar I figured. I decided to let her know. She kept her eyes on the road but glanced at me a few times waiting for my answer.

"'I soon reach' is a Turks and Caicos Islands phrase. Bahamians will say it too. The two nations are separate but nearly everyone in the world doesn't really understand that. It basically means I'll be there soon, or I'm coming. It has no differential on time and distance. Someone could say to you 'I soon reach' and could be a block away or weeks away. I think Dan may have been intending to see you soon."

My comment made her tears finally spill over. We were nearly at the turn on Coral Reef Drive. I instructed her to turn left. The sensor on my visor triggered the guard gate arm in the resident lane of the complex and we drove into the Royal Harbour Yacht Club.

"I'm ahead on the right. 6211. The one with the ivy vines over the garage door."

She had regained her composure as we got out of the car.

"You live here?"

"Yes," I said as I started wobbly up the stairs to the front door.

"This is amazing. The place is beautiful. Not much of a fruntchard but it looks great," she said as she started up the stairs behind me.

I stopped just short of putting the key in the lock and looked back at her a few steps below me.

"Fruntchard?"

"Yes, a fruntchard. Like the backyard but the front? A fruntchard?" she said, narrowing her eyes at me. "I swear Cade, you ain't got the good sense God gave corn. You need to spend some time in the Mason Dixon line and get some sunshine culture."

I turned the key in the lock.

"Addison, this is Miami. Sunshine and culture are things we have an abundance of. We may not have a singular culture but if you want the United Nations of cultures in thongs, hair extensions, Brazilian butt lifts, and aloe-soothed sunburns we're your dream destination."

I was going to try and get onboard with the whole southern gentleman manners thing but stepping aside so she could enter the condo first would be awkward. The front landing at the top of the stairs was tight and once inside she'd have no idea where to go. Besides, she already had me pegged as an uncultured oaf. Why ruin perceptions now?

In the air conditioned coolness of the condominium, the smell of the widely Miami-used cleaner *Fabuloso* was strong. The doctor who owned the condo arranged for housekeepers to come in once a week and clean. They came in last Friday, but I hadn't been home much since Saturday morning. The place still smelled of the fragrant cleaner.

"What's that smell? It's divine!"

"It's Miami culture," I said as I put down my keys in a ceramic bowl near the kitchen. I reached into a cabinet and poured myself a two finger pour of Jameson in a rocks glass.

"Can I get you anything?" I asked her.

"No thank you. One of us needs to stay even keeled. Can I have a tour instead?" she asked.

I showed her the entire condominium. I showed her the spare bedrooms and told her to make her own choice for tonight. I may not be a good southern gentleman, but I did show her I had spare toothbrushes, toothpaste, soaps, clean towels, tampons, and even saline solution and shot glasses for contact lenses. She gave me a sideways look. I reminded her that CVS was a few miles away and like the boy scout motto I try to "be prepared."

She marveled at the rooftop deck. After a few minutes of taking in the view, she decided to turn in for the night. Before going down to one of the spare bedrooms she reminded me that we needed to go back and get her car early in the morning. Fighting school buses, frazzled carpool parents, and the hordes of commuters on a Monday morning was something I didn't want to even contemplate.

"Thinking of morning traffic is harshing my mellow," I said.

"If I don't get my car in the morning you'll know a whole different definition of harsh," she said with a giggle.

She wished me a goodnight before going downstairs. I sat in one of the plush chaise lounges. I said a silent toast to the moon as I was grateful to be exactly where I was and not in a coroner's metal drawer like Macario Santos Higuera.

I went through the entire shooting event in my mind. It was a series of steps and missteps that created each and every action. If

Trentlocke had brought his cigarettes with him, when I took the red traffic light the blue Chrysler driver laying on his horn causing Trentlocke to look up, the bridgetender being a credible witness, Officer Antonia Baker not overreacting, even contending with Detective Borkowski was a part of the whole equation. Good or bad, every part of the day fell into its own place in the total sum of what happened. Many would think of it as karma.

The way my life has been unfolding I felt as though I have karma on speed dial. I just hope she'll pick up each and every time I call.

In the moonlight I looked at my hand holding the rocks glass, the Jameson slightly rippling. This was the same hand that punched a police sergeant yesterday, and held a smoking gun over a dead man earlier today. The universe can be tricky to understand.

This juncture of my life, and yet again the intersections of mayhem, malevolence, and magnanimous action could all come from the same person. The drug world has no room for introspection. I told myself to snap me out of it. I reminded myself that it was all about eyes forward and mind focused. Each day is different from the previous one. The best thing we can do is keep moving ahead. One smudgy bloody footprint in front of the other. Whose blood? It didn't matter so long as it wasn't my own. Tonight, the wife of a DEA agent was probably crying herself to sleep with enormous relief for the safety of her husband, and another woman was one flight below me probably crying herself to sleep with enormous grief for the loss of her former husband. The immeasurable disparity being the common bond between both women.

The sun would be up in the rapidly approaching morning. I needed to be up with it if for no other reason than to bring Addison to get her car. Major Brunson said for me to stay out of the office. I fully intended to adhere to the edict. I set a wake-up alarm on my Nokia 9110 cellphone and downed the remainder of the Jameson. The burn was instantaneous. The buzz enhancement I hoped would be forthcoming. I gingerly removed myself from the chaise lounge. Running and jumping down metal stairs and falling outside of

Duffy's Bar had made me sore. I easily found my bed in almost the same fashion the asphalt found me outside of the bar.

I had no idea how soon I fell asleep. I do know the shrill pitch of my alarm made me wish that whatever time it was I fell asleep I wish I had done it hours earlier. I stared at the ceiling contemplating how sick, tired, worn out, or spent I would be today. I knew that Addison would want to get home and get her day underway so I scooted across the bed until I was on my side on the very edge of the bed then shifted my body weight to sluggishly tumble out. The slow roll permitted my feet to hit the ground first. This method of getting out of bed afforded me the opportunity to lean back against the box spring and mattress if I was unsteady on my feet. If I was able to rise up from the crouching position it foretold of my sobriety. I actually did a little of both.

I waddled into the opulent marble bathroom and turned on the shower. The etched glass-encased shower stall quicky fogged up with steam. I stepped into the hot shower, steadying myself by holding onto the shower head, letting the water stream down on me, gathering my faculties and assessing my condition. There were no dry heaves, no puking, no overtly throbbing headache, and no obscuring fogginess of the brain. I looked at those as indicators of either a victory or a testament to eating a Death Dog late at night.

I towel-dried may hair, brushed my teeth twice and then I dressed in a pair of jeans, a light gray t-shirt, and a pair of tan Dockers. I went downstairs. Addison was sitting on the couch, freshly showered, wearing her clothes from last night. She looked relived to see me up and moving.

"Good morning. How are you feeling?" she asked me.

"I feel good. How about you?"

"That bed in your spare bedroom is really comfortable. The shower was great. I appreciate your hospitality. Thank you," she replied.

I felt the need to explain myself, knowing full well I fell over and should not have been driving. Yet deep down inside I knew it wouldn't change my future coping skills or my penchant to do stupid things.

"Addison, if drunk me did or said something stupid, you've got to take it up with drunk me. Don't tell sober me because we don't know what happened. We weren't there."

She sighed. "Male avoidance has been the downfall of more relationships, careers, and kingdoms than any economic upheaval, plague, or advancing army."

"Is that a fact, Eisenhower?" I said as I rummaged about the kitchen.

"Don't be messing with President Eisenhower. I like Ike. He created the nation's interstate system. A precursor to the need for the NTSB, therefore indirectly making me employable," she said.

"Who created the NTSB?"

"Lyndon Johnson through the Department of Transportation Act," she said.

"That about seals my interest in this conversation. So as far as you were concerned when the feds called you said, 'It's NTSB for me,'" I said from the kitchen.

"Beggars can't be choosers. Like I mentioned when we met, I had options but the NTSB seemed to be a better choice. The aviation industry is growing constantly with more commercial, passenger, and private aircraft every year. It came down to long term stability. Unfortunately, mishaps occur. Weather, pilot error, manufacturing: Every air disaster is one of those three things. Plus, the NTSB oversees rail lines, transit, and even mariners. Mostly it's aviation. Admittedly there are more airplanes in the water than there are submarines in the sky."

I was busy in the kitchen leaning over the sink soaking a thick wad of paper towels in ice water that I planned to put over my eyes and use on my face as a bracing wake-me-up aid. Addison joined me in the kitchen.

"This place is spotless. It's like you never cook in here," she said marveling at the cleanliness of the Viking range and oven.

"My favorite cookbook is a takeout menu," I said as I started splashing the icy water from the sink on my face.

"Do you really think giving yourself frostbite is going to remove the toxins in your body from drinking? Science and the understanding of how the body metabolizes alcohol must not have been on your academic agenda. Ever! With as much as you drank, I'm surprised you don't need sunglasses to open the refrigerator."

I was still bent over the sink trying to quash the clamoring voices in my head, and the addition of Addison's voice joining in was not helping me in any shape or form. I couldn't quiet the chatter in my brain, but I could quell her if I could get her back to her car. I straightened up and used a dish towel to wipe my face and neck. I looked at her.

"You ready to go get your car?" I asked her.

I sensed her reluctance to leave. I understood it. The condominium was a great place. I'd become partially desensitized to the wonderful views and opulence, but she knew as well as I did that she needed to retrieve her car before some business owner called the tow truck company back to tow it. A different dispatcher and an indifferent tow truck driver could result in the car saga regenerating itself over again.

"Yes I am," she said more as an affirmation to herself than as an answer to my question.

As we got into the Land Cruiser she asked about stopping for coffee on the way.

"Do you like Cuban coffee?" I asked her.

"I do. But I also like sleeping sometime in the next three days. I'll pass on Cuban coffee."

Cuban coffee was the sustaining lifeblood of nearly everyone in the drug trade. Its highly caffeinated properties made many a user call it "Cuban crack cocaine." Those who hadn't built a tolerance to its sensory jolt were sometimes actually terrified of the caffeine elevations and the boosted awareness that inhibited their ability to wind down. I, on the other hand, due to my tolerance level could drink it as a night cap and be fine.

"Is there a Starbucks nearby?" she asked.

The time foretold me that traffic would be heavy going to retrieve her car. I surmised we had a choice. We could sit in traffic or actually do something that appeared counteractive to a conventional travel route. I could drive south on Old Cutler Road, against the heavy traffic flow where there was a Starbucks on the corner of Richmond Drive. We could get coffee almost immediately. The traffic would bleed off very soon. We'd actually make better time. As I made switchback turns on residential streets avoiding the main thoroughfares, I proposed that option. She readily agreed to the idea, and I'd resumed some control of the morning. We drove westbound on Coral Reef Drive past the vast 114-acre decommissioned Florida Power and Light property. The drive was beautiful. Addison was seeing it for the first time in daylight. The hibiscus, bougainvillea, frangipani, different palm species, and towering oaks seemed to have her mesmerized.

The intersection of Coral Reef Drive and SW 67th Avenue is a three-way stop. Where 67th Avenue ends is a wide turn-out where parents drop their children off for the nearby Westminster School. Buses and private transport vans were dropping students off, too. The crossing guards were having a heck of a morning moving kids, buses, and cars. The crossing guard noticed I was the only car coming west on Coral Reef Drive and held traffic briefly so I could get through the intersection. I was thankful for the reprieve. I drove right past a maroon Oldsmobile Bravada idling in the turn-out.

Chapter Eighteen

STARBUCKS IS ON the west end of a very small cluster of stores that borders the lush Deering Estate. We both went inside the coffee shop and within minutes we were walking out. I got a double espresso. It was the closest thing I could get to a Cuban coffee so long as I doctored it with sugar. I used enough sugar to make Addison admonish me about the dangers of sugar. She got a Latte with Stevia and we got back in the Toyota. I pulled out of the parking lot.

There is no defensive driving in Miami. In Miami, it's offensive driving. Miami drivers would pass you in a car wash if they could. I pulled up to the stop bar at Old Cutler Road. I had my head turned south waiting for one of the very few benevolent South Florida drivers who would kindly let me merge into the slow-creeping traffic. I studied the line of cars like an apex predator. Similar to how a speedy baseball runner on the third base bag will stare intently for the steal home sign, I was hoping for the sign to merge. I had confidence. I could do it. I just needed the sign. I ardently scanned the traffic for the slightest indication from a driver to give me the go ahead. I don't know if the driver was kind in nature or just not paying attention, but I saw a gap in the traffic. I squeezed into an opening that most people would never attempt outside of Miami. I blended into the traffic with such quickness it would have made

George Jetson proud. Addison gasped at my quick intrusion into the line of cars. Her gasp caused me to look at her.

Turning my attention from her back to the road, I saw the maroon Oldsmobile Bravada pulling out of the Shell station across from Starbucks. Unfettered by traffic, the Bravada was now south-bound on Old Cutler Road within a mile of where we were in stop and go traffic. Numerous schools vie daily for the same roads to be conduits used by stressed parents navigating their mornings. Those same parents are contending with petulant kids, unforgiving clock-watching bosses, and the myriad of everything that can go right and wrong with dropping kids off to school. I needed to let go of my suspicions, paranoia, and self-preservation concerns. I wish I could have hitched all of those feelings to the maroon Bravada, and have them tool down the road away from me. I undoubtedly recognized that my central nervous system and waking mind was toxically polluted by the VIN lifestyle. I was seeing threats from a housewife in a car who probably had Skittles rolling under her car seats. I was thinking a parked SUV with sun-melted crayons in the car's carpets was a danger. I believed that every car I saw was an adversary when the reality was it was more than likely a child-seat ferrying conveyance for a time-challenged parent. I needed to get that part of my own psyche under control.

My mind and my heart were being ravaged by the volatility of my career. I'd been suffering the anxieties, fears, and conversational recriminations of my job seeping like fetid water into my soul. I was on autopilot, moving just a few feet at a time as the car in front of me also inched along, internally grappling with these feelings of slow simmering ravaged disorder that had become my life. It was Addison who snapped me out of my sinking fugue.

"Is it always like this?" she asked.

I didn't know how to tell Addison about the feelings inside of me. It wasn't something that I often talked about, especially to someone who I barely knew. I didn't think she could fully understand what was going on inside of me. I stayed quiet, wondering how to articulate what it was I was feeling inside.

"Is it always like this? The traffic. Is it always like this?" she asked again.

I was running a dialogue in my head as I followed the car in front of me, crawling at a snail's pace along the road. I thought she was asking me about what was playing in my head. I was relieved that her question was a harmless query about the traffic.

"Oh yeah. Yeah. It can be heavy until it starts bleeding off about a mile away."

It was at that moment my cellphone rang. It was the VIN office. Major Brunson had told me to stay out of the office. I answered the phone despite what he'd told me. Coming from the VIN office it was more than likely our general secretary, Ileana Portillo. She is a Cuban American, twice-divorced, single mother of two, whose pronunciation of certain words is a horrific mash-up of English with a heavy Spanish accent. It's a way of communicating that most people in Miami abide by. A combination of English and Spanish, creating a further fusion of words that we affectionately refer to as "Spanglish."

"Hello?"

"Ah...eh *buenos dias*, Cade. A man called two *tines pero* for *ju*. He says he need to talk with *ju*."

"What was his name and what does he want?" I asked her.

"*Coño* Cade! How do I know to think what he wants? He asked for *ju*. *De oficina es* busy like crazy gone over. *Ju* want the message or no?"

"Ileana, yes tell me his name and number. I'll figure it out."

I cradled the phone on the crook of my neck as I pulled a pen and scrap of paper out of the center console.

"*Esperar. Necesito tener mis ojos.*" [Wait, I need my eyes (glasses)].

When she got back on the line she said it was Jason Cordicio and gave me his number which I wrote down. I thanked her and asked if there was anything else I needed to know.

"No. Okay. Then *ju* have been told," she said as she hung up on me.

Traffic was still moving better. I told Addison I needed to make a phone call and it would only be a minute. I dialed Jason Cordicio's number.

"Hello?"

"Mr. Cordicio, this is Cade Taylor. My office said you wanted to talk with me."

"Oh yes, thank you for calling me back so soon. I need to talk to you about what happened Saturday morning," he said as I slid my eyes briefly over to Addison, who appeared to be deep in thought looking out the car window.

"So how can I help you, Mr. Cordicio?"

"Jason. Please call me Jason. My wife is really rattled by all of this. I was wondering if we could meet somewhere and talk about what happened."

"Today isn't very good, Jason," I said.

"She's climbing the walls and to tell you the truth, so am I. Can you imagine if that guy fell through our screen enclosure into our pool? I talked to Tessie. She's also freaked. He missed our houses by a few *yards*! Some things have been going on the past few weeks… Airplanes flying overhead low and stuff. Can we meet tomorrow?"

"Well…"

"Please, Detective," he said.

"Okay, but can it be in the morning? My days stack up sometimes."

"Yes, of course. How about we meet in Pinecrest at Wagon's West for breakfast, say 8:30?"he suggested.

"Okay. I'll see you at Wagon's West at 8:30 tomorrow."

Traffic was easing up and we were starting to make progress.

"Hot date?" asked Addison.

"Hardly. That was one of the residents who was there when we were called out Saturday morning. His wife is freaked out by it all and he wants to talk about some things that have been going on the past few weeks."

"I heard you say Wagon's West, is that a new restaurant?"

"If you think 1981 makes it new, then yes. It's been around for a long time. A serious local following," I said.

"Cade, last night we never fully established whether or not you're going to bring me in on the investigation."

"I said last night and I'm saying it again. It isn't my investigation. In a very short time I've seen the DEA, and DSS, all get involved with Miami Dade. We're lucky Miami P.D. didn't want to claim a piece of it since my shooting occurred in their city. Because it's an extension of Macario Santo Higuera shooting at Trentlocke and actually hitting a DEA agent, I think Miami will avoid this like a root canal. I still have to give a statement to Miami Dade Homicide. I can only put that off for so long. They'll come knocking. This is getting complicated. Truth be told, an ex-wife from another federal agency may not be a component they'll want to entertain."

"I'm not asking to be entertained or pandered to. I'm asking to be brought in so that I can assist. I shouldn't have to defend my federal importance to a local VIN detective who clearly can't see a separation of personal and professional attitudes," she barked.

"You're right. You don't have to explain to me. Just call the DEA or Miami Dade and say, 'Hi, I'm the woman who was married to the DSS agent and I want to be involved in the case because I know about ailerons, wind speed, and thrust reversers.' I'm sure they'll see there's no conflict of interest there."

"Cade, you're like one of those Russian nesting dolls. You're full of yourself. With or without you or your precious consent, I will *not* let this go."

We were pulling up to her car. The boot was removed from her tire. She reached into her bag for her keys.

"Thank you for the ride. We are *not* through," she said as she got out of my car and into her own.

She drove off with nary a wave or look. She drove north on Red Road. I turned the Land Cruiser around in the parking lot and happily headed in the opposite direction. I decided to take Red Road nearly all the way south to get home. I picked up my cellphone and called the VIN office.

"*Veen.*"

"Hello Ileana. It's Cade. Is Gary there?"

"*Oye Dumbolito!* I just spoken *contigo. Ju* think I don't know *ju* nasal voice? Gary *llame* and say he be holding up in *muy* big bumper to bumper he said. You know *tráfico en la calle?*"

"Yes Ileana, I get it. Gary will be delayed for work because of traffic. Can you have him call me please?"

"*Si*, Okay then," she said as she hung up on me.

Gary was Gary Fowler. Gary is our in-house financial administrator. I always call him "Big G." It had nothing to do with his size or girth, but simply a nickname I heard a guy once call his buddy in an elevator in Chicago. Although nearly the same age as me, he likes to call everyone 'dude,' a holdover from his days growing up in Hobe Sound, Florida's surfing Mecca. He has a buzz cut and the straightest, whitest teeth of anyone in the department. He also has a bar code tattoo at the base of the back of his neck and a small "F" tattooed on his right middle finger. He once told me that when he waves his hand in greeting or when accepting a volley of directions from someone he doesn't care for, the tattoo signified inwardly to him that he could "give a flying fuck." He had a master's degree in finance from Florida International University. He is a serious standup guy who has helped me on many things before.

December in Miami can be quite lovely. The entire winter can be seasonally wonderful. There's normally low humidity with more sunny warm days than cold days. Today was looking to be a day of sunshine and slight breezes. I was still feeling the effects of last night's bout with the fine folks who make Jameson. I was also up for a little more mental decompression. In my head I tabulated how many beers were back at the condominium and I decided to get some more. The gods of efficiency were smiling down upon me—along the way past Sunset Drive was a Farm Store. Created in the 1960s, the Farm Stores were small buildings with drive-up lanes on either side. They sold food staples and dairy products. They also sold beer.

I pulled up to the Farm Store. The attendant was waiting for me to speak first. It was quickly evident that the smiling friendly clerk spoke didn't speak English. Being a native Miamian this didn't faze me. We always seem to find a way to communicate amongst ourselves in this large metropolis.

"*Dame llaves por favor.*" I said. [Give me keys please.]

"Keys" was common Cuban slang for Beck's Beer because the German beer has a key on the label and on the wrap around the bottle neck. The accommodating clerk handed me a chilled six pack of Becks through my car window. The beer came with a small paper bag in case I chose to drink and drive. Somehow, somewhere, people came to believe that if you put a beer in a small paper bag no one would know you were drinking and driving. I chuckled at the idea of slipping one of the frosty bottles into a paper bag. Within fifteen minutes I was driving through the gate at the Royal Yacht Harbour Club and my phone rang as I pulled up to the condominium. It was the VIN office again.

"Hello?"

"Is this the one and only Cade Taylor?" said Gary.

"Hey, Big G. What's the good word?"

"You tell me. I was just in Brunson's office and he was talking about a shooting that took place yesterday. Would you happen to know anything about that?"

"Big G, right now unless there's something to say, there's nothing to say."

"Okay. I get it. Well, when you *can* say, will you let your good friend Gary I Can Keep a Secret Fowler know?" he asked me.

"See that's where we're alike, Big G. I can keep secrets, but the people I tell them to obviously can't."

That made Gary laugh. We shared some small talk when he decided to ask what it was I needed.

"Can you look around and let me know if you can find anything on this guy Emmanuel Servais? He came up in one of investigations but we don't know much about him. Can you fire up that computer of yours and channel your inner sleuth, see what you can find?" I said.

"Servais. First name Emmanuel. Is he French?"

"I have no idea. Like always Big G, my eyes only. My eyes only."

"You got it, Kemosabe. Later."

I left the six pack on the ground by my front tire. I went inside and changed into a tropical print bathing suit and brown sandals. I chose a plush large beach towel from the linen closet and I filled a vinyl soft-sided cooler halfway with ice. I didn't see myself as a problem drinker but I did see myself as an experienced drinker. I kept a bottle opener in the cooler. I went out the front door and wiggled the beers into the cooler, then walked to the pool. The day was postcard perfect. It was Monday. Children were still in school. The Christmas break was still at least two weeks away. It was quiet, peaceful, and languidly serene by the pool, no one was there. The only sound was the soft murmur of the pool pump and skimmer working in unison. The first beer was really smooth, cold and crisp. The pool has a designed ninety-degree corner between the shallow end and the deeper end. In the cutout corner is a poolside planter with three large, well-landscaped palm trees. It was my favorite aspect of the pool. I stayed in the shadow of the palms drinking beers and marveling at the blue sky and green palms above me, as if they were above me just for my own use and enjoyment. I basked in the peacefulness, letting the beers help free my mind of concern and worry. I did give some thought to Addison Hope and the internal struggle she must be fighting. I recalled what she had said to me.

"I'm haunted. I mean, full-on wracked with guilt that I was just yards away from him as he lay under those tarps and I didn't know it was him."

She must have been doing an emotional high wire act without a net. I took another highly desired, but equally detrimental swig from what was now my third beer. I felt for her in many ways. She must be tortured over the way her life had inexplicably intersected with the death of her ex-husband. I made a mental note that if I should see her again, I would be accommodating and less defensive.

I was surprised I hadn't heard from Llyod Trentlocke. I wasn't overly concerned about Miami Dade Homicide Detectives Bukowski and Clifford. There was always a chance of an investigation going sideways. I didn't foresee that happening with my killing of Macario Santos Higuera. There were witnesses, ballistics, car crashes, Trentlocke's testimony, and a DEA agent shot. I was confident that there would be an inquest, but that there would also be a predetermination hearing. Predetermination is exactly what it sounds like. They'd predetermine an outcome before even asking me about the shooting. It would be a formality. Years from now I'd be an unnamed participant in a teaching story Detectives Bukowski or Clifford would relay to young, eager police academy rookies.

The late morning had given way to early afternoon and I was downing my sixth beer when my cellphone rang, the VIN office again.

"Hello."

"Cade, this is the wakeup call you requested from the Gary Fowler hotel."

"Big G, tell me you got some good news," I said.

"Well seeing as you aren't here and Brunson has been on the phone with Miami Dade Homicide, I would venture to say you're insulating yourself somewhere, chilling away from everyone except probably your favorite bartender."

"I'm my own poolside bartender today."

"Ah, and what are we numbing with today as we float in the pool?" he asked.

"Becks."

"*Am Morgen ein Bier und der Tag gehört dir*," he said.

"What? What was that? German? Big G, you speak German?" I said, astonished at his language skill.

"Yup. I had to take a language at FIU for my undergrad. I figured I'd learn Spanish in Miami whether I wanted to or not, so I chose German. Probably not one of the top ten answers on the board. I sound like I got a loogey in my throat every time I speak it, and it rarely impresses the opposite sex. Not a very useful or flattering skill to speak the national language of a country smaller than Montana."

"No, I think it's cool. Wow, I learned something new about you today. So what did you say in German?"

"'Drink a beer in the morning and the day is yours,'" he said.

"I like it. I like it. I'm going to have to tuck that one in my pocket and use it sometime."

"So before we get into this Emmanuel Servais, how many beers have you had today? I don't want to have to repeat myself an hour from now because you can't remember the call."

"In dog beers I'm just under a year old," I said.

"Cute. Well, there isn't anything about Emmanuel Servais anywhere."

My expectation of useful news fell. Gary could usually find things that most people can't. He was a whiz with the computer and tried any and all ways to get information.

"But…." he said in a long drawn-out way to get me excited again. "Good news and bad news."

"Give it to me right in that order," I said.

"The good news is I found a Lambert Joseph Emmanuel Servais," he said.

I pumped my fist in the air a few times, phone against my ear with the other hand. "That has to be him! How many Emmanuel Servaises can there possibly be? Great job, Gary!"

"Well, I think the bad news might make you pee in the pool. The bad news is Lambert Joseph Emmanuel Servais is the former Prime Minister of Luxembourg and he died in 1890."

Chapter Nineteen

"THERE HAS TO be more than that?" I said, refusing to believe what I'd heard.

"Well, it isn't like it is a super common name. That's it. Whatever or whoever you're looking for once ruled Luxembourg and died over a hundred years ago."

"Could there be someone named after him?" I asked him.

"I'll see what kind of prime minister he was and if anyone is named after him. Keep in mind how the names Adolf and Fidel have fallen off of the popularity scale. But I'll see if there are any descendants or people named after him," he said.

"Thanks, Big G. I appreciate it," I said, contemplating what my next investigative lead could be.

"I'll get with you later. Enjoy the beers in the pool."

"It's a cheap ride to Heaven." I said hanging up.

Unless I decided to go back up to the condominium and restock the cooler I was pretty much done drinking beer in the pool. Restocking did cross my mind. Drinking alone never bothered me. In many ways I preferred it. My pace. My thoughts. No judgment or inconsequential conversation to interrupt my solitude and peace. The alcohol has become an accelerant to get me from vicious thoughts and memories to vacuous thoughts and remembrances. That's what

I told myself. Like any accelerant, there's a burn factor. A chance for the accelerant to turn on me.

I'm not there. That's not me.

The alcohol deluded me into a peaceful place sooner than if I'd tried to process my feelings without it. Alcohol was a beguiling, spiteful enchantress who entices and promises but in the end only delivers more heartache and despair. Mental haze becomes a mental maze. Like a rat in a laboratory grid, the repetitive running along the same obstacle-laden lines don't equate to progress. It just wore me out. A housefly that keeps crashing into a closed window adjacent to an open door is working hard but not working smart.

I was working hard on myself, but I wasn't working smart. I'd learned my own *this has got to work* version of compartmentalization. Overthinking always worked. Sometimes it was just me and my thoughts that helped me tuck away my fears and emotions. Other times it was me and copious doses of alcohol. Lately I'd felt the compartmentalization meter jitter and skitter to the alcohol side more than before. I'd adopted a self-proclaimed expertise in shielding myself from all that matters. I'd navigated the tricky art of keeping one foot in the world of dangerous reality that was a perpetual attachment to my job, and another foot in the world of secretive escapism.

In order to escape I must cut the cords to my haphazard life.

The alcohol at first helped me erect a barrier, shutting down and shutting off all the unpleasantries, regardless of where they charted on the psychological damage scale. It seduced me into forgetting the things I deeply yearned for. It walled me off from the things that kept me grounded: a sustainable relationship, caring friends, and a supportive family were what I needed. Not a growing penchant for drinking.

Walking back to the condominium I tried to make sense of how this whole case had caromed off the rails. Why was a Philadelphia mobster and two drug runners so fearful of someone named Emmanuel Servais? DSS Special Agent Dan Stallings wrote to

Addison Hope that if something happened to him, authorities should look for someone named Emmanuel Servais. Now Gary was telling me the closest name he could find to Emmanuel Servais was the former prime minister of Luxembourg, Lambert Joseph Emmanuel Servais. A prime minister that died in 1890. How did it all relate to ninety kilograms of cocaine that fell from the sky alongside Dan Stallings? DEA Special Agent Zammit said the kilos had similar markings on them as kilos previously seized in Philadelphia. He said the drug trade and all organized crime in Philadelphia was run by a ruthless leader named Ray Caruso. The Caruso crime family had Philadelphia locked down and all the other east coast crime families were fearful of Ray Caruso.

Yet Ray Caruso was an enigma. No one could describe him. No one ever claimed to see him. Macario Santos Higuera wouldn't be able to tell us anything and any investigative leads may have died with him.

This entire investigation was something I never wanted to be a part of and yet here I was, trying to appease Major Brunson, assist Miami Dade Homicide Detective Llyod Trentlocke, and as of about 9:30 this morning, avoid Addison Hope.

I changed clothes and plopped down on one of the chaise lounges on the rooftop terrace shaded by the roofline. I soon fell asleep.

I was awakened by my cellphone ringing at 4:30pm. I'd been asleep for at least five hours. The call was from Brunson's office. I let it ring a few times as I cleared my throat and sat upright. I wanted to appear as wake as I could.

"Hello."

"Cade, be available to meet me and Agent Zammit. Tonight. 7pm at Deli Lane in South Miami."

"Okay. What's going on?" I asked him.

"We want to talk over a plan we've come up with. You don't need to bring nothing but yourself. Be on time. I don't want to be waiting on you."

"Understood."

"What?" he said.

"I mean, I understand," I said.

"See you then."

7:00 tonight. That was good. Gave me some time to nap a little longer, shower and then be on my way. Traffic would also have weaned off. Deli Lane was a café just a few blocks from the Farm Store where I purchased the beer earlier. If this meeting with Major Brunson and Agent Zammit ended early, I might be able to swing back through the Farm Store for more Becks. To have on hand at the condominium.

That's what I told myself.

At 7pm Major Brunson and Agent Zammit were sitting at an outside table. The exterior was lit by strings of overhead Edison lights.

"Cade how are you doing?" Zammit asked as I sat with them. "On behalf of everyone at the DEA, we're very fortunate you showed up when you did. It could have all been worse for everyone—"

"Including me," said Llyod Trentlocke as he pulled up a chair and sat to my left.

"Oh hey, I wasn't told you'd be here," I said as I stood to shake his hand.

Both Trentlocke and I exchanged a big hug and knowing smiles. Pleasantries were exchanged around the table. When the waiter came we ordered and then Major Brunson got the agenda underway.

"Cade, as you know Miami Dade is the largest police agency in the county. Detective Trentlocke has made some great in-roads on the case so I'm going to turn the table over to him, then Phil and I will take it from there," said Brunson.

Trentlocke had a thin manila folder with him. Inside of the folder were four sets of papers each stapled at an angle across the right top corner. He distributed a set of the papers to each of us.

"We were able to get fingerprints off the motorcycles from the garage yesterday. Our crime scene people are good. They are really good. In the bikes' tire threads they found soil samples, coral rock dust, and pieces of pine needles. This morning they went out to the rock pit adjacent to Marin Avenue in Coral Gables and collected soil and pine needle samples. Granted, those things can be found in other parts of Miami Dade County, like the Rockdale section near the Falls Shopping Center and around Metro Zoo, but *those* samples mixed with the coral rock dust and salinity of the soil are very consistent with the rock pit. These motorcycles were recently at the rock pit. Three riders. Three bikes. The first motocross bike on the sheet in front of you is from a lime green 1995 RM125 Suzuki, prints on that bike came back to Macario Santos Higuera. We found his prints all over the bike most notably the gas cap, gas tank, both handlebars, and the rear struts."

"Same guy that shot my agent and shot at you," said Agent Zammit.

"And the same fucking asshole that Cade shot and killed yesterday," said Brunson.

After some brief discussions from Brunson, Zammit, and Trentlocke about the shooting that bordered on congratulatory remarks, Trentlocke steered the conversation back to the papers we were holding.

"Second page is similar to the first. Soil, coral, pine, all consistent with the rock pit. Prints were checked along the same areas. The bike is different—it's a 1997 blue Yamaha YZ125. Gas cap, gas tank, handlebars, rear struts, and front forks were all dusted for prints, barely any were found. Like I said, our technicians are good. They were able to get a few partials off the handlebars and a very good thumb print on the shifter. It took a little time to come back from the Automated Fingerprint Identification System but it did finally come in around 5:00 this morning. The prints belong to a Pennsylvania resident, Alvize "The Blister" Palmisano.

"The *Blister*?" said a startled Brunson.

Trentlocke had a booking picture of Alvize "The Blister"

Palmisano. He laid it on the table. We passed it amongst us. I studied it intently.

"Yeah. Get this. He did time at Rahway State Prison in New Jersey for backing his car over some guy three times. Somehow the guy lived. The victim refused to testify. The state booked him anyway for reckless endangerment. It was weak, but New jersey thought he'd talk. Palmisano never did. He did his small time and he was released. The file from the corrections officers at Rahway say he got the nickname 'the Blister' because he always shows up after the job is done. He's done stints at Rahway and at Eastern State outside of Philly. The guy's thirty-six years old, born and raised in Philadelphia. His full file should be on my desk by tonight. We're having some issues getting the file from Rahway because after over 100 years they decided to change the name of the prison to East Jersey State Prison last week, which means fax numbers, phone numbers, everything is being changed too. Personally, I think with the change, lots of people are avoiding doing their job. Don't worry we'll get it, but we've made a positive I.D. It's him."

"What did he do in Pennsylvania to get sent up the river?" asked Zammit.

"I guess that blister nickname is pretty accurate. They found three rival mobsters all tied up with bed sheets and stuffed into a car trunk. Philadelphia State Police Forensics said they were in the car trunk a few hours before they were each shot in the head."

"This guy Palmisano, *the Blister*…they got him on the murder charges?" blurted Brunson.

"They linked the purchase of the car's tires to him. He bought them ten months earlier. Palmisano claimed he sold the tires on the black market. He said he had nothing to do with the car or the murders. He had a partial alibi. The jury didn't buy it and he got a conspiracy charge. The FBI had a wire on a supper club on Passyunk Avenue in South Philly. Some old wise guy died of liver failure. Members of the Ray Caruso crime family were heard on the wire saying the old guy killed the three in the car trunk and the FBI bought it hook line and sinker. They charged the dead wise guy posthumously with murder and cleared the case. In doing so they sprung the Blister out of the pen. Two years later a confidential informant told the Organized Crime Bureau of the Pennsylvania State Police that the Caruso mobsters knew about the wire and knowingly hung the murder rap on the dead guy. They knew their disinformation campaign would get the FBI to leap at it."

"Any idea where he is now?" asked Zammit.

"He could be anywhere in South Florida, Philadelphia, who knows? It doesn't take long to go underground or get out of town." He sighed. "Moving on, bachelor number three gets really interesting," said Trentlocke.

"The third guy? The one I heard called *Dedos*?" I inquired.

"Yeah, Dedos. The one they called Dedos is missing two fingers on his right hand. How he lost the fingers we don't know. We think that is why they call him Dedos. His real name is Washington Sanchez—"

"Wait. Hold on. The guy is actually named Washington Sanchez?" asked Zammit.

"I'm Homicide. You'd be surprised at what names I've seen. Usnavy Martinez? His mother named him that because the U.S. Navy rescued her from a leaking makeshift raft in the Florida Straits. I've seen Nosmókin Burke because when he was born the first thing his mother saw was the "No Smoking" sign in the delivery room. So as far as I am concerned, Washington Sanchez makes total sense," said Trentlocke.

Brunson was mildly amused. "I always liked Rudyard Kipling. I'm going to encourage my son to name our next grandchild Gunga Din Brunson," he joked.

Everyone shared a brief laugh and the waiter arrived with everyone's entrees. Brunson and Zammit started eating but Trentlocke wasn't touching his food. I could tell there was more to what Trentlocke was telling us. I knew Llyod. He had a bigger story to tell.

Trentlocke went on: "So, yes, we identified Washington Sanchez by his eight fingerprints, they were on all three motocross bikes. I'd venture to say the Blister is in charge. Macario Santos Higuera and

Washington Sanchez are the workers. Both of their fingerprints are on the front forks, and rear struts and all over the three bikes, so we think they did the loading and fueling of the bikes. Fortunately for us, Washington Sanchez has been in and out of the Miami Dade jail system frequently. He's been arrested for stupid stuff like drunk and disorderly, trespassing after warning, minor drug charges; he was even arrested at a Home Depot on a battery charge for ramming a shopping cart into a store manager as Sanchez tried to shoplift a shop vac."

"'Shoplift a shop vac.' Say that three times fast," joked Brunson.

Trentlocke gave a slight smile. "Miami Dade Corrections had a consistent address on his multiple arrest forms, we got the address around 8pm last night. It's in the county, the house is at 1401 Southwest 75th Avenue. We were able to muster a combination of TNT and homicide teams to conduct surveillance on the house around ten last night. Detective Meaghan Clifford and I stayed back at headquarters and drew up a search warrant for the house and an arrest warrant for Sanchez. At two in the morning we were able to get a very sleepy, and I might add, very cranky Judge Robert Lenz to sign the warrants and we executed the warrant at 5am today. Brief knock and announce, then our team busted the front door off of the hinges and we went in—"

"Did it cross your mind to notify us since one of our agents was shot?" Zammit snapped.

"Time was of the essence. Once we had the warrants signed we needed to move fast. We felt that Sanchez might know that Santos Higuera was dead and he might flee—"

"What did you find?" interrupted Brunson.

Trentlocke hesitated for a moment, eyes trained on the three of us.

"Pink Mist."

Chapter Twenty

"**Y**OU GOTTA BE fucking kidding me!" said Brunson as he laid down his fork and sat back in his chair.

Pink Mist is a military and law enforcement term for when someone is shot in the head and their blood and brain matter disintegrate into a wide splattering pink mist in the air or against a wall. Death is instantaneous and the projectile that was used to kill is usually from a sniper rifle, hunting rifle, or a close-range shotgun blast.

"It was a shotgun. There was very little left of him above the bridge of his nose. We think he may have met his maker sometime around 6:00 last night. There was an open can of SpaghettiOs on the kitchen counter. He got whacked before heating the can up on the stove," Trentlocke said.

I was trying to process what Trentlocke was telling us.

"You're saying that two of the three people I overheard at the rock pit on Saturday night were both dead before nightfall the next day?" I asked Trentlocke.

"Cade, After Macario Santos Higuera shot at me and hit one of the DEA agents, you took him out and someone took out Washington Sanchez. I'd say it was very wise of you to have laid low when the Blister, Sanchez, and Santos Higuera arrived at the rock pit. This is a lot of violence in a short twenty-four hours. I'd wager if they'd seen you, they'd have tried to kill you."

"Do you think the Blister or one of the other members of the Caruso crime family killed Sanchez?" asked Zammit.

"Could be," said Trentlocke with a shrug.

I recalled what Alvize "the Blister" Palmisano said at the rock pit to Higuera and Sanchez. He said "youse two" would need to deal with Emmanuel Servais. That he was "gonna need some convincing."

"Or it could be Emmanuel Servais."

"Who the hell is Emmanuel Servais?" Brunson grunted.

"At the rock pit. The guy Llyod identified as the Blister Palmisano was ripping into Santos Higuera and Sanchez about the load of cocaine not being in the water. He told them they were going to have to deal with somebody named Emmanuel Servais. It sounded like all three of them were scared of whoever Emmanuel Servais is. More so, Santos Higuera and Sanchez. It was like Servais was some sort of intermediary between the Caruso crime family and the cocaine."

"Cade, did it ever cross your fucking increasingly shrinking mind that maybe that information could have been of value yesterday when we met at the police station?"

I recalled what major Brunson had said to me as we walked into the meeting.

"Don't say a word. Don't say a fucking word unless I ask you myself. You got it?"

I didn't want to inflame Major Brunson even more. If Trentlocke and Zammit knew that Brunson had censored the meeting it would be a big break in trust.

With a deep breath, I steadily said, "As I recall, there was a lot going on in that meeting."

When no one replied, I went off with the string of incidents and information I'd been flooded with in that short time, just to keep them in check and let them know I had a better grasp of the situation than they apparently thought I did. I always did, and Brunson knew it.

"We started with the NTSB's Lawson Dreyer lecturing us about how intelligent he is, and how he figured the whole situation out based on his worldly investigative experiences. Then we had a meeting *after* a meeting once he and the NTSB lackey left. Llyod starts talking and then the Regional Director of Diplomatic Security Services, Brad Mitchell, comes in from a rushed flight from Key West, all frenzied from losing Special Agent Stallings. He jumps right into the meeting and drops a bombshell on all of us—but especially Phil. He tells us Agent Stallings had actually been working undercover moving cocaine right through Phil's Caribbean swimming pool. As if that isn't enough, he informs us that Stallings had infiltrated the operation to such an extent that he believed the profits from the cocaine sales were going to a northeast crime syndicate. This same crime family need I remind you all is funneling the money into an unknown presidential candidate's campaign."

I paused and took in a reading of the table. They were listening. I could tell they were tabulating the events in their own minds. I continued.

"The narcodollars are to help the candidate get an early lead in the primaries and slide right into the White House. In return, the newly elected president would help get casino laws get passed in Pennsylvania. All the love birds from the Poconos on down to the geriatric retirees in a three-state area would flock to the Keystone State to lose their money in mob-run casinos. Mitchell takes off, and then Lloyd gets a jump on an address and we were out of there. With all due respect, it was a little heavy and a little rushed," I blurted.

Obviously completely forgetting that he'd told me to not say anything in the meeting, Major Brunson didn't let up on the gas.

"Cade, if you have any information that you're still holding, you need to be out with it now. When you're in a hole the best thing to do is stop fucking digging."

I waited a beat to measure my response. Major Brunson had

obviously also forgotten what he had said to me on the phone Saturday evening.

"Cade, have you ever thought to consider that the conversation between you and me wasn't about you conveying information to me, but me conveying information to you?"

Or had he?

"That's why I sit in the biggest office in this shitastrophy we call a police department. I have a solid memory and drop my cards only when needed."

I needed to answer him. The table was awaiting my response. Was Major Brunson truly unaware of what he'd said to me or was he so far in front of the conversation that I hadn't caught up yet? When you let the cat out of the bag it is a whole lot easier than trying to get him back in the bag. I figured it was best to take my chances.

"NTSB investigator Addison Hope was on the scene Saturday morning. The NTSB pulled her back because she'd once been married to Dan Stallings. I learned yesterday that she received a Christmas card from Stallings. It was postmarked from the Bahamas. In the card he told her he was into something really big. He said it was 'Watergate big.' He said if anything ever happened to him to tell the authorities he was chasing a criminal named Emmanuel Servais that if anything ever happened to him the authorities need to find this guy Emmanuel Servais."

"What island was it postmarked from? How did you learn this if the NTSB 'pulled her back' as you say from the investigation?" asked Zammit, eyes narrowed.

"She told me last night. She doesn't know which island the card was postmarked from. All she could tell me was that it was a pretty stamp."

My comments caused Trentlocke let out a low whistle which was barely audible over Brunson's spontaneous profanity laced tirade about me consorting with Addison Hope. Trentlocke leaned forward, his jaw clenched for a second. "Wait a minute. You were talking with an NTSB investigator even though we did our best to keep them out? An NTSB investigator, I might add, who was once *married* to the central part of our investigation? You did all of this last night?" Trentlocke's agitation was alarming, but not unexpected.

I repeated the exact phrase he said to us moments ago.

"'Time was of the essence.' Yes, last night while you were getting warrants drawn up and neglecting to tell any of us about it," I said.

Zammit was becoming increasingly agitated. "Fellas, it's evident that everyone wants results, but let's get those results as a unified team. The DSS is running an operation in *my* area of responsibility; Cade, you're communicating with an NTSB investigator who might be a little too close to the flame; Llyod, you're serving warrants and checking addresses without the DSS. Let's get on the same sheet of music here." His voice rose more and more as he spoke.

"Enough!" Brunson yelled, slamming his hand on the table. "Enough of the bullshit! I can tell when someone is speaking shit fluently. Cade, Llyod. Quit hiding behind the *I didn't know* bullshit. We got us a real fucking problem here. Way too much coke has been coming through here on its way to Philadelphia and we need to find out who this server guy is—" said Brunson.

"Servais. It's Servais," I corrected him.

"Cade, I don't care if it is David fucking Letterman. We need to get to him before he gets to any of us or interferes with what we're trying to do here."

"I asked Gary from the office to look into him. He came up pretty much empty. The closest match he found was the former prime minister of Luxembourg was named Emmanuel Servais and he died in 1890. So that's pretty much a dead end," I said.

A more composed Zammit said, "Gentlemen, we need to get past this 'dead-end' mentality. In lieu of what we've learned tonight, I think I can speak for Major Brunson when I say we've formulated an operation to flush out any of the Ray Caruso crime family members here in South Florida. Hopefully it will lead us to this man, Emmanuel Servais and whatever his role is in these homicides."

Trentlocke looked at me and I looked back at him. Inwardly, I was very hesitant but outwardly I showed no emotion.

"Good. Let's lay the plan out," said Brunson.

Chapter Twenty-One

"**B**OTH AGENT ZAMMIT and I have come up with a plan. Llyod, we'd be greatly indebted if you got onboard with us. You aren't under our command...but Cade you are," Brunson said pointing his finger directly at me. "If you want to catch a fucking rat you have to think like a fucking rat," he continued.

Zammit chimed in, "Llyod, there were way too many people on the scene investigating the shooting death of Macario Santos Higuera. We can't keep that information down any longer. The media will be knocking any minute now. I'm actually surprised it hasn't happened yet. We need to get in front of this and not behind it. We need the Miami Dade Police Department in on this *with* us, so we've spoken to your director and he's greenlighted it."

"What's the plan?" asked Trentlocke.

"We created a press release for the media. It says that only five kilograms of cocaine was seized, not ninety. Only five. We also mention that a day later the same unidentified Coral Gables detective who seized the five kilos killed known drug trafficker Macario Santos Higuera on a Miami street. Cade, you'll never be identified. There will be enough slip-ups in the press conference to give the Caruso family an idea of who you are..." said Zammit.

"So, I'm bait," I said.

"You're live bait, and we intend to *keep* you alive," said Brunson.

"Why only five kilos?" asked Trentlocke.

"The Caruso family knows there were ninety kilos. We'll tell the media an unidentified detective turned in five kilograms, they'll think Cade has the other eighty-five. They'll also know Cade killed a member of their transport team. He killed one of their contractors *and* he's holding eighty-five of their kilos with a street value just north of two million dollars. We hope to draw them to Cade so that we can take them all down," said Zammit.

"Cade, how do you feel about it so far?" asked Brunson.

"I'm listening," was all I could muster at the moment.

"The public information office of the DEA will give a detailed news release to the local, national, and international press. In the press release we'll put in some breadcrumbs for the Ray Caruso crew to pick up on. The press release goes out at noon tomorrow. It will be too late for the story to get lost in the midday news, but right on time to be the lead story on the five and 6:00 newscasts. We will hold a press conference at two in the afternoon at DEA headquarters. The Coral Gables Police public information officer will be there as well as the Miami Dade Police public information designee. A 'joint agency win' is what we're calling it. Five kilos of coke off the street and a known drug trafficker killed, all due to the good work of an unidentified Coral Gables detective. Major Brunson will be called upon to speak and say the detective is on administrative leave pending the outcome of the investigation. On a hot mic Brunson will turn to me and intentionally mention that 'he's probably at his hangout, Sam's Hideaway Tavern.' We hope the media will pick it up and run with it. Loose lips sink ships. There are moles in the media and in police departments. The word we hope will get back to the Caruso crime family," said Zammit.

"You think they'll come to Sam's Hideaway Tavern looking for Cade?" asked Trentlocke.

"Cade, are you familiar with it?" asked Brunson.

"Uh well…"

"Seriously. Is there a fucking bar you don't know in Miami?" asked Brunson.

"I'm not familiar with it," said Trentlocke.

Zammit said, "The tavern is on U.S.-1 just before the eighteen-mile stretch into Key Largo. It's literally at the southern tip of Krome Avenue. It's considered a dive bar. The tavern claims proudly that they are 'the oldest southernmost tavern on the mainland USA.'" said Zammit.

"They open at one in the afternoon and close at two in the morning," I said almost inaudibly to the table.

"Hot damn! I knew he'd fucking know the place," Brunson guffawed.

Agent Zammit pulled up a black leather fanny pack the size of a shaving kit from under the table. I thought it was the way he chose to carry his gun. He pulled a thick envelope out of it and slid it across the table to me.

I opened the envelope and looked inside. It was cash. Mostly 100-dollar bills with a smattering of twenties mixed in. I made a mental inventory and closed it, then slid the envelope towards Llyod.

"There's $15,000 in the envelope. Make these goons think you already sold five of their kilos. Use it as credibility money," said Zammit.

Brunson was quick to add, "The money came from the DEA. It isn't from our property room. No need for any fucking receipts for our asshole city manager. We don't care what the hell you do with it."

"Buy drinks, strippers, bet on games of pool. We don't care what you do as long as you look like you just came into new money and you expect to have even more money soon. Another reason for the cash is—" said Zammit.

"Sam's Hideaway Tavern only takes cash," I finished for him.

Brunson shook his head with a chuckle. "You know your watering holes. We fucking checked about the cash only policy. We're calling this one 'Operation: Hideaway.'"

"Suppose they come to the tavern and find Cade. Then what?" asked Trentlocke.

"We'll have the bar and the entire area completely staked out. We secured a house on an open three-acre parcel six blocks west of the tavern. Miami Dade will have a helicopter and a spotter staged there on standby in case they need to be airborne. Cade will tell them he has no plans to go back to the department. They'll lean on him for the eighty-five kilos and Cade will let it be known he already sold five of them. He'll negotiate a buy-back and delivery fee for the eighty remaining kilos substantially lower than street value. It will be a bird in the hand proposition to them. If they provide the buy money, Cade will deliver at least ten real kilos so we can make the drug charges stick. The rest will be seventy sham kilos," said Zammit.

"Sham kilos?" asked Trentlocke.

"Shams. Fakes. We're not going to risk losing eighty kilograms. They may think they're buying back their own load. It'll piss them off but they won't be dead in the water on their plans," Zammit said.

Trentlocke's suspicion was painfully clear in his eyes and tone. "So you have this entire tavern locked down with surveillance, and even air support, but you're still concerned there could be a loss of the cocaine—which could very much mean a loss of Cade. What's your plan when they take possession of the coke and then decide to kill Cade?" he demanded.

"Llyod, this is a homicide investigation with a strong predication of narcotics. Your homicides are directly tied to the importation of these kilograms by the Ray Caruso crime family. We need to get these hoodlums roped in and maybe even this Servais guy will turn up too. It solves all of our problems. Cade does work for Major Brunson. The DEA doesn't get a choice to back out; Cade has a choice. There's always a chance that if the work doesn't suit him, he can walk. We at the DEA don't have that opportunity. Chances have to be taken in our line of work. We try to mitigate the risks but it's *cocaine*. The cocaine world is fraught with changing dynamics. We're covering this the best way we can," said Zammit.

"What if you drive my homicide suspect underground and I have an unsolved case on my desk? Putting Cade out there like some sort of goat tied to a pole in the Serengeti is wholly dependent on you—and *everyone*—doing their job correctly without any missteps," said Trentlocke, shaking his head.

I leaned over, tapped Trentlocke on the hand. "Llyod. It's okay. Like Phil said, there' always a chance of something going wrong and I have the opportunity to say no. But my choice is clear."

I turned my attention from Trentlocke to the entire table.

I'm in," I said to everyone at the table.

Zammit and Brunson broke into wide smiles.

"We're gonna get these bastards," said Brunson.

"Cade you'll be wearing a Kel pager," Zammit said as he slid the pager to me over the table.

A Kel is a listening device disguised as a pager or cellphone so my back-up could hear everything. They were named after the ultra-secretive Kel Corporation: a company so secretive they wouldn't even acknowledge their Massachusetts headquarters to Wall Street investors. I examined the Kel. I turned it on and then off. It was fully charged.

I said, "A little sidebar. One of the residents on Conde Avenue who awoke Saturday morning to the sight of what was left of Dan Stallings called the police station today wanting to speak to me."

"Tessie?" asked Trentlocke.

"No, her neighbor Jason Cordicio. He was the guy from 601 Conde Avenue in the jean jacket and the board shorts. Anyway, he said his wife and his neighbor Tessie are still freaked out about the whole situation. A lot of hypothetical talk about what would have happened if Dan Stallings fell through his pool screen or actually hit his house. That kind of stuff. He said there's been some things going on the past few weeks. Planes flying low overhead and stuff. I figured he might have dates or times and we can get an idea of the frequency or pattern of the air drops. So I told him I'd meet him for breakfast tomorrow and see what he has to say," I said.

"Good idea. Any information could help. But we start Operation: Hideaway when Sam's Hideaway opens tomorrow. I don't expect anybody connected to Ray Caruso to catch on for a day or so. Use your time at Sam's Hideaway to establish bragging credibility in the place," said Zammit.

"You said this place is open until two in the morning?" asked Trentlocke.

"Sometimes they'll extend the hours if they're having good cash flow and a decent clientele, like overworked FPL line men. Lots of motorcycle clubs like to stop in on their way to or from the Keys. They actually have a twenty-four-hour liquor license. Generally speaking, their hours are until two in the morning."

Trentlocke turned to me.

"Two in the morning! Cade, we were in the same police academy class together. We've had some disagreements and trust issues, but we're still brothers in arms, especially after what happened yesterday. I'm your ride or die…until 9pm."

Chapter Twenty-Two

TRENTLOCKE AND I saw that there weren't many adjustments to be made to the operations plan once we'd looked over the printed copies. The surveillance teams were positioned in ideal locations. The names of many of the agents and detectives were foreign to me. According to the plan, if I stepped outside the tavern and put my hands on my hips, they were to send someone in to check on me. If I bent my elbow up towards my head and clasped it with the other hand it was a sign that I was in big danger. If I said the word "spectacular" into my cellphone or into the Kel mic, it meant I was in serious trouble. That would have everyone associated with *Operation: Hideaway* barreling through the doors.

"So, I show up sometime around one in the afternoon and everyone will be in place?" I asked Zammit.

"Pretty much. Remember we don't do the press conference until two, so we have no idea if the nugget we plant will germinate. It's better that you're already establishing a local presence and continual appearances at the tavern until we can determine if they're picking up what we're putting down."

"I have the take-down word and the body signs down. I'll take the ops plan home, look it over again and then get rid of it. My only issue is that I don't know any of the take-down cover people. Can we have a color of the day and switch it up each day?" I asked.

"What's a color of the day?" asked Trentlocke.

"All the friendlies, the back-up cops and agents will have the same color on. It could be a bandana, a baseball hat, a shirt but it has to be the same color so that they all know and recognize each other, and most importantly, Cade can see it and know," said Zammit.

"Let's just do it now," said Brunson.

Very quickly it was agreed that green would be designated the color for tomorrow. At the conclusion of each day the team would pick a color. I'd get a one-word text message notifying me of the color for the next day. It was suggested I also wear the color of the day for anybody who may have a challenge recognizing me.

The plates were cleared, the bill was paid. It was time to go. Trentlocke would still be investigating the murder of Washington "Dedos" Sanchez. We all shook hands and went our separate ways. Brunson walked with me in the parking lot while Trentlocke and Zammit went the other way.

"Cade, I don't sugar coat shit. I ain't no fucking Willy Wonka. I don't have an enemy in the world but none of my friends like me either. I can be bluntly fucking honest. If standing up for yourself burns a bridge, well, I have waterproof matches just to make sure the fucker gets lit. So hear me when I say, this ain't some vacation for you to slosh your goddamn mind away. The DEA and I are serious about getting this Caruso gang of thugs out of Miami. I'm not thrilled about this NTSB chickadee being in your ear. If you can dump her, then do so."

"She might have value. She says she can access certain federal data bases and stuff most can't."

"You figure that one out on your own. You might need to evaluate what her contribution can actually be. From where I sit, I see all show and no go from the NTSB. That's just the fucking pragmatic me talking. People think common sense is a gift—for me it's a punishment. I have to contend with all of you fuckers who don't have it. Speaking of a lack of common sense, you ever square up with Sergeant Rainer?" said Brunson.

I recalled my telephone conversation with Brunson. Always had an affinity for remembering conversations down to the syllable, but these words were ones that stuck, regardless:

"So you two imbeciles find a way to play nice on my playground or as God is my reluctant witness, I will have you both walking Miracle Mile looking for pedicured dogs shitting on our lovely fucking pink sidewalks. Understood?"

"No, I haven't had the chance to see him yet," I said.

"Fuck it. We have bigger fish to fry. I'll talk to him. I don't need to remind you to be careful going forward. These guys mean business. Over two million dollars' worth of business. Don't be all macho and not use your back up if you need to and don't corner someone that you know is meaner than you."

"Understood."

He glared at me in silence.

"I understand," I corrected myself.

He got in his car and drove away, leaving me in the shared parking lot between Deli Lane and B.T.'s Gentlemen's Club. B.T.'s is a sanitized version of the name everyone calls the strip club.

"The Booby Trap" is what everyone called the long-tenured strip club. The pink neon lights glinted off of the parked cars in the lot as I watched Brunson's taillights get further away. Agent Zammit's words came back to me:

"Buy drinks, strippers, bet on games of pool. We don't care what you do..."

The *we don't care what you do* sounded very appealing.

I walked to the Land Cruiser and opened the rear cargo compartment where I opened the envelope and took out eight crisp new hundred-dollar bills. I slipped the bills into the front pocket of my pants. I pulled back the thin carpet mat in the rear of the Toyota and wedged the remaining cash, the Kel, my badge, the ops plan, and my gun in the void around the spare tire. I pulled the carpet back into place and smoothed the thin fabric flat before I closed the rear compartment and locked it. I scanned the rooflines of the strip club and Deli Lane for any security cameras that may be trained on me or the Land Cruiser. There were none.

I thought it was a good idea for Agent Zammit and Major Brunson to toss a big red herring at the media for anyone who might pick up. I needed to make those odds even better.

Headquarters for the DEA is at least fifteen miles north of the Booby Trap. Sam's Hideaway is about twenty miles south of where I was standing in the glow of the strip club. Time and distance have a lot to do with the quickness of information being disseminated. I thought it would be better for *Operation: Hideaway* if I planted some seeds of my own, see if they germinated too.

Diamond tread silver aluminum sheet metal covered the entire rear door. It reflected the neon enticingly. It also hid scuff marks, fingerprints, and nicely cleaned up the bloody nose prints of unruly clientele the bouncers had to forcefully remove. Next to the door was half a sheet of the same grade of aluminum with the entrance to B.T.'s Gentlemen's Club clearly written in blue and pink paint. The pink mailbox next to the door was a nice touch. If you ever wondered what Mattel would envision a Barbie's Strip Club to look like, then this was definitely it.

I pulled on the door and stepped into a very darkened room. The first thing I saw were three big guys in black B.T.'s Gentlemen's Club polo shirts. One of them was about my age, the other two looked like University of Miami football linemen recruits who didn't make the team. They glanced at me.

"Twenty dollars," said one of the younger big bouncers.

I always found it ironic that strip clubs demand a cover charge to see women with no coverings. I made a slightly exaggerated production of fishing out the wad of hundreds from my front pocket. I extracted one of them with a bored, detached look on my face as I viewed the space behind him. I held up the hundred between two of my fingers. The three bouncers noticed the wad of cash but chose to act nonchalant. The bouncer gave me back eighty dollars in change in ripped and tattered tens, and fives—bills cycled continuously through G-strings and sequined thongs during the night. The small bills were intended to encourage tipping the dancers. At the end of the night, the dancers would exchange the bills with the manger for larger bills. The grimy sequence of small bills from direct hands to indirect female anatomy repeated again and again each and every night.

I stepped through the door-sized metal detector into the club. I pretended not to notice that the metal detector was not plugged into an electrical outlet. *Down in Mexico* by Death Proof was playing on the sound system. I felt like a bandito walking into a barrio brothel.

Three girls were on the small dance floor. They were totally naked except for red bandanas around their necks, an ode to the song lyrics. The sexy dancers were making a show of dancing around a sombrero on the floor of the stage, full of laughs and smiles as they paraded their beauty. Eight men crowded around the stage to ogle the women. Like Whack-a-Mole, one of the men would pop up from his seat and slip a bill into one of the dancer's garters and as soon as he sat down a different guy would pop up and repeat the routine. The rise and fall of the men was almost comical as they competed against each other to rid themselves of money.

The décor of the place was an abundance of glass and mirrors designed to make the space look bigger. It also reflects the shiny baubles and beaded miniscule garments the strippers discarded as soon as the music started. The ceilings and floor were painted black with day-glow stage paint strategically placed on steps and corners so the dancers could navigate in the dark.

I passed close by the older bouncer. In the mirror I saw him briefly hold his hand up to his forehead like he was a shark with a dorsal fin. None of the bouncers thought of me as a shark. The hand gesture was actually mimicking a tomahawk as he covertly informed the bartender and dancers that walking in was a *good one to finan-cially scalp*. Before I was able to take a seat at the bar, two of the seated strippers between me and the bar were on me. One was brunette, the other was a bottle blonde. Judging by their ample busts I wouldn't be far off if I predicted each of them has a passport with Colombian stamps from their visits to Bogota for cheap plastic surgery. The first to talk to me was the brunette.

"Welcome to B.T.'s. I'm Krystal with a K. Oooh, you must work out," she purred as she put her hand on my arm.

Not Cristal, Chrystal, Cristol, or Krystle...but Krystal.

"I'm Cade with a C."

"Cade? I like that. Does your wife like your name?"

"I'm not married," I said.

"Oooh, even better," she said as she took the bar stool on one side of me.

The blonde advantageously took the bar stool on my other side.

"I'm Kandy with a K," she said, seductively close to my ear.

Not Candy, Candi, Kandi, or Khandi...but Kandy.

Both women were beautiful and barely dressed. They used a lot of feminine charm to try and hold my attention, cooing little sentiments in my ears with smiles and giggles. They applied light touches to my neck and head. They also used effleurage strokes along my shoulders and back. Kandy ran her hands through my hair.

"Whoever cuts your hair must be a master. Do you like that word? *Master*?" asked Kandy mischievously.

"Only when I'm cutting bait on the boat," I said.

The perplexed look on her face was priceless.

The Mexican hat dance on the stage had ended. The three dancers with their fists loaded with cash barely had the dexterity to blow kisses and simultaneously promise to return to the gullible men who just spent cash for false affection and adulation.

"Stormy, Cassidy, and Tiffany to the Diamond Stage," the DJ announced.

Backstreet's *No Diggity* started playing through the loudspeakers. From behind a curtain emerged three different strippers. One with really short hair, almost cut military-style. I didn't see any attraction to a stripper who looked like Sergeant Carter from *Gomer Pyle* but I wasn't interested in the Diamond Stage anyway. I wasn't interested in Kandy with a K, or Krystal with a K. The K girls were just a vehicle to get me to the bartender. That's who I was actually interested in.

Spotting the three of us at the bar, the bartender ambled over. He was a little paunchy with a receding hairline in the front, but he grew his brown hair long in the back, which he put in a tight ponytail. He was wearing a polyester black vest over a long white sleeve shirt. There might have been a bowtie earlier in the evening but he now just wore his collar open.

"Hey partner, what can I get you? Remember it's a two drink minimum."

"Buy your ladies a drink?" Krystal asked me.

The dancers in strip clubs will often get a poor sap to buy something like a "Champagne Cocktail," "Cheetah Juice," or a "Vegas Bomb." These drinks are often incredibly overpriced and very light in alcohol—mostly ginger ale and grenadine. I feigned total ignorance to the ruse. The strippers make more money dancing. The fawning over me was intended to make me have a connection with them when they danced. It was also an obligatory chore to make money for the strip club by persuading me, the customer, to buy expensive drinks.

"What are you ladies drinking?" I asked them.

Almost in unison they both said, "Gentlemen Parlors!"

The bartender started to move to make the drinks. "Hold on buddy, come back here," I said to him. A bit chagrined, he came back to me, giving the K strippers a look of dissatisfaction at their inability to get me to buy drinks.

"First off, I'm Cade. What's your name, my friend?"

"Butch."

"Nice to meet you, Butch. Just how much are those Gentlemen Parlors?" I asked him doing my best to come across as a guy full of cash but with a reluctance to spend it.

"Twenty each," he said.

The affection from the K strippers had magically ceased during our conversation. I looked at both strippers on each side of me. I hooked them with reticence and then sprung reckless generosity on them.

"Well in that case, how about two each for these incredibly beautiful women and a shot of Jameson for both you and me?" I said.

The smiles returned to everyone's faces. We toasted each other. The women rubbed their bodies against me. Even Butch was happy to clink his glass to mine in a bonding moment of testosterone-driven joy. An hour later I was on my second Jameson. Both Kandy and Krystal had gone off to do their tour on stage and I watched them from the relative safety of the bar. They both gave me long looks from the Diamond Stage. This was a good time for me to talk to Butch.

"Hey Butch, who do you like more Kandy or Krystal?"

"Oh, you know. How can you have a favorite? They're all good," he said being diplomatic and coy.

"Up until about a few days ago I wouldn't have been able to sit here and take in all this wonderfulness," I said.

"Excuse me? Am I in the presence of a scratch-off lottery winner?" Butch laughed.

"Butch, let me tell you. Sometimes it just falls from the sky," I said, feigning the onset of inebriation, making me an even easier mark for all of them.

"Out of the sky, huh? How's so?"

I leaned forward conspiringly. "I'll let you in on a little secret. *Everyone* digs for gold. They're sweating in the hot sun, moving dirt. I can attest that real gold can fall right out of the sky and you don't have to go to Colombia to get it. *Cartagena Cargo*, if you know what I mean!" I said holding a finger to one of my nostrils.

"I know what you mean," he said with a big smile.

"Fell from the sky, let me just say it was like white square boxes of Kleenex. Talk about being in the right place at the right time!" I said.

"You have any of that cargo on you right now?" he asked with an expectant smile.

"Not in my pockets. How could I have ninety tissue boxes in my pockets? Actually, it's eighty-five tissue boxes. I turned five of them into the cops just to keep them from looking at me."

His eyes went wide. "You turned five into the cops? Are you crazy?" he said, already calculating the street value of five kilograms of cocaine in his head.

"It keeps them from looking at me and looking for more. They think I'm a model citizen!" I laughed. "From my eighty-five I already sold five of the Kleenex boxes to some guys down at Sam's Hideaway."

"The joint on the way to the Keys, right?" he asked.

"Yup."

Seeds planted.

All the elements were in place for a bumper crop. My name, my hangout, and the product I have and how I got it.

"You don't say…" he said, looking past me at the bouncers by the door. Their eyes met.

Once finished dancing, Kandy and Krystal went backstage and returned to the bar thirty minutes later. Now naked, they only wore stiletto heels. They stood on either side of me, anticipating more cash would come their way. I could see that I'd accomplished what I had set out to do when I chose to come into the strip club.

I closed out my tab. I tipped Butch with a crisp DEA supplied hundred-dollar bill. Just before I left I slipped Butch a twenty to give to the DJ for a "special Cade music request." Kandy and Krystal saw the money being bestowed and true to form, they put on even more of an act of fawning over me. I gave Kandy and Krystal each $150.00 which they gleefully put in their garters.

"That's for the next song. I want you both dancing for me and the boys," I said, motioning to the other men in the room.

The DJ got on the loudspeaker and called Kandy and Krystal to the stage "for a special Cade music request."

I was happy to have my name broadcast to the room.

More seeds planted even deeper.

Both strippers made a point to kiss me on each cheek as they rubbed and clung onto me, pressing their naked bodies against me tightly. They returned to the stage and the DJ spun my special request. I chose a little rocking number from way back—Mean Gene Kelton and the Diehards' catchy riff *My Baby Don't Wear No Panties.* The deep, driving blues beat got the entire club energized. Kandy and Krystal were really enjoying the song and many of the men were on their feet, adding even more cash to their garters.

"My baby wears garter belts, my baby wears spike high heels,

My baby wears fishnet stockings, she's always dressed to kill.

My baby likes to tease me when she's dancin' on the floor.

She sneaks me a peek, says do you want to see some more, cause…

My baby don't wear no panties—ask me how I know.

(How do you know... how do you know...)

I said my baby don't wear no panties—ask me how I know.

(How do you know... how do you know...)

She said she likes that natural feelin' and she knows it turns me on."

With Butch paid and both Kandy and Krystal relegated to the Diamond Stage, I could leave the club without any delay. I stepped through the still-unplugged metal detector. I nodded my head to the bouncers near the door as I passed by them and stepped into the parking lot, making a beeline for the Land Cruiser. I was using the car's remote to unlock the doors when I heard a voice call out to me from behind.

"Where ya going?"

I turned to look behind me. It was one of the younger football player sized bouncers walking towards me. My gun was deep in the spare tire well and I knew I wouldn't be able to get it with him coming at me. I changed my direction and headed for the passenger side of the Land Cruiser.

"Home. Have a good night," I said over my shoulder.

"Not so fast. You still have a bill to square up," he said as he came closer.

"I'm sorry, what?" I said as I got adjacent to the rear passenger door.

"There's a communication fee for talking to the girls. You still owe $200," he said as he neared the front of the Land Cruiser.

"You're serious? You want to charge me for talking to the dancers?" I said as I opened the rear passenger door.

"How about you put that hard thing between your legs in the backseat, and yes, I am talking about the tire iron."

I opened the rear car door and grabbed the tire iron. I covertly tucked it lengthwise behind my right arm as I quickly stepped out of the door frame. The bouncer was now standing near the front quarter panel and still walking towards me.

"Two girls. $200," he said, now at the front passenger door.

He held a small aluminum baseball bat at his side and raised it like an extension of his arm to point at me. He was three feet away.

"You care about your teeth?" he said, holding the bat out in a direct line, pointing it at me.

Anytime someone threatens you with a long item as a weapon, like a pool cue, baseball bat, or even a tennis racket, most people's natural inclination is to flinch or stand upright. The attacker needs to pull that weapon back before coming forward to have maximum effectiveness as he strikes you with it. The reality is as quickly as you can, you need to close the gap between the attacker and you, preventing them from getting a big wind-up to deliver a damaging blow.

I pounced into the space between us. The speed I used completely startled him and I was able to wrap my left arm over his extended right hand holding the bat. I locked my left arm hard down on his arm, pinning it against my body until I was right up against him, chest to chest. His striking arm and the bat were firmly against me. His natural inclination was to move back. That's exactly what I was hoping for. I swept his leg with my right leg as I hit him in the chest with the tire iron held crossways in my right hand. I didn't need a big wind-up to use the tire iron. With his right arm locked and his legs taken out from beneath him, he landed with a loud *thud* on the asphalt. He must have played sports at some time in his life because he instinctively tucked his chin into his chest to keep himself from hitting his head on the ground. I still had his right arm and the baseball bat pinned behind me as I stood over him. I twisted the curved tire iron in my hand and put the flanged end of the tire iron right against his throat, just above his clavicle. I applied enough pressure to compromise his airway. It was like holding a forged metal spear to his throat. He coughed and gagged. His tongue involuntarily laid outside of his mouth. His eyes bulged with fear and pain.

"Drop the fucking bat or I'm going to stake you to the parking lot like a beach umbrella," I spat, sneering at him.

I heard the aluminum bat bounce harmlessly onto the parking lot. I could hear it rolling a few feet away. I let up on the pressure of the tire iron just enough to allow him to swallow.

"You move, you breathe, you even blink and I'll pierce you like a stuck pig. You have a choice. Fractured collarbone, crushed windpipe, broken nose...or better yet, do you value your teeth?" I asked him as I once again pushed the edge of the tire iron down.

He was compromised. He also was too scared to choose one injury over another.

"Don't leave it up to me, sport. I'm a multiple choice kind of guy. I usually choose all of the above." I tightened my grip.

He started crying and begging for mercy.

"Is your collarbone and the ability to eat solid food worth $200? Tell you what. I'm going to move back. You're going to sit up and you're going to tie your shoes together. Don't even think of doing something funny because I'll crack your kneecaps, shatter your shins, or just plain ol' smash in your fucking skull. You better be quick and tie good knots or I'll put you in the hospital."

I backed up off of him. He sputtered and coughed but he sat upright and untied his shoes.

"Faster or I'll carve out your kidney with this tire iron," I barked at him.

He fumbled, then tied his shoes together with multiple knots. Sitting there, looking at his shoes tied together, the tears really started flowing.

"Scoot on your butt away from my car or I'll run you over."

Like an Olympic bobsledder he bounced on his butt at least one full parking space away from me and the Land Cruiser. I quickly picked up the baseball bat and threw it along with the tire iron into the backseat. I already knew there weren't any security cameras in the parking lot. Having him sit with his shoes tied together, it would take him some time to be able to get up. I didn't need him running to the other bouncers before I could leave. If he even tried kicking off his shoes I was fully prepared to break as many of his bones as I could. I told him so from the open window as I got ready to pull out. I put the Land Cruiser in drive and left him in the parking lot as I peeled out.

Chapter Twenty-Three

I DIDN'T NEED SOME "I got cut from the football team" loser putting a dent in my plans. He had a choice. He could get his shoes untied and go back into the strip club. He could tell the other bouncers he wasn't able to find me in the parking lot, or he could go back in and tell them how he got dish ragged out there. I'd guess he would choose to say he never found me and save face. A face he almost lost to a tire iron.

I intended to go home and get some rest so I could become a bar fly for at least the next week. That was my plan. I recalled what I thought when I saw the scraggly man wearing the faded American flag baseball hat as he sat outside on a bench behind the Keg South Tavern. He was smoking a cigarette and drinking a Pabst Blue Ribbon.

Day drinking would take you into the twilight of the day and unfortunately to the twilight of your mind.

I thought this inane assignment was not what I needed. Not what I needed at all as I fell further into the deep drinking cistern of my own doing. I needed it like a camel needs a hump. This was a deeply funded permission slip to play hooky from work and drink for half a day. I could feel myself slide even more into the twilight of my mind as my own personal tipping point teetered. I'd need to strike a balance between sobriety and case objectivity.

The drive home would be quick. Once again it was nearly a straight shot south on Red Road. I'd be home in a matter of minutes. Still enough time to think about what Trentlocke said about Dedos being murdered in his home.

It sounded like the shotgun obliterated his head.

I pulled over at the intersection of Chapman Field Drive and Red Road. I felt it necessary to have my gun nearby and accessible. I retrieved the cash, the Kel, my badge, the ops plan, and my gun from the tire well. I gave some thought to putting the tire iron in its proper place near the spare tire but opted to keep the tire iron in the backseat. It served me well tonight. Why not keep it in the backseat in what cop-speak calls my "lunge-able reach."

Putting the carpet in the back of the Land Cruiser in place, I looked at the baseball bat—an aluminum twenty-five inch Louisville Slugger. It was a child's bat, small, easy to conceal. It even said "Official Tee-Ball" on it. I chuckled at the where it said in a faded blue band at the top, "Feather Weight" and "Big Barrel." It may be a bat intended for children to play with, but it could do serious damage to someone.

Further south on Old Cutler Road I pulled into the Chapman Field parking lot. I did a slow-moving wide circle in the parking lot and tossed the bat out of the car window. I figured some kid could find it at tee-ball practice tomorrow and be very happy. I left the park and drove home. Morning would be upon me soon. I needed to meet Jason Cordicio at the Wagon's West restaurant.

The next morning I awoke feeling like I'd been in a roller derby the night before. My head hadn't caught up with my body and was quick to start piecing my day together before I'd even gotten to move.

The police department's psychologist once said, *"Your meticulous chronicling of everything from reciting directions in your head, to recalling the minute details of every conversation, to speaking with overexaggerated clarity is a trauma response, Cade. An exertion of control in a life where control is a farce."*

In any case, I immediately remembered that the color of the day was green. I put on a green t-shirt from Scott Gray's Top Bunk Bar in

Lake Forest, Illinois. I tugged on some jeans, and put on a dark blue Hartford Whalers baseball hat. My instincts told me to take the red swatch of fabric that I pulled from the kilograms of cocaine in the evidence room. I tucked the swatch into my back pocket. I also put the picture of the single kilogram on the ground that I'd taken in the same back pocket.

I stowed the Kel listening device, my badge and my gun in the center console of the Land Cruiser, then headed to Wagon's West. It was in the Suniland Shopping Plaza in Pinecrest. I luckily dodged much of the school traffic by taking back roads through Pinecrest on my way to the restaurant which was smack dab in the middle of a very long strip shopping center. The entire shopping center's front parking lot spanned the length of the plaza along highway US-1. There was a Bank of America branch, a large U.S. Post Office, a slew of small clothiers, nail salons, and restaurants in the shopping center. It was so large that there was even a Walgreens only a few store-fronts down from a CVS. Unbeknownst to a lot of people there was a smaller parking lot on the backside of the shopping center, as well as a breezeway cut through right by the Suniland Auto Tag Agency and Pete's Barber Shop.

I parked in the smaller, less populated backside parking lot. I walked through the breezeway. Wagon's West was just a few businesses down on my right. It expectedly had a frontier wagon logo on its menus, walls, and advertisements. The narrow inside of the place had a motif with a lot of wood. A counter bar was on the left side of the quaint diner with red vinyl bar stools bolted to the floor in front of the counter that faces the hectic kitchen. Using the space as efficiently as possible, on the right side of the narrow restaurant was a row of booths, and a step up after the first four booths towards the back of the restaurant. There was a small hostess stand by the front door. The enterprising ownership was able to squeeze in two booths by the front window which were plastered with hand bill advertise-ments for various events, resulting in the restaurant's sorely lacking natural light. Even with the hanging overhead lights it was still a semi-dark place.

I stepped into the air-conditioned coolness of the restaurant expecting to see Jason Cordicio. I stood by the hostess stand scanning the restaurant for him. The way patrons interacted with the staff and each other I could sense the restaurant was patronized frequently, if not daily by the same regulars. As expected, it was crowded. I looked behind me towards the two booths near the window. One booth had three men wearing identical Picket's Heating and Cooling Company shirts—undoubtedly a work crew fortifying before they set out on their service calls. In the other booth was an old man with wire-rim glasses perched on the end of his nose reading today's issue of the *Miami Herald*. The old man was eating a steaming bowl of oatmeal, a small amount of the oatmeal on his chin and dribbled onto the table. Through the pitch of multiple voices, occasional laughter, constant jocularity, clanging silverware, and jostling dishes filling the air, the waitress who was doing double duty as a hostess whisked by, telling me she'd be with me "in a moment." She filled the old man's mug with coffee as he looked up at her with appreciation. She dabbed his chin with a napkin. He still beamed at her as she walked back to me. She grabbed a laminated menu and searched for a booth to seat me.

"I'm expecting someone, so I'll need two menus please," I said to her.

"No problem, Sugar. Let me see if Wanda has an opening in her section," she said as she stepped towards the back of the restaurant. She stopped abruptly when she noticed that the second booth in the row of booths was open. "Sugar, I'm going to put you here in my section. I didn't know they had this table cleaned so fast. I'm Darlene. This your first time here?" she said as she sat me in the booth.

I chose to sit facing the door as I waited for Jason Cordicio to show up.

"No, I've been here before."

"Well, you must have slipped past me. What can I get you?"

"Just two waters for now, please," I said.

She hurried away. The din of the restaurant took hold again. I halfheartedly perused the menu as I kept my eye towards the door, waiting for Jason Cordicio to show up. He was late. I tempered down my annoyance. I smiled nicely at Darlene when she brought two ice-filled plastic glasses of water.

"You need a minute to wait for your friend?"

"Yes. Sorry."

"Baby doll, ain't nothing to be sorry about. I'll come back by." She went to the front of the restaurant by the hostess stand.

The old man with the oatmeal held his hand up to signal her. They spoke briefly across the small space between them then she went behind the counter and returned with an orange juice for him. Just as she set the plastic glass down, in walked Jason Cordicio. He immediately spied me and came right to the booth. I started to get up to shake his hand but he motioned to me to stay seated.

"No offense. I just washed my hands," he said as he sat across from me.

"Germophobe?"

"Lately it's taken a back seat and I'm full-on insomniac. Both me and my wife." He picked up the menu but didn't bother to look at it as he laid it aside. "This your first time here?" he asked.

He said it the same way that Darlene had asked me. I decided to answer him the same way.

"No I've been here before."

"I'm here nearly every day. I'm as regular as everyone in here," he said, looking towards the counter. "Darlene is the best. I like Wanda too but she talks too much. I hate seeing my order up in the kitchen and she's off talking a storm with somebody."

"Understood. I mean, I understand."

"You know what you want?"

"I'm still deciding," I said.

"The hotcakes are great here," he suggested.

Darlene came back to the table with her pen and pad in hand. "Good morning J," she said to Jason.

"Darlene, this is my new friend Cade," he said motioning to me across the table.

"Good morning, Cade. Do you know what you want?"

"Jason recommends the pancakes—"

"Hotcakes. The hotcakes," he corrected me.

"I'll have the hotcakes with bacon please," I told her.

She smiled sweetly at me and then turned away and headed towards the back of the restaurant.

"You're not eating?" I asked him.

"Oh, that," he said with an embarrassed smile. "Like I said, I'm here nearly every day. She knows my order by heart."

"So, Mr. Cordicio, what is it that I can help you with?"

"Jason. Once again, please call me Jason. I hope I can call you Cade. It's just us guys here talking, no pretenses."

Being a detective, especially a VIN detective in South Florida, is anything but pretense. Titles matter, especially in conversations. It helps with the hierarchy of conversation. Sitting here in a wooden booth with a padded backrest and a varnished hard wooden seat was not the hallowed halls of Parliament, or the storied chambers of the U.S. Capitol. Dropping titles was fine by me.

"How can I help you, Jason?" I rephrased.

"It's really weird. This whole thing has been like a bad dream. One day you're living your life like a normal person and the next day there's a guy's *leg* in your driveway. I always heard this kind of thing was very Miami. We've been here five years and I just never thought *we'd* experience it. The realtor who sold us the house said Coral Gables was very safe!"

The house.

He said, "the house." Not our house. There was no possession or ownership. He was already distancing himself from his house. That kind of talk was very indicative of someone who's contemplating moving.

"My wife is totally freaked. She wants us to move."

"Jason, I hear you. I'm in the conversation with you, but I'm struggling to understand what it is I can do or say to alleviate you of your feelings. I recognize that this is definitely another 'only in Miami' story, but the fact it happened so close to your house is happenstance."

"I don't think it *is* happenstance. For the past couple of months there have been more and more low-flying planes. At first I thought it was just my imagination or that I was being overly sensitive. After talking to my wife, I found out she noticed it, too."

I remembered what he had told me that morning about the sleeping arrangement with his wife.

"I have a deviated septum. I snore a lot. My wife often times moves to the spare bedroom in the middle of the night."

"Jason, if I recall correctly you said you had sleep apnea and you sometime sleep in a different room from your wife," I said, purposely choosing to say "apnea" over "deviated septum."

"I'm not entirely sure what it is. I snore. The doctors told me a deviated septum, not apnea," he said.

Touché, Jason. Consistent response to what he told me.

"The spare bedroom, is it adjacent to the primary bedroom?" I asked him.

"It's a four-bedroom house. The bedroom we intended to be the spare is actually the bedroom that our son Lucas claimed for himself when we moved in. We wanted the spare to be the furthest bedroom from the main one, but now it's Lucas' bedroom. My wife says she can hear me snoring through the walls, so when he's at college she sleeps in his room. He'll be back in a few days when he finishes his finals." He laughed a little. "She'll either invest in good earplugs or at the very least take the bedroom between us and Lucas. Come to think of it, if *I* had been using earplugs, I wouldn't be having this discussion with you! I also wouldn't have heard Tessie screaming. My God, it sounded like she burned her hands on the hinges of the gates to Hell. It scared the shit out of me."

Darlene appeared at the booth holding two plates of food. One plate had a delicious-looking stack of hotcakes with steam rising from them. With a friendly smile she put the plate of hotcakes in front of me. The second plate was a spinach and cheese omelette with hash browns and rye toast. She put that down in front of Jason. She reached in her apron and pulled out a bottle of green jalapeno tabasco sauce which she also put in front of Jason.

He thanked Darlene and said, "They started carrying bottles of the green sauce mainly because of me. Darlene is the best. Did I tell you that already?"

"Yes you did," I said.

As we ate, I tried to explain to Jason that air traffic patterns were not something that I or the Coral Gables police had any control over. I tried to assure him that as a lifelong native of Miami, people falling out of airplanes were very rare, even for South Florida. I made a point of telling him that I could understand how finding body parts splattered across his neighborhood was definitely a ghastly and disturbing event. I explained that Lloyd Trentlocke went the extra mile to try and find a logical explanation. I told him about flying with the Miami Dade police helicopter and searching the bay and the mangroves for a parachute or an ultralight aircraft. He took some comfort in knowing that extra efforts had been made to find a logical explanation for the shocking Saturday morning he'd experienced.

"I'm very grateful that our kids weren't there to see it. Of course, Lucille Amanda went and called both our son and daughter about it. She really pissed me off with that one. I had to reassure the kids it was not a common thing—"

"And now I'm reassuring *you* that it's not a common thing. I don't foresee this ever happening again," I said.

"Thank you. Thank you for taking the time to be here. Seeing you just made it all easier," he said.

All was calm and at ease. He seemed to feel better about it all. I did too. At least until a moment later when Addison Hope walked in the front door.

Chapter Twenty-Four

S HE STOPPED BY the hostess stand and began looking around. I could feel my blood pressure ratchet up like a rocket. I hurriedly reached into my front pocket, pulled out a twenty and a ten—the remnants of the change from my time in the strip club last night—and put the thirty dollars on the table.

"Jason, breakfast is on the City of Coral Gables. I'm sorry, but I'm going to need to go. I just saw an old contact walk in."

He instinctively turned in the booth to look towards the door. He had to have seen Addison Hope standing there. I gave another quick apology as I maneuvered out of the booth. I walked very fast towards her. She smiled at me.

"Weren't you wearing a hat like that when I met you?"

I didn't even answer her. I slipped my right arm under her left armpit along her ribs. I moved my arm around her waist very quickly. It was done with such speed that anybody watching would think I was hugging her but I grasped the back of her blouse with my right hand. I swiftly turned her 180 degrees so that we were both facing the front door. I used a small amount of force to walk to the front door with my arm around her waist. I pushed open the restaurant door with my left hand and ushered her with my right hand out the door into the morning sunlight. I continued the modified perp walk with her for a few feet until we were out of sight of the busy restaurant.

"What is *wrong* with you, Cade Taylor?" she chastised me.

"What's wrong with *me*? What could possibly be wrong with me? I just opened the door for you. Isn't that what a good southern woman wants? Oh, I'm sorry. Maybe I should have asked you first, just like you should have asked me before barging into a meeting I was having," I said, trying unfruitfully to conceal my agitation.

"I just don't understand—"

"No. What you don't understand is the meaning of 'stay out of it.' What *you* don't understand is this is not your case. What *you* don't understand is that people are working on your behalf and on behalf of multiple agencies. You think you can just come in uninvited and do your best Scarlett O'Hara impression, toss a few *I declare*s around and it will all be fine. Well it isn't lady. It isn't. Stay in your lane… Better yet, stay in your own airspace or whatever it is you NTSB people do."

"You have a distorted sense of judgment, Cade Taylor," she managed to say in the midst of my tirade.

"Let me tell you about judgment. My judgment of this situation and my judgment of you is rooted in experience. Good judgment comes from experience, the same experience that's born from *bad* judgment. You coming here today, this morning, that's bad judgment on your part. You lack the experience to know that. So I used good judgment to remove you from what could have been a bad experience for you and me. See how that works?" I hissed, still feeling the ratchet of my blood pressure percolating.

One of the three men in identical Picket's Heating and Cooling Company shirts came walking out of the restaurant. I thought we were safely away from the front door, but he had to do a slight side shuffle to get around us. As I silently made space for him I remembered Jason's call to me yesterday and how I agreed to meet him.

"Okay. I'll see you at Wagon's West at 8:30 tomorrow."

Addison had been in the car, overhearing my conversation.

"I heard you say Wagon's West, is that a new restaurant?"

"Addison, I don't know where you parked but I'm in the back. Walk with me now. By the way that isn't a request. Let's go," I said as I started walking along the shopping center towards the breezeway.

"I really don't want to," she said.

"I really don't want you to either," I said over my shoulder as I continued walking away from her.

I kept walking. I never looked back. I needed to move. I needed to move without interruption. I needed to have a moment to keep me from raging at her. I could not believe Addison's audacity, to glean the tidbits she did from my telephone conversation, and use my meeting with Jason Cordicio this way.

The more I walked, the more I cooled down. I'd had incalculable amount of VIN-related meetings with people in multiple locations all over Miami. Meeting Jason was a pretty benign moment. It was practically a breakfast without any bearing on anything. I couldn't placate his feelings and he didn't tell me anything that Brunson, Zammit, and I hadn't deduced already.

The closer I got to the opening of the breezeway the more composed I became. By the time I rounded the corner into the breezeway I reasoned that even if Addison had sat in on the meeting, so long as she didn't say much, it probably would have been a non-event.

I sat down on the bench outside Pete's Barber Shop. There was a cooling breeze blowing through the opening, hence the name breezeway. Addison was pacing a good distance behind me. My time on the bench helped to mentally walk me off the ledge of my own anger even more. She sat on the bench next to me. We sat in silence.

"Addison, I have a lot of agitating people in my life. When I have an opening, I'll call you, but right now I'm full up," I said.

"Well, shit fire and save the matches," she said.

"What the heck does that mean?"

"It means I'm just so shocked that you have agitating people in your life. Ever think that maybe *you're* the agitator, Cade Taylor? Did it ever occur to you that you're either the fire or kindling to all of your own *agitation*? Where was the harm?" She turned her body towards me while I looked straight ahead. "Where was the harm if I'd been part of the breakfast meeting? What would you have done if I'd been there first and then you showed up? Were you going to pull me out of the restaurant? Drag me from the table?"

"There are no tables, only booths," I said.

"Does it matter? See! That's what I'm saying. It's the remarks, the smirk from you that lights everyone's fuse."

"Addison, you missed the meeting you were not invited to. Is there something that precludes you from going on with your day, or are you here so you can grace me with your presence some more?"

"Let's have a reset," she said.

"*Why* would I be interested in a reset, Addison? Every time you NTSB windbags get on a scene you demand every resource available. You cordon off an area just barely smaller than the state of Rhode Island. Me? I don't have that luxury. My business is up and close. Conducted over tables, administered in parking lots, located in back alleys, handled in hotel rooms, and anywhere else it damn pleases. I don't have a defined space to work in. My work comes to me and I come to my work. So, it is as you say in the south, so *peachy keen* that you think my meeting was about something that involves you. Guess what? That isn't always the case."

"Again. How about a reset?"

"Okay Addison, what is it that you want now?"

"I want what I've been saying all along! I want in. How hard is it for you to understand that?"

"Didn't *your own people* at the NTSB pull you back from this? Sunday morning! Sunday morning, didn't they keep you out and instead send your subordinate Lawson Dreyer to the Coral Gables Police Department?"

Her mouth dropped open just a little. "What? Dreyer was dispatched to a meeting in the Gables?"

"Yes. He was there with some other NTSB snotnose. We had a meeting at ten in the morning. You told me they wanted you at the office at 9:30. You said they were bringing in another investigator from Ashburn, Virginia to work with Dreyer. Remember? You accused me and Trentlocke of throwing you under the bus. I figured they were keeping you out because of your relationship with Dan."

"That's what they said when they told me about Dan, but I didn't know Lawson was in a meeting about all of this," she said.

"Really?"

"Really."

"Well, he was there alright. He had a hairbrained idea that Dan was killed accidentally in some sort of stunt. He was convinced that Dan threw a parachute out of an airplane. He told us Dan must have dove out of the aircraft to retrieve the parachute and put it on in the air in some ballsy feat, said he'd seen it done in previous investigations over the Mojave desert," I told her.

"What? That's preposterous! There are so many things wrong with that theory. Did he even factor in altitude, speed, pressure, and darkness? It's *inconceivable* that he even considered it a plausibility."

"Last time I checked he works for you. He's your guy, not mine," I said.

"I haven't seen any reports from him about this at all," she said with consternation.

She began searching inside her bag for her cell phone. I could see that she was authentically miffed.

"Hold on. Hold on, Addison. Don't go making a bunch of calls. You wanted a reset, well here's your chance for a reset."

"What do you mean?" she asked.

"Just by association with me you know more about this case than anyone at the NTSB. You want in? Here's your first opportunity. Trentlocke, the DSS, the DEA, definitely none of us need the aggravation of another bloated federal agency shoving and demanding their way into things. Good Lord, if the entire NTSB is anything like you and Lawson Dreyer you'll exhaust all of us, and we'll get nowhere. Dreyer said he wanted to put a bow on this investigation and wrap it up. He left the meeting asking for reports from Trentlocke."

I fibbed a little about exactly how Dreyer left and how we made no attempt to refute his assertions. As I sat on a bench in front of the barbershop at the current moment it wasn't prudent to inform her that we were happy to see Dreyer leave the meeting and go off chasing his own tail in a circle. Addison had learned from our time at Duffy's the inroads we'd made in the investigation and that Macario Santos Higuera was dead. She also knew that Santo Higuera was part of a three-man crew involved in the importation of kilograms of cocaine.

"Do you remember I told you that Macario Santos Higuera was with two other men?" I asked her. She nodded. "Do you remember I told you that all three of them were terrified of a guy named Emmanuel Servais?"

"Yes. Emmanuel Servais. The same name that Dan wrote in his Christmas card to me," she said as she adjusted her position on the bench to face me better.

"Miami Dade Homicide identified both men through fingerprints on motorcycles from the crime scene where the DEA agent was shot. One set of prints is connected to a known Philadelphia mobster nicknamed 'the Blister—"

"The Blister? You gotta be kidding me. How'd he get a nickname like that?" she blurted, interrupting me.

"I don't know if it was from his own guys, or the correction officers from his time in prison, but they call him the Blister because he always shows up after the work is done."

"Cute," she said.

"His real name is Alvize Palmisano. They think he's probably killed a few guys in his day but has always found ways to beat the wrap and do little, if any, prison time. We think he's part of the Ray Caruso crime family I told you about at Duffy's."

"I'm listening," she said.

"The second guy that Miami Dade Homicide identified is a Colombian national called Washington Sanchez. They located him early yesterday morning. He was found in his house killed by a shotgun blast to the head at close range. Of the three that we know are connected to the cocaine shipment, the same shipment Dan was the kicker on, two are now dead."

"I don't know much about cocaine. What makes this particular shipment so identifiable as being the exact kilos of cocaine that Dan was kicking out of the airplane?"

"They all have identical markings. The Blister was insistent on retrieving the kilos. When they came up empty it rattled the three of them. We have confirmation from the DEA in Philadelphia that *these* kilograms with *these* markings on them have been seized previously from other Caruso crime family members."

"What markings?" she asked me.

"When cocaine is shipped into the United States the drug cartels will often comingle shipments. It's the way they differentiate which kilos are allocated for who. The drug cartels stamp them or write on them. It could be symbols or letters but when it reaches our shores, the people responsible for distributing the cocaine will know what parcels of the load go to who. In this case the entire load is committed to the Ray Caruso family. The intel is solid from the DEA in Philadelphia. What we've learned in these scant few days support that as well," I explained.

"What did the kilos of cocaine have written on them?" she asked me.

"It's more of a weird rectangle symbol with circles and the same number, 215. 215 is the area code for Philadelphia. The symbol...we still don't know what that means."

"Rectangle with circles? Are the circles smaller and below the rectangle in the bottom corners of it?" she asked me.

I eyed her suspiciously. Her asking me about the symbolism was eye-opening. Her nearly perfect description of the symbolism was very suspicious.

I was flummoxed about how I should answer her. I figured it was ridiculous to not try and get some sort of verification, especially if she somehow could recognize the symbol on the kilos. I leaned back a tad and pulled the Polaroid picture of the single kilogram from my back pocket putting it face down on the bench. I slid it to her. She put her hand on the Polaroid, but before she flipped the picture over she looked me in the eye for a beat. She overturned the picture. She looked at the picture and I could see instant recognition register in her eyes. She smiled and handed me back the picture.

"Hobo."

"Hobo?"

"It's Hobo code," she said.

Chapter Twenty-Five

"**H**OBO? LIKE A bum?" I asked her.

"Many people lump hobos, tramps, and bums as one in the same. Truthfully there are some very minor distinctions. Everyone thinks of these as related terms, but they aren't. A hobo travels and is willing to work; a tramp travels, but avoids work if possible; a bum neither travels nor works," she said.

"What is this? Some sort of southern lexicon you have going here?"

"Cade, I told you when we first met," she said with an amused grin. "I'm with the NTSB. Our domain includes railroad, transit, highway, marine, pipeline, and commercial space. I've been to about nine different railroad classes and seminars in my career. Hobos have their own language and terms. They also use symbolism to communicate to other hobos that may be traveling through behind them. They leave coded symbols on railroad cars, trees, telephone poles, and the sides of buildings. Wherever they think another hobo might see it."

"What do these messages and symbols say?" I asked her.

"They can say anything. Three wavy lines means barking dogs are present, a cat means the lady of the house is sympathetic to hobos, a diamond with a line at the top of the diamond means danger, every symbol is universally known and understood. If you don't know hobo code you'll think you're looking at elementary graffiti. Not so. Everything is intentional."

"The rectangle with the two circles under it, what does it mean?" I asked her, pointing at the photo.

"Well, you can barely see it in the picture but at the top left of the rectangle is a tiny line. See it?" she said, holding the picture out.

"I see it now, but I thought it was just a little overage of the ink on the rectangle."

"No, It's intentional. That's the hook. This symbol is a railroad car. The area code in the railroad car to me means these kilos were intended to be put on a railroad car and taken to Philadelphia by train."

I sat there dumbfounded. DSS Special Agent Brad Mitchell told us that Dan Stallings' reports told of air drops of cocaine from deep south in Miami Dade County all the way up to the Lake Worth Inlet in West Palm Beach. I told Addison as much.

"Lake Worth inlet by Peanut Island, right?" she asked me.

"I guess so, I'm not super versed on Palm Beach."

"Well, I am. That's a straight diagonal run to F45," she said.

"F45?" What's an F45?" I asked her.

"I'm sorry, I'm talking NTSB. F45 is the location identifier for the North Palm Beach County General Aviation Airport. Just like your Tamiami Airport here in Miami is TMB," she said.

"Shit."

"What?"

"There's an airport in Pompano Beach just off of the intercoastal waterway."

"Yes! Its location identifier is PMP. I know it well," she said.

"The Florida East Coast railroad goes right near all of those airports. We just say FEC. The FEC at one time went all the way from St. Augustine to Key West," I said.

I remembered what I heard Macario Santos Higuera say to the Blister at the rock pit when they were discussing the color of the plastic wrapping on the kilos of cocaine.

"It was only blue because that custom inspector held us up on the red sheeting. We had to use blue on the last one. We always use red because of the white stones."

"The kilograms were wrapped in red mylar plastic," I said as I pulled out the swatch and laid it on the bench.

She picked up the swatch and studied it intently. Her eyes started to mist. She was probably thinking that the piece of red plastic in her hand may have been one of the last things Dan touched before he died. She ran the red plastic between her fingers. I genuinely felt bad for her. I stayed silent until she very abruptly handed it back to me as if by not touching it she could disavow herself of her feelings. I put the piece of plastic back in my rear pocket.

"Addison, you said you can be a source of information. You said you can cut through the government channels and red tape. You said you can *do things*. Most importantly you keep saying you want in. You want in? Here is your chance," I said.

"Yes. Tell me. Anything. I want in."

"The information we were able to gather was that the owners of the cocaine are using mostly bright red plastic wrap to encase the kilos into manageable bundles. They've used blue plastic before but their choice of color is the red plastic I just showed you. There was mention that they 'always use red because of the white stones.' So if you're telling me the markings on the kilos are hobo code for railroad cars, is it possible that these loads are being put into open air freight cars and then have white gravel or stones put on top of them to conceal them as they get shipped to Philadelphia?"

"It's very possible," she said.

"Tell me what can you do with trains? What government channels can you look into?" I asked her.

"I can look into which trains and train cars are being used to ferry livestock from the Department of Agriculture. I can get into the Department of Energy files and see what cars are being used for natural gas, chlorine, coal, shale or any other fuel or chemical source. I can see the frequency and final destinations. FEC is only going to go to Jacksonville, from there—even though it's still an FEC rail car—it could be running on a CSX route, or an Old Dominion route. If I had to lay it on the line, pardon the pun, I'd say it is CSX. They go straight into Philadelphia. Did any of the kilograms have a small fireball or flame on the hobo rail car symbols?" she asked me.

"I don't know. There were ninety kilos. We were busy trying to get them gathered up and hauled away. I took a picture of only one. Why? What does the fireball mean?"

"A fireball means a 'hotshot.' It's a way to say the train is hauling priority freight, the train rarely makes any stops so therefore the train covers more terrain quicker. The hotshot is the equivalent of a cannonball run. If those kilos get put on a hotshot they could be in Philadelphia in under twenty-four hours."

"Where are you parked at?" I asked her.

"Dadgummit, Cade Taylor! You led me to think I could be of help and now you just raked my magnolia shrubs to get what you want!" she said, shaking her head with exasperation.

"You're in, but you're in with me. No NTSB Lawson Dreyer types, and no paperwork until we're done with this. I'm putting my neck out there bringing you in on my side of the huddle. Don't you be calling plays from the sideline or running a half back option on me, got it? You're with me and keep it on the down low."

She slowly smiled again.

"What I need you to do is to gauge the distance from all these airports to the FEC railroad yards. We got Tamiami Airport and North Palm Beach County General Aviation Airport as two very good potential starting points aligned with good drop spots into water. We both think the Pompano Beach Airpark is another good source. Go through your NTSB network, start plotting distance and feasibility of what waterways and airports are in line with each other. Do *not* overly alert an air traffic controller. Then measure those findings up against the distance to rail yards. Let's see which rail yards are being potentially used to load the cocaine onto the rail cars. It's a probability versus plausibility equation. If you can look into FEC and CSX schedules, look for Philadelphia-bound trains—especially the ones that are hotshots. Can you do that and get us started?"

"Yes, absolutely," she said.

"Now once again, where are you parked?" I asked her.

"I'm in the front," she said, sounding a little stunned that she'd finally gotten through to me and was part of the investigation.

"Come on. I have to be somewhere after 1:00. I'll walk you to your car."

We started walking back in front of the storefronts. There were Flanigan's restaurants across both Miami Dade and Broward counties. There was one here in the Suniland Shopping Center.

The main branding color of the well-known eateries was kelly green.

When we got to the front door of Flanigan's we made a quick stop inside. From the hostess stand I purchased a green t-shirt, size medium. Then I walked her to her car.

I opened her car door for her.

"I'm impressed," she said.

"I'm picking it up…slowly."

She started the car. I handed her the green shirt after she opened the window.

I said, "I'll be kind of land-locked the next couple of afternoons. If we should meet up again later today, you'll need to come to me. Be sure to wear this green shirt today."

"Why?"

"It reminds me of all the good times we've had," I said as I walked away.

Chapter Twenty-Six

IT WAS TOO early to go down to Sam's Hideaway Tavern. I was in that in-between stage of when I needed to be somewhere and when I didn't need to be somewhere. I decided to go back home and maybe get a cat nap in before I made the trek down to deep south Miami Dade County.

On the drive home I thought about the conversation I'd had with Addison. I was as certain as was she that the method of getting the cocaine to Philadelphia on trains was ingenious. Especially if you were able to get it on a hotshot fast-moving train. There are so many rail yards in Philadelphia, a good smuggling ring could get their contraband moved and hidden with extreme ease. If the Ray Caruso crime family had even an inkling there was a problem they could cause a rail disruption anywhere between South Florida and Philadelphia. It could be a stolen car, abandoned and left at a railroad crossing in Georgia; a broken safety gate in North Carolina; a dumpster fire in West Virginia, burning across the tracks. Anything to get the train to stop or at the very least slow down. Ray Caruso's confederates could board the open-air freight car, pull the kilos out of the gravel or stones and throw them off the train. Their biggest vulnerability would be the actual drop shipment from an airplane into the water. This we know as a fact. Once they had the kilos it would be an easy "cannonball run" to Philadelphia.

Whoever Emmanuel Servais was, he was definitely still out there. I gave some thought to Washington Sanchez and his eight fingers. He'd probably held them up in a last-ditch effort to save his life. The Blister threatened him at the rock pit, and for what? So Sanchez could live only a day later?

I wasn't thinking the Blister killed Sanchez. The Blister was just as scared of Emmanuel Servais as Macario Santos Higuera and Washington Sanchez were. It wasn't like Higuera was killed for losing the cocaine load, and he didn't die at the hands of Emmanuel Servais. Because I killed him.

For Servais it was probably fortuitous that I killed Santos Higuera. One box checked off of the tally sheet. I wondered if the Blister even knew that both of his rock pit cronies were dead.

DSS Special Agent Mitchell said that the seizure of the ninety kilograms would set back the Ray Caruso family, but it wouldn't cripple them. A "set-back" wouldn't be enough to abate the lost cocaine and untimely death of two drug smugglers. These disruptions may lead to the whole case rapidly proliferating even more.

I passed a small, three-acre tract of mango trees that undoubtedly one day would yield to developers and their plans to build a house on every available parcel of land in Pinecrest. I thought about what Addison had told me about Dan's holiday card.

He'd foretold of something being "Watergate big."

He said if anything ever happened to him to tell the authorities he was chasing a criminal named Emmanuel Servais. He punctuated that if anything ever happened to him the authorities needed to find this guy, Emmanuel Servais.

Emmanuel Servais. That name continued to waft and swirl around the murder of Washington Sanchez and the kilos of coke. The only thing Big G could find was that there once was a Lambert Joseph Emmanuel Servais and he was the prime minister of Luxembourg. And he died in 1890. That was of little help. It was definitely not a common name.

This was becoming a dead end without any rhyme or reason.

The only thing that made Dan Stallings' comment about something being "Watergate big" was what DSS Special Agent Brad Mitchell said about the cocaine being sold to a crime family in Philly. That they'd use the profits to get a presidential candidate in their pocket for the 2000 election. He said the crime family was "building a war chest" to finance a candidate through the early primaries before the election that was still a year away.

"I think Dan knew this. And the guy who stands to gain from it all is Emmanuel Servais."

I ran through the events of Watergate in my head. The Democratic party housed their campaign headquarters in the Watergate office and hotel complex. In 1972 there was a break in that was traced back to high-ranking members of President Richard Nixon's re-election committee. It would lead to the downfall of President Richard Nixon. Years later, the word "Watergate" was synonymous with political crime and corruption. If what Brad Mitchell said was accurate then there was a presidential contender with ties to a presidential contender somewhere who has ties to the most powerful and elusive crime organization.

I was nearing the entrance to the Royal Harbour Yacht Club. I called the VIN office hoping to get Big G on the phone. After three rings I heard:

"Veen."

"Good morning, Ileana. Is Gary in?"

"Esperar."

"Hello, is it me you're looking for?" Gary sang into the phone a few seconds later.

"When did you become a Lionel Richie fan? What's up with Ileana, she didn't even say hello?"

"Did she say *Veen*?" he asked.

"Yes."

"Well then, she said hello. Besides, she's weeping over the *telenovela* she's watching. I can't tell exactly what's going on but I gather some guy just found out his mother gave him up for adoption. The gardener's daughter who he loves is actually his half-sister or something so he can't marry her even though it would mean if he *did* he'd have to give up the money his family has held awaiting his return from a sailboat, and—"

"Okay. Okay, I get it. I shouldn't have asked," I said. "Big G, do you recall Watergate?"

"Well, I was a kid but yeah, I remember it. I think the lesson from that is burglars know the price of everything and the value of nothing."

"Could you do me a favor and just check around the news channels and news sites you like and give me an idea of who's thinking of running for president?" I asked him.

"Well I could, and I'd love to just do a little cursory look for you. There is one hang up. Major Brunson has already requested a deep dive on the same thing. I'd much rather just sniff around then stick my whole face in it like he wants. You know what he says, he sits in the biggest office for a reason. So why do you and the Prince of Profanity want this information?"

"What did Major Brunson say to you?" I asked, trying to mask my surprise that Brunson and I were dialed into the same train of thought.

"You want to know what he said exactly?"

"Yeah. What did he say *exactly*?"

"'Gary, can you do this? I'm not the fucking city's long-term solution for its lack of resource planning. That's why we have you.'"

"He actually said that? Oh man. Did he say anything else?"

"I asked him why he needed it. He told me he'd be mailing out W-2s on January 2nd to all the people who've been in his fucking business this year."

"Not working out too well I see," I see.

Gary huffed a little. "Since you're both asking me to spend my time being a political analyst, you care to fill me in on what exactly is going on here?" he asked.

Gary had always been very good to me. An invaluable asset to me personally and the VIN unit as a whole. I didn't fully know how much I should tell him, especially since I was doing a huge reach back on a very thin theory. Major Brunson, I suspected, was thinking the same thing as me. We were both trying to see if we could develop another inroad to whoever Emmanuel Servais was.

I had to tell Gary something. "We're just trying to get in front of the inevitable visits we'll see in the city by candidates in the next year and half. It's partly for Dignitary Protection and just so we can get a good idea of who's who."

"You're full of it, you know that?" he said.

With a sigh, I gave in a little. "I'll make a deal with you. When you find out what Major Brunson wants, you tell me. Then I'll clue you in. I promise."

"Okay. Since we're so chummy about clueing each other in…" He lowered his voice. "Let me clue you into the fact that as I sit my happy butt up here. One floor below me Miami Dade Homicide is reviewing your file and talking to Lieutenant Maddalone," he said.

"I expected a visit sooner or later, although I thought it would be later than sooner. Let me guess, a big guy who looks like a Salvation Army donation box with a head?"

"You got that right. There's also a real pretty homicide detective with him."

"Let me guess again," I said with another sigh. "A young woman. Wavy dark hair, big smile and a black ink tattoo of a seashell on her left wrist?"

"I didn't notice that tattoo, but she has a pretty cool flower geometric tattoo on her right elbow. I'm a tattoo kind of guy. I notice those things. He looks like a door stopper and she's a traffic stopper." he said.

"Tread lightly, my friend. They know all about killing and hiding it. Big G, I'm hoping you understand that when I *can* say, I will say, but it just isn't today."

"You're a poet and you don't even know it. Later," he said by way of signing off.

I pulled in front of the condominium. After dropping my keys into the artisan-created glass-blown bowl by the foyer, I plopped down on the couch and pulled a billowy pillow up behind my head as I stretched out. I intended to nap until I felt like going down to Sam's Hideaway Tavern.

I knew that Major Brunson and DEA Agent Phil Zammit would like me to be in Sam's Hideaway when they opened at 1pm. That just wasn't going to happen. There are two things I know: Cops and bars. Just because a bar opens at 1pm doesn't mean that the opening minute is the best time to go in and establish congenial rapport with strangers. There needs to be people there. People who have been drinking for a while. People inebriated enough to want to talk. Drinking people. The kind of drinking people who want to tell me their life story as I buy them drinks. People who have clouded judgment and clear opinions.

As for the cops, I'd venture to say that many of them were just being told today what their assignment was. They'd look on the map and curse and swear that they have to drive to the near-bottom of Miami Dade County while some guy they don't even know played benevolent money-loaded drinking buddy to the entire bar. They'd ask other detectives and agents to cover for them until they could get down there. They'd beg out of it to attend their kid's soccer practice, judo lesson, after-school parent teacher conference, the excuses are varied. It would make no difference. The excuses are only limited by their ability to sell the untruth. They'd find any and all excuses to avoid sitting in a car for nearly twelve hours. Some would use the proximity of the Florida Keys Outlet Mall to do early Christmas shopping. I can almost guarantee that one or two would break off from the surveillance in search of a bathroom only to curl back and go down to Key Largo for a quick beer and a sunset view.

I didn't expect to hear from Addison or Gary anytime soon. I fell asleep rather quickly and awoke with a start at 3pm. Agent Zammit and Major Brunson had probably just finished their press conference. The news wouldn't start hitting the airwaves until 5pm at the earliest.

I sat upright on the couch and collected my wits. Within thirty minutes I was back in my car, taking Old Cutler Road as far south as I could and then merged south onto US-1. Old Cutler Road terminated north of the Cauley Square Historic Village. I turned south and drove past the historic village of shops, eateries, and gardens that make up Cauley Square. The landscape for the next couple of miles was generally gas stations, fast food restaurants, tire stores, dollar stores, and auto part stores. The next big identifier to me was Coral Castle built by five-foot-tall, one-hundred-pound Latvian immigrant Edward Leedskalnin in the 1930s. He built a compound from immense thousand-pound coral rock and oolite hunks of rock, working primarily in the moonlight away from prying eyes. He used rudimentary hand tools. His engineering techniques still confound scientists and engineers to this day. The entire home and grounds were an homage to his unrequited love who never journeyed to South Florida to join him in his castle. The toil he endured and the unrelenting heartache he must have lived with made me thankful for accessible shots of Jameson Irish Whiskey. I'd rather nurse my floundering emotions without calluses on my hands.

I whizzed past the Coral Castle knowing that Sam's Hideaway would be coming up on my right in less than a mile. That's when my cellphone rang.

"Hello."

"Cade, I was going to go back to the office but traffic is a mess. The reason I hate being in fucking public is because the public is in public."

"Major, how did the press conference go?"

"I gotta hand it to Miami Dade and the DEA, they sure know how to get those beady-eyed reporters and cameras to come out. Phil says it was a success."

"Well, that's what you wanted, right? Success?" I said.

"Cade, success is like being pregnant. Everyone congratulates you but nobody considers how many times you got fucked."

"I never thought of it that way but...well, okay," I said.

"Cade, hear me out. It's great they have a helicopter standing by and a bunch of people pulled from their cases to be out there today. As time goes on, I wouldn't put a lot of trust in a bunch of multi-jurisdictional dipshits watching my back. Some of these guys are as dumb as scuffed bocce balls. You keep your wits about you. I know for a fact that if Lieutenant Maddalone gets his socks in a sweat going to a shooting scene in downtown Miami, I can tell you that a shooting at the bottom end of the county will go over like a pregnant pole vaulter."

"Sam's Hideaway does claim they're the most southern bar in the U.S. mainland."

"Why does it not surprise me that you fucking know that? Listen up. We set a big fucking trail of chum in the water today with the press conference. Let's hope we get a Great White or at the very least a Philadelphia tuna. Oh, and another thing—the assistant U.S. attorney was there. He said you have the green light to make, or not make, any ancillary cases that come from you cavorting with the high echelon of Miami society. He'll walk it in or walk it back. Your discretion. Keep me posted." And he hung up.

The high echelon of Miami society.

If the high echelon of Miami likes to drink in a flat roof cinder block bar adorned with repetitive alarms, surveillance cameras, and Miami Dade trespass warning signs advertising that the entire place is accustomed to having trouble, then I guess the highbrow of Miami would be inside. I hoped the high echelon also like central air conditioning, still running wall air conditioners chiseled into the walls, exposed piping, rusty hurricane awnings, faded paint, a welcome sign strategically placed over a no trespassing sign, trash cans on either side of the door, a worn and faded asphalt parking lot in front, and a mailbox just in case anyone at the bar needs to get their latest court appearance notice. The bar was faded yellow with hand-painted palm trees on each end of the tightly built bunkerlike rectangular drinking oasis. It was tucked back off of US-1, nearly hidden from view. Thankfully looming over the bar, a large billboard touted the services of yet another Miami attorney's legal competence.

When I pulled up to the bar there were still parking spaces in front. I chose the furthest parking space at the northern end of the parking lot. I knew the bar would inevitably fill up with cars and motorcycles, and I wanted the surveillance units to have a clear view of the Land Cruiser. A cluster of propane tanks and electrical transformers were pushed together on a raised concrete slab in front of my parking space. The entire mishmash of potential explosive trouble had a barbed wire-topped fence around it. I studied it briefly through my windshield. I had never seen such a configuration before. I clipped the Kel to my belt under my shirt and stuffed my right front pant pocket with cash. I left my gun, police identification, wallet, and badge under the driver's seat. I made a point to stand outside of the Land Cruiser—near the back of the vehicle at first. I wanted to provide the surveillance units an opportunity to get photos of me and the license plate. I leaned against the rear of the Toyota with my hands in my pockets pretending get some sun and much-needed vitamin D on my face. I took off the Hartford Whalers baseball hat so that the watching units could get clear pictures and views of me with and without the hat. After a few minutes of standing outside in clear view I walked to the front door of the bar.

Painted in bold letters on each end of the bar's roofline were the words "Cocktails" and "Cold Beer." Above the front door was a sun-affected green sign with a frosty beer mug between two leaping dolphins. SAM'S HIDEAWAY TAVERN was boldly written above the elementary, but effective mural. If there was any doubt, the moniker "the oldest Southernmost Tavern on the Mainland USA" was below the leaping dolphins. If that didn't scream "here we are," then nothing would. As I went to pull on the front door I saw the faded message painted on the wall to the left: *If your I.D. is hokey, you might end up in the pokey!*

Being in a dive bar for a day has its own appeal. Being *paid* to be in a dive bar for a day is appealing. Oddly enough the idea of being paid to be in a dive bar for *days* was not so appealing.

I stepped into an interior that reeked of a collective collision of scents like no other dive bar in Miami. Sweat, beer, ammonia, and frying oil all fought to be the dominant odor. There was a mishmash of adorning lights. There were neon rope lights across the tops of every shelf, pin lights along the bar, Edison lights across the ceiling, and too many beer posters and advertisements to even try to count. There were two well-worn pool tables towards the back of the bar. A tucked away alcove housed two video poker games with accompanying chairs for the relentlessly determined gambler who was insane enough to think a big payout awaited them at the last tavern in the mainland USA. The most promising thing in the bar was a well-stocked jukebox. The bar has a transcendent vibe that's welcoming, intimidating, cautionary, and alluring at the same time. I found a comfortable stool near the back of the bar that afforded me the ability to see people walk in and still have time to size them up as friend or foe before they got too close to me. The bartender was a tall guy with a ruddy complexion and unkempt sun-streaked white-blonde hair. He was lanky and had a scab on his left elbow. The bar towel was slung over his right shoulder. He was a southpaw. I was sure the scab on his elbow came from breaking up a fight or enforcing one of the many signs posted about bad behavior and ejection from the bar. He didn't even try to say hello. He just stood in front of me awaiting my drink order.

"*Soy perdido.*" [I'm lost.] I said.

"Buddy, this might not be the bar for you. *Comprende*? If you're on your way to the Keys there are plenty of *Margaritas y turistas* for you," he said.

Among the plethora of beer posters, banners, and advertisements was a tabletop-size neon sign for Ballantine Ale.

"I'll have a Ballantine Ale."

He wordlessly looked back over his shoulder at the Ballantine neon light.

"Sorry buddy, that's an old sign. We don't have Ballantine Ale."

"Make it a Heineken please."

He put an ice-cold green bottle of the unmistakable Dutch beer in front of me.

"Start a tab please. Tell ya what, my name's Cade. What's your name?"

"Trevor. My name is Trevor. Buddy, we don't keep tabs. We're a cash only bar here. If you need cash we have an ATM by the door."

"ATMs are too much trouble, Trevor. I'll make a bet with you," I said as I laid two 100-dollar bills on the bar. "Start a tab with these Ben Franklins and I'll go you one better. Take twenty off the top as a tip, but if you can tell me what the logo is on my hat I'll double your tip."

He looked at me suspiciously. He eyed the $200.

"Buddy, I'm from Kearney, New Jersey. I hate the Devils. I hate the Rangers. I'm really not much of a hockey fan but for forty bucks I can sure recognize the logo for the Hartford Whalers."

I slid the $200 towards him. "Forty bucks for you and start a tab with the 160 left over."

"You're going to drink $160 worth of booze?" he said with a slight shake of his head.

"I want to be the town drunk," I said.

"Good luck. In this place, people take turns."

"I might make some friends. Who knows? You want to give me some of that cash back in quarters for the jukebox?"

He came around the bar and punched in a series of numbers on the jukebox.

"First five songs are on me," he said as he walked back behind the bar.

I looked over the music options. I saw a few nice selections to choose from. The first choice I made was The Rolling Stones' *Mixed Emotions*. I hammered down the first Heineken as Mick Jagger and the boys sang.

"You're not the only one
with mixed emotions
You're not the only ship
Adrift on this ocean."

I asked Trevor for another Heineken.

"You have any intention of being in the Keys today?" he asked.

"Nah, the place is nothing but *Margaritas y turistas*," I replied.

He laughed as he put the next beer in front of me. I slowed down on the Heinekens as the bar started to fill up with patrons over the next few hours. They seemed to come in from all walks of life. Some came in on motorcycles; others looked like they'd spent the day fishing on the open ocean for dolphin or wahoo. A few pulled up in work trucks from a hard day of pulling wires, laying pipes, or digging trenches. There were some who straggled in from a down the street bus stop or found their way in on rickety, rusty bicycles. Many of them were local. I'd say that *everyone* in the bar was local except me. A skinny, sunbaked woman with black hair tied back sat beside me. I estimated she was sixty years old. She wore a bright pink t-shirt, cut-off denim shorts and a pair of cork sandals. She ordered a gin and tonic from Trevor. I told Trevor to put it on my tab. He willingly did so but with a *stay away from her* look on his face. She thanked me for the drink.

"Are you PADI certified?" she asked me.

"I'm sorry, what?"

"Are you PADI?" she asked me again.

The slight hesitation as I tried to understand her non-contextual question was all she needed to pick up on the answer she was looking for.

"Forget it. You ain't PADI."

"What's PADI?" I asked her.

"Professional Association of Diving Instructors. I work at Captain Slate's in Key Largo. We just had two dive instructors quit today. I was wondering if you were PADI?" she said.

"Here you go, Machete," said Trevor as he put the gin and tonic before her on the bar and walked away.

"Excuse me. Did he just call you *Machete*?"

"Yeah. People don't forget," she said just before taking a long pull on her drink.

"I'm sorry, what?" I said again.

"People. Don't. Forget."

She drew it out in such a way that she clearly was not interested in telling me and she didn't think I was very bright. I don't know if it was the gin or the coldness of the drink she was savoring more, but she downed the gin and tonic rather quickly. I motioned to Trevor and he concocted her another. Once again he put the drink in front of her and walked away. She looked around and realized I'd bought her second drink. She raised her glass to me in gratitude. I acknowledged her by tipping my Heineken bottle in her direction.

"Thank you. I don't think I've seen you in here before," she said.

"I'm looking for a new home and this place called to me," I said.

She looked around at her familiar bar and tried to see what was so attractive about the place to me.

"You should get caller I.D.," she said, shaking her head.

We sat in silence for a beat as she once again took a big gulp of her drink. She put her head back slowly, letting the gin and tonic slide down her throat. She then turned toward me in her bar stool.

"What's your name?"

"Cade. My name is Cade."

"Is that with a C or a K?"

"It's with a C. What's your name?" I asked her.

"My momma and my poppa named me Elizabeth, but since I was old enough to hear everyone talk, I've been called Betty."

"Machete? They call you Betty Machete?"

"Like I said, people don't forget."

I kept my eyes on her and sat silently. She felt my gaze and felt compelled to tell me more.

"Me and my then-husband, Errol, had an itty bitty house in the Redlands. It was small but it sat on three acres of lychee and mango trees. Out by the pump house there was a big thicket of Florida holly bushes. They got bigger by the month until finally all of my nagging about it got to Errol. So we both went to work on the bushes one Sunday afternoon. Errol had a steel cut blade and was cutting the bottom of the bushes. I had a machete. I was whacking at the top. Well, the darn fool raised up and I got him at the hairline. Sixty-four stitches and a scar that looked like a map of the Mississippi River. We broke up shortly after that. It's okay. He wasn't ever really the same again anyway. Ever since then, I went from being Betty to Betty Machete. People don't forget."

I told her it was an interesting the story. She said it was something she'd gotten used to and when she was younger it kept the sloppy drunks and lecherous men away from her.

"It has its advantages. When I go to Circle K to get my Winston Lights or a Mello Yello, most men who know me open the door for me. I want to be clear—I said Mello Yello. I don't drink that Mountain Dew stuff."

"Mountain Dew? What's wrong with Mountain Dew?"

"It's a meth-head drink. Mountain Dew and meth. M and M. They go together like salt and pepper."

I made a quick scan of the bar to see if anyone was drinking Mountain Dew. It didn't appear at least on the surface there were any meth heads in the bar. Betty and I kept company talking for a good hour before she excused herself.

"Thanks for the drinks. You ain't like most of the men I see in here. You got charasma."

"Charisma?"

"You get the point. Gotta go. I got a hungry racoon to feed."

She slid off of her bar stool, her spindly tanned legs straightening as she sought her equilibrium.

"You have a pet racoon? What's his name?"

"Revolver," she said as she disappeared into the thick crowd.

Revolver and Machete. It sounded like a spaghetti western movie title.

Over the next hour I met an assortment of people who sat in the bar stool next to me. Some stayed for as long as fifteen minutes while others only a few minutes. It was the lucky stool. I bought everyone a drink who sat in it. I met Toby, a herpetologist at Miami Metro Zoo; Clarence a real estate advisor with a big appetite for tequila; Kiley, a self-proclaimed lipstick expert; Paul, a pool cleaner who likes to be called "PPC," and Ronnie an unlicensed but as he says, "a really good" caterer. Ronnie wasn't very good at saving my seat when I went to the cramped tangerine-tomato-colored men's room. Rather than deal with the sullen fellow sitting in my seat, I chose to step outside and check my cellphone. I'd missed a call from Addison. I called her back. She answered the phone on the first ring.

"Addison, it's Cade. What's up?"

"Cade, I've plotted the locations of small airports in relation to the FEC railroad tracks. I think you'll be surprised. When are you available for me to show them to you? Is now a good time? I can meet you somewhere."

"Tonight's not good. How about sometime tomorrow before 1pm."

"You shoved me out of breakfast. It looked like my kind of place. Can we meet there in the morning? Say 9am?" she asked.

"Coming from the Roads section you'll need to leave early," I said.

"I did it today, I'll do it tomorrow. See you then," she said as she hung up.

I looked back at the vapor streetlight affixed over the bar's front door. It cast the parking lot in a soft, pumpkin-tinged light. The place was full. I'd run through my bar tab with Trevor. It would take some time for the planted seeds by Brunson, Zammit, and myself to sprout. The surveillance units would need to get into their rhythm and schedule. I was willing to wager the helicopter crew would love to go back to Tamiami Airport, and put their chopper in the hangar.

Once I was settled into the driver's seat, I texted the number I was given from the ops plan. I pressed the numbers for the cancel code into the phone and effectively told the surveillance units we were done for today. I wheeled the Toyota out of the parking spot and I sat there facing north. In a matter of minutes I saw headlights across the street and north of me at the gas station. I counted five cars pulling out. They were all heading north on US-1.

Chapter Twenty-Seven

A T 8:55 AM I walked into Wagon's West for the second day in a row. It was like my own version of the movie *Groundhog Day*. The old man with the wire rim glasses was in the same window booth reading the *Miami Herald*, his oatmeal placidly steaming in front of him. I recognized the three Pickets air conditioning and heating technicians. They were in the same booth they were in yesterday.

All of them locals.

Including Jason Cordicio. This time he was sitting at the counter. Partially turned away from me, I didn't think he saw me come in. I took off my Hartford Whalers hat and held it down by my side. If he noticed me I would say hello. By taking off the hat I was trying to reduce the chance of him recognizing me. As I approached, I spied Addison in one of the back booths. Her head was buried in the menu and she didn't see me. Better yet, she hadn't made the connection that Jason was who I'd met yesterday morning. I thought I'd be able to slip past him when I heard him call out to me.

"Cade! What brings you in here?"

Busted.

I turned back to Jason. He was nearly finished with his spinach and cheese omelet. The bottle of green tabasco sauce in front of his plate was like a miniature marker of his place in the restaurant.

"Morning, Jason. Breakfast brings me here. It's good seeing you again," I said as I tried to shuffle away towards Addison.

He motioned me to lean in closer to him. I leaned towards him. We were very close.

"Was that *you* they were talking about on the news last night?" he said very quietly.

"News? What did they say on the news?" I asked, feigning ignorance.

"Channel Ten said that the guy who fell out of the airplane was a drug smuggler and that they recovered five kilograms of cocaine practically from my backyard. Right near the bay and the rock pit behind my house! Lucille Amanda says it all makes sense now. *Drug smuggling*? In Coral Gables? In the sky? I mean, that's crazy!"

"Jason, I couldn't tell you. I've decided to take a few weeks off. I'm just not in the loop. Enjoy your breakfast. Take care," I said as I put my hat back on and parted from him.

I made my way back to Addison who looked up and smiled. I sat down across from her.

"They have nearly everything on the menu. It's quite extensive," she said.

"The pancakes are pretty good."

"I don't see pancakes. It does say hotcakes."

"Hotcakes, pancakes, flapjacks, griddle cakes, does it really matter?" I asked her.

"Words are important, Cade."

Darlene, the waitress from yesterday arrived at our table and took Addison's order. I ordered the hotcakes. Darlene smiled at me in recognition. When Darlene left, Addison jumped right into the purpose of our meeting, pulling out a folder. She opened the folder and presented the papers to me. On top was a map of the south-eastern tip of Florida with red dots, blue dots, and black lines all over it.

"The red dots are all FAA small municipal airports. The blue dots are FEC railyards where trains either stop or experience track switches. The black lines are air routes into the airports from the east," she explained.

"Okay."

"Taking into account what I've been able to learn about weight and size of large, multiple kilograms of cocaine shipments... Certain trains are scheduled to go to or at least through Philadelphia. Of those trains only one is scheduled per week to bring rocks, pebbles, concrete dust, or silt north to Philadelphia. It's a cannonball and it leaves the Miami FEC railyard at 9pm every Sunday night," she said.

"Words are important," I muttered to myself as I studied the papers.

On the third paper I saw three stars on the overlay of railroad tracks between the Miami FEC railyard and the next junction station in neighboring Broward County.

"What are these three stars here on the tracks?" I asked her.

"Those are chokepoints where the train slows considerably as it leaves the Miami rail yard. Adding train cars, multiple busy thoroughfares, their crossing gates, backing the train up to pick up other train cars, even neighborhood noise ordinances against train whistles... All of those things will cause the train to slow to a creeping crawl for a few minutes before it revs up and starts high tailing it to Philadelphia."

"So the cocaine doesn't have to be loaded on the train in the FEC Miami center where there are lots of security and cameras. It can be loaded on board any one of these chokepoints," I said almost to myself as I studied the papers.

"Yes, I suppose so. I'm not sure entirely how," she said.

"Three to five-man teams. Two on the ground, three up on top of the open gravel car. One guy gets on the ladder of the railcar midway up. The other's on the ground, handing him the satchel-loads of cocaine. The guy on the ladder hands it up to one of the three on top of the gravel car. The third guy pulls it up to the top while the other two are shoveling divots and holes in the gravel to bury the satchels just below the surface. A hundred kilos could be loaded in less than five minutes on the stalled or extremely slow-moving train. If they're worth their weight, they'll mark the train car in hobo code. When the train gets to Philadelphia the off loaders will know exactly which railcar to get the cocaine from. It's beyond simple," I said.

"Beyond simple, you say?" she said, raising her eyebrow.

"The shipment that fell into the rock pit was kicked out early Saturday morning. They tried to retrieve it Saturday afternoon before the salt it was packed in dissolved and the kilos naturally floated to the top—"

"The kilos were packed in salt?" she interrupted.

"Yes. It's a smuggling technique called the 'Real McCoy.' The contraband, whatever it may be, is densely packed in salt. When the salt starts to dissolve in the water, the contraband will rise to the surface. So if they dropped it Saturday, they tried to retrieve it Saturday, and then they planned to put it on a cannonball freight train on Sunday, that may mean that the Ray Caruso crime family might not have a storage place. They're looking to get it and move it as soon as they can."

"You think they're using the FEC railyard or maybe one of these chokepoints?" she asked me.

"Unless they have someone on the inside—which is highly possible, considering the volume of money and cocaine we're dealing with—yes that is a very good possibility. I just keep thinking they're short haulers. They don't want, or have, a suitable place to hold the coke for extended periods of time. If they could afford to pay off an FEC official or security team then they could afford a suitable stash location. I think they're trying to stick to old mafia codes of *no drugs ever*. They're failing miserably at it. Do you know anything about these identified chokepoints?"

"Funny you should ask. I went out late yesterday and looked at all three locations. The one that struck me the most was at East 11th Avenue and East 47th Street. I think it's eastern Hialeah because the numbering system of the roads changed."

"Sounds like the city of Hialeah. They have their own road numbering system that's counter to Miami Dade County," I said.

Darlene placed our breakfast orders in front of us with a smile and walked away. The hotcakes looked just as delicious as they did yesterday.

"So why East 11th Avenue and East 47th Street?"

"The train definitely comes to a stop there. I guess East 49th in Hialeah is actually Northwest 103rd Street in the county. There's a backlog because of the intersection at Northwest 103rd Street. On East 47th there's a short, paved stretch of road that leads right to the railroad tracks. It's a dead end between two warehouses. There are no windows or doors from the warehouses that face this dead end street. The whole dead end street can't be more than forty yards long. Big enough for trucks, a semi, or a couple of cars. There's a chain link fence topped with barbed wire to keep people from accessing the railroad tracks. But guess what?"

"What?"

"There's a *single* chain link gate right in the middle. Painted in front of the gate is a bright orange circle with a looping arrow coming off the bottom of it. It's pointed at the gate," she said.

"What does that mean?" I asked her.

"It means *this way* in hobo code."

"Did it ever cross your mind that it could be a symbol from hobos to each other that it's a great place to catch trains?" I asked her.

"Of course it did. Why would the Ray Caruso group reinvent the wheel on this? The train stops there. The egress is there. It's a known hop-on and hop-off spot. I think it works nicely, especially since you just said you think they're short storage guys. This works really well."

I pretended to be engrossed in the hotcakes as I mulled over

Addison's words. It made a lot of sense. It was possible. More importantly, it was *plausible*. She kept sneaking peeks at me expectantly, waiting for affirmation and validation.

"Addison, great work. I think you may be onto something," I said.

She beamed with pride.

"So what's the next step? What are we doing today?" she asked me.

"*We* aren't doing anything. I have to be somewhere in the afternoon that will probably carry me into the night. Keep formulating your ideas. I think you're onto something there. Seriously, really good work."

"Cade, don't *think* of parking me on the sideline."

"No, it's all good. I'm just committed to being elsewhere today for a period of time. What did you ever learn about the airplane that carried your ex-husband?"

The mention of Dan caused her to purse her lips briefly. She folded up the maps and pushed them off to one side on the table.

"It gave a call sign for a private aircraft from the Bahamas. It opted to change direction as it neared Tamiami airport. The pilot told air traffic control it had to divert to Miami International Airport because of a pet quarantine issue."

"What does that mean?" I asked her.

"It means they were saying they had an animal on the airplane that wasn't properly vaccinated and they went to Miami International Airport because they have the facilities there. The aircraft diverted and flew east past Miami. It went back to the Bahamas. It never landed in the U.S. Both air traffic control towers passed it back and forth. By the time they realized it was leaving our airspace and going back to the Bahamas it was a non-issue, it went back to its airport of origin."

"Where was that?" I asked her.

"MYX4, also known as Big Whale Cay Airport. It's not much bigger than an average main street in any small town. NTSB thinks of these types of flights as training flights. Pilots look for the lights of a city, they fly to them, turn around and then plot their way home. We're on friendly terms with the Bahamas so very little is done if they don't actually land in the U.S."

"You said it was registered in the Bahamas."

"Tail number SG N29. Cessna 402."

"Who owns it?" I asked her.

"An LLC in New Mexico. Ever try to get ownership from the state of New Mexico? Good luck. New Mexico is the only state that requires no names of LLC owners to be on file anywhere. We have no idea where the airplane is now, who flew it, who flies it, or who actually owns it."

"I thought you had back channels?" I teased her.

"Cade you like to melt my butter over any little thing you can. I think I've done a pretty good job in the past twenty-four hours," she said, betraying that she felt a bit insulted.

"You have. Absolutely. Don't let my teasing get to you. On the odd chance anybody else flew from here to Big Whale Cay can you check all small aircraft flights from Key West to Fort Lauderdale Sunday until around three in the afternoon? Macario Santos Higuera died around three and I'm sure it all shut down after that."

I reached into the pocket of my jeans and pulled out a wad of cash. I peeled enough bills off the wad to sufficiently cover our meal and leave a generous tip for Darlene. The color of the day was orange. I was wearing an orange University of Miami t-shirt.

"Will you call me later if you find anything about those flights? I think we're onto something with that East 11th Avenue address in Hialeah. It makes sense. Why risk security, cameras, and paying people off when you can just put it on a temporarily stalled train away from prying eyes? Call me later." I said.

As I left the restaurant I made quick notice that amongst all the regulars—the old man with the oatmeal, the three Pickets air conditioning mechanics, and the rest of the locals—were still there. Only

Jason Cordicio was absent. As I neared the breezeway my cellphone rang.

"Hello?"

"How'd it go last night?" Major Brunson asked me.

"It went well. I think I made some inroads with the locals. When I go back today I'll see who was there from yesterday and forge those relationships deeper."

"I had to be at city hall this morning for the final meeting about *Santa's Village at Miracle on the Mile Event* this year. Every year this city puts out that garish Christmas-themed phony fucking village for all these overindulged fucking rug rats and their pushing and shoving parents. Road closures, detours, extra cops, what a pain in the ass. I was almost late to the damn meeting because of all of these damn school zones between my house and city hall. Fucking school zones! Elementary school I understand. The kids are little, and extra care should be taken. Middle school gets barely a pass with me. If you haven't learned about cars and roads, well it's just going to be harder on you going forward. The one that gets me is high school. High school! Do high schools really need a school zone? Let me tell you, if I hit you with my fucking car and you're in high school I did you a big fucking favor because your survival rate in life was not that high to begin with."

"Understood. I mean, I understand."

"I got a friend. He grew up in St. Augustine. Can you believe they actually have an elementary school across the street from a fucking alligator farm? Holy shit fuck! If that had been me and the iron heads I went to school with, half of those fucking imbeciles would have never made it to sixth grade," he said.

"Yeah, I went to school with some people who took chances too," I said.

"Oh, excuse me. You don't take chances yourself? Remind me who I'm talking to? Oh, I know, I'm talking to the detective that's the reason why the fucking Miami Dade Homicide detectives were here going through his file yesterday," Brunson said.

"Did you have anything to say to them?" I asked.

"I told them that they should look at the most recent file on you they've got and quit wasting time. There hasn't been a long enough duration for anything to really change. Aside from that, we'll just see if what we put out in the press conference yesterday someone puts two and two together."

"I'm just leaving a restaurant in Pinecrest. The Coral Gables resident whose yard Dan Stallings landed near was there. He said he saw it on Channel Ten. I think it might take root."

"You got everything you need? What do you got to wear that's orange?"

"A jumpsuit from Miami Dade Corrections."

"Well, you'll fit right in, won't you?"

"I'm wearing an orange UM t-shirt."

"Good. I can't help you drink Mai Tais with some of the most dental-averse people in Miami Dade County, but I can help you in other ways," he said.

"I think I'm okay," I replied.

"Keep me posted and check in."

The line went dead as he hung up the phone. I drove back home and essentially repeated the same routine as yesterday. I texted the surveillance units that I'd be in place by 5:30pm. There was no use in having them and a helicopter standing by for hours if I wasn't going to be there.

Filling an insulated thermos with ice and water, I went down to the swimming pool. Someone had left behind a purple inflatable float behind. Opportunity and desire collided. I languidly floated in the pool, dozing off and on, waking only when the jets pushed me against the ladder in the deep end. Occasionally I took some pulls from the thermos to hydrate and have a fluid reserve in me to ward off the libations I'd be indulging in later on. The hours meandered away and I went home to change back into my jeans and orange University of Miami t-shirt.

I drove deep south for the second day in a row, same routine as the day before. After I pulled into the parking lot, I stood near the back of the Land Cruiser to allow any new surveillance units to see me before I went inside Sam's Hideaway Tavern. I found an open bar stool. Trevor was tending bar again. He immediately strutted over to me.

"Dude! Back for more pain?" he laughed.

"Let's start the pain session with a cheeseburger and fries," I said.

"Something to wash it all down with?" he said as he jotted down my order on a little pad of paper.

I looked around the bar and saw that there were only six other people in the place. I laid $300 down.

"I'll start with a Heineken and buy a round for everyone else on me."

There was the clang of a bell from behind the bar and the small number of drinkers gave a collective cheer. Within the next hour I ate a very good cheeseburger, met a guy named Ligore who told me he'd once been on the Canadian national chess team, had a grizzled old guy firmly declare to me that the annual Ernest Hemingway contest in Key West was rigged, and I managed to lose a twenty dollar bet in a game of billiards to Ediberto the sales manager for the Largo Honda car dealership. I went back to the bar and ordered a second Heineken.

"Did you lose to Ediberto?" asked Trevor as he served the second beer to me.

"Yeah. He says he works at the Largo Honda dealership."

"Largo Honda may say they have no sharks in their advertisements, but that guy is a definite pool shark. Forget the dealership. With him, he's a stealership," said Trevor.

Losing a game of pool to a car dealership manager was not a big deal for me. Victors like to talk. Losers slink away. I needed to forge relationships as often and as quickly as possible. I kept the drinks coming for everyone around me. I repeated the same plan as the day before. Whoever sat in the bar stool beside me became my new drinking *compadre*. It was nearing 10:00 and the place was full of sweaty drinking people. There were seven guys in the place, all wearing some sort of pseudo motorcycle club vests. The large crest on the back of their vests had flaming falling dominoes in the center. The top rocker said *Near Saints,* And the bottom rocker said *Near Sinners, Miami, FLA.* They sported doo rags, grimy jeans, motorcycle boots, and any other regalia they could adorn to look as similarly different from each other as possible. They were definitely not one-percenters. I think if an actual Outlaw or Pagan biker stepped into the bar these guys would crap in their pretense pants.

The place was packed. It was becoming too crowded. People were jostling against me and each other.

It would be very easy for someone to shove a fish filet knife right into my ribs.

I needed to get away from the deep crowd of people. I got Trevor's attention, closed out my tab leaving the fifty-dollar balance as a tip for him and made it to the front door where I stood just outside, letting the vapor streetlight over the door cast me in a soft tangerine glow.

I walked to the Land Cruiser and picked up my cellphone to check for messages or missed calls. There was a voice message from Addison. I texted the code for ending tonight's surveillance to the group leader before calling Addison back. Within minutes I once again saw headlights turn on in the neighboring gas station and small businesses. The detectives in those cars, all anxious to get home, wasted no time in pulling out and heading north. The parking lot at Sam's Tavern was full of cars but there was no one else outside except me. I dialed Addison's number. It was nearly 10:15pm. She answered on the second ring.

"It took you long enough to call me back."

"Addison, I told you I would be busy into the night."

"Pass. I'll give you a pass on this one," she said.

"How about I just pass on this altogether and you can try and call me in the morning?" I said.

"No. Don't. I'm just frustrated. I went out to the East 11th Avenue choke point, the one with the gate. Remember?"

"Yes. I remember. It's at East 11th and East 47th Street in far eastern Hialeah."

"Guess what?"

She seemed to have a penchant for saying that a lot. I didn't know if that was a southern thing or her way of speaking. I did know I was tired. I rubbed my eyes. "I don't know, Addison. What?"

"The pass-through gate to the train tracks. It has a huge padlock on it."

"Okay," I said, a little perplexed.

"The gate is locked but the gate hinges have no pins in them! People are accessing the train tracks by lifting the gate up and then putting it back on the hinges. Anybody just giving it a quick look would think the gate is locked."

"Could be anything, Addison. Kids playing in the trainyards, workers seeking a shortcut to another bus line, or yes, even hobos hitching the rails."

"It could also be cocaine smugglers putting it on trains to Philadelphia! The *same* smugglers who killed Dan. I think we should meet again."

"I don't think we should meet again, Addison."

"Yes we should!" she demanded.

"Not tomorrow. I have a lot going on. I'll meet you Friday at Wagon's West again for breakfast. Let's give it a rest for a day. Like we discussed, see if you can find anything about small aircraft flights last Sunday morning. There could be more than one load of cocaine. We might have missed one. I'm working with my boss and a guy in our office trying to gather as much information as we can. Give me a day and we can sort it all out."

"Cade, I think you're freezing me out. You're giving me busy work to do."

"No, Addison. I'm not, but we are hitting a lull. Just hang in there. Okay? Good night," I said as I hung up.

I sat in the Land Cruiser, contemplating my next course of action. The music from inside Sam's Hideaway faintly followed me as I sat there thinking. I reclined the seat a little. I tried to clear my head of my dive-bombing wandering thoughts, and tilted the rear view mirror to afford me an unobstructed view behind the car while I was reclined. I blinked to make sure my eyes were not playing tricks on me.

Tucked into one of the darker spots in the parking lot was a maroon Oldsmobile Bravada.

Chapter Twenty-Eight

THE SURVEILLANCE AND backup units had already been cut loose. It had been at least ten minutes since I watched the last headlight fade northbound into the night. I was between a rock and a hard place. If I called the units back it would easily take twenty minutes, and I'd get some very disgruntled detectives, all because I was suspicious of a maroon Oldsmobile Bravada.

At least on the periphery, I needed to play this one on my own.

I retrieved my gun from under the car seat. I stuck it in my waistband at the small of my back and pulled the orange shirt down to fully conceal the gun. I was perturbed to be wearing such a bright color, but if there was to be a return of the police units I needed to be in the color of the day.

I exited the Land Cruiser and cautiously walked a widening arch around the Oldsmobile. I approached the large SUV from the back. It had a Florida license plate.

NTA 36B.

I stepped further back towards US-1 and stayed out of the bright lights of the bar's parking lot as I dialed the Coral Gables police station.

"Coral Gables Police and Fire, Operator J.R. Richards, how can I direct your call?"

"Jeanie Rae, this is Cade Taylor."

"Cade? Punch anybody today?"

"No, but I would have liked to. Jeanie Rae, can you run a tag for me please."

"What is it?" she asked.

"November Tango Alpha Thirty-Six Bravo."

I could hear papers rustling and the sound of her teletype machine spitting out information in the background.

"November Tango Alpha Thirty-Six Bravo, NTA-36B comes back not on file."

"Stay on the line. I'm going to try and get the VIN off the dashboard. Be ready to write it down."

I held my gun low along my thigh as I cautiously approached the Bravada from the rear. The car was empty. There was enough light cast from the bar's parking lot for me to read the vehicle identification number. Jeanie Rae wrote it down as fast as I could say it. She wanted to read it back to me but I'd already moved away from the car into the shadows of the parking lot. I waited on the line for her to come back to me with any information. It took her two minutes.

"Cade, you there?"

"Yes, I'm here."

The Oldsmobile is registered to Center City Investments, 4000 Locust Street, Philadelphia, Pennsylvania 19104. It should have a Pennsylvania tag on it. Alpha, X-Ray, Tango, Eighty-Eight, Forty-Two. AXT 8842. "

"Thank you, Jeanie Rae. Can you print that and forward it to Gary Fowler in VIN, Please?"

"Will do. Remember, no punching, Cade. Anger management helps," she said before she hung up.

I tucked my gun back into my waistband and climbed back into the Land Cruiser. I drove it across the street to Rick's Yellow Bait Shop, tucking the Toyota in behind the bait shop's pungent dumpster. Then I walked quickly back to the parking lot at Sam's Hideaway.

I wandered amongst the various cars, work trucks, and motor-cycles in the parking lot. My biggest interest was in the work trucks and the motorcycles. They usually carried some sort of tool, a screw-driver, secreted in the back of the truck or magnetically affixed to the underside of a bike. As luck would have it, I found exactly what I was looking for in the bed of a marine engine repair truck. Amongst the empty soda cans and rusty marine parts there was a discarded pair of rusty needle nose pliers.

Grabbing the pliers, I returned to the Bravada. I crouched down by the rear passenger tire and stuck the open prongs of the needle nose pliers into the tire valve stem, then clamped the pliers down. The end points latched onto the valve stem. I rotated the pliers counterclockwise, six revolutions until the valve stem pulled away. Air hissed from the tire as it deflated.

I went to the driver's side of the Bravada. Knees bent, my back straight against the SUV, I leaned my back against the rear quarter panel above the tire well. I gripped my hands up under the tire well and using all my leg strength I put my back into lifting the SUV up and down. Within a few lifts and drops of the SUV, the car's alarm started screeching. Simultaneously, the horn honked in a steady pattern as the headlights flashed.

I pulled my gun from its place behind my back and with gun in my hand, I jogged over to the front door of the bar. I opened the door with my left hand and held it in place as I stood outside against the exterior wall, hidden behind the open door. I could hear the patrons in the bar rumbling about the door being open and all the noise the Bravada was causing. Luckily for me, the Bravada was facing the front door. The flashing headlights lit the interior of the tavern up in beats. Trevor cut the music to the jukebox and loudly exclaimed that "Whoever owns that piece of shit, go out there and turn it off or I'll break the alarm myself."

Someone from inside the bar tugged on the door to close it. I released my hold but stayed pressed up against the wall. The Bravada's horn and alarm were still blaring along with the pulsing headlights when the bar door opened. A stocky man stepped out. He was holding a keyless entry remote in his hand. He walked towards the Bravada, pushing buttons and grumbling about the alarm. I left my secreted spot and walked briskly behind him. He was able to get the alarm silenced. Before he could turn back towards the bar I put my gun right up against the center of his back.

"This is my gun, and that is your spine. You even think about moving and you'll never give a standing ovation ever again. Any questions?" I grunted close up in his ear.

He instinctively put his hands in the air.

"Lower your hands by your sides," I said, pressing the muzzle of the gun firmer against his vertebrae.

He was genuinely scared. I could also tell that by his reticence he was a fighter. If given the chance he'd try to turn the tables on me. He was definitely the type to have made his bones.

This was probably a made man in the Ray Caruso crime family.

A sudden rise in volume of the music in the bar indicated someone had opened the door, probably to come outside right to the parking lot. "Walk to the car and don't turn around or I swear one of those drunk idiots in there will use you as alligator bait tonight." I nudged him with the gun to walk forward to the Bravada.

Within a few steps we were in the dark shadows of the parking lot, at the rear of the Bravada.

"Spread your legs, extend your arms wide across the bumper and put your forehead on the bumper," I commanded him.

I'd moved the Glock up to the base of his skull and pushed firmly to assist him in lowering his head to the bumper until he was splayed across the back of the Bravada. He wasn't a young man. In a few minutes it would become uncomfortable, but for now he was able to comply with my demand.

"Who are you? What do they call you?" I asked him.

"They call me lots of things but right now you can call me 'Deacon' 'cause I'm gonna prophesize your imminent death," he snarled at me.

I pressed the back of his leg hard against the bumper with the bottom of my foot and he collapsed onto one side in the gravel parking lot.

"Tell you the truth, I'm tired of standing," I said.

I sat on the rear bumper and put my feet on top of him, holding him down hard against the gravel as I rested my elbows on my knees. I kept the muzzle of the Glock pressed hard against his forehead. I immediately recognized him from the picture Trentlocke had showed us.

The man I was crushing my heels into was Alvize "the Blister" Palmisano.

"You know my friends don't think I'm all together up here," he said, alluding to his head.

I stuck the barrel of the Glock against his lips and forced the first inch of the barrel into his mouth.

"My friends think I'm fucking crazy," I replied. I pulled the Glock back just enough to expose his gum line. "You floss? You might have a little perio going on there. Now, why are you following me?"

"You're a dirty cop and you got something that belongs to us—"

"Ex-cop. As for insulting me in my prior occupation, well that seems less than fair. I don't have anything that belongs to you or whoever you work for. What I do have is a newfound entrepreneurial spirit. What I have is eighty kilos. I'll sell those eighty kilos to anyone, including the previous owners, for a flat $700,000. Cash! Now, I know they're worth a whole lot more, I don't have the time to piece it out. There were ninety kilos. The cops got five of them. I already off-loaded another five to a buyer who wants more. You want the other eighty? Then it's 700 cash by sundown day after tomorrow. I'm giving you *two* days. After that, me and the kilos are on the open market."

"You're bluffing," he said.

With my free hand I retrieved the swatch of red plastic wrapping from my pocket. I dangled it in front of his face. I could see the recognition register in his eyes. I then shoved the end piece of the plastic into his nostril.

"You ain't got no idea who you'se fucking with," he said bravely.

I leaned down, closer to him and hissed, "Let me tell you who I'm fucking with. I'm fucking with some sewer-level soldier in Ray Caruso's family. A guy who's so highly thought of that Ray Caruso has you out here in this beer bunker watching *me* while the rest of your so-called crew is drinking Cristal at the Forge on South Beach. Listen closely, you northeast piece of shit. You tell Ray Caruso and the rest of your greasy friends I am *not* to be fucked with. You make sure Emmanuel Servais gets the message too."

He blinked. "What do you know about Emmanuel Servais?" he said.

"I know you're scared shitless of the guy. I know that Macario Silva Higuera and Washington Sanchez are both dead and I know *you* are Alvize 'the Blister' Palmisano. That's right, Alvize. I know more than you might think I do."

I could see the surprise in his eyes. I pressed the gun deeper against his upper gums until they started to bleed. I ignored the little thrill I felt knowing that he was tasting his own blood with each swallow. I used my other hand to rifle through his clothes. Surprisingly he didn't have a gun on him.

"Good boy. No gun. As an ex-con you can't risk getting picked up on a weapons charge by the po-leece down here in Florida. Here me good. 700,000, here, in two days at 5pm, or I'm selling the eighty kilos."

I stood up, making sure to press my full weight into him as I did. I told him my cellphone number. I made him repeat it five times.

My blood was pumping faster than I expected. I didn't want to be *enjoying* this. I had to question for a second if this was the only thing I actually *did* enjoy anymore. "If I ever see you again and you don't have the 700,000 I'm going to put a bullet right through both your elbows and both knees. I'll leave you in the Everglades. We got things in there that they haven't even discovered yet. Now roll under your car and get up in there as far as you can before I change my mind," I said.

He rolled under the rear bumper and pressed himself up under the rear axle. The tire was flat. He wouldn't be driving anywhere soon.

I left him there, burrowed under his car. I jogged over to my car at the bait shop. I turned south on US-1 and did a heat run on Card Sound Road, going as far as the bar Alabama Jack's at the county line. I waited for an hour at Alabama Jack's before heading back north. Knowing that the Blister had been camped outside of Paradise Point waiting for me, I drove to Coral Gables where I parked on Alcazar Avenue. I retrieved my go bag from the rear of the Land Cruiser and checked into the Hotel St. Michel. I used some of the cash from the DEA to pay for the room.

The government is great at making everyone pay. Tonight the DEA would be paying for my slumber. If I'm fortunate enough to fall asleep. I thought to myself, how much have I paid? It feels like I have paid with the near loss of my life countless times, several in the past few days. I've also paid with my emotions which are deadened and stale. I have paid with my personal relationships of which the fact there were disturbingly few did not go unnoticed by me. When do I stop paying? Is paying with my sanity at this juncture, the final end point or will there be more dust ups in parking lots, more nefarious people, and yes even more shootings?

My mind was doing wildly divergent spins and flips as I tried to sort all the parcels of my life in the past few days. I tried to quell my mind and sleep. I needed to be in the office to brief Major Brunson, and figure out my next course of action.

Chapter Twenty-Nine

I WALKED INTO THE VIN office early the next morning, freshly showered, and wearing clean clothes. I intercepted Charlene as she was walking to Major Brunson's office.

"I'm going to need to see him as soon as I can," I told her.

"That doesn't mean he'll see you as soon as *he* can, but I will let him know," she said as she continued walking down the hall.

I cooled my heels waiting in the VIN office. Gary walked in and did a double take, surprised to see me in the office.

"Ileana's out today. She's taking the day off to rest her foot, said some woman stepped on it at Santa's Enchanted Forest. You ever been to that place?" he asked me as he sat down at his desk.

"Santa's Enchanted Forest? No."

"Every night people go out to Tropical Park and see animatronic Santa's. Easily 120,000 people, all in separate cars. I don't know about you, but I don't think the spirit of Christmas is a skinny Santa, scantily clad lady elves, and the aroma of churros frying. It just isn't the ideal version of the North Pole if you get my non-snow drift," he said.

"Bah humbug, Big G."

"I thought I'd have a peaceful day with Ileana out. Are you here to ruin my idealized version of peace and tranquility?"

"Well, I guess that depends. You have any luck with the political candidates?" I asked him.

"Funny you should ask. I'm supposed to be in Brunson's office in ten minutes to discuss it," he said.

"Care if I tag along?" I asked.

"It'll save me the trouble of telling it twice. Brunson might have a different opinion but I'm cool with it," he said as he started going through the postal mail and interagency mail on his desk.

"What's this Center City Investment in Philadelphia query?" he asked me, eyebrows furrowed.

"That came up last night. I was hoping you could help us go further with it and get some ownership information."

Gary smiled slyly.

"I had three political candidates that I thought warranted looking into. Now I think I'm down to one."

We walked down the hallway to Major Brunson's office. Charlene was behind her desk in the outer office. She immediately informed us that Major Brunson was with someone else. Before we could sit down, Major Brunson bellowed through the door, asking if Gary was present. She picked up the phone and answered him on the intercom, telling him I was there with Gary. He obviously opted to forego the phone and just yelled through the door again.

"Send them in."

Charlene looked at us as she put the receiver back in its cradle. She didn't even bother to tell us to go in. I led the way and Gary followed. When I opened the door it rubbed against the carpet. Major Brunson was sitting behind his desk. Phil Zammit was seated across from him.

"Cade, Gary come in. Gary, take the open chair. Cade, pull up a chair."

We sat in a row . I noticed the latest hot sauce on the credenza behind his desk.

Raging Lava Hot Sauce.

"Gary, with us is DEA Special Agent Phil Zammit. Agent Zammit is the regional supervisor of OPBAT, which is a combined partnership of the DEA, the Coast Guard, Customs and the Bahamas designed to fight drug smuggling to and from the Bahamas," said Brunson.

"Gary, nice to meet you. OPBAT is an acronym for our joint task force Operation: Bahamas, Turks. Our OPBAT Operations Center is in Nassau," clarified Zammit.

"Phil, Gary here is one of our best. Quite the fucking utility player. Very sensible and reliable."

"I think he just said I'm a Honda Civic," Gary said under his breath to me.

"Phil, we can talk freely in front of Gary. I asked Gary to give me a rundown on political candidates that are coming out of the gate quicker than the others so we can try and identify which candidate might be benefiting from the Ray Caruso crime family. Gary, what do you have?"

That's when I interrupted.

"Major, if I may, I'd like to go first. It might help Gary with his own information."

"Why not, Cade? It's your fucking meeting and your fucking office. Oh wait, hold on, it's the biggest office in the damn place! All *my* stuff is in it! Maybe this isn't your meeting and maybe, just *maybe* this isn't your office! Don't let any of those things get in the way of you hijacking a meeting that, if I recall, you were not penciled to be in. By all means, go ahead with your latest edition of Cade News."

I exhaled, reminding myself to keep my composure.

"I think the press conference worked. I had an encounter with the Blister Palmisano at Sam's Hideaway last night—"

"Why didn't the surveillance units report it?" asked Zammit.

"It happened after they were cut loose."

"What? You shut it down for the night and stayed behind? What the fuck is actually wrong with you, Cade? Every time I have hope for you some psychotic fucking twist causes my lower colon to spasm!" shrieked Brunson.

I looked at the hot sauce bottle behind him. In my head I seriously wondered if I was actually the reason for his lower colon spasms.

"I was leaving the parking lot when I saw a maroon Oldsmobile Bravada in the parking lot. It looked like the same Bravada we saw a few days ago at the end of my street—"

"Who's this *we* you're talking about?" asked Brunson.

"Me and Addison Hope."

"God*damn* it, Cade! Didn't we discuss keeping the NTSB out of this fucking thing?" shouted Brunson.

"Hear me out. There's a lot to say and I think you should hear it first. She actually didn't notice the Oldsmobile. I did. I saw it on Coral Reef Drive and then a few minutes later it was on Old Cutler Road. As for Addison Hope, she was able to bring some information to the investigation that we would have never made a connection to."

"Like what?' he shrieked with his face reddening in anger.

"The markings on the kilos. I showed her a Polaroid of one of the kilograms and she deduced the odd rectangle marking on it signified a train. There's an actual code in symbols and pictures used by hobos who ride the trains. She knows how to interpret the signs. She then correlated the small municipal airports in Miami Dade and Broward counties and their distance relation to the FEC railroad tracks. Did you know that because of certain gate crossings and switching tracks there are choke points where the trains slow, and sometimes completely stop, after they leave the rail yard? Well, she discovered that there's a highball express, a 'cannonball run' is what they call it. She discovered that there is a highball express cannonball run that leaves Miami for Philadelphia every Sunday." I said leaning forward in my chair tapping my finger on his desk with every point I expounded on.

"Cade, get your greasy fingers off my desk. Do you know what I think? I think you've let this damn NTSB investigator's struts and flaps get to your head. I think you're compromising yourself and everything me and Phil are trying to accomplish here. Hobos? Really? Fucking *hobos*? Do you think Ray Caruso and his thugs are hobos?"

"No, of course not. They're smart enough to use a conveyance we haven't seen before and use the language and symbolism of that conveyance to move product from Miami to Philadelphia."

"*Conveyance*? What kind of shit talk is that? Just say what it is. It's a fucking *train*. A goddamn choo-choo!" he barked.

I began to feel exasperated. I took a deep breath. I needed to tell my side of the investigation in ways that would convince Major Brunson and Phil Zammit to listen.

Words are important.

"Addison Hope is an investigator with the NTSB. Her back door portals are completely different than ours, to information that we may not have. The Ray Caruso mob definitely knows that I'm holding eighty kilograms of their cocaine. They think I sold five of them. They are not happy. They also think I've separated from the police department. They think I'm looking to sell the eighty kilos so I can take the money and run. They're also aware that I know about Macario Santos Higuera, and Washington Sanchez no longer being among the living. I let it be known that I'm aware of Emmanuel Servais. They're a little confused. The Blister doesn't know I heard their conversation at the rock pit, I used a lot of what they said to make them think I know more than I do. I think they bought it. Especially when I showed the Blister the red wrapping from the kilos—"

"You showed him the red wrapping from the kilos? How?" asked Zammit.

"Before the kilos were impounded I cut off a small swatch of the plastic. I thought I might need it in the future for credibility, and I was right. As for showing him… Well, I actually didn't *show* as much as shove it to him. I wedged it into his nose."

From the corner of my eye I saw Gary slump in his chair. He knew there would be an onslaught of profanity from Major Brunson.

The Major's words were oral missiles and Gary wanted them to fly over his head rather than get hit with the venomous tirade.

"Cade, that doesn't explain a fucking reason why you're in the shit with the NTSB and we have this stinking shit all over us!" he yelled.

"Yes it does. The NTSB oversees railways as well as aviation. She's versed in the running of trains and knows the decades-long symbolism of hobos. She interpreted that the kilos are being put on a train. The night drop that killed Dan Stallings was early in the morning on Saturday. The freight train to Philadelphia leaves on Sunday. The Caruso family wants to get the cocaine and move the kilos as fast as they can. Sunday is approaching and they know I have their cocaine. They also know that I'm looking to sell it back to them at a price that still gives them a decent profit. They'll want to get this done before Sunday night."

"While you were shoving plastic up his nose, what price did you negotiate?" asked Brunson.

"An even flat $700,000. It's low enough to still give them a profit margin and a figure they can put together in forty-eight hours. I gave them until 5pm tomorrow to make the deal work."

"We'll need to get people in place down south." Zammit said to Brunson.

"They won't want to be south. They were only down there because either they picked up the cues from the press conference, or they'd been following me. Addison Hope pinpointed that there's a choke point in northeast Hialeah at East 11th Avenue and East 47th Street. They'll want to do the exchange somewhere in north Miami Dade. We already have the Blister on drug trafficking; anything extra is just that. Extra. We need to find out who Emmanuel Servais is. We know nothing about him or Ray Caruso," I said.

"How are they supposed to contact you to set up this meet?" asked Zammit.

"I gave the Blister my cell number. I have the battery out of the phone right now."

"Now why the fuck would you do that?" asked Brunson.

"They knew where I was before the press conference. Before they knew for sure I had their cocaine. They obviously want this cocaine badly. They were going to hit the ground running looking for it. I pulled the battery because I have no idea what extent they'll go to find me. Not only do they think I've separated from the police department but they think I'm a dirty cop. To them I'm one rung up on the ladder of disgust from pedophiles. I'll put the battery back in when I'm away from the police department. I'll see if I have missed calls or if they call."

There was a lull in the conversation. Gary cleared his throat and we all turned our attention to him.

"Major," Gary said, "you asked me to look at both the Democratic and Republican parties for any presidential candidates that may be outpacing the competition. I had my eye on three candidates but after talking with Cade this morning I'm looking primarily at one candidate."

"Who's that?" asked Brunson.

"The maroon Oldsmobile Bravada that Cade saw last night is actually a vehicle registered in Pennsylvania. It had a bogus Florida tag on it but it belongs to an investment firm in Philadelphia called Center City Investment. There is a Republican candidate in New Mexico who in a *Time Magazine* article last year boasted about his college-age daughter getting a summer internship at Center City Investment. She was the first female intern in the firm's history. The Republican is Senator Neil Garner Elbin. His daughter Felicity Elbin was the intern. Neal Garner Elbin's home district is in the Las Cruces area of New Mexico. There's money there. Where he's ruffled feathers is that he has made references to Las Cruces being a smaller upscale version of Las Vegas. The people of New Mexico said a hard no to that and he was forced to sign a bill that there would be a moratorium on casinos and card rooms in New Mexico," said Gary.

Both Zammit and Brunson looked at each other.

"Gary, do you think that having an agreeable disposition to

casino gambling could be a hindrance to a candidate vying for the presidency?" asked Zammit.

"I was a finance major in college, not a political science major, but I'd venture it is probably one of those *not in my backyard* things," Gary said.

"So where is this Neil Garner Elbin in the polls?' asked Brunson.

"Nobody has officially announced their candidacy yet. He isn't pulling away so much as it seems he has solid financial backing allowing him to travel and meet people and businesses more than anyone else this early in the race," said Gary.

I sat there listening. I think both Zammit and Brunson were thinking the same thing as I was. Ray Caruso money was paying for all of Senator Elbin's travels. It was then that I remembered what Addison Hope had said to me.

"Tail number SG N29. Cessna 402."

I'd asked her who owned it.

"An LLC in New Mexico. Ever try to get ownership from the state of New Mexico? Good luck. New Mexico is the only state that requires no names of LLC owners to be on file anywhere. We have no idea where the airplane is now, who flew it, who flies it, or who actually owns it."

"The airplane that Dan Stallings was pushed out of was registered to an LLC in New Mexico. It's a Cessna 402. Addison Hope tracked it to a small airport in Big Whale Cay in the Bahamas," I said.

Zammit took immediate interest.

"I'll call our operations center and get a Bahamian chopper in the air to Big Whale Cay within the hour."

"Who owns the LLC?" asked Brunson.

"Major, I can tell you from my finance background that New Mexico LLCs are nearly impossible to find ownership records. They don't register the officer's names with the state in New Mexico," said Gary.

"Then Satan said, 'put the alphabet in math.'" said Brunson.

"Major, I'm sorry, what?" asked Gary.

"It's a fucking expression, Gary. An expression for when something is hard and somehow it gets harder," Brunson replied.

I felt I should try and say something to get us all back on track and focused.

"The way I see it is, we have their cocaine. The very same cocaine the Ray Caruso crime family wants to sell to prop up their candidate Senator Neil Garner Elbin. They want Elbin to get in the White House so that they can get 1600 Pennsylvania's support on building casinos in eastern Pennsylvania. They don't intend to finance his whole campaign, just give him enough money to get him moving before big PAC inquiries and financial disclosures become an issue. Before the media spotlight shines too harshly they want to get Senator Elbin out in front of the others. I think the best thing to do is start taking out the stacked blocks we know about."

"What are you thinking?" asked Zammit.

I licked my dry lips, leaned forward, I inwardly noticed that I was getting excited about my own plan. I parked that realization for later and plowed right in with my ideas.

"Phil, I'm thinking with your OPBAT team and with Addison Hope's help, we retain and hold the Cessna 402 in the Bahamas. We notify Llyod Trentlocke that we may have the airplane Dan Stallings was thrown from. We get Trentlocke to put an additional hold on the airplane for Miami Dade Homicide. We pile on. We cause the LLC to spin. So we take at least one airplane out of the potential fleet, but more importantly we send a message that we are *onto* the LLC in New Mexico," I blurted.

"Damn Taylor maybe there is more to you than constant fucking aggravation. I like it. Let's Elmer Fudd this bastard," said Brunson.

"Elmer Fudd? Major, you watch Elmer Fudd?" asked Gary.

"Gary, you nimrod, I got fucking grandkids. Elmer Fudd it. You know how Elmer Fudd sticks his shotgun in every hole to flush out Bugs Bunny? Let's flush them out of every hole."

Zammit had a big smile on his face. "We have a southwest asset forfeiture group in Santa Fe. I will call their chief and get a team to start sniffing around the good Senator's holdings and finances. Another shotgun in the hole so to speak."

Brunson said, "What about the Center City Investment group? Gary, can you check for officers and any holdings or investments they may be in? We'll do the same with the Philly bastards. Rattle them, shake them up. I want New Mexico, the Bahamas, and Pennsylvania to have no idea where it is all coming from. Let's get the Ray Caruso syndicate looking at everyone and everything sideways."

"Sounds good," I said.

"Cade, when these shitbird mobsters call, you accelerate this exchange. Tell them you have another buyer who's cash ready. Make it clear you're in full off-load mode. If they've got to scramble to make the purchase it will cause *more* commotion. Another shotgun in another hole. Let's tilt these fuckers on their axis," said Brunson.

"What about Trentlocke? Won't he be pissed?" I asked them.

"He's still busy with those homicides. Besides, we're now moving towards a full drug and money investigation now. Brad Mitchell called this morning. He's on his way to Washington DC to assist with the funeral ceremony for his fallen agent. We're doing this with the DEA. Everyone has their marching orders. Cade, if the Blister calls you get this $700,000 deal to go today! Make it happen today. Keep them jumping. As soon as you know it's going I need to fucking know. Let's meet back here in two hours," said Brunson.

***

TRAFFIC WAS BACKED up south on Lejeune Road as I approached Cartagena Circle. Growling internally and feeling agitated with the Blister and the delay in hearing from him, I made a split decision to turn east on Ridgewood Road. I continued east until I was at the end of the intersection of South Prospect Drive and Pullen Ave. It was very quiet and secluded. If anyone connected to Ray Caruso was tracking my phone, I wanted to be close as to Biscayne Bay. If they pinged my phone the location would show me being in the bay instead of on land.

Being very removed from the vicinity of the police station, I felt comfortable slipping the battery into my cellphone. I'd missed three calls from Addison Hope.

"Cade Taylor, you keep ducking me like an ex-boyfriend in a supermarket," was how she answered my call.

"I'll keep going down the aisles I think you won't be in."

"Very funny."

"I recall saying I'd meet with you on Friday at Wagon's West," I said.

"Yeah, but I needed to tell you, the cannonball that runs to Philly on Sunday is still a go, but there's a *second* train that goes tonight at 8pm. It has only one stop, in Baltimore."

"Hey, I want to ask you about Washington DC—"

It was at that moment that another call was trying to come in on my cellphone.

"Addison, I'll call you back, I have to take this call," I said as I switched from her to the incoming caller.

"Hello?"

"Is this the scum rat bastard that's been selling off our hard-earned squares of happiness?"

I immediately recognized the Blister's voice from our little impromptu meeting last night.

"I told you I have eighty left. The other buyer who wants what I have left is a lot nicer than you," I said.

"I'm not here to be nice. Nice guys are nice. I'm not one of those. I'm more of a nice *enough* guy but only when I need to be. Youse don't understand—I ain't gotta be nice to you."

I recalled the tact that Major Brunson wanted me to take.

"Cade, when these shitbird mobsters call, you accelerate this

exchange. Tell them you've got another buyer who's cash ready. Make it clear you're in full off-load mode."

Cause more commotion.

Another shotgun in another hole.

"Let's tilt these fuckers on their axis."

I opted to punt. I hung up on him. If Major Brunson knew I just hung up on the designated frontman for the Ray Caruso crime family I swear he'd have a coronary. My phone rang again within twenty seconds.

"Did youse just hang up on me? Do you have any idea—"

Click.

I did it again. This time it took a good minute before he called me back. When the phone rang, I made my intentions known from the onset.

"Listen, you wayward psycho. You talk to me again like I'm some sort of street monkey, you can hang whatever deal you *think* we have on your dick. I got a west coast connection that wants in. When they want in, that means you're out. The only way to keep them from being in is for you to be in first. See how that works? It's like one of those revolving door things you freezing nut sacks use in Philadelphia. Get in before they do, or you're out. Now if you so much as disrespect me one more time on this telephone, I'm west coast-bound and down. Now speak. Speak!"

He paused for just a second. "I think we's got off on the wrong foot here—" he started to say.

"The only foot we got here is mine heading west if you don't say in or out. You're wasting my time, Alvize."

"Yo, yo, yo, take it easy there. No using names on the phone. It ain't no secret, we ain't very copacetic but that don't mean we can't help each other out here. We's looking to alleviate you of any potential disruptions you might be having, ya know with the time difference and all on the west coast."

"I'm listening," I said.

"We's proposing $620,000. Ya know, for the aggravation we's incurred on account of us not having ready access to our merchandise."

"Hear me out. It's $700,00 for my time and energy to haul your merchandise out of that rock pit. I had to dry it and walk away from a municipal pension. It's 700 and be grateful I don't tack on storage and transportation."

"*Grateful*? Oh, you can believe me you, we's really grateful. So grateful that we's gonna handle the transportation. You just have to deliver. Tonight!" he barked into the phone.

"Tonight? If you want it tonight it'll be $720,000. I need the extra for a car wash and gas."

"No can do, we's got margins to cover and—"

Click.

Major Brunson would definitely be in full-on cardiac arrest if he knew I just hung up on the Blister over $20,000.

I put the car in gear and pulled away from the idyllic corner of Pullen Avenue and South Prospect Drive. I retraced my drive on Ridgewood and my phone rang just as I neared Maya Street. I turned onto San Vicente Street and pulled over adjacent to the homes that comprise the Dutch South African Village of Coral Gables.

"Hello."

"Yous gotta stop hanging up. It ain't good for your health. You want 720—"

"It's about to be 740 if you don't get it right this time," I said.

"How's about you and me get more friendly? Let's settle at $710,000. Whattya say? We get what we's want and you don't have to worry 'bout no granola-eating west coast dirty hippies."

"They aren't hippies and they aren't dirty. Never let it be said I'm not reasonable. I was reasonable letting you live last night, wasn't I? By the way, you get your tire fixed?"

"Yeah it was the damndest thing, the valve stem was pulled out. Can you imagine, a perfectly good tire with a valve stem problem? Not like the old days, I tell ya. You could get a tire and use it as mold for cement. Makes a pretty good sinker in the Delaware River. I miss those days. Maybe they'll come back soon, huh? Wouldn't that be something?" he said.

"I'm sure. Well, I have, as you say, the squares of happiness."

"I got 710,000 baseball trading cards. Let's meet tonight, I'll trade cards for happiness," he said.

"Sounds good to me," I conceded.

"I'll tell ya how we's gonna do it…"

Chapter Thirty

WHEN I CALLED Major Brunson and told him of the plans laid out by the Blister, all the other meetings for the day were scuttled. We went into full-go mode. The Blister set an exchange of money for the cocaine to be at 9pm.

That meant a certain amount of scrambling and confusion on our side.

"If they have to scramble to make the purchase it will cause more commotion..."

When Major Brunson said that I wish he would have been more specific about exactly who would be experiencing more commotion. Putting this deal together with a time limit looming was distressing. The Caruso family only had to show up with $700,000. We had to confer with a continual series of lawyers and U.S. attorneys about the removal of the eighty kilograms from our property room. At one point as myself, Brunson, Zammit and other DEA agents sat in on a conference call with yet another assistant U.S. attorney, droned on, Major Brunson slipped me a note. An excerpt from a William Shakespeare play.

Henry the 6th, part 2, Act 4, Scene 2

"The first thing we do, let's kill all the lawyers." ~ Dick the Butcher

I was actually shocked that he knew this excerpt. I couldn't mask my total surprise. From his seat behind his desk he formed a square in the air with his index fingers and mouthed the words to me *"biggest fucking office."*

The plan was becoming more operational. We were able to get permission to release twenty kilograms from our property room. We'd fill the rest of the satchels with sham kilograms of cocaine. The AUSA was concerned about us losing the entire eighty kilograms. Quite frankly, I think the DEA was concerned too.

Agent Zammit provided four thick Hefty bags. We put fifteen fake kilograms with five real kilograms of cocaine in each bag then loaded them into the back of my Land Cruiser.

The Blister wanted to do the exchange on the East 49th Street bridge that spanned the railroad tracks. The bridge is the border line between the City of Hialeah and Northwest Miami Dade County. The numbering system changes from East 49th Street to Northwest 103rd Street in the middle of the bridge. The DEA did a quick scouting of the area. They determined that the Blister wouldn't throw the satchels over the bridge to a railroad car because of the high concertina wire fencing in place on either side of the bridge. The Blister said he would stage a car accident on the span of the bridge. The Blister instructed me to be there exactly at 9pm. I was told to drive with the kilos eastbound to the top of the bridge, the phony car crash would be facing west . There was a three-foot concrete divider between east and westbound traffic. Under the pretense of aiding their staged accident, I'd stop abreast of them. His guys would take the kilograms out of my car, put the cash in my car and we'd all be on our way in opposite directions. The whole exchange should take place in less than a minute.

Our plan was rudimentary. The DEA would be in place in various stages along the route. They arranged to have four marked Florida Highway Patrol cars with us. Two of them would be covertly parked a few blocks west in Hialeah; the other two would be parked east in Miami Dade County. Miami Dade Aviation would have a helicopter at the ready at nearby Opa Locka Airport. Llyod Trentlocke was able to get us ten officers from their TNT team. The TNT detectives would be staged in two-person teams around the meet location.

The DEA and TNT were confident that the kilos would never make it off of the bridge.

Their concentrated efforts were on the bridge and the road. If anything was to go wrong I was instructed to get down between the Land Cruiser and the raised concrete median. They'd have a visual on me the whole time. If necessary, the takedown word would be "west." If I said any sentence with the word "west" in it, the takedown teams would descend upon us.

While the kilograms were being assembled and sorted a large order of food was brought in from the nearby Canton Chinese restaurant. I tried to eat, but I was too tense. Years before I'd read an article about the contents of someone's stomach causing sepsis when that person suffered an abdominal gunshot wound. I nibbled on Chinese noodles and slowly slurped wonton soup.

The DEA agents and the TNT detectives suited up in raid jackets and tactical vests. At 7:30pm we left the police station. The agents and detectives drove to eastern Hialeah and bordering Miami Dade County to their assigned positions. I stood by while Agent Zammit and Major Brunson loaded the kilos into the back of the Land Cruiser. They put two suitcases we'd removed from the property room in behind the kilos. The suitcases were filled with telephone books, intended to slow the removal of the kilograms from the car.

Not to mention that a hand that holds a suitcase is a hand that can't hold a gun.

Brunson looked at me intently when he filled me in on the logistics. "Cade, we're going to go up to North Dade in a formation. Two Florida Highway Patrol cars in front, then you, then the other two FHP cars. I'll be in the lead FHP car; Phil will be in the one in the rear. We're going to keep it tight. Don't let anyone get between us. We're taking the Palmetto Expressway north. We'll pull over and all split up when we get close."

I was surprised Major Brunson was going out with us on this

operation. He got into the passenger seat of the lead FHP car. In formation, we all drove north on the Palmetto Expressway and exited at West 49th Street. Driving in Hialeah was an exercise in the most optimum semblance of social Darwinism, except it surely seemed that everyone behind the wheel of a car was an idiot. We pulled into the parking lot of Hialeah High School. Agent Zammit and two of the FHP cars hung back. As 9pm drew closer they would move closer to the bridge.

Major Brunson and the trooper exited their car and came over to me in the Land Cruiser.

"Cade, let's do our best to make this go as smoothly as it can. Safety doesn't happen by accident. If it breaks into a shitstorm, think of yourself as the third monkey on the gangplank to Noah's Ark, and it's starting to rain. You fight like a motherfucker. Don't worry about *nothing*. Either put people in a trauma center or center trauma on them," Brunson said gruffly, close to my face.

It seemed my late change in temperament wasn't entirely terrible in Brunson's eyes. I hadn't thought of it as self-preservation before then.

I was left, sitting alone with twenty kilograms of cocaine in my car, hoping a curious Hialeah patrol officer wouldn't show up and delay me. I tried to visualize the meeting and I prayed for a safe outcome.

The clock on the car's dashboard said 8:53pm.

I put the car in drive and eased into the eastbound Hialeah traffic. My biggest delay would be if I got stuck at a red light at East 8th Avenue. As I approached the intersection, the light was green.

8:57pm. Although still a few blocks away, the bridge ahead of me was visible. I could see the sequential arch and rise in the streetlights in the dark sky. I instinctively rolled down the driver's side window. The glass wouldn't stop a bullet. If I was fired upon, I didn't need shattered glass flying into my eyes.

I slowed down to look up at the top of the bridge. In the westbound lane against the center median it looked like a minor fender bender had just taken place. A light metallic blue Mitsubishi Montero looked like it had been rear-ended by a silver Volvo 940. I neared cautiously and slowed to a stop beside the two cars. Two men stood between the Montero and the wall. They watched me closely as I drove past at a crawl. Fifteen yards east of the "accident" was Alvize "the Blister" Palmisano, holding a canvas athletic bag. One of the two men loudly told me to stop when the rear cargo compartment of the Land Cruiser was even with the rear compartment of the Montero. The Blister stood motionless yards from the front of my car as one of the men shouted at me again.

"Open the back!"

I pretended to not hear him and asked him to repeat what he'd just said. Before he could answer, a man who'd been crouched down between the Montero and the three foot high concrete median wall sprung up and leveled a sawed-off shotgun right at me face.

"Turn the car off! Open the back and raise your hands slowly, asshole, or you're fucking dead!"

The only thing between us was the dividing concrete wall. The barrels of the shotgun were pointed right at my head. It would be a definite kill shot if he pulled the trigger. He was sweating. He also exuded the determination and competency of someone who had done this before. The gun looked like an enormous cannon to me.

My eyes must've been big as saucers. I was terrified. The kilos, the money, the Blister, none of it mattered at that moment. My only thought was to stay alive and do exactly what they said.

I raised my left hand, and with a silent head nod conveyed that I was turning the car off with my right hand. I turned the car off and in doing so, dropped the keys on the floor by my feet. If they chose to steal my car I wanted to delay the chance of them getting away quickly.

Fear raced through my veins like liquid electricity. I was feeling jittery, and queasy. I tried to keep the man with the shotgun as calm as I could so that he wouldn't intentionally or accidentally turn my head into pink mist. I knew enough to give the verbal takedown signal.

Please let the Kel be working.

"This ain't the Wild West. You don't need to shoot me like we're in a Wild West movie," I stammered.

"Keep your hands up! Open the door from the outside. Get the fuck out *now!*" he shouted at me.

The other two guys had jumped the retaining wall. I did as he demanded. The Blister was smiling. I heard the rear cargo door of my SUV being opened. The two guys would probably grab the suitcases first.

I couldn't risk them finding the telephone books and think they were being ripped off. I needed to tell them the cocaine was in the Hefty bags. I was talking as I opened the car door exactly as I was instructed to. The gun looked even bigger to me as I started to step and out of the Toyota.

"Don't shoot. The coke's in the garbage bags. The suitcases are for my brother out west. Don't shoot. The coke's in the garbage bags."

They threw the two suitcases to the side against the concrete barrier. One landed upright, the other one pitched over and stopped at an angle against the wall and the rear tire. I started to step out of the car, keeping my hands up. I needed the shotgun-wielding gangster to see I wasn't a threat. He switched the shotgun to his right hand and cradled it in the crook of his arm as he straddled the wall, steadying himself with his left hand. He kept the shotgun pointed at me.

He intended to come onto my side of the bridge.

As his left foot touched the ground, he briefly wavered. The shotgun turned momentarily away from me.

I seized the moment.

I swung the car door open as forcefully as I could, smashing it into his shin and knee with a sickening *crunch*. He hollered in pain. I yanked the door back and then thrust it forward again, hard and as quick as I could.

I slammed his leg between the door and the wall four times. The force shattered his tibia, fibula, and kneecap. He bent over, screaming obscenities and howling in agony. He fell back to the ground on his side of the wall. The shotgun went with him as he slipped out of my sight.

Blue lights tore up the bridge from both directions.

I stepped to the wall to see that the shotgun was still in his hands as he writhed on the ground. He tried to aim it at me.

"If it breaks into a shitstorm think of yourself as the third monkey on the gangplank to Noah's Ark, and it's starting to rain. You fight like a motherfucker. Don't worry about nothing. Either put people in a trauma center or center trauma on them."

I whipped my Glock out from behind my back and shot him twice in the torso. He went rigid briefly, and then went completely limp.

It looked like a swarm of blue fireflies were winging in from both sides of the bridge. The two men at the rear of my car started running west down the bridge. One of them tried to cut back across to the west side of the wall but a Dodge Stratus driven by one of the Miami Dade TNT detectives clipped him. He tried to run diagonally towards the safety of the sidewalk that awaited him across the two lanes of traffic and flipped up, bouncing across the hood of the TNT detective's car. His body crashed down. He smashed against the windshield before tumbling off of the Dodge. He hit the ground with a solid *thud*. He wasn't moving. Blood trickled from his ears and nose.

The detective slammed on his brakes. The car had skidded to a stop with the rear tires running over the dead man's left arm. The other off loader from the back of the Land Cruiser was near the bottom of the bridge. He was on his knees with his hands on his head. A DEA agent and a different TNT detective had him at gunpoint.

Everything happened in a poof of mere seconds. I turned to the right to see Palmisano. He was still on my side of the bridge. He still held the bag. With his free hand he had reached into his waistband and pulled out a shiny, chrome-plated handgun.

I dove over the strewn suitcases on my left as he fired three shots at me. One round struck the Montero's hood. The second round caromed off the wall and whistled past me as I hit the unforgiving asphalt. Roadway grit rubbed against me like sandpaper.

The third round penetrated clean and clear through the first suitcase which exploded into cloth and paper particles that drifted up and floated above me. The bullet went through two of the suitcase's thick telephone books and came out the backside, lodging in the second suitcase, failing to penetrate the jumbled phone books inside.

I'd barely taken a breath when I peeked up to see him running west along the sidewalk towards the bottom of the bridge in the direction of East 10th Avenue. I took off after him. A sea of blue lights and loud sirens were approaching me from both directions.

Palmisano saw the police converging towards him. He had an alternate plan already devised. He knew there was a cut-through in the concertina wire near the bottom of the bridge.

He threw himself into the jagged fence opening with the force of a college linebacker trying to make a goal line stand. The fencing made a jangling noise as he fell headlong through the serrated opening, catching his shirt, until he tore himself away, nearly ripping the garment from his arm. He hit a grassy berm with the grace of a wounded elephant before rolling head over heels down the dry, dirty incline.

There was an abrupt twelve-foot drop down to where East 11th Avenue dead ends.

I continued running after "The Blister." When I got to the opening the fence was still wavering from Palmisano barreling through it. I eased through it with substantially less personal injury than he surely did and slid down the grass-mottled, rock-strewn embankment.

At the concrete lip twelve feet above the street I lay down on the edge. I hung my left side over the ledge and spider-dropped onto the ground. I caught a glimpse of him as he ran down East 11th Avenue. I heard the loud *screech* of train brakes being released as the FEC train was starting to pull away from the choke point where

East 11th Avenue and East 47th Street converged. It would take the train some time to make noticeable movement, but the fact that the process started was not good. The train would increase its speed and momentum exponentially as more rail cars began rolling. Palmisano could hop on any one of those cars and hop off somewhere else. He would vanish into the night. East 11th Avenue was dimly lit, only two streetlights on the entire street. Their light was highly compromised by the awnings, overhangs, fencing, and buildings. The businesses were all in a tight row on both sides of the street ringed with litter. If there was ever a street that in South Florida represented a lack of urban planning mixed with shoddy code enforcement and filthy industrial commerce stacked upon itself than East 11th Avenue is it. At night the street looks eerily Dystopian. It was nearly devoid of any vegetation. Dumpsters and overflowing garbage cans jut into the roadway. Numerous junked and cannibalized automobiles were haphazardly parked upon any available piece of the avenue. Dingy, dented garage doors were shuttered tight with chains, locks, burglar bars, and cables. Wind-torn banners hung, nearly unreadable, from bent fences and rusty porticos. Each business had their name emblazoned in worn flaking paint across the rooflines of their unkept, faded, sun-scorched building facades. Wooden pallets, corroded forklifts, and random stacks of tires seemed to hold up some of the businesses.

Palmisano kept running. The bag was slowing him considerably but he gamely carried on. He was battered from the fall to the avenue from the embankment, his gait visibly anguished but determined. I kept him in sight, all the while holding back enough paces because I was wary of him stopping and taking more shots at me. With each step I mentally calculated which piece of debris or machinery I could duck behind if he started shooting at me. I realized quickly that this overly industrialized block was longer than we both initially calculated.

He turned the corner towards the railyard at East 47th Street.

Not one DEA agent or TNT detective at the intersection. Not one.

I'd *told* Brunson and Zammit that Addison Hope had scoped the intersection and noted it as a gateway for the Caruso criminals to use as a transport location for the cocaine. I'd told them. Then again, they hadn't want to listen to anything Hope had to say. Or myself, apparently. All those meetings, and crucial information goes ignored.

And now, unbeknownst to many of us including myself, East 11th Avenue and the next street over were not through avenues. I could hear the sirens but the agents didn't know how to get to where Palmisano was running.

Why hadn't they listened to me?

As I approached the corner I had to be cautious. I stayed on the east side, my gun held out in front of me as I neared the corner. I used my phone to dial 911. Immediately a Miami Dade police dispatcher answered. I told her who I was, that I was in front of a business in a white building with 4707 in black letters next to the raised front door and a small set of steps,, and I told her to send units my way. I hung up as soon as I could.

I glanced around the corner with my gun ready to fire. Sweat soaked my shirt. I could feel my own pulse pounding in my neck and chest.

The building across the very narrow stretch of East 47th Street was dark gray and would afford me better concealment than the white building I was leaning against. I made the decision to dash across the street and put myself against it. To my left, the train rolled very slowly out of the railyard. The gate that Addison told me about was pushed wide open, hanging precariously on one hinge. Parked in the short spit of paved street that lead to the fence and gate to the yard were trucks from a neighboring drywall business. I used the trucks as cover and concealment as I weaved between their large chassis. The train was now moving at what I would consider to be a quick walk.

Palmisano could be anywhere in the rail yard. This wasn't boding very well for me. He certainly heard the sirens approaching too. I surmised he might look to get on the first car he could before the train was stopped by authorities, K-9 dogs were called, or a large contingency of officers showed up. Even if he rode the rail car only 1500 yards he could get off and escape unseen.

Time was critical.

I made the choice to enter the rail yard and take a chance on guessing which car he may be in—or even worse, on top of.

The sirens were getting closer. I heard the reverberating *thump thump thump* of the Miami Dade helicopter which must have lifted off from its staging spot at Opa Locka Airport.

It was now winging towards me.

The helicopter's search light illuminated the fetid puddles and grease-stained ground around me, its bright halogen light locked on me as the spotter in the helicopter found me.

I kept flashing my hand three times, showing all five fingers.

Fifteen

Fifteen

Fifteen

I continued signaling the airborne craft in police code that I was a cop. Even as I moved into the railyard looking for Palmisano I kept my left arm raised, all five fingers opening and closing in three beats. Eventually they understood who I was. They widened the illumination of their light off of me and focused the intense light onto the rail yard.

The train was gaining speed. Palmisano was likely in one of the cars ahead of me. If he was on top of a rail car the helicopter would spot him. There were five tanker cars hitched in a row but it was unlikely he'd be in one of those—but there *was* a pale brown CSX open box car in front of the tankers.

I started jogging towards the CSX rail car. I passed the first tanker car. The entire train was pulling away from me. I needed to be faster.

I was able to catch up to the fourth tanker car. The train's speed was now equal to my own running pace.

I was getting tired.

The train was gaining momentum. I was getting slower. The train was getting faster. The helicopter was arcing across the night sky, its spotlight splaying across the section of train I was alongside.

I decided to take a chance. I chose the open CSX box car as Palmisano's possible hiding place. I was twenty-five yards away when I shot a three-round burst into the moving open rail car.

The bullets zinged and ricocheted within the corrugated metal interior. My bullets created a Major Brunson Elmer Fudd effect. Palmisano jumped out of the car like a cockroach fleeing an aerosol insecticide. The fall appeared to aggravate his recent injuries even more. He collapsed on the ground right near the rails, trying to gather his wits about him. I transitioned my shooting position from the rolling CSX box car to him. I had my gun trained on him. My Glock was held firm in my hands. I had my dominant eye on the front sights of the weapon pointed at him.

"Don't you fucking move!" I yelled.

It was at that moment that the Miami Dade helicopter had swung around to our side of the train. Its search light houses a colossal 1600 watt bulb. All of its 30,000 torch-lumens made daylight of our position.

I wasn't anticipating the flash of brightness. It briefly blinded me. Somehow in the moment of my temporary blindness, Palmisano managed to scamper away. He rolled under the moving train to the other side of the increasingly quick-moving train.

If I pursued him, if I miscalculated my own attempt I'd be obliterated by the train. He could also be on the other side of the train waiting to shoot me.

The train was picking up speed. It was a very long train full of box cars, container rail cars, flat rail cars, and tanker cars. I chose to start running in the opposite direction of the moving train. I ran south as the train rolled north. I saw a flat open train car and I used the attached three-step ladder to get up onto the flat car. No sooner was I on it than I hopped off onto Palmisano's side of the tracks. The noise of the train and the sound of the helicopter banking in the western sky created a deafening crescendo of noise. I crept along the moving train trying to blend in against the rail cars, keeping my gun in front of me, ready to shoot.

Within forty yards of walking alongside the train I saw Palmisano. He was crouched down with his gun in his hand, intently watching under the train wheels, looking for me to emerge. When an open box car rambled by him he'd raise up from his crouch and point his gun into the open void of the box car. When it passed he'd crouch down again, looking for me to emerge from under the moving wheels. He fully intended to shoot me on sight.

Approaching him was treacherous. The tracks were built upon gravel, shards of granite, slag, discarded pieces of metal, bolts, screws, railroad spikes, clips of wire, chipped wood, and an occasional dented soda can or broken bottle mixed in. It was all loose under my feet as I slipped and fumbled closer to him. Pieces of frayed lumber and bits of iron that had been removed or broken off of trains were carelessly discarded along the tracks. The debris rubbed against my ankles as I closed in on him while he intently searched for me in the dark. All of a sudden he had a survivalist epiphany. He looked to his left and saw me.

He was very quick. He fired two rounds at me, I could see the muzzle flash from his gun. The squeaking of the train on the tracks was loud but the gunshots were ear-splitting. My first instinct was to move to my left and I hit the side of the momentum-building train. The force of the moving boxcar bounced me ten feet to my right, knocking the wind out of me. It hurt like hell and opened a gash behind my left ear. Blood quickly seeped out of the wound and started soaking my shirt. I thought I'd been shot, the sticky dark blood pumping out of me slowly, throbbing. I tried to reason what had happened; my ears were ringing; my mind was cloudy. I was woozy. The entire left side of my body hurt. I tried to get up and fortunately for me, I was unable to do so. It would have made me an even easier target for him.

He fired three more rounds at me as I struggled to my feet. The rounds crunched into the gravel at my feet and changed trajectory in all sorts of directions around me.

The helicopter came around the southern side of me. Palmisano must have seen the blood pouring from my head; he charged at me with the gun in his hand. I was easy prey to him. Somewhere in being blindsided by the train I lost my grip on my Glock. I had no idea where it was. I tried to make myself as small as I could, pressing myself into the pitted, rock-strewn ground. I crawled across the stones to get even closer to the moving train. The industrial smell of metal shavings, iron, warped wood, and the rocks themselves filled my nostrils.

He stood over me and pressed the muzzle of his gun against the back of my head.

"This is my gun, and that is your brain stem. You even *think* about moving and youse'll never give a standing ovation ever again. Any questions?" he said, mocking me. "Youse recall saying that to me you dirty fucking pig. How's it feel now? You rat fucking fink piece of shit. I swears to God If I find out youse killed any of my guys… I'm gonna shoot you in the kneecaps and throw you under this fucking train. It ain't the Everglades but it'll be the same for you like youse swore youse was gonna do to me," he spat.

My arm was tucked under my body. He pressed the gun against my head hard. I needed to think of something fast.

I grunted a lie.

"My gun is pressed against my balls,"

He wanted my gun. He knelt down on top of me, digging his knee hard into my back, gun pressed against my head.

"Pull your arm out slowly."

"I can't, you're pressing my hand and gun even more into my balls," I gasped.

He eased off my back but still stood over me. The train was now running four feet away from us at a very good clip and I thought the helicopter had lost sight of me. It was overhead but shining its light hundreds of yards away. The sirens were still wailing, but it was meaningless to him. He knew they were all lost and they had no idea where either of us were.

"Roll on ya side, slow."

I squirmed as I painfully lifted a few inches off the ground and turned onto my right side. He leaned down over me, baring his teeth, holding the gun inches from me. The space beneath me became more exposed. He intently looked for my gun.

"You ain't got no gun," he laughed.

Amongst all the debris, I'd landed on a railroad spike—and concealed it in my hand. He was three feet above me. My back on the ground, I hurled the spike with as much force as I could muster and caught him just above his eyebrow.

Stunned, he staggard backwards. Blood gushed from his forehead. He must have been seeing stars from the impact of the solid iron against his skull. I kicked him as hard as I could in the knee cap. He screamed in pain. He crashed onto his back still holding onto his gun. We were now both prone on the ground, laying in opposite directions.

Partially on my side, I whipped a bunch of pebbles at him. I spun on my side, onto my stomach and awkwardly leapt on top of him, concentrating all my strength on his gun hand. I laid diagonally across him with both hands wrapped around his right wrist. I banged his hand against the ground multiple times, but he held steadfastly onto the gun. With his other hand he threw rabbit punches at the back of my head. One of his punches hit the gash behind my ear and it hurt so bad I thought I was going to vomit. I caught him twice under the chin with elbow uppercuts. He was tough. He still firmly held the gun. I wanted to eject the magazine from the weapon but I couldn't risk releasing my grip on his wrist.

"You fight like a motherfucker. Don't worry about nothing. Put people either in a trauma center or center trauma on them."

I sank my teeth hard into his right shoulder until I felt thick muscle grind between my teeth. He screamed loud obscenities. He went berserk with adrenaline-spiked strength. He lifted himself and me a few inches off of the ground.

That was the advantage I needed.

I slammed his hand down harder from the briefly elevated height, and he released his grip on the gun. I grabbed it and rolled off of him to my left. I was still practically astride him when I fired one round that bore into him under his right armpit.

The fight immediately went out of him. He ceased moving. I pushed away from him.

He was still alive. His breathing was heavily labored. Trying to catch my own breath, I checked him for an exit wound. There was none. The bullet had torn into him and lodged somewhere in his chest.

He struggled to focus. I watched him. His gaze was unsteady and his eyelids fluttered. Blood pulsed from his mouth frothy with lots of air bubbles in it. He was aspirating and drowning in his own blood. Surprisingly, he had enough air in him to say a few finals words.

"Youse dead. Emmanuel Servais is gonna kill you."

Chapter Thirty-One

I T WAS 4:30 AM and I was still in the rail yard.

I was sitting at a command post comprised of tents, generators, tables, and chairs. TNT agents, DEA agents, Miami Dade paramedics and nearly everybody who was on duty in the northside district of the Miami Dade Police Department were there. The paramedics said I might have a slight concussion. I always thought that was a lame term for *it looks kind of serious but he isn't showing any effects from the injury, so instead of saying he might be slightly fine, let's say he has a slight concussion.*

Major Brunson had been sitting with me the past hour. He ran interference with Lieutenant Maddalone who'd arrived an hour ago to take possession of my Glock. It took a K-9 unit and its handler nearly thirty minutes to find my Glock. When I brushed against the rolling train the weapon must have bounced underneath it onto the rails. I never would have been able to retrieve the handgun even had I known where it was. It was scratched but still functional.

My entire left side ached like one enormous bruise. The paramedics wrapped cool packs across my bare torso with ace bandages to help reduce swelling. Half of the attending paramedics advocated me going to a hospital to be checked out. The other half were from the "you're tough you can stick this out" theory of medicine. It was Brunson who demanded I go to Doctor's Hospital to have X-rays taken.

A Miami Dade team of homicide investigators was having a lengthy quiet conversation with Agent Zammit off in the corner of one of the tents. The DEA supervisor was supporting that my shooting of the shotgun-wielding gangster and the death of the other gangster from the TNT agent's car on the bridge were all under the purveyance of the DEA. He staunchly defended his position that my killing Alvize "the Blister" Palmisano was an ancillary part of the entire investigation. It was an argument he was losing—especially since the TNT officer behind the wheel of the Dodge Stratus was a Miami Dade detective.

Major Brunson eventually intervened. He pulled Phil Zammit over to where I was sitting.

"Phil, they're going to do the investigation. It doesn't matter. They'll make recommendations based on their findings and we can read them, file them , or shit-can them. What do we care?"

Reluctantly Zammit shook his head in agreement. Phil relayed to me and Brunson that they had Palmisano's bag. There was only $80,000 in it. The rest was paper stacks with real one hundred dollar bills showing on top. It was a "Jamaican Roll."

"Three dead. All criminals. Over what? Us scamming them with fake kilograms and them scamming us with fake money," said Zammit.

Brunson said, "This is a dirty business. Figuratively, and tonight, literally. Look around you. Cade is fucking filthy. I feel dirty. The whole place is black dust and goddamn rusty air."

I was way beyond tired. I more than ached all over and I just wanted to go home. I was confident that days earlier the Blister was parked down the road from my place. If Palmisano had known exactly where I lived, he would have been in my condominium complex. He'd been fishing, hoping to see me. He probably was going out of his pea-sized Philadelphia brain looking at all the passing cars. The way life had been going for the Blister he would eventually have had to atone to Emmanuel Servais. That atonement would have most likely led to Palmisano's demise. The way I saw it I just did Emmanuel Servais a big favor by killing Palmisano. I wasn't worried about what he said about Emmanuel Servais killing me. I wasn't worried about him knowing where I lived.

Zammit said to me, "Cade, one of my agents will give you a ride to Doctor's Hospital in your car. Another agent will follow you. The Land Cruiser door is a little dinged. It was part of the shooting investigation. They just released it since you didn't shoot from it. They went all through it looking for any prescription pills, illegal drugs, or alcohol."

"Did they find any?" I asked, deadpan.

"What?" shrieked Brunson

"It doesn't hurt to ask?" I joked.

"If you check out okay at Doctor's Hospital, then go home," said Brunson as he handed me my car keys.

I thanked him for the keys. We all sat together, either talking or pretending to talk to keep everyone else away. Ten minutes later two young DEA agents walked up and Zammit said, "Your ride is here."

I said to Brunson, "Major, Gary's looking up some things for me. Can please make sure his cellphone is on today?"

"Go home, Cade."

"I'm just saying, can he be available, even after hours?"

"If you're asking about the goddamn overtime, yes. I'll sign the papers but don't you be calling *anybody*. You need to be in the hospital recovering, or home recovering. I'll check in with you later. Now go the fuck home, Cade!"

The ride south to Doctor's Hospital was quiet. The streets were devoid of traffic and we made very good time. One agent went inside with me while the other agent parked my car. The DEA agent who accompanied me spoke to the ER nurse who seemed to have an infatuation with his tiny badge. I say tiny only because the Coral Gables police badge is large compared to most agencies. The attending emergency room doctor commended the paramedics on the job they'd done treating me. He said the wound behind my ear "could use a stitch or two, or I can butterfly it. You might have a scar." I opted for the butterfly bandage. The X-rays came back negative for fractures but the doctor talked a lot about something he called "*soft tissue damage.*" He reiterated that I'd be sore for a few days and to expect some stiffness, advising against any exercise or high-action activity for at least ten days. He sent me home with a bottle of maximum strength Ibuprofen.

"Come back if you need anything. As an ER doctor I never see follow ups normally. Usually I just treat em' and street em.'"

To my surprise, the DEA agent waited for me. I actually think it had more to do with the nurse whose telephone number he was able to obtain. He drove me around the parking lot as we looked for my car. On the second level of the parking garage, we found the Land Cruiser.

"This must be the end of the road. Thank you," I said as I gingerly exited the agent's car.

I stood outside the Land Cruiser until he drove off. I didn't want him to see me wince and gasp as I tried to slide myself behind the wheel. I got into the SUV with deliberate and painful movements. The contents of the car were still primarily intact. Miami Dade homicide investigators didn't disrupt the interior too much. I gave it a quick perusal. The tire iron was still in the backseat. I made a mental note to secure it later in the trunk space. The exterior of the Land Cruiser was a mess. The car was covered with fingerprint dust and adhesive splotches from tape, especially the driver's side door. I took the back way around the hospital and University of Miami on San Amaro Drive out to Red Road. At the Mobil station at Red Road and US-1 I purchased a car wash. It hurt like hell to lean out the open driver's window and press the numbers on the car wash keypad, but it was necessary. I emerged with a clean car, wishing the same could be said about me.

I pulled up to the opulent condominium in Paradise Point. I went inside. I felt like a foreigner in my own home. My clothes were grimy and caked with dirt, grass stains, rust streaks, and black marks. I smelled really bad. I caught a glimpse of myself in the hallway mirror; I looked like a coal miner who'd gone to war. As I stripped in the laundry room, I debated throwing my clothes in the washing machine or throwing the clothes in the trash.

I decided that I wanted as few remembrances of the night as I could. My memories would haunt me enough. I didn't need to relive them each time I saw the shirt or pants from tonight. I took them off and put them in a separate garbage bag. I absent-mindedly tied the garbage bag into a knot.

Thirteen times.

Thirteen knots.

My mind was not in a good place. I was *weepy*. I found my breath was laboriously halting, like I was about to sob. Blinking like crazy, felt my face crumpling and my eyes watering. I was tentative to even move about the unit. It felt safe not moving. God, I needed to rest.

I also needed a drink.

Some armchair psychologists would correct me and say I didn't *need* a drink, I *wanted* a drink. I wanted to tell the armchair psychologists that they needed to shut up. Until they firsthand watched people die, especially die from their own hand, they might want to keep their opinions to themselves. I'd *need* them to do that as much as *want* them to do that.

I shuffled to the standup bar, reached into a cabinet with a groan and gave myself a two finger pour of Jameson in a rocks glass. I downed it quickly because I felt I *needed* it and I *wanted* a second one quickly. I had the bottle in one hand and the second pour in my other hand. I was clad only in my underwear. Again catching a glimpse of myself in the mirror, I let out the sob I'd been harboring.

My appearance was startling. It reminded me of a picture I once saw when I was traveling through North Carolina, on the sports page of *The Winston Salem Journal*. They printed a picture of the University of North Carolina at Greensboro men's lacrosse goalkeeper. He was in his underwear. He'd made seventeen saves in a college game, and he had seventeen discernable bruises everywhere the ball had struck him. I felt the same way. My injuries were visible, raw, red, swollen, and ugly. I felt just as ugly on the inside.

I took the bottle of Jameson, the rocks glass and my cellphone upstairs with me. Every step felt like climbing a mountain, every movement a fight. *Everything is a fight.* I took full advantage of the multi-headed shower. Sitting on the marble bench in the shower, I let the water pour over me. I must have been in the shower for forty-five minutes. No measure of water or soap could make me feel clean. I felt dirty in my soul, I wanted to scrub myself from the inside out. From the shower window I saw the sun breaking over the calm water of Biscayne Bay. I turned off the shower. I didn't bother with the directions on the Ibuprofen bottle, I just tossed back four of them. I knew enough to stop drinking but I planned on sleeping anyway. I'd just eased into bed when my cellphone rang. I'd meant to turn it off.

It was Addison Hope. Stifling the feeling of rising tears again, I cradled the cellphone against my cheek.

"Hello," I said with my hand over my eyes.

"Good morning. I have a lot to show you at breakfast today, I'm on my way. Traffic is a heavy, so I may be a little late."

"Um, Addison I'm going to have to cancel."

"What? Why?"

"I'm feeling under the weather," I said hoarsely.

"Are you sick?"

"I feel like I got hit by a train."

"Hardly! Seriously, lets meet," she said.

I wanted to hang up and sleep in the worst way. Nothing seemed to matter except getting rest. Shutting down, shutting off.

"Let's push it back to dinner tonight..." I barely got out as I turned the cellphone off.

I WOKE UP with a groggy slow opening of my eyes. I didn't know what time it was but by the shadows on the wall, it was nearing sunset. My sleep had been deep but with very intense dreams. I didn't remember any of them. I hadn't moved in the bed hardly at all from when I conked out, shortly after saying goodbye to Addison. The cellphone was still inches from me on the bed. I tried moving. It was painful and very slow. When I'd finally gotten myself upright with both feet on the floor, I turned on my phone. I trudged into the shower again, nearly repeating the sequence exactly from earlier that morning. The message light on the cellphone blinked continuously as I showered.

After the shower, wrapped in a towel, I went out to the bedroom terrace and flopped into a chaise lounge. There were three messages from Addison, all of them inquiring about dinner. There were two messages from Gary. I called Gary back first.

"VIN," he answered the office phone.

"Ileana still out?" I asked him.

"Dude, you sound like you got wiped out in the pit," he said, reverting to his surfing lingo.

"Don't I know it."

"Ileana went home already. Major Brunson told me to stay a little longer in case you called back. I think the old man knows you better than you think. I'm making overtime watching *Jeopardy* on Ileana's TV."

"Thanks for hanging in there. Big G, what else do you know about this New Mexico senator?"

I heard him typing on his computer keyboard.

Within a few minutes he spoke.

"I bounced between the search engines of Yahoo, Dogpile, Northern Light, and Google. A lot of the information is redundant. They all point to the same articles and knowledge bases. Neil Garner Elbin went to the University of New Mexico. He got an undergrad degree in urban planning, and went on to get an MBA at New Mexico State University. That's where he met his wife, Cecilia. They have a son, Cody Elbin, thirteen years old. They have a daughter, Felicity

Elbin who's nineteen, she's studying finance at Drexel University. Elbin started his political career as a councilman in Deming, New Mexico. Four years later he was elected mayor, he was mayor for two years. He left his second term to run for state representative in district two, won by a large margin and after yet *another* four years he ran for state senator and won. Since being a senator he's staunchly defended the White Sands Missile Range, he's beefed up the New Mexico National Guard, and has sat on multiple defense committees, and foreign diplomatic committees."

"Foreign Diplomatic committees?" I asked him. "Do you think you can dig any deeper and see if Neil Garner Elbin made any visits to embassies, or appointed people to positions, I mean anything related to him and foreign diplomats."

"For the overtime, I'll do anything. Call me later," he said.

I called Addison Hope back.

"Cade Taylor, you're going to make the devil wish he never took you in," she said.

"Addison, what does that mean?"

"You're rude and I'm starving."

"How am I rude, I've been sleeping."

"Well, it was rude you didn't call me back. Whether you were sleeping or not. I am hungry and getting angry. That makes me *hangry*."

"Okay, Addison. I hear you. Where are you now?"

"I'm at Dadeland Mall. I just bought shoes."

I needed to think of something we could eat for dinner that would be near me and not hard on me getting in and out of the car. I didn't want to park in some far-off parking lot and walk dozens of yards to get to a restaurant.

Guadalajara Mexican restaurant had a small parking lot and quick access in and out.

"Do you like Mexican food?"

"Yes!" she said enthusiastically.

"Head south on US-1. There's a Shell gas station at SW 132nd Street. Turn onto 132nd and behind the gas station is a Mexican restaurant called Guadalajara. I'll meet you there. If you get there before me, get a table and order me the *El Zarape* with chicken."

"I most certainly will not. That is not a proper way to dine. I will wait for you," she said, agitation in her voice.

"Addison, I'm having a tricky day here, and it's Friday night. They get crowded. If you get there first just get a table. If you're so inclined, I already know what I'll be having. *El Zarape* with chicken please." I hung up.

It took me twenty minutes to put on a pair of jeans and a long sleeve black Henley shirt. Putting on shoes was an exercise in pain tolerance and determination. I grabbed my gun, badge, and cellphone then clambered slowly into the Land Cruiser. In the fading light of the day, I could see the dents and scratches on the car door. Ramon, the rental agency manager, was not going to be too pleased. I'm not entirely sure where dented cars fell on his list of enjoyable things but I was almost certain this would be way down on the bottom on the list.

I stepped into the restaurant and Addison had already secured a table near the front windows of the restaurant. There was a heaping basket of crispy tortilla chips and two ramekins of fresh salsa on the table, as well as two menus.

"Oh my God! What happened to you? You look like you got hit by a train!" she cried out in astonishment.

"I tried to tell you that," I said dismissively.

"You look terrible. Are you okay? What happened?"

"We had a late, rough night last night. Did you order the *El Zarape*?"

"I know what you said. Actually I thought you might change your mind so I held off on ordering," she said.

"Words are important," was all I could mutter before the waitress appeared at our table.

I ordered a Pacifico beer and the *El Zarape con pollo*. Addison ordered *Bistec Tejano*. The waitress took immediate pity on me. She came back with an ice cold Pacifico beer and a side plate with a cloth napkin that she'd soaked in ice water and wrung out. I wrapped my hand around the Pacifico and immediately knew I would be wanting a second beer. I motioned to the waitress with the bottle.

"Muchos Gracias, otrava por favor." [Thank you, another one please.]

"So what happened to you? It looks painful," she said as she leaned across the table.

"It is painful. Last night we were up in north Dade…" I started to say just as my cellphone started ringing. "Excuse me Addison I need to take this."

"Big G, any news?"

"I think you might want to stay by the phone. There's all kinds of stuff coming up."

"Like what?" I asked.

"Like our Senator friend from New Mexico two years ago had a bunch of Greenpeace-type people jeering his motorcade in Luxemburg. They were tying themselves together with cables and locks, blocking the road. When his motorcade was stopped they started breaking all the windows of the cars and tried to pull him out."

"What did they want with him?"

"His home district in New Mexico oversees the White Sands Missile Base. The protestors wanted all short range and long range missiles scrapped. From the article I'm reading it got pretty violent and dangerous for Senator Neil Garner Elbin of New Mexico."

"Okay…"

"So, check this out…he was rescued by long term resident D.S.S. Agent *Brad Mitchell* who led a team from the U.S. Embassy. They got the Senator and his advisors out of the crowd and into the safety of the embassy. Get this! The embassy is located at 22 Boulevard

Emmanuel Servais L-2535 Luxembourg City, Luxembourg. The boulevard of the embassy Brad Mitchell spent most of his time on is named *Emmanuel Servais!*"

Chapter Thirty-Two

"CALL BRUNSON. CALL him now! Tell him what you just told me. I'll be standing by."

I hung up the phone. Addison could see the change in my demeanor.

"What? What is it?" she asked me.

"Why aren't you in Washington D.C?" I asked her.

"Washington D.C? Why would I be there?"

"You tell me!" I angrily said back to her.

"I don't like your tone and I don't know what you are talking about." she retorted back.

"Who is the Regional Director of the Diplomatic Security Service Special Agent Division?"

"I have no idea." she said.

"When they called you into the Miami office and told you about Dan's death, who did you speak to?"

She was taken aback by my demeanor but she answered without hesitation.

"I thought that you and Detective Trentlocke had filed a complaint against me. With the news I got I would have taken a complaint over hearing Dan was dead any day. The Miami Regional

Director Dee Buchanan called me into her office. She was very kind. She offered me some tea, and then she very delicately told me about Dan's passing away. She was very kind."

"This Dee Buchanan, did she have anyone else with her?" I asked her.

"No. Why?"

"You didn't meet with Brad Mitchell?"

"Who is Brad Mitchell?"

I thought back to what Brad Mitchell said in our meeting before we went out to the warehouse where Macario Santos Higuera started shooting at Trentlocke and the DEA agent.

"In the meantime, our office is going to send a delegation to the NTSB to talk with Dan Stallings' ex-wife. She needs to know the entire State Department and myself are supporting her."

He worked with Dan. He was Dan's boss."

"I've never heard of him. Why do you keep asking me if I am going to Washington D.C?"

"Brad Mitchell told us yesterday he couldn't attend a briefing because '*he is on his way to Washington D.C to assist with the funeral ceremony for his fallen agent.*"

Our food arrived at the table.

"I haven't heard a word about a state funeral for Dan!"

"You said you had a lot to tell me. What did you find about aircraft flying in and out of South Florida last Sunday? I asked her.

"There were a lot of flights mostly going in and out of Pompano Beach airport, and Opa Locka airport. Tamiami airport had a few but they were related to flight schools."

Specifically Key West. Anything government or otherwise from Naval Air Station Key West?"

She looked over her notes.

"No. Nothing."

I recalled what Brad Mitchell said when we first met him.

"Good morning. I am Brad Mitchell. I am so sorry for being late I just flew in from Key West and there was a delay leaving. Please accept my apologies for being late. The agency and I are incredibly distressed over this whole situation. I met our jet at the Naval Air Station Key West. My driver got a little lost in Coral Gables and got us here as soon as he could."

My cellphone rang. It was Major Brunson.

"I just spoke to Gary. What are you thinking?" said Brunson.

"I think that Brad Mitchell has conveniently been unavailable every time we have set out to make a move on the Ray Caruso Crime family. I also think he sent Macario Santos Higuera out to the warehouse on Flagler Street. He set Macario up. Brad Mitchell had no idea we were going to be there until Trentlocke and you confirmed the address from the license tag. Remember what he said? *I'd like to get some of my people on that as well. This is a federal agent we suspect was pushed from an airplane.'* He left. He was a no show. None of his people were there." I said.

Brunson spoke next.

"I think he's a fucking worm. After what Gary told me it makes sense. Ray Caruso gets his boy Senator Neil Garner Elbin into the God damn White House and they fucking get their casinos in Pennsylvania. Where does that leave Brad Mitchell?" he asked me.

"He probably gets appointed to the United Nations, Secretary of something, who knows! Senator Elbin will definitely take care of him. Mitchell's been the go between for Ray Caruso and Senator Elbin the whole time. Diplomatic channels, encrypted communications, the whole black passport thing. His briefcase and suitcases never get searched. This guy's been playing us and killing off all the dead wood in the Caruso family that is interfering with their push for the White House. He was stationed in Luxemburg. The embassy address in Luxemburg is on Emmanuel Servais boulevard. He's been using that name as his alias." I said.

I looked at Addison across the table. She had stopped eating and was wide eyed when she heard the name Emmanuel Servais.

"I got a confirmation from Addison Hope at the NTSB. There were no flights Sunday morning from Naval Air Station Key West to Miami. Remember he said he had flown in and was late due to his driver? I'm calling Bullshit. He is in Miami and he has been in Miami this entire time. I suspect he killed Washington Sanchez too. Do you remember what Dan Stallings wrote to Addison Hope?" I said.

"Something about Watergate."

"Dan Stallings wrote it. He said it was 'Watergate big.' He said if anything ever happened to him to tell the authorities he was chasing a criminal named Emmanuel Servais. If anything ever happened to him the authorities need to find this guy Emmanuel Servais."

"Cade I got you and Phil. We can't depend on anyone else." he said.

"We also have Trentlocke and Addison Hope." I corrected him.

"I'll set up yet another fucking weekend morning meeting for tomorrow. Me, you, Phil, Trentlocke and bring Addison Hope too." he said.

The line went dead. Addison Hope stared at me looking for an explanation.

"Addison, Brad Mitchell was Dan's supervisor. He knew the inroads Dan was making in dismantling the cocaine smuggling ring. We think Macario Santos Higuera pushed Dan out of the airplane. We also think that Macario and a guy named Washington Sanchez were sent to retrieve kilograms of cocaine that were also kicked out of the very same airplane…"

"The Cessna 402 tail number SG N29?" she said.

"Yes the Cessna. The Cessna as you know is registered to an LLC in New Mexico. We aren't having any luck finding the true ownership but we have discovered that a New Mexico Senator named Neil Garner Elbin is contemplating running for President in 2000. He is doing some hand shaking, baby kissing, and meet and greets. The Ray Caruso family is looking to get casinos built in eastern Pennsylvania. We think that before the media and others start looking at campaign finances the Ray Caruso crew is propping

Senator Elbin up financially. They are hoping Senator Elbin can get out of the gate faster than the other candidates. Ray Caruso had a lieutenant named Alvize "The Blister" Palmisano. He oversaw the retrieval of the cocaine. We suspect thanks to you, that it was being put on trains out of South Florida for Philadelphia. Palmisano died last night."

I made an overt gesture indicating to Addison to look at me.

"I killed him in the trainyard last night."

"Oh my God!" she said in horror.

"So Brad Mitchell the D.S.S Regional Director and Dan's boss has a connection to the Senator and we think he has been acting as an intermediary between the Senator and the Ray Caruso Crime Syndicate. For all we know he may have set up Dan to be killed." I said.

She slumped back in her chair.

"My Major wants a meeting tomorrow morning. You wanted in? Well he has officially requested you be there at the meeting. You're officially in. He will call me back when he gets the meeting set up."

She looked at me.

"Don't you find it odd?" she asked.

I had wrapped the still chilled empty Pacifico beer bottle in the cold wet napkin. I was holding the cold empty bottle to the back of my neck. Removing it from my neck only to drink the second Pacifico.

"Find what odd?"

"The whole airplane thing. The Cessna 402. How is it that they got the kilograms into the target rock pit but Dan missed all of that mangrove and bramble. If he had been thrown out while the airplane was over the mangroves it may have taken months if ever to discover his body." she said.

"What are you saying Addison?"

"I'm saying that Dan may have fought or he may have been

pushed on the first shove but somehow flying in the dark the airplane needs to know where they are." she said.

"Don't they have those altimeters and things like that?" I asked her.

"It goes beyond that. It's a Cessna 402 coming in from the Bahamas. The aircraft has radar and instrument readings but they have no way of knowing which way the wind is blowing. That is why every airport has windsocks. It is seriously necessary if you're looking to drop bundles out of a moving airplane into a rectangular stretch of water. You have to know the direction of the wind." she said.

I hadn't really considered wind direction as being important. It made sense. I remember when the Miami Dade Police Helicopter pilot tried to bring me back to my car he had trouble with the wind. The kite surfers were loving it but it was concerning to the pilot. It now makes logical sense what the helicopter pilot said.

"*I can tell by the kite surfers that the winds have picked up and are switching back and forth.*" I heard him say through the headset.

"Addison if you don't have a windsock what is some of the better ways to tell which the way the wind is blowing?" I asked her.

"In many places that are remote they will light fires. Then the pilot can tell wind direction by how the smoke blows." she said.

I looked at her. She looked at me.

"Addison I smelt smoke when we first arrived on the scene."

I could smell the faint whiff of smoke and wondered if we were investigating a fire or arson.

"You smelt smoke?" she quizzed me.

"Didn't you?" I said.

"I don't remember I was too busy keeping Detective Trentlocke from smacking Lawson Dreyer."

"The street is tucked in off of Old Cutler Road. I even made a joke to one of the firemen about them not being able to find the street because they probably never get calls for service there."

Jokingly, I said to one of the firefighters "How'd you find your way here? I'm surprised you guys even know where this street is."

"We get called here all the time. That woman you were talking to always complains about her neighbor burning logs in an outdoor backyard firepit." said the firefighter.

"He actually told me they get called there often because of one of the neighbors, Teresita Esteban DeHoya. Everyone calls her Tessie, and she calls the fire department routinely because her neighbor Jason Cordicio keeps burning logs in an outdoor fire pit." I explained.

"Isn't he the same guy you sat down with at Wagon's West?" she asked.

"Yes. Come to think of it he said something peculiar when I sat down with him. It was peculiar because of the way he said it."

"What did he say?" she asked me.

He thanked me for meeting with him. Then he said, *'seeing you just made it all easier.'*

"What do you think that meant?" she asked me.

"I don't know. The man I killed last night in the trainyard. He was parked down the street from us when we left my place and we went to Starbucks. He had an idea where I lived but he didn't have the exact address. When we left Starbucks I saw him driving on Old Cutler Road."

"You didn't say anything to me?" she said.

"There is so much traffic for schools at that time I thought I was being paranoid, but I later saw him two nights ago in the same car." I said.

"Let me see if I got this straight. This guy Jason Cordicio might be lighting fires in a firepit to signal the dopers the wind direction so they can make their air drops. Your fire department has been called out previously because of the fires. Could he have told that guy where you live?" she asked.

"I don't think so. I saw the suspicious car the day before I met with him."

"Maybe the guy eyeballing you lost you and he called Jason Cordicio. Maybe he told Jason to set up a meet with you so he could start following you again." she said.

I downed the last remnants of the second Pacifico Beer. I mulled over what she had been saying to me. It made sense in its barest form but I couldn't figure how Jason Cordicio would know where I lived. I don't even own the place. "There is no record of me living in Paradise Point. Very few people know I live in the Royal Harbour Yacht Club." I said.

"Does Major Brunson know you live there?" she asked.

"I think so." I said.

"What about Trentlocke?"

"No, well at least not until recently. On the scene last Saturday he was giving me grief about the geography of the southern part of Miami Dade and Coral Gables. I mentioned my place to him…oh shit…no way!" I lamented.

"What?"

I sat their quiet and dumbstruck.

"What? What is it?"

I was talking to Trentlocke and Jason Cordicio walked up behind me. I think he heard what I was saying."

"I'm in the Royal Harbour Yacht Club, you know Paradise Point." I said.

"Excuse me detective is there anything you need from me? I'd like to check in on my wife." said Jason Cordicio who unbeknownst to me had walked up behind us.

Chapter Thirty-Three

ADDISON JUMPED INTO my car. I started driving us to Jason Cordicio's house at 601 Conde Avenue. The entire drive over I mulled over all of the things he'd told me that I had overlooked. His son Lucas attends Temple University. Temple is in Philadelphia. His daughter Lanie lives in Haddonfield, New Jersey, just outside of Philadelphia. I was fuming at my own stupidity. How could I have been so stupid? Addison could sense my self-loathing.

"You can't beat yourself up over this. Besides, there isn't much left of you to beat up. You couldn't have known that Jason Cordicio had a Philadelphia connection. When you met him we were all dealing with Dan's death scene. There's no way you could have put these things together," she tried to assure me.

I called Gary. I got his voicemail. I left a message:

"Big G. Hey, sorry to bother you again. Can you go into Dun & Brad Street financials and do a deeper look at Center City Investments in Philadelphia? I want to know if you see a guy named Jason Cordicio attached to them. When I met him he told me he did finance and mergers. He said he helps venture capitalists identify suitable acquisitions. Thanks. Call me back," I said.

I must have been really amped up. I was doing seventy miles an hour on Howard Drive as I approached Old Cutler Road, gripping the steering wheel until my knuckles turned white, my anger settling in.

"Cordicio set me up! Palmisano could have killed me if things had been just *slightly* different. It's going to be hard to prove that lighting fires is part of a drug trafficking conspiracy but I'll let the assistant United States Attorney worry about the charges. I'm taking this fucker to jail *tonight*. I'll charge him as a conspirator in Dan's death too," I said as I tore into Conde Avenue and pulled up in front of Cordicio's house. Given my injuries and soreness I stepped out as quickly as I could. Addison walked with me to the front door—and we both noticed the door had been severely damaged, and splintered from its door frame. I grabbed Addison by the arm and pulled her back from the door as I simultaneously reached for my cellphone. I walked Addison back to the car while I called the Coral Gables police dispatch. I requested uniform patrol cars to meet me at 601 Conde Avenue with regard to a possible break in. I told Addison to wait in the Toyota Land Cruiser until the police units arrived.

"You're just going to leave me here? Alone! Don't you have a backup gun or something you can give me?" she protested.

"No. Sit tight. The police are coming. There's a tire iron in the backseat if you think that will make you feel better. Now stay here." I closed the car door with her inside the Toyota.

I drew my Glock and walked up to the front door of the residence. I listened intently but heard nothing. I put my right foot against the bottom of the door and pushed it open slowly.

I slipped further into the opening with my gun leveled and ready. Each inch it opened I filled with my weapon at eye level ready to shoot. When the door was open wide enough to step inside I did a quick peek, then curled in around the door. Inside the door and using it as protection, I scanned the interior.

A struggle had certainly taken place. There was broken glass and an overturned chair near the front door. Books, papers, and family photos were strewn about the floor. I slowly stepped away from the door. A low watt nightlight in the hallway was all I had to see with as I moved deeper into the house.

Noises came from somewhere to my right.

I cautiously walked towards the noises. They amplified as I got closer. There was an end table lamp on in the living room. Moving through the living room I came to a doorway that led into the dining room. And looking into the dining room I could see Jason Cordicio.

He was tied to a chair. Gagged with a gold napkin tied tight across his mouth. He'd been beaten. Welts and bruises covered his face. He was wet from sweat. His entire face was flushed in crimson red from exertion.

He looked as though he'd struggled bravely but was now tired and beaten. He was nearly unconscious. That's when I heard the voice.

"Jason. Jason! Look, don't you want to see your wife? Come on, she's going to put on a show for us. It's called the hot curling iron hokey pokey."

I was able to sidestep in the semi-darkness and see through the doorway a woman I assumed to be Jason's wife, Lucille Amanda. She too was tied to a chair. She didn't have the same signs of being beaten like Jason but she was definitely being terrified.

I caught a glimpse of Brad Mitchell when he moved across the front of her to plug the curling iron into the wall socket.

"Jason, it's going to be great." He started to ghoulishly sing, "You put the curling iron in, you pull the curling iron out. You roll it over your eyes and you shake it all about. Come on, Jason sing along with me..." teased Mitchell.

Where *are the police units and* what *is taking them so long?* I wondered.

I needed to get into a better position to take Brad Mitchell out if I could. I maneuvered a few inches to my right—and stepped on some broken glass. It was enough noise for Brad Mitchell to take notice. He dropped the curling iron and immediately pulled out a Sig Sauer pistol.

"Who's there. Who the fuck is there?" he screamed.

I put my sore left shoulder against the door jamb and pointed my Glock right at him. I now had a better look inside the dining room. The place was a mess and Brad Mitchell was crouched way low behind sweaty terrified Lucille Amanda, holding the gun to her head.

"Cops are on their way. Everyone knows about you, Mitchell. They know about Macario Santos Higuera and Washington Sanchez. It's over. Give it up."

"Fuck you, Taylor. You're bluffing. You took out the Blister. No jury is going to believe anything like you think they will. My attorneys will show that the Blister killed everyone. I'll take you and this piece of shit Cordicio out and we're all back in business again. So long as we don't hurt daddy's little girl, right honey?" he said, shoving the gun harder against Lucille Amanda's head.

I slid a little further into the doorway. Amanda Lucille was now crying hysterically. The gag in her mouth strained to contain her sobs.

I spat at him, "You ratted your own agent out. You got no future, Mitchell. Give it up before you just hurt more people you don't have to."

"Taylor, I'm going to take great pleasure in killing you. You and that DEA cowboy Zammit got in the way of some real good planning. How do you think this will end? Huh? How are you going to survive after you get Ray Caruso's daughter killed? How's that going to end for you, Taylor?"

Lucille Amanda Caruso.

In the distance, the sirens began. They were still far away but they were coming. I could see in Mitchell's eyes that he heard them, too.

"This only ends one way, Mitchell. With me standing over your pine box."

No sooner had I said those words when I spied Addison Hope stealthily approaching behind Mitchell. She raised the tire iron high in the air and came crashing down with it on the back of his skull. Mitchell immediately blacked out. He crumbled to the floor, dropping his gun and his grip on Lucille Amanda. He was knocked out cold. Lucille Amanda was trembling with a mixture of fear and relief. The sirens were very close now. In the dining room now, I put my foot on Mitchell's gun, securing the weapon. I looked at Addison who was looking down at Mitchell. She still had the blood-speckled tire iron in her hand. She looked at me. Then she quietly spoke.

"I soon reach."

Chapter Thirty-Four

FOUR DAYS LATER, and I'd been granted much necessary time off from work. I was finally starting to move with minimal pain and discomfort.

It took five hours for Brad Mitchell to become conscious at Jackson Memorial Hospital. Addison Hope really thumped him with that tire iron. The attending doctors were concerned about brain swelling but that had all passed. He was conscious and talking... and talking he most certainly was. He'd been talking to the State Department and to the DEA.

Two days ago, without any discernible reason, New Mexico Senator Neil Garner Elbin held a press conference from Taos, New Mexico. He said the needs of his family come first and he would not be running for President of the United States in 2000. He said, "Any conjecture I was intending to run was just that: conjecture. After exploring the sentiment of the country and seeing firsthand the rigors of a political campaign for the highest office in the world, I have decided to step away from the race for the Presidency and focus on my health, family, and home state. The great state of New Mexico!"

I spoke to Addison Hope on the phone yesterday. She was flying out to Washington DC to address any questions the NTSB might have. She would also be going to Prosperity, South Carolina to attend Dan Stallings' funeral. She spoke of Dan in very endearing terms.

"Now I'll have to live with the fact that I'll remember him longer than I knew him."

I needed palm trees and eighty degrees. I booked a few days at Tranquility Bay in Marathon Key. I figured between the resort and Burdines, one of my favorite bars, I could find the physical and mental recovery I needed. I'd always felt that the lower the latitude the better my attitude. I packed a medium size bag of shirts, underwear, bathing suits, and shorts. I threw on a t shirt, a pair of jeans and tucked my hair behind my ears under a dark blue Hartford Whalers baseball cap. I wasn't ready to go through the hassle of swapping out the car yet. Ramon from the car rental wouldn't be in any hurry to get a dented car that he couldn't rent.

I loaded up the Land Cruiser. The morning light was breaking across Biscayne Bay. As I started driving out of the Royal Harbour Yacht Club I could see the school traffic was building. It would be like this all the way down to US-1. I decided to take the Don Shula Expressway to the Florida Turnpike which would drop me a few hundred yards from Sam's Hideaway. I made a note to myself to not even think about stopping in on my way back from the Florida Keys. This was going to be Cade time.

I zig-zagged my way through Pinecrest working my way to the entrance ramp for the Don Shula.

My phone rang. It was the police station.

"Hello."

"Cade, it's Scott Rainer."

"Hey Scott, I've been meaning to call you. I'm sorry I lost my cool and hit you. That was uncalled for, and I apologize."

"Thank you, Cade. I'm glad we're square, but that's not why I'm calling. A woman who lives down south called today. I thought you'd be interested."

"Okay, who was it?"

"A resident. Her name is Teresita Esteban DeHoya. She lives at 600 Conde, right across from 601 Conde Avenue. She called Code Enforcement first and they forwarded it to us. It was probably a good ninety-minute delay. There was a moving truck at 601 Conde Avenue the same house you were at days ago—"

"Yes, yes, I know. Go on," I said anxiously.

"I guess the truck had been there in the middle of the night—in clear violation of our ordinances, she repeatedly reminded our units. Between the code enforcement delay and with our patrol units in shift change, by the time we got a unit there the place was cleared out and the moving truck was gone. By the way, uniform patrol got today's court bulletin. The owner of 601 Conde Avenue Jason Cordicio, bonded out on a $750,000 bail. Some attorneys from an investment firm in Philadelphia bonded him out at 1am last night."

"Center City Investments."

"Yeah, that's them. You know of them?"

That's all I heard as I threw the cellphone down. I pulled a spine jangling tight, tire-squealing U-turn. I raced to Wagon's West. I screamed through intersections and passed cars in the swale. I drove with a mixture of lunacy and urgency. As I hoped, there was an open parking spot in the rear of the shopping plaza. I partially ran and partially limped through the breezeway. I turned towards Wagon's West.

The restaurant was packed with people. I made quick notice that amongst all the patrons the old man with the oatmeal, the three Pickets air conditioning mechanics, and the rest of the locals were still there, too. I scanned the booths and the counter for any sign of Jason Cordicio. I looked over people's heads and past the staff. He was nowhere to be seen.

Then I saw it—an open bar stool at the counter. The remnants of a spinach and cheese omelette with hash browns and rye toast was on the dirty plate. The toast was nearly gone except for the crust of one slice. In front of the plate was a bottle of green jalapeno tabasco sauce. I must have just missed Jason Cordicio.

Darlene the waitress told me she had an opening in her section near the front door. I sat down in the booth.

I was stunned. Jason Cordicio had not only bonded out of jail but he had fled. I was just trying to collect my thoughts. The old man had finished with his oatmeal. He looked at me, noticing my hat.

"Hartford Whalers, huh?" he said in a raspy voice.

I was still submerged deep in my thoughts, but I muttered a simple reply.

"Yeah, Hartford Whalers."

"That's good," he said.

Darlene came by and asked me if I was ready to order. Distractedly I just said, "I'll have the hotcakes and an orange juice."

I sat there feeling low and dejected. Fifteen minutes later she came back to the table with my order. She had tears in her eyes. She was trying to hold back the floodgates. I asked her if everything was okay.

She wiped the corners of her eyes and told me "Actually…everything is great. One of my favorite customers just gave me $500 as a going-away present. I wasn't expecting that and I wasn't expecting him to be moving."

"Who was that?" I asked her.

"R.C. He always sat in the booth by the window, with oatmeal."

I looked up and the old man was gone.

"R.C.?" I said.

"Yes, R.C. Ray Caruso."

THE END

Milton Keynes UK
Ingram Content Group UK Ltd.
UKHW010606060224
437337UK00010B/312/J